Jessica Fellowes is an author, journalist and public speaker, best known for her work as author of five official companion books to *Downton Abbey*, various of which have hit the *New York Times* and *Sunday Times* bestseller lists. Former deputy editor of *Country Life* and columnist on the *Mail on Sunday*, she has written for publications including the *Daily Telegraph*, the *Guardian*, *The Sunday Times* and *The Lady*. Jessica has spoken at events across the UK and US, and has made numerous appearances on radio and television. She lives happily in London and Oxfordshire with her family, an energetic Labradoodle and two chickens.

D1438015

JESSICA FELLOWES

–THE–
MITFORD MURDERS

sphere

SPHERE

First published in Great Britain in 2017 by Sphere
This paperback edition published in 2018 by Sphere

1 3 5 7 9 10 8 6 4 2

Copyright © Little, Brown Book Group Ltd 2017
Written by Jessica Fellowes
The moral right of the author has been asserted.

*All characters and events in this publication, other than those
clearly in the public domain, are fictitious and any resemblance
to real persons, living or dead, is purely coincidental.*

A CIP catalogue record for this book
is available from the British Library.

ISBN 978-0-7515-6718-2

Typeset in Electra by M Rules
Printed and bound in Great Britain by
Clays Ltd, St Ives plc

Papers used by Sphere are from well-managed forests
and other responsible sources.

Sphere
An imprint of
Little, Brown Book Group
Carmelite House
50 Victoria Embankment
London EC4Y 0DZ

An Hachette UK Company
www.hachette.co.uk

www.littlebrown.co.uk

FOR SIMON & GEORGE
BEATRIX & LOUIS

Je est un autre.

Rimbaud

PROLOGUE

~~~~~

12 *January* 1920

Florence Shore arrived at Victoria station at 2.45 p.m. in a cab. It was an extravagance, all the way from Hammersmith, but one she felt she deserved. The style of arrival befitted her new fur coat, a birthday present to herself that she had worn for the first time only the day before to impress her aunt, Baroness Farina, over China tea and ginger thins, her aunt apologising for the lack of cake.

Florence had been at this station only twenty hours earlier, when she returned from the day trip to her relation in Tonbridge, and now she was heading back in almost the same direction, to St Leonards-on-Sea, where her good friend Rosa Peal lived above a teashop. Besides the birthday and the fur coat – reason enough for anyone to take a cab rather than the two buses it would take to cross the city – Florence was excused her choice of transport thanks to her substantial luggage: a dispatch box, a large suitcase, her vanity case, an umbrella and a handbag. Furthermore, on the question of reckless spending, it was only two months since she had been

1

demobilised so she had spent few of the extravagances she might have allowed herself since inheriting money from her sister five years before. Not to mention she had her savings. That decided it, then – Florence hailed a porter. She would tip him handsomely, if he bore her cases without complaint.

'To platform nine, please,' she told him, 'by the third-class carriages.' Her self-indulgence had a limit.

Free from her loads, Florence adjusted her neat fur hat and shook out her long skirt. The pre-war fashions suited her figure better; she wished occasionally she could stand to lose the corset but she couldn't get used to it. The one time she had walked out without her stays she had felt as if she were parading down the street naked. According to ritual, she patted her handbag, held on to her umbrella for walking support and marched with purpose to the ticket office. She did not have time to waste.

There was a post office in the station, and she wondered if she should send a note to the porter at her lodgings to let her know she had gone away, but decided against it. She could write from St Leonards, after all. She carried on towards the ticket office, relieved to see that there were no long queues, and stood behind an agreeable-looking young woman at stand number six. Florence admired the slim figure before her, glossy hair swept up and tucked into a large hat, trimmed with navy satin. The fashion for bobbed hair had not yet quite swept the capital in the way she had seen in Paris, though she suspected it wouldn't be long. Speedily, the woman bought her ticket and, on completing her transaction, gave Florence a fleeting smile before going on her way.

Florence faced the ticket officer, a bearded man in a cap behind glass. She briefly wondered how the railway authorities permitted beards, then reminded herself that he could have facial disfigurements from the war that he wished to disguise. It was common enough, as she knew all too well.

'Yes, ma'am?' he prompted. 'Where to?'

'Third class to Warrior Square, St Leonards, please. Returning a week today.'

Florence saw him glance at her war medal and he gave her a look as if to say: You're one of us. What he actually said was: 'Platform nine. You're in time for the three-twenty. It's a fast train to Lewes, where it separates – front carriages to Brighton, rear carriages to Hastings. You want to sit in the back.'

'Yes, I know,' said Florence. 'But thank you.'

'Six shillings, then.'

She already had her bag on the ledge before her; the correct change was swiftly fetched from her purse. Deft, even in gloved fingers, Florence handed the money over and received in turn the small, stiff rectangles. Carefully, the return portion was secreted in the bag, the outward-bound ticket she kept in her hand, the clasp snapped shut.

Back out on the concourse, Florence looked up at the station clock – it was not yet on the hour but she knew the porter would be shivering on the platform with her bags, so she decided against a quick dash to the station's cosy tea room for a cup of tea. The way before her felt vast and empty, more like an aeroplane hangar than a train station. The bleak chill of January had long killed the jollity of Christmas, let alone the novelty of a new decade. They'd looked forward to a post-war life for so long, only to find that nothing could be returned to the way it was before. Too much had changed; too much grieving had been done.

At least the journey ahead was not a long one and Rosa would be ready with a hearty supper when she arrived – generous slabs of bread and thickly spread butter, carved slices of honey-sweetened ham and a glass of ale, probably followed by a wedge of unsold cake from the teashop, warmed with a dollop of homemade custard. After a week or two at Rosa's, Florence's corset always had to be loosened by an inch. Strangely, recalling this feast – a memory that could be trusted after many visits to her friend – did not stir Florence's appetite. Hot, sweet tea was all that she wanted right now, but no matter. She had had worse deprivations.

She continued her walk towards the train. Number nine was a sort of half-platform, running along the far right side of the station so that one had to walk through platform eight to get to it. As she moved along, stately but sure, like the *Lusitania* departing from Liverpool, she thought she recognised a figure out of the corner of her eye. It gave Florence a start. Did he know she would be at Victoria? The man was slight, angular and frayed at the edges – a wooden life raft to her ocean liner. His back was half-turned away and his hat was pulled down low so that she couldn't be sure if he had seen her. Florence picked up the pace, her heart quickening. She spotted her porter up ahead, waiting patiently by her bags, and she calmed herself. She had only to get on the train; in less than twenty minutes she'd be on her way.

Florence caught the porter's eye and held it as she approached him, unnerving him rather. It made her feel safer to look at him, even though he was nothing but a stripling. He scratched at his chin and nervously pulled at his cap. Something tugged in Florence's mind at seeing his edginess. She was about to dismiss it when someone came into view, on the porter's right: Mabel.

The boy made guttural noises. 'Ma'am, sorry, ma'am, this lady wanted to take your luggage but I wasn't sure . . . ' He trailed off.

Mabel moved forwards. 'Florence, dear. He wouldn't take my tip.'

Florence did not reply but spoke directly to the porter. 'That's quite all right. You can go now. Thank you.' She gave him a shilling with finality and he walked off, relief on his face. She turned to Mabel. 'What are you doing here?'

'That's no way to greet your old friend, is it?' said Mabel, smiling. 'I just thought I'd help you. I know how particular you are about where to sit. And you have so much luggage, you couldn't manage alone.'

'I had a porter, as you can see. I can manage perfectly well.'

'I know. But there's no harm in accepting my help. Now, stay there, I'll check the compartments.'

As they had been standing there the train had pulled in. With the porter dismissed, Florence stayed by her bags while Mabel opened the first of the third-class carriage doors and then the other. She soon returned.

'You'll have to go in here. There's no one else, so you can sit where you like. There's a lady in the other one and she's sitting facing the engine. She won't move.'

Florence was silent, her features smoothed over, as hard to read as an ancient tombstone, the etchings barely visible after centuries of rain and wind. Mabel picked up the large suitcase and the dispatch box, dark red leather with faded, pale corners, battered after years of accompanying its owner around France. Florence had already picked up her vanity bag, small and navy blue, its key in her purse. It had been a present from her aunt, bought from Asprey in Bond Street when Queen Victoria was still on the throne.

The compartment Mabel had chosen was indeed empty of another soul, and had already been swept clean of the usual passenger detritus since its last journey. Two padded benches faced each other and there was only one other door, on the opposite side. Once the train was moving, nobody else would be able to get in. Mabel put the case under the first seat on the right-hand side, facing the engine. The dispatch box she put next to the space where Florence was to sit. Florence took off her hat and put it on the box beside her.

'Have you got anything to read?' Mabel asked, reaching forwards to look in Florence's handbag but was warded off with a sharp movement. 'You'd better sit down. You haven't got long now.'

Florence still said nothing but sat down in the seat that Mabel had appointed for her. It was in the far corner; from the platform she couldn't be seen easily by anyone looking in. It wasn't yet dusk but the light was dull, the sky the same dirty marble as the concourse floor. Thankfully the steam pipes would warm her up before too long. There were gas lamps in the compartments but they wouldn't be lit until Lewes. Reading in this light was not impossible but not particularly comfortable for a woman her age – fifty-five years old as of the day before. She had decided to retire when the war ended and now, she thought, she had only her old age to look forward to.

Mabel straightened up, looking as if she was about to say something, when there was a stirring behind her, causing her to jump. The door opened and a young man, of twenty-eight or perhaps thirty years old, stepped inside. He wore a light brown suit of tweed and a hat. Florence couldn't see an overcoat, which one might have expected on someone travelling to the coast in January, but perhaps there was one slung over his arm and she just didn't notice it. He had no luggage, no walking stick nor even an umbrella. He sat down on the left, by the window, diagonally across from Florence, his back to the engine.

They heard the station guard's whistle blow – the five-minute warning.

Mabel moved towards the door and the man stood up. 'Let me,' he said.

'No, thank you,' replied Mabel. 'I can do it myself.'

She pulled the window down with the leather strap, leaned outside to turn the handle and pushed the door open. Florence remained seated and did not acknowledge her travelling companion; a newspaper lay on her lap, her reading glasses perched on her nose. Mabel stepped outside, pushed the door shut and stood on the platform looking in. It was not long before the guard blew his final whistle. The train moved off, slowly at first, then gathered momentum steadily until by the time it reached the first tunnel it was rolling down the line at full speed. That was the last time anyone saw Florence Nightingale Shore alive again.

PART ONE

1919–1920

CHAPTER ONE

Christmas Eve 1919

Weaving in and out of the throng along the King's Road, her thin coat pulled tight around her neck against the sharp wind, Louisa Cannon walked with her head down, her feet light on the pavement. The outlines of the street may have faded to the encroaching darkness but the crowds were no sparser. Pairs of shoppers dawdled in front of the pretty windows, decorated with electric lights and enticing Christmas treats: coloured cardboard boxes filled with Turkish Delight, their vivid pink and green jellied cubes almost glowing through the heavy dusting of icing sugar; the pale, glazed faces of brand new porcelain dolls, legs and arms stiff in starched cotton dresses, paper-thin petticoat lace peeping out from the hems in extravagant layers.

Just behind her, the grand department store Peter Jones had put a tree in every window that faced out on to the street, red and green ribbons carefully tied on to the branches and wooden decorations hanging down from the dark green firs: miniature painted rocking-horses, spinning silver stars, golden eggs, striped candy canes. Each item a perfect facsimile of a child's fantasy brought to luscious life now that war and rationing was over.

A man stood before the shop, his hands clasped behind his back, his face bathed in the soft light of the windows, and Louisa wondered if he was distracted enough not to notice a hand slip into his pocket and feel for a wallet. Her uncle's parting words had gone around her mind in a loop since the morning: 'Don't come back without a decent lot. It's Christmas, there's plenty about.' He must have been leaned on by someone else because he had been particularly bad-tempered and demanding lately.

As she got near, the man turned abruptly and stuffed his hands in his pockets. She should have minded but what she really felt was relief.

Louisa tucked her chin in further, dodging around the laced boots and patent leather shoes on the pavement. Besides her uncle, she was on her way back home to her mother, who was lying in bed, not quite ill but not quite well either – grief, hard work and hunger contrived against her lean frame. Lost in thought, Louisa felt the heat before she saw it coming from the chestnut stand, the bitter smoke hitting her empty stomach.

A few minutes later, she peeled off the hard, baking hot skin a tiny strip at a time, using her front teeth to nibble at the sweet nut beneath. Just two for herself, she promised, and she'd take the rest to Ma and hope they wouldn't have cooled too much by the time she got back home. She leaned against the wall behind the stand, enjoying the warmth of its fire. The chestnut seller was jolly and there was a happy, festive atmosphere. Louisa felt her shoulders relax and realised she had had them hunched over for so long, she'd stopped noticing. Then she looked up and saw someone she recognised walking along the street towards her: Jennie.

Louisa shrank back and tried to hide in the shadows. She stuffed the bag of chestnuts into her pocket and pulled her collar up higher. Jennie came closer and Louisa knew she was trapped – she couldn't walk off without revealing herself. Her breath quickened and, in a panic, she bent down and pretended to fiddle with her bootlaces.

'Louisa?' A hand, gloved against the winter, touched her gently at her elbow. The slim figure wore a fashionable velvet coat, loosely cut and embroidered with peacock feathers. If Louisa's green felt coat had had the merit of flattering her narrow frame before, it merely sank into drabness now. But the voice was friendly and full of warmth. 'Is it you?'

There was no escape. Louisa stood and tried to look surprised. 'Oh, Jennie!' she said. The closeness of a crime nearly committed and the arrival of her old friend made her cheeks burn with shame. 'Hello. I didn't realise it was you.'

'It's so lovely to see you,' said the young woman. Her beauty, which had been burgeoning when Louisa last saw her, had now blossomed into something both magnificent and delicate, like a cut-glass chandelier. 'My goodness, it must be – what? Four years? Five?'

'Yes, I suppose so,' said Louisa. She put her hand around the chestnuts in her pocket, absorbing their heat.

Another figure suddenly came into view, a girl two or so years younger than Louisa, with dark hair hanging down in loose curls past her shoulders, green eyes peering out beneath the brim of her hat. She was smiling, apparently enjoying this reunion between friends.

Jennie put her hand on the girl's shoulder. 'This is Nancy Mitford. Nancy, this is my oldest and dearest friend, Louisa Cannon.'

Nancy stuck out a gloved hand. 'How do you do?' she said.

Louisa shook it and had to steel herself against curtseying. She may have had a warm smile on her face but she had the posture of a young queen.

'Nancy's the daughter of good friends of my parents-in-law,' Jennie explained. 'Their nursery maid has run off and the nanny is worn out, so I thought I'd lend a hand.'

'She ran off with the butcher's son,' Nancy interrupted. 'The whole village is in uproar. It's the funniest thing I've ever heard and Farve has been spitting fireworks since it happened.' She burst into giggles and Louisa found them quite infectious.

Jennie gave Nancy a mock-stern look and continued what she was saying. 'Yes, anyway, so we've been out to tea. Nancy's never had a mince pie at Fortnum's before – can you imagine?'

Louisa couldn't think what to say to this, never having had one either. 'I hope you enjoyed it,' she said at last.

'Oh, yes,' said Nancy, 'it was delicious. I'm not often allowed to eat a piece of Catholic idolatry.' She twirled a little on her feet, whether in parody of girlish excitement or sincerely, Louisa wasn't sure.

'How are you? How are your parents? You look …' Jennie faltered, only slightly but just enough. 'You look very well. Oh dear, it is cold, isn't it? And so much to do – Christmas tomorrow!' She gave a little nervous laugh.

'We're fine,' said Louisa, shifting on her feet. 'The usual, you know. Marching on.'

Jennie took her arm. 'Darling, I'm running a bit late. I said I'd get Nancy back. Can you walk with us so we can talk some more? Just for a minute?'

'Yes,' said Louisa, giving in. 'Of course. Would you like a chestnut? I bought them for Ma but couldn't resist having one or two myself.'

'You mean they're not yours?' said Jennie and gave her friend an exaggerated wink and a nudge in the ribs. She forced a smile out of Louisa at last, revealing her neat row of teeth and brightening her tawny eyes.

She peeled them a nut each, Jennie holding hers with the tips of her fingers before popping it into her mouth, Nancy copying her. Louisa took the moment to appraise her friend.

'*You* look well. Are you?'

Jennie did not laugh again but she smiled. 'I was married last summer to Richard Roper. He's an architect. We're off to New York soon because he wants to get away from Europe. Too broken by the war, he says. There's more opportunity there. Let's hope so, at any rate. What about you?'

'Well, I'm not married,' said Louisa. 'Couldn't do it in time to catch the vote, so I decided against it altogether.' To her pleasure, Nancy giggled at this.

'You tease,' said Jennie. 'You haven't changed a bit.'

Louisa shrugged. The comment stung, though she knew Jennie meant nothing mean by it. 'No, nothing much has changed: I'm still at home, Ma and me scratching about for work as ever.'

'I'm so sorry. That is hard on you. Can I help you out a bit? Please.' Jennie started to fish about in her bag, a delicate square hanging on a silver chain.

'No. I mean, no thank you. We're fine. We're not completely alone.'

'Your uncle?'

A cloud passed over Louisa's face but she shook it off and smiled at Jennie. 'Yes. So we'll be fine. We *are* fine. Come on, let's walk along together. Where were you going to?'

'I'm dropping Nancy off, then meeting Richard. We're dancing with friends at the 100 Club – have you been there? You must go.

It's all so different now and Richard is the most daring sort of man. I suppose that's why he married me.' She lowered her voice, deliberately conspiratorial. 'I'm not quite like all the other wives . . .'

'No, it doesn't sound as if anyone else from around our way would be in that crowd. But you always were so much more of a lady than anyone else. I remember how you insisted on a starched nightdress. Didn't you pinch some starch from my ma's cupboard once?'

Jennie clapped a hand over her mouth. 'Yes! I'd forgotten all about that! I told your mother I'd work as her assistant and she laughed me right out of the room.'

'I don't think washerwomen have assistants,' said Louisa, 'though I help out often enough. Believe it or not, I'm quite good at darning these days.'

All the while, Louisa was conscious of Nancy's green eyes watching them both, taking it all in. She wondered if she ought to be alluding to Jennie's less-than-aristocratic background in front of her but decided that Jennie was so incapable of any form of fib that Nancy probably knew about it anyway. At any rate, Jennie didn't seem to be showing any embarrassment.

'Your ma's still working, then?' said Jennie, sympathy in her eyes. 'What about your dad? Not still up and down those chimneys, is he?'

Louisa gave a tiny nod. She didn't want to explain to Jennie now that he had died only a few months ago.

'Mr Black and Mrs White we used to call them, didn't we?'

The two young women giggled and leaned their shoulders and heads against each other for a second, back to being the schoolgirls they'd been together in pigtails and pinafores.

Overhead the stars started to pop out in the clear black sky, though they lost the competition to the street lamps. Motorcars drove noisily down the street; frequent toots on the horn could not be translated easily, sounding alike whether impatient at a slow car or a friendly beep of recognition at a pal on the pavement. Passing shoppers were bumping into them with their laden bags, irritated at the young women interrupting the steady stream of the crowd with their slow-moving island of three.

Jennie looked at her wristwatch and then sadly back at her friend. 'I've got to go. But please, can we meet again? I don't see enough of my old friends . . . ' She trailed off. It didn't need to be spelled out.

'Yes,' said Louisa, 'I'd like that. You know where I am – the same old place. Have fun tonight. And merry Christmas! I'm happy for you. I really am.'

Jennie nodded. 'I know you are. Thank you. Merry Christmas to you, too.'

'Merry Christmas,' said Nancy, with a small wave, and Louisa waved back.

With Nancy beside her, Jennie turned and started to walk along the King's Road, men stepping out of their way as they parted the waves like Moses.

CHAPTER TWO

Christmas had always been a cheery pause in the winter months for Louisa, but this year, without her father there, neither she nor her mother had had the heart to carry out their own small traditions. There had been no decorations hung in the flat, no tree fetched from the market. 'It's only one day,' Ma had muttered.

It was just as well, thought Louisa, that they had more or less gone on as if it were an ordinary Thursday. Her uncle, Stephen Cannon, had slept until midday and barely muttered tidings of festive cheer to his niece and her mother as they sat close to the fire – Louisa reading *Jane Eyre*, her mother knitting a dark green jersey – before heaving himself into the kitchen in search of beer. Stephen's dog, Socks – a long-legged black-and-white mongrel with silky ears – lazed at Louisa's feet, having the best time of all.

When Stephen sank into the armchair, Winnie picked up a dropped stitch and edged a little closer to the fire. 'We've got a joint of pork for dinner,' she said, her head only slightly turned towards her brother-in-law. 'And I was given a small Christmas pudding by Mrs Shovelton.'

'What she give you that for?' said Stephen. 'Bloody snobs. They'd never give you half a crown extra, would they? Be more use than a pudding.'

'Mrs Shovelton's been good to me. You know I had to take two weeks off when your brother ... when Arthur ...' Winnie gave a hiccup and looked down, breathing deeply, keeping panic at bay. The worry had got worse lately and not all of her mistresses were so understanding when their washing came back a day later than promised.

'Sshh, Ma,' said Louisa. 'It was very nice of Mrs Shovelton to give it to us. I think I've got a few coins to put in it, too.' She glared at her uncle, who shrugged back at her and took a swig of his drink.

Thankfully, after the pork and potatoes, Stephen had announced he was going for a kip in the chair. Louisa and her mother had wrung out all their Christmas spirit in one concentrated joint effort over the pudding. Louisa had put three halfpennies in and a sprig of holly on top. There was no brandy to light and they briefly wondered if a splash of beer would have the same effect but decided against.

'Merry Christmas,' Louisa had said over the first spoonful, held triumphantly in the air. 'Here's to Dad, eh?'

Winnie's eyes had filled up but she smiled at her daughter. 'Yes, love. Here's to Dad.'

They'd finished off the pud, not bothering to leave any for Stephen, and cleared up together, their almost identical figures moving against each other in a well-worn pattern as Louisa washed and Winnie dried in the cramped kitchen. Stephen woke up only to grab his coat and say that he was going to the pub, slamming the door behind him and Socks, who trotted after him. Mother and daughter resumed their quiet activities and went to bed as early as they felt they could decently get away with – nine o'clock at night.

Through the walls they could hear the next-door neighbours begin a rousing chorus of 'Good King Wenceslas' and knew it would be the first of many.

Some hours later, Louisa felt Stephen shaking her shoulder as he woke her from a shallow sleep.

'What is it?' she whispered, not wanting to wake her ma beside her. She ran through in her mind all the people she might need to receive news about in the middle of the night but she was hard pressed to think of any. Mrs Fitch next door on the other side, who had minded their old cat when they'd gone to Weston-super-Mare for five days a few years ago? Mrs Shovelton? But if something had happened to her, couldn't it wait till morning? All the grandparents were long dead – Louisa had been 'a lovely surprise' to her parents, forty and forty-six years old when she was born. But Stephen put his fingers to his lips, slightly off-centre, and gripped her shoulder firmly, pulling her out of bed.

'All right! All right, I'm coming,' she said in a loud whisper, rubbing her face to wake herself up. Ma turned on her side, a rasping sigh as she breathed out. 'Keep your hair on.' She walked into the kitchen, where Stephen was waiting for her. 'What?'

'There's a man in the front room,' said Stephen. 'He wants to see you. He's letting me off a small debt for the pleasure. So make sure you give it to him.' His blank face gave way to a smirk at his own joke.

'I don't understand.'

'You will when you get in the next room. Get.' He shooed at her like a stray dog that was bothering him for scraps.

'No,' said Louisa. She'd grasped his meaning. 'No. I'll tell Ma.'

In a single, violent movement his large, flat hand smacked her straight across the cheek and Louisa almost slipped to the floor in her bare feet. Her dressing gown was not quite tied around her cotton nightdress as she tried to straighten up, her hand out, groping for the kitchen table, when she was hit by a second slap, the back of his hand this time, on the same cheek. She felt it burn; an ache in her jaw started to throb. There were no tears, her eyes were dry, her throat drier.

'Your mother doesn't need to know. She's got enough to worry about, ain't she? Now, for the last time – get in there.'

Louisa looked at her uncle for a long, cold moment. He stared back and thrust his chin at the door. This ... she thought. It's come to this.

Stephen had been the only one to notice her change from being a child. Once or twice he'd told her she 'wasn't just a pretty face' and she'd accepted the faint praise with pleasure. Now she understood.

She pulled her hand away from her cheek and wrapped her dressing gown tighter around her, retying the knot firmly. Then she turned around and walked into the next room, closing the door behind her softly, so as not to wake her mother.

Standing by the fireplace, the embers long gone out, was a man she recognised from the pub down the street when she'd gone to fetch Stephen home for dinner: Liam Mahoney. Her throat closed.

His eyes were narrowed slits, his mouth set in determination. She stayed by the door, her hand on the knob. She thought: So long as I'm holding on to this, I'll be all right.

In the near-blackness it seemed as if every other sense was heightened. She could smell the ale on his breath, the sweat that seeped out of every pore; it even seemed as if she could smell the very dirt beneath his fingernails. There was a shuffling sound behind the door: Stephen, bending his ear down to listen.

'Come over here, girl,' said Liam, and his hand moved to his belt buckle, the brass gleaming in the half-light.

21

Louisa didn't move.

'Not a very well brought-up young lady, are you?' he said.

Louisa's knuckles turned white.

His tone softened. 'There's nothing to be afraid of. I just want to take a look. Your face could be your fortune, you know that?' He chuckled as he came towards her and reached out a hand. Louisa flinched and crossed her arms.

'You're not looking at anything,' she said. 'Whatever it is you want, I'm not giving it to you. Touch me and I'll scream.'

The man barked a laugh. 'Shush. There's no need for all that. Look, the thing is . . . ' He lowered his voice and bent his head to talk directly into her ear. She smelled the alcohol and the sweat again, and closed her eyes. 'The thing is, your uncle owes me money. All you have to do is one small job and I'll forget it. You come down to Hastings with me and I'll have you back in two shakes of a lamb's tail. Nobody around here need know.'

Louisa was still standing close to the door. She thought she heard Stephen – a stifled noise. She pictured his fist in his mouth.

With one hand Liam pushed her back against the wall. Fear set in then. Her hands flew up and she tried to pull him off but he was stronger, catching them in one hand, then sliding his other hand down her side, feeling her curve at the waist, her hip bone.

Louisa went still. She looked past his head at the window opposite, where the curtains were drawn but no longer met in the middle, shrunken by the years. Through the gap, a lamp glowed yellow, flickering gently. The road was empty. She stared at the pavement, the tufts of grass that grew between the cracks. She tried to go inside the cracks, to crouch in the darkness there. She'd been there before, where she was safest.

Then there was a sound from the stairs – Ma calling.

Abruptly, Liam pulled away and she slumped, taking deep

breaths. Stepping back, he did up his jacket buttons and pulled up his collar. 'Just a night in Hastings,' he said. 'It isn't a lot to ask.'

She wasn't aware of much after that, just him in the hallway and murmuring voices. Then Stephen's footsteps, heavy and erratic up the short staircase. At last, silence.

Mechanically, she put herself in motion, going to the kitchen, boiling water in the kettle and carefully making tea. She warmed the pot, poured milk into a jug and took out a porcelain cup and saucer from the back of the cupboard. Her father had bought the blue-and-white china set for her mother just before she was born. That made the cup and saucer older than she was – nineteen years old at least, and they looked less chipped and cracked than she felt.

It was only as she sat at the table, the cup of tea poured out before her, that she allowed herself to cry, but not for long. She wiped her face with the flat of her hands and shook her head. The time had come to do something. With a start, she remembered Nancy Mitford saying that the nursery maid had run away. There was a chance they could still be looking for someone. Jennie would know. From a drawer in the kitchen Louisa found some paper and a pencil, and then began to write the letter she hoped would change everything.

CHAPTER THREE

◦◦◦◦◦◦

12 *January* 1920

When Louisa and her mother emerged from the back door of Mrs Shovelton's white painted house in Drayton Gardens, their concentration was on their heavy loads. Louisa, wanting to spare her mother any more burden than she absolutely had to bear, had squashed in almost half as much again in her own basket.

Jennie had replied to Louisa's letter and told her to write to the Mitfords' housekeeper, Mrs Windsor. *And darling,* she had added, *I think you'd better mention any work you've done with children, if you have it. There are six in their nursery.* That had been almost two weeks ago. With no word from Mrs Windsor and no nearer to another solution to getting rid of her uncle, there was more weighing on her mind than a laundry basket. The biting wind made them dip their heads and the glare of the metallic winter sunshine, still low in the sky, burned their necks as they walked steadily to get the day's work back home.

Over the road, Louisa spotted her uncle Stephen in his pork pie hat, leaning against a lamppost and smoking a cigarette. He threw it down when he realised they were about to walk past him. Socks was there, too, obediently sitting on his haunches by Stephen's feet. He moved to go to Louisa but was stilled by a short whistle from his master. Stephen gave him a titbit from his pocket and patted his silky head. Then he fixed a smile on to his face that radiated absolutely nothing at all. Louisa saw all this but kept close to her mother, looking fixedly ahead to where the main road lay, with its people and cars. Witnesses.

'Oi, oi,' he shouted after them. 'Aren't you going to say hello, then?'

Louisa's mother turned around to look at him. She squinted at him in puzzlement. 'Stephen? It's not payday, today,' she said.

'I know.'

'So why are you here, then?'

'Can't a man come and say hello to his dear old sister-in-law and lovely niece?' said Stephen. He moved towards them, his face empty, Socks padding behind him. Louisa felt something pass through her and wondered, briefly, if she might faint.

'I thought I'd come and give you a helping hand,' he said as he took Louisa's basket. She resisted for just the smallest moment but he tugged it easily out of her hands. He turned back to Winnie, his mouth turned up at the corners, no teeth showing this time. 'Help you get back to the flat nice and quick.'

Winnie looked at him blankly, said nothing and continued to walk in the direction she was going in, towards her home and against the easterly wind. Stephen stood back on the pavement, as if to let her pass like Sir Walter Raleigh throwing his cloak down for Elizabeth I. Louisa watched her mother's weak back and rounded shoulders hunch her basket up an inch and started to go after her. She didn't see her uncle put the basket down on the pavement behind her before his hand shot out and grabbed her at the elbow.

In a low voice he said, 'I *don't* think so, do you?'

In that moment, Winnie turned the corner and lost them both to the noise of the traffic and loud clip-clop of a carthorse. Louisa knew her mother wouldn't look back.

Stephen said, 'I know what you've been up to.'

'I haven't been up to anything. Let me go.' Louisa pulled her arm but Stephen's grip got tighter. He started to walk them both away from the main road.

'You can't leave the washing there!' said Louisa. 'They'll charge Ma for it and we'll get no pay. If you must take me with you, at least let me take it back to them first.'

Stephen considered this for a moment then shook his head. 'They'll find it. We're barely ten yards from the front door,' he said. But, in looking at the basket sitting in the middle of the pavement, he had loosened his grip.

Louisa slipped her arm out and started to run, back towards the house. She wasn't entirely sure what she was going to do when she got there – she didn't think she'd have the nerve to knock on the front door. Mrs Shovelton's butler probably wouldn't even recognise her as the washerwoman's daughter, even though she'd been collecting the linens with her mother for six years. Even if he did recognise her, he would be so outraged at her appearance and at her standing on the front steps – so clearly a servant and not a visitor of the family – he was likely to slam the door in her face.

Dismissing the idea as fast as it had come, Louisa ran past, moving ever further away from her mother, towards a cobbled mews street where she might lose her uncle to the shadows, if not to a lack of sure footing on the slippery round stones.

But her hesitation at the house's steps was fatal and this time Stephen caught both her wrists and held them behind her back. Her face twisted in pain, and she buckled her elbows and knees, trying to pull herself away. Stephen gripped her small wrists together, both easily held in just one of his large hands, the other grabbing a handful of her hair and the back of her neck. She caught a glimpse of the dark yellow nicotine stains on his finger-nails and her stomach turned.

'I wouldn't try that, if I was you,' he sneered. 'You're coming with me.'

Louisa gave up trying to fight him. He was bigger and nastier than she was; she wasn't going to win. He felt her submit beneath his grip and relaxed his hold on her neck, though he kept her arms behind her back. A woman walking smartly on the other side of the street, heels clipping like a dressage pony, gave them a quick glance but carried on.

'Good girl,' said Stephen, soothingly. 'If only you listened to me more, we wouldn't have to have all this trouble.'

As if he were a policeman and she a criminal, he marched Louisa down to the end of the mews and out on to the Fulham Road, where he hailed a taxi. If the driver was at all concerned to see a man in workman's boots and a patched-up woollen coat forcing a young woman in a plain outfit and cheap hat into his cab, together with a dog, he didn't show it.

'Victoria station,' said Stephen to the driver. 'And look sharp about it.'

CHAPTER FOUR

12 *January* 1920

Guy Sullivan's long frame was bent nearly double with laughter, his hat was threatening to fall off and he could feel the seam of his jacket stretched to bursting point. 'Harry, stop! I can't take any more.'

Harry Conlon looked as if he was considering whether to stop or continue this delicious torment of his friend. They had stolen a quick tea break in the stationmaster's office at Lewes, where they had been sent down to investigate a missing pocket watch. The stationmaster, Mr Marchant, was well known for summoning the London, Brighton and South Coast Railway Police for non-existent crimes on an almost weekly basis.

'Nonetheless, lads,' Superintendent Jarvis had solemnly reminded them, 'that doesn't mean that this time he's not in the right. *Never assume* – not if you want to make decent policemen. Remember the turkey who believes the sight of the farmer's wife each morning means he's going to get his feed, only to find he was wrong—'

'On Christmas Eve. Yes, sir,' Harry had interrupted.

'Er, yes. Quite right. On Christmas Eve. Well done, Conlon,' Jarvis had grumbled, clearing his throat. 'What are you standing around for, then?'

Harry and Guy had speedily exited the Super's office, a narrow room that barely contained its occupant's leather-topped desk and wooden chair but nevertheless had the atmosphere of Court One at the Old Bailey to anyone summoned within its smoke-stained walls. The office led directly on to platform twelve at Victoria station.

'What did you do to put the boss in such a good mood with us, Harry?' asked Guy.

'I don't know what you're talking about,' he replied, smirking.

'Yes, you do. Bob and Lance usually get this one. It's not an investigation so much as a nice day out. I was all ready for another morning resetting the signal box.'

'Don't get too excited. It's a bloody freezing day in January, not exactly an outing by the sea in June,' laughed Harry. 'But I *may* have made sure the Super had a nice box of his favourite cigars at Christmas . . .'

As new recruits, Harry and Guy had been paired together when in training for the railway police force four years before. They were not an obvious choice for a partnership at first sight: Harry had apparently stopped growing when he was twelve years old yet had the kind of blond good looks that might have passed for a matinée idol in a dim nightclub. Indeed, he had tried that trick quite a few times, with occasional success. Guy was tall – 'Lanky,' said his mother – with high cheekbones, a flop of pale brown hair and a gap between his teeth. Thick, round specs were always slipping down the bridge of his nose. Yet they had each responded to the other's easy humour and forged their friendship as two men who had been excluded from the war – Harry because of his asthma, Guy because of his extreme shortsightedness.

The morning he had returned home without his orders but a letter of exemption instead flashed into Guy's mind with disarming regularity. In 1916, one brother was already dead, killed at the start of the war in the Battle of Mons. Two more brothers were in France, deep in the trenches, their stoic letters home betrayed by shaky handwriting. His father worked long shifts at the factory and his mother had turned into a colourless wisp of a woman, slipping into the shadows of her own home, hardly making a sound, let alone talking. Guy had stuttered at the eye test; desperate not to fail, he guessed at the answers but the letters had jumped and blurred before him, and he had known it was hopeless. Walking back to number eight Tooley Street where his mother waited for him, the rain had poured, water trickling down the back of his shirt, soaking him to the skin. It wasn't enough when he wanted physical pain, something – anything – to let him stand alongside his brothers and their courage. Standing before the front door and trying to find strength to push it open, he was cloaked in humiliation. Even the tears of his mother, sobbing with relief into his chest, were not enough to stop him wishing he could pack up and go to war.

Signing up to the LB&SCR Police had given him purpose, a spring in his step, even if it hadn't done away with the smirks altogether. When Mrs Curtis from number ten had congratulated him on passing his policeman's training, she had not been able to stop herself from remarking, 'The railway police – not *proper* police, is it?' Last year, his three brothers had returned home – Bertie, the youngest, having joined up six months before the end – and all had taken up work as bricklayers and hod-carriers. Guy had been happy to see them all safely back and thought his smart uniform and policeman's helmet would earn him a smidgen of respect from his siblings, but when he had been forced to admit that some of his duties included watering the hanging baskets at the station and resetting the signals, the ridicule had started again and never stopped.

When Guy and Harry walked into Mr Marchant's office that morning, they found the stationmaster pacing around with a pocket watch in his hand. 'Ah, there you are!' he said, his squirrel face twisted with concern. 'You're just too late again. I opened my desk drawer five minutes ago to find the pocket watch inside.'

Harry threatened to burst out laughing and Guy gave him as stern a look as he could manage through his thick lenses.

'I see, sir,' said Guy. 'Do you think it was replaced when the thief heard you had reported it stolen?'

Mr Marchant stopped pacing and stood absolutely stock-still, looking at Guy as if he had told him the meaning of life. 'Do you know, I do! I think that's exactly what happened.'

Harry had to pretend to busy himself with finding his note-book, hiding his face and doing his best to muffle snorts that were threatening to escape. Guy managed to carry on as he took notes from Mr Marchant and nodded as seriously as he could, but when the telephone rang he finally allowed himself to catch Harry's eye and smile.

'Sorry, lads,' said Mr Marchant, 'there's a delay on the train from Bexhill. I've got to go and deal with it. Help yourselves to a cup of tea.'

No sooner was the door shut behind him than Guy and Harry exploded. 'Is he completely off his rocker?' said Harry. 'A war medal, a five-pound note, a fountain pen and now a pocket watch all mysteriously found in his desk drawer hours after he's reported them stolen?'

'Please, don't,' said Guy, doubled over, eyes squeezed shut. 'My stomach hurts.'

Harry drew himself up and started to contort his face like the stationmaster's. 'Is that the police?' he began, as if booming down a telephone, 'I've got a very, very serious crime to report . . .'

Which is how it happened that neither of them heard the door of the office fly open.

CHAPTER FIVE

～⁀✎

12 *January* 1920

In the taxi, Stephen held Louisa by her wrist, her arm twisted behind her back, though not as firmly as before. When the motorcar slowed down at a crossroads, she thought about trying to leap out but was intimidated by the general cacophony of the streets. Trams shuttled up and down their metal rails, sparks flying from the wires overhead; buses leaned slightly as they rounded corners, the Pears Soap poster beneath two or three cold passengers on the open-top upper deck. Boys, who should be at school, marched up and down the pavements with sandwich boards proclaiming the news: LLOYD GEORGE RAISES TAXES AGAIN and BABY LEFT ON CHURCH STEP. A pre-war relic – the horse and cart – stood like a statue at the side of the road, a fresh heap of manure the only testament to the animal's life force. Young men and middle-aged spinsters wobbling on bicycles would suddenly appear at the side of the cab, occasionally glancing in through the window to see a grim-faced man, his face set straight ahead, hat pulled low over his forehead, an unsmiling woman beside him.

Louisa's heart was hammering fast in her chest. Socks lay on the floor of the cab looking relaxed but his ears were pulled back.

Her uncle was a man she knew too well not to worry about where he was taking her. Louisa's father had been the youngest of six children and Stephen had been the black sheep, leaving home as soon as he could, resurfacing only when there was a funeral. 'And not because he's paying no respects, neither,' her father had said. 'Only because he thinks there might be a payout from the will, or at least the chance of palming an aunt out of a few coins.'

During the years of her childhood, Stephen had come several times, always outstaying his welcome, both her parents too weak and unwilling to ask him to leave. Besides, they were working all the hours they could and when Stephen offered to walk Louisa to school in the morning, they took it as a favour earned. They never found out that he took her to railway stations instead, teaching her 'from the school of life', as he put it, picking pockets from the rich – or at least anyone with a decent-looking coat. She certainly learned lessons but none that she told Ma about. Stephen kept her quiet with a supply of barley sugars and the oily sensation of guilt. Her parents had enough to worry about, didn't they? Bitterly, she remembered that often she had been pleased with his attention when she'd got so little at home. She didn't like doing what it took to make him smile at her but she'd do it anyway. Sometimes he'd give her a shilling – 'A share of the profits,' he'd say with a smirk – and she started to save the coins in a jar hidden beneath her bed. One day she'd have enough to leave home, she'd thought.

So it hadn't been entirely surprising when Stephen had shown up at her father's funeral and come to the small wake afterwards at the Cross Keys pub. Socks was with him this time, a young but already well-trained dog, and Stephen had won Louisa's sympathy when he told her he was just like the dog he'd had when he was

34

a boy. She knew the story, having been told it often, usually after Stephen had had a few too many and was feeling morose. As a child, he'd found a stray on the streets and taken it home, and though the whole family had taken to the dog, it was only Stephen that it followed around, sleeping by his side every night, keeping him warm as he lay on the floor of the bedroom that was shared by all six children. When his father kicked it out of the house for stealing the precious leftovers of a stew, Stephen's heart had broken. Socks was just like that dog, Stephen said, and they would both smile at the mutt, tail thumping on the pub floor.

Winnie had been distraught after the funeral, and when Stephen offered to help take her back to the flat, Louisa had forgotten to be on her guard and was grateful for the extra pair of arms. It had been late and ale had been drunk, so it would have been churlish not to give him her bed for the night – she could easily share with her mother, she'd said.

As usual, over the next few days, the right moment or the right words couldn't be found to ask Stephen to leave. Winnie and Louisa avoided talking about it to each other, as if to discuss it out loud would make his presence in their flat too much of an uncomfortable reality. Stephen never gave them any money, but sometimes he would bring back to the flat something he'd bought, or possibly won, off someone at the pub – a cut of beef or some mutton – so they couldn't complain that he hadn't contributed anything to the meagre suppers Winnie cooked. He always cut a chunk off for Socks before he ate any himself. Stephen never made any mention of where he had come from the day of the funeral or what he had been doing before he'd turned up – it had been two or three years since he'd last been around – and they knew better than to ask.

Over the weeks, they'd learned to tolerate his presence and

adjusted to it in the way one adjusts to a pain in the knee: at first it niggles every time you move, and then you start to forget it's even there. Apart from the fact that he had taken over Louisa's room and came home drunk most nights, the sum contribution of his personality to their domestic life was largely made up of surly grunts and a deeper imprint in the armchair where Arthur used to sit and Stephen now slept off the worst of his hangovers after lunch, Socks at his feet.

In the cab, Louisa thought about her mother – she'd be wondering what had happened. At the same time, she knew Winnie wouldn't be doing much about it. She had the laundry to get done and she'd be more worried about the missing basket. Perhaps she would return to Mrs Shovelton's to see if it was there. More likely she'd return the washing she did have and meekly accept the loss of the job, apologising for their carelessness as she backed out the door, despite the many years of laundry where not so much as a single handkerchief had ever gone astray. Louisa loved her mother but sometimes she resembled nothing more than one of the pillowcases she so faithfully washed and pressed: clean, white, smelling of Lux flakes and existing only to provide comfort for others.

As the facts stood, nobody knew that Louisa was in a taxi heading for Victoria station with her uncle. The trains from Victoria went south, she knew that much. Her stomach lurched, empty as it was. She looked sideways at Stephen but his face remained stony.

'Where are we going?' she asked, in a voice firmer than she felt.

'Never you mind,' said Stephen. 'You'll find out soon enough.'

'At least let go of my arm – it hurts.'

'And let you jump out?' As if to make the point, he jerked on her wrist again, sending a shot of pain up to her shoulder.

'We're here now, anyway,' he said as the taxi juddered to a stop at the station's entrance, opening the door with one hand and still holding on to Louisa with the other. She was dragged out and stood beside him as he dug in his pockets for change to pay the taxi. He leaned in through the window, handed the money over and pulled Louisa away as the car drove off.

'That's three and six you owe me now,' he said to his niece. It was almost a skill how someone like him could persuade himself that nothing he spent was for him but was always owed back – as if he was a saint who did only favours for others. Once, she'd been shown a negative for a photograph and marvelled at the perfect inversion of light and shadow in the image beneath the glass; Stephen was exactly like that.

This reminder of her uncle's absurdity took her fear away. There was no reasoning with an unreasonable man. She wasn't going to be able to talk her way out of this and she hadn't the physical strength to cut free of his grasp. She had better go along with it for now and keep alert to the first chance she spotted to outwit him. He wasn't very clever so it surely wouldn't take long.

'Uncle,' she said, and he turned to look at her without breaking their pace. 'At least could you hold on to my other arm? This one is starting to hurt.'

Stephen paused, trying to work out if this was one of her tricks. He grunted assent and swapped his hands around, holding her other arm and moving to her right side without ever letting go of her completely. Louisa shook her left arm out, feeling sensation return to her fingers as the blood flowed freely again. As he moved to her other side, she noticed a piece of paper sticking out of his coat pocket. She couldn't see much, just a corner, but it was the creamy colour and thick texture that she noticed. An envelope. Stephen wasn't a man to receive letters; certainly not ones of quality. She moved her head back up before he could realise that she'd seen it. She knew, she absolutely *knew* what it was, and she had to get hold of it.

All around them were the usual busy travellers of a main thoroughfare station. First-class and third-class passengers alike moved in and out of the grand entrance, like bees around a hive: country naïfs arriving to seek work in the city where the streets were paved with gold – or so they hoped; top-hatted men off to inspect factories in the north, and bowler-hatted men following in their wake, leather briefcases swinging against their matchstick legs.

At any other time, she would have enjoyed the scene: the flower stalls, the newspaper stands, the porters wheeling stacks of luggage. How much had she longed to be one of those people? Buying a ticket and confidently boarding a train that would take her across the country, speeding through fields and valleys to arrive somewhere no one knew her and anything was possible.

Instead, she was jerked roughly by her uncle as he bought two tickets – 'One-way, third-class' – to Hastings. She vaguely heard the ticket officer go on to say that there was a short platform at Lewes, the first stop, where the train divided.

'Hastings?' said Louisa as they walked away. *Liam Mahoney* rang in her head.

'I've got friends we'll be staying with for a while. Now shut up.'

Louisa went quiet, she needed to focus on the letter that she had to get from Stephen's pocket. If that letter was offering her an interview for the nursery maid's job, that was her lifeline. She had to grab it.

She kept silent while he manoeuvred her to platform nine, where there was a train already waiting. Stephen chose a rear compartment, with just one other passenger – an old woman who quietly wept into her handkerchief and barely seemed to notice them. With a whistle, a hiss and a jolt, the train set off and only then did Stephen relax his hold on his niece. They sat beside each other, Louisa bolt upright and stiff, telling herself not to glance at Stephen's pocket. Her uncle pulled his hat down lower, folded his arms and stared out of the window.

As the train steamed along, Louisa looked out at the disappearing London skyline, the grey net curtains in the windows and the blackened bricks of the houses south of the river. It wasn't long before they gave way to Sussex's flat fields of stubbly brown earth, neatly divided from the pale sky by even lines of hedges. Farmhouses were dotted both near and far from the train line, sometimes allowing passengers a close up of milk churns by a barn door waiting to be loaded on a cart, at others revealing only a smudge of chimney smoke. Emerging from the first tunnel, Louisa couldn't help but admire the sight of a group of brown and white cows lying together in the corner of a field with a single bull standing before them, like a lazy parliament and its prime minister. There were two more tunnels, each pitching the train into near darkness, making the sound of the train wheels oppressively loud in Louisa's ears.

Now, thought Louisa. Take the letter *now*.

Her left hand lifted slowly and with her fingertips she faintly felt the thick wool of Stephen's coat. She traced upwards to the edge of his pocket, her elbow pressed against her waist, her heart beating so hard she felt sick. But just as her forefinger and thumb came together to pinch the corner, the compartment was thrown into light again and she jerked her hand down.

Stephen felt the movement and looked at her sharply, but she settled her face in repose, staring ahead. Patting his pockets as if looking for something, she saw him stealthily check the letter was there before he pulled out his tobacco pouch and started to roll a cigarette. Soon, grey clouds of smoke filled the compartment. The old lady gave a small cough but did not interrupt the rhythm of her weeping. When Stephen was almost down to the stub, the red glow threatening to burn the tip of his thumbnail, Louisa became aware that the train had started to decelerate. As the wheels turned more slowly, her heart drove a faster beat, reverberating in her chest until she could feel it pulsing in her throat. The train stopped and Louisa stood up suddenly.

'Really, Uncle,' she said, all sunshine and smiles, 'you're being very rude. This poor lady can hardly breathe.'

The old lady looked at Louisa. Stephen reached up an arm but Louisa pretended not to notice and opened the window, smiling at her fellow female passenger as if in mutual sympathy. She could feel the bangs of doors opening and closing further down the train as various passengers got off and on, then the platform guard called out the name of the station – Lewes. Louisa pushed the window as far down as it would go and, turning sideways, slipped her right arm outside to grab the handle.

'Siddown!' said Stephen, standing, as she knew he would, and stepping towards her as he flung his cigarette to the floor. Socks leapt up. Louisa heard the guard's whistle blow, long and loud. The train gave a whistle in reply and she felt the bump as the wheels started slowly up again.

There was no time to think. Louisa took the letter from her uncle's pocket as he came near, just as he'd taught her, then pushed open the door and jumped down on to the tracks, rolling away as the train built up speed, the train door flapping and her uncle standing at the gaping doorway, his face crumpled with fury, his mouth opening and closing meaninglessly as the hiss of steam drowned him out.

CHAPTER SIX

⌒

12 *January* 1920

In their laughter, Harry and Guy hadn't noticed a guard run in through the doorway of the stationmaster's office.

'Sir, sorry, sir, there's a girl on the tracks,' he babbled, then pulled himself up straight when he saw their uniforms. 'Sorry, Sarge,' he said to Harry. 'I thought you were Mr Marchant. Can you come? We need help.'

Harry and Guy quickly straightened their helmets and Guy did up the top button of his jacket. They attempted to mask their disarray with an overly serious tone.

'What's the problem, sonny?' said Harry, even though the guard was, at most, only two years younger than he was and a good six inches taller.

'It's a young lady, sir,' said the guard, moving back towards the door. 'She's on the tracks. We think the train had already started moving when she jumped and she's in pain. We need to move her quickly.'

The two policemen started to run and the guard pushed ahead

of them, eager to lead the way. It didn't take them long to get to the end of the platform, where they spotted the woman in question – she was a hundred yards away, down on the ground, one leg splayed, the other bent inwards. She was clutching her leg and her face was scrunched in pain, though she wasn't making any noise. Her hat had slipped down the side of her head and Guy could see strands of dark brown hair straggling at the back of her neck. Her boots were scuffed and she wore no gloves. She looked wretched but also, thought Guy, clocking the fact in the way that a young man must, she was pretty.

It didn't take long for the men to heave her up to her feet, slight as she was.

'I'm so sorry,' she said, shaking with the shock of the fall. 'I didn't realise how fast the train was going.'

Before long, she was up on the platform and sitting in the station café with a cup of sweetened hot tea before her. While the guard went to find the nurse, Harry stood by the door – on lookout, he said – while Guy pulled up a chair next to her.

'Right, miss,' said Guy. 'We'd better take down a few details.'

'Why? I haven't done anything wrong, have I?'

'Strictly speaking, no, miss. But it was a dangerous thing to do. And we need to write a report,' said Guy, reddening very faintly. 'So could you tell me your name, please?'

'Louisa Cannon.'

'Address?'

'Flat forty-three, Block C, Peabody Estate, Lawrence Street, London.'

'Occupation?'

Louisa gripped the letter in her hand – she hadn't had a chance to read it yet. 'Washerwoman. That is, I help my ma out. But it's not what I'm always going to do.'

Guy smiled. 'No, Miss Cannon.' He paused. 'It *is* miss, isn't it?'

'Yes.'

The blush went a little pinker.

'Where were you travelling to?'

'Hastings but I ...'

'What?'

'Nothing. I was going to Hastings.'

'Why did you jump out of the train, then? Did you want to get out at Lewes? Sometimes people don't realise the platform is shorter than the train. It's happened before.'

'Oh, yes, I mean ... yes, I was going to Lewes ...' Louisa's voice trailed off again.

Guy looked at her kindly. 'And you nearly missed your stop? Was that it?'

Harry gave him a sharp look.

'Yes, that's it. Ow.' She winced and gripped her leg.

'The nurse will be here soon, miss,' said Harry. 'Try not to move too much.'

'I don't need a nurse,' said Louisa. 'I need to go.'

'Just a few more questions, Miss Cannon,' said Guy. 'Were you travelling alone?'

Louisa looked at him. 'Do you really need to know all this? I have to go.'

Guy put down his notebook and pencil. 'Harry,' he said, 'could you go and find out what's happened to that nurse?'

Harry understood. He left.

'Tell me what's happened,' said Guy. 'You're not in any trouble, we just need to make sure nothing is wrong.'

The soothing tone was almost too much for Louisa. She felt as if she hadn't heard someone talk gently to her like that for months, if not years. She was still holding on to the envelope, which was addressed to her. 'I need to read this,' she said.

43

'Go on, then,' said Guy. 'Take your time.'

Slowly, Louisa drew the piece of paper out of the envelope and started to read the looping handwriting in black ink. She gave a start. 'What day is it? It's Monday, isn't it? What time is it?'

Guy looked up at the clock in the café. 'It's three o'clock, almost exactly. Why?'

Louisa lost her composure altogether at this. 'I'm never going to make it!' she cried. 'My one chance to get away, to do something – and now I can't. I can't. *Ow.*' She clutched her leg and took a deep breath. 'Look,' she said, and gave Guy the letter.

He read it. 'I think you can make it,' he said.

'But I'm such a mess – look at me!'

Guy looked at Louisa. He saw the slim figure, the fine, pale complexion, the shine on her cheekbones and large brown eyes, wet with tears. But he was a policeman – he also saw the bedraggled hat, half of its brim coming away, the cheap coat and boots that needed new laces and a polish.

'Do you really want this job?' he asked.

'Yes,' she said, looking at him directly. 'Very much.'

'Right,' said Guy. 'In that case, we'd better do something about it. Wait here.'

'It's not as if I can go anywhere, is it?' Louisa grimaced but there was a gleam in her eyes.

As Guy was going out, Harry returned, this time with the nurse in tow, and while Louisa was being examined, Guy went to the stationmaster's office to make some enquiries. By the time Louisa's bandage had been wrapped around her sprained ankle, Guy was back, waving a small piece of paper.

'I've got the train times for you; you can definitely make it,' he said.

'Make it to what?' asked Harry.

44

'Her job interview,' said Guy, suddenly aware he knew far more about this young lady than his policeman's duty warranted.

The nurse stood up and packed the last of her things into her bag, gave Louisa a few brief instructions on looking after her ankle and left.

'What's going on?' said Harry, noting the colour on his friend's face. He gave him a broad grin, which Guy didn't return.

'Miss Cannon,' began Guy, 'I don't want to cause you any offence but I think perhaps you need to . . . well, if I might suggest, you . . .'

'What?' said Louisa.

'Yes, *what*?' said Harry, thoroughly enjoying himself.

'I think your boots need a polish, miss,' Guy blurted. 'I could do them for you at Victoria station; I've got all my kit there. And Harry and I . . . I mean, Sergeant Conlon and I are on our way back there now. Aren't we, Harry?'

Louisa suppressed the urge to giggle. Guy saw this and tried not to look offended. He knew most men his age had a sweetheart and Harry had tried to fix him up with a dancer or two from the 100 Club, but he'd never got further than choking his way through a Whiskey Sour and going home.

'Why would you do this for me?' said Louisa.

Guy's cheeks flushed again. He cleared his throat. 'Humph, well, call it civic duty. But we'd better get going if you're to get the right train. You see, you need to get the . . .'

He rambled on about trains to London and across London to Paddington and out again to Oxfordshire, in time to meet the groom at half past five, but Louisa wasn't listening. The idea that she might be able to do this, that she had been given a chance to change her life, was overwhelming in its richness of possibilities. Like trying to eat an entire chocolate cake in one sitting – it was glorious but it threatened to be beyond her ability to achieve it.

'Stop, Sergeant . . . ?'

'Sullivan.'

'Sergeant Sullivan. Thank you for all this. Truly.' She gave him a brief smile. 'There's no need to take me anywhere. I can get there by myself. I'm very grateful to you. Goodbye.' Louisa stood up, wincing only slightly and started to walk out.

Guy made a movement as if to stop her but Harry gave him a look and the two men let her go.

'If you're sure, Miss Cannon. Here, take this,' said Guy, and he handed Louisa the train times he had written down.

Louisa took it with a nod and put it in her pocket, next to the letter. She had nothing else on her but a handkerchief and she knew she didn't have long – her uncle Stephen would be catching the next train back to Lewes to find her.

A few minutes later, Louisa was waiting for the next train back to London. Looking up and down the platform, her eye soon fell upon a well-dressed middle-aged gentleman, clearly bound for the City. He was wearing the uniform of a man who worked for a bank: bowler hat, tightly furled umbrella, leather briefcase, spats. She waited for the signal she needed – yes, there it was. Every man could be relied upon to do this as he waited for a train to arrive: pat his coat pocket to check his wallet was still there. Louisa walked towards her quarry, her heart beating fast, trying not to limp. She didn't want to do this but unless she did, she wasn't going to get a bite of that cake.

'Oh! I'm so sorry, sir! I wasn't looking where I was going!' Louisa burbled as the gentleman looked at her crossly, his briefcase knocked to the ground and papers spilling out. Louisa kneeled on the floor to pick the papers up, the city gent bending down with rather more difficulty beside her.

'It's fine,' he said gruffly. 'Let me do it.'

'Oh, yes, sir,' Louisa continued. 'So sorry again, sir.' In the midst of the confusion and her gabbling, she slipped her hand in his pocket and had just caught the wallet in her grip when she felt a light touch on her arm.

'Miss Cannon?' It was Sergeant Sullivan, looking at her, bewildered. 'Is everything all right?'

Hastily she pulled her hand out of the man's pocket, without the wallet, and stood up. She looked down at the man, still reaching for his papers, and without thinking said sharply, 'Excuse me, sir! I will not!'

The city gent looked up at her, confusion on his face, but said nothing.

Guy flashed a stern look at him before walking Louisa away, steering her by her shoulder. Harry was a few steps behind them.

'What happened there?' asked Guy tenderly. 'Did he make an improper suggestion to you?'

Louisa, flustered now at her lie and wondering why she had done it, shook her head. 'It's nothing,' she replied. 'Nothing I can't manage.' Much to her consternation, she could feel guilt rising.

Guy threw a look back at Harry, then turned to Louisa, her hat askew, her leg bandaged. She looked like a sparrow with a broken wing. 'Do you need some help?'

Louisa turned away. She'd ask anyone but him. He was a policeman, after all.

'I don't know why I'm about to say this but why don't I lend you a little money?' said Guy. 'I can issue you a pass for the trains; you don't need to buy a ticket. And I've got a few coins on me so you can buy yourself a sandwich for the journey. Maybe a bit of boot polish, too.' He grinned.

Louisa relented. If it meant getting that job . . .

'I'll pay you back,' she said. 'I mean it—'

'Don't mention it,' said Guy. 'So long as you can get to that interview. Wait here, I'll get the pass.'

They had reached the stationmaster's office, where Guy left Louisa sitting on the bench outside, Harry standing beside her. Embarrassment suffused her body; she could barely look at him. Guy came running out of the office a quarter of an hour later, though it felt much longer. He thrust the passes and some shillings into Louisa's hand, dismissing her half-hearted protests.

'We've got to go,' he said to Harry. 'The Super's been on the telephone – there's an incident at Hastings station. He wants us to find out what's happened. I don't know any more than that.'

Guy turned to Louisa and she could see he was distracted by this excitement. 'I'm sorry,' he said. 'I hope you make it to the interview. I hope you get the job. Perhaps—'

'Yes, I'll let you know,' said Louisa, smiling at him. 'I can write to you at Victoria station, I suppose? Sergeant Sullivan, isn't it?'

He nodded. 'Thank you. Goodbye ... and good luck.' Guy turned to Harry and the two of them ran off, the tall and the small, answering the call of duty.

CHAPTER SEVEN

~~~~~

12 January 1920

It was a bleak scene that greeted Guy and Harry that afternoon. The sun had gone from the sky and an early evening chill had descended with the dusk in the twenty minutes it took for their train to pull into Hastings station. They hurried across over the bridge to the next platform – they had been told the incident was on number one – and saw the 3.20 p.m. from London Victoria that was not now going to reach its final destination. Infuriated passengers had been herded off and put on another train, diverted from the drama that had happened right beneath their noses by thoughts of missed appointments and suppers that would go cold.

A cluster of men was standing on the platform by the last compartment, its door held open by a young porter. Most of the crowd were unashamed gawkers but Guy identified the stationmaster, Mr Manning, with his distinctive dark green livery and gleaming brass badge. He was talking to another man in a hat, a policeman. Close by them stood three working men in dusty clothes, caps on their heads, hands jammed in their pockets, whispering to each other.

Guy quickened his step and broke up the conversation with what he hoped was an authoritative tone: 'Mr Manning, sir, we're Sergeants Sullivan and Conlon from the London, Brighton and South Coast Railway Police. Superintendent Jarvis sent us. What's happened here?'

Mr Manning looked up at Guy with a serious face that betrayed his upset. He opened his mouth to speak but was stopped by the man from the East Sussex force, Detective Inspector Vine, who wasted no time in introducing himself.

'Thank you, *Sergeant*, but we've got everything in hand. The ambulance is here and they're taking away the victim.' He ran an index finger over his moustache and nodded at Guy peremptorily.

'Absolutely, sir. But we need to make a report for the Super,' said Guy resolutely. He moved towards the open carriage door, where a station guard stood, keeping the crowds away. The moustache on the lip of DI Vine seemed to curl a little tighter as he took a step back to allow them through.

They peered inside the narrow compartment, where the gas-lights threw off a sharp glare that illuminated perfect spotlights, giving Guy the sensation of a dressed stage. It took him a moment or two to adjust his eyes to the dim outlines. Two men dressed in ambulance uniform were heaving a woman on to a stretcher. She still wore her fur coat but it had fallen open to reveal her old-fashioned black crêpe dress and laced patent boots. Her head flopped to the side, showing a wide streak of dark, dried blood, her mouth was slightly agape, her hair disarrayed.

It was raining women in peril that day, thought Guy.

'Is she alive?' he whispered to Harry.

'I think she must be,' he whispered back. 'Look.'

They watched as the woman raised one of her hands, fluttering her fingers, like a chicken walking after its head had been cut off.

The men bore the stretcher out through the carriage door, bracing themselves as they did so against the crowd outside.

Once the ambulance men had left, Guy and Harry stepped inside. 'There's blood on the floor,' said Guy, aghast.

Harry looked at the blood, a smudge of dark red, then at the empty space where she had sat. There was a worn-looking leather case beside it, a hat clumsily placed on top, with a black handbag. The *Illustrated London News* was lying awry on the seat, with blood smeared on the folded side, as if she had held it to her head, perhaps to stem the flow. Another suitcase was below the seat. There was a navy blue vanity case too, open, showing a glimpse of white clothing inside. On the floor was a pair of broken spectacles, two pieces of a snapped hair comb and a page of newspaper. Guy wrote down each item in a list. It seemed a rather pathetic summary of a woman's life. He noticed another large smudge of blood on the wall where her head had been.

'Look in her handbag,' said Harry. 'It might say who she was. I mean, *is*.'

Guy looked: there was a purse with no money inside it, a notebook with a few faint pencil notes he couldn't read in the dusk, the return portion of her train ticket and a National Registration Card identifying the owner as Florence Nightingale Shore, Queen's Nurse, of Carnforth Lodge, Queen Street, Hammersmith.

Overcome, Guy's eyes grew wider behind his glasses. 'It's a murder investigation,' he said.

'Not yet,' said Harry. 'She's still alive. Let's hope she pulls through. Come on, we'd better talk to the others.'

Outside, there was a commotion. Passengers had seen the body being carried out and it had created amongst them a wave of fervent whispers, and one woman had fainted. Mr Manning found himself surrounded by DI Vine and the two guards from the train – introduced as Henry Duck and George Walters – as well as Guy and Harry. There was a loud discussion as to what should happen next but no one seemed to be listening to anyone else.

Mr Manning turned to DI Vine. 'Will you take the woman's things away, Mr Vine? We've got to get this train moving or there's going to be delays on the line all night.'

'It's *Detective Inspector* Vine, actually, Mr Manning,' he replied. 'I'm sorry to disappoint you but this train is now a part of our investigation. We won't be clearing anything away.'

Guy felt an agitation that confused him. The attack had happened to someone else but it had infected the air with something sour and acrid. A little apart from them were the three working men, no longer talking to each other; they smoked and looked at their feet.

DI Vine beckoned Guy and Harry over. 'I need to take these three into the station. They got on the train at Polegate Junction but didn't raise the alarm until Bexhill. They're saying they thought she was asleep at first and then just as they got to the next stop they saw the blood on her face. Let's take one each. The station's only a few minutes' walk away. But be careful, lads – these might turn out to be our murder suspects.'

CHAPTER EIGHT

12 January 1920

Louisa got back to London after darkness as the frost had settled in for another long night. She gripped the letter in her pocket. She knew she'd missed the interview time – 5.30 p.m., already an hour gone since – but she would go there anyway. She had nothing, quite literally nothing, to lose.

Using the shillings Guy had given her, she bought an Underground ticket to Paddington – the letter had instructed her to catch a train to Shipton – and a hot cup of tea with a slice of buttered bread. Only when she held the mug did she realise how frozen her fingers were. In the public washroom at the station, she splashed water on to her face and tried to smooth her hair down. An elegant lady beside her, adjusting her hat, gave her a barely hidden look of disdain.

At the platform gate, Louisa's chest tightened as she showed the pass Sergeant Sullivan had given her, but the guard waved her through and she was on her way. There was only blackness beyond the windows, no view to show her the fading horizon of London. Exhausted, Louisa closed her eyes and tried to sleep.

When it seemed that she had slept but a minute, Louisa heard the guard coming through, announcing the next stop as Shipton. As she walked out on to the platform it was only 7 p.m. but the desolate scene and the cold made it seem much later. There was a pub in view and Louisa went in to enquire for directions to Asthall Manor. The old men at the bar looked at her quizzically.

'What business you got there, then?' the publican asked.

'I'm there about a job,' said Louisa, caught on the spot. 'Please, will you tell me the way?'

'Seems a funny sort of time to have an interview.'

'Please,' said Louisa. 'Could you just tell me the road I need?'

An old farmer swigged the last of his ale and said he'd give her a lift most of the way – it was time he got home to his supper anyway. He warned her she'd still have to walk another half an hour or so on the dark road. Louisa almost fell to her knees in gratitude but made do with a 'thank you'.

When the farmer dropped her off, the clouds had gathered above and she felt the first few drops descend. She thought about sheltering under a tree until it passed but she knew she was going to arrive at the house far too late as it was. If she could have, she'd have slept outside until morning but it was too cold. At least the temperature stopped her from thinking about the ache in her ankle. She blew on her fingers and walked as fast as she could, staying in the middle of the road, out of the way of strange shapes that seemed to lurk in the hedges, startling her at corners. A couple of cars came past, beeping their horns to make her leap to the side, their lights sweeping over her and briefly illuminating the falling rain.

At last – God alone knew what time it was – Louisa saw the long stone wall with an archway and iron gates that the farmer had told her to look for. He told her that was the entrance to the house from Asthall village, which went to the back of the house. Clearly he had understood she would not be knocking on their front door.

The back door was opened to her timid knock by a young maid, dressed in a uniform of blue and white *Toile de Jouy* with a white linen apron and an organdie cap threaded through with black velvet ribbon, tight curls barely contained beneath. Louisa knew that what she saw was a bedraggled, wet girl with a broken hat, worn-out boots, a bandage coming loose and a face red raw from the winter. She shivered, unable to speak instantly. The maid continued to look at her, though not unkindly.

'Good evening,' said Louisa. 'I know it's late but I was expected – I had a letter from a Mrs Windsor to come here for the job of nursery maid.' She went to her pocket and pulled out the crumpled letter to show the maid the unmistakable crest embossed at the top.

'Blimey,' said the maid, 'I don't know what Mrs Windsor'll say about this. You'd better come in quick, it's horrible out there.'

Louisa fought back a sob as she stepped into the kitchen and was put in a chair close to the heat of the wood-burning stove while the maid went to fetch Mrs Windsor. A cook gave her a glance of concern but was otherwise busy finishing her preparations for the family's dinner. Louisa could see there must only be minutes until it would be served.

Mrs Windsor came through shortly, in the same uniform, with a handsome head of dark hair showing a few strands of grey below her cap. She looked stern as she approached Louisa, who stood immediately and then wobbled as the blood rushed from her head.

'Louisa Cannon?' said Mrs Windsor. She did not offer a hand.

'Yes, ma'am,' said Louisa. 'I know I must look—'

She was interrupted. 'I'm afraid whatever your story is, I can't allow you to meet Her Ladyship. You shall have to return home. I'm sorry, Miss Cannon, but I'm sure you understand.'

Shame pricked Louisa's skin. She nodded, silent. There didn't seem much point in saying anything. Mrs Windsor left the room, calling out only to the cook that she would ask the family to go through to the dining room now.

Louisa watched her leave and found she couldn't move. She was aware of the rain drumming on the window, far heavier now than when she had been walking along the road, and of the cook bustling about the kitchen, putting plates on the table and stirring a huge pot of something that smelled delicious. Louisa felt the emptiness of her stomach, the dryness of her throat.

'Come and sit over here,' said the maid, 'out of Mrs Stobie's way. I'm Ada. You don't have to go just yet. Let's get the supper out and then we'll see what we can do.'

Numbly, Louisa allowed herself to be led to a bench at the side of the kitchen. She pressed herself into the corner to make herself as small as possible, and watched the cook and the maid as they served supper. Mrs Windsor came in once more to fetch something and saw her, but said nothing.

When she'd finished serving up, Mrs Stobie gave Louisa a bowl of stew and told her to sit at the table to eat it. No one was unkind but she felt like a stray cat being given milk before it was shooed away. Still, she started to feel a bit more human – feeling returned to her toes, the dampness on her clothes started to dry out. This didn't change the fact that she didn't know what she was going to do next.

As Louisa was sitting at the table, trying not to scrape her spoon noisily at the bottom of the bowl, a girl with long, dark hair and startling green eyes walked into the kitchen. Nancy.

'Mrs Stobie, Nanny says please may we have some hot chocolate—' She stopped, spotting Louisa. 'You're here.'

Louisa stood hastily, the chair scraping on the flagstone floor. 'Yes, I'm here.'

To her amazement, Nancy laughed. 'Goodness, you did cause a ruckus. Old Hooper went down to the station and you weren't there! What happened to you? I was a bit embarrassed,' she carried on talking at a furious pace, 'seeing as I was the one who had recommended you. So I am glad you've shown up. Do tell.'

'Well, I . . .' Louisa began, though she hardly knew how she'd go on. To hear that she had caused Nancy embarrassment made her want to throw herself under the table and lie there until everyone had gone. As she began an explanation, she was cut short by the cook, who told Miss Nancy to mind her own beeswax and motioned for Louisa to sit back down. Nancy rolled her eyes when the cook's back was turned but didn't pursue the question. There was vitality in that face, thought Louisa, a hunger for more . . . more what, she didn't know, but *more*. She recognised it in herself.

'Have you met Muv? I mean, Lady Redesdale, my mother? She's having dinner now, so I expect not. Afterwards will be a bit late. Perhaps tomorrow? Do you have somewhere to stay?' Nancy had pulled up a chair and was sitting opposite Louisa, elbows on the table, an earnest look on her face. Mrs Stobie coughed in disapproval but continued to busy herself with the boiling milk.

Louisa was suddenly aware of a whole, huge house beyond the kitchen door. A house far bigger than any she'd ever been in, with a family all together, happy and healthy. She remembered what she had been told about them by Jennie, in the letter that had given her their address – five girls and one boy, another on the way. A lord and a lady for the parents, and a nanny in the nursery. A nursery! When Louisa and her mother collected the laundry from Mrs Shovelton, they rarely got further than the back door. So she'd only seen what those houses looked like in illustrations: fine paintings on the walls, silk-covered sofas with plumped-up cushions, thickly tufted rugs and blazing fires. There'd be a gold-framed looking-glass hanging in the hall and vases of freshly cut flowers brought in from the garden. And now this girl, sitting in front of her, with brushed hair and a velvet collar on her dress, a knitted cardigan over the top. The idea that Louisa could be a part of this house for even a minute was patently absurd. She could no more work here than be a nursery maid in Buckingham Palace. She'd better leave, and soon.

Louisa stood abruptly and picked her hat up off the table, trying to hide the fact that the brim was hanging off the crown. 'Sorry, miss,' she said, 'I'd better get going.'

She stepped away and said thank you to the cook. Before anyone could move or say anything, she'd opened the back door and walked outside. The cold hit her anew and the rain hadn't stopped. She still didn't know where she would walk to but she thought she could follow the road back to the station and there would be shelter there, at least. In the morning, she'd have to steal a few coins for the train journey home. The thought of home, and who would be there, waiting for her, almost made her retch but she carried on, her head bent against the weather. The tears streamed down her face. If it wasn't for her mother, she'd have lain down in the ditch and waited for death.

She had been walking only a few minutes, still following the curve of the wall, when she heard someone shouting her name. Louisa turned and saw Nancy running along the road, her cardigan held over her head, a rather pointless attempt to keep the rain off. Louisa stopped and stood still, unable to believe it was happening until Nancy stood right before her.

'Why didn't you stop sooner? I was calling you!' said Nancy, catching her breath.

'Sorry,' said Louisa, stunned.

'Come back,' said Nancy. 'Come and stay the night. I've persuaded Mrs Windsor that you'll look a whole heap better after you've had a bath and a sleep. Then you can meet Lady Redesdale in the morning. Come *on*. It's pouring and I'm freezing cold.'

Unable quite to believe it, Louisa walked back with Nancy at her side as the young girl chattered, telling her that it was so silly of them to send her away into such a filthy night. It wasn't as if they'd managed to find anyone local who wanted the work and they were in desperate need of a nursery maid.

'Not me, of course, I'm sixteen,' said Nancy, talking at the rate of a wind-up toy. 'But there's Pam, who's thirteen, she's always playing house; then Deerling is ten; Bobo is five; Decca is three; and Tom's eleven, but he's at school. And Lady Redesdale's expecting again. She's sure this one is a boy. He's going to be called Paul. That's why we need a nursery maid; poor old Nanny Blor can't do it all by herself.'

'What funny names,' Louisa exclaimed and then clamped her mouth shut. She hadn't meant to say that out loud. But she wanted to laugh, at all of it, at the sheer bloody relief of it.

Nancy giggled. 'Oh, some of those aren't real names. It's just that hardly anyone gets called by their proper names here. Muv and Farve – that is, Lord and Lady Redesdale – call *me* Koko because my black hair when I was born reminded them of the Lord High Executioner in Mikado. You'll soon catch on.'

'I hope so,' said Louisa.

'How old are you?' asked Nancy abruptly as they turned back into the drive.

'Eighteen,' said Louisa.

'Then we shall be friends,' said Nancy as they reached the back door. 'Will you be able to start here straight away? Oh, here comes Mrs Windsor. I'd better hop to it. See you later!' She gave Louisa a wink and dashed away.

*

The next morning, having been given a bath and a hairbrush, and a night's sleep in an empty servant's bedroom, her clothes miraculously washed and dried by the time she woke, Louisa was shown to the morning room to meet Lady Redesdale, who was seated on a pale pink sofa. Louisa trembled with nerves but she knew this was it, her only chance. She had to make it work.

There were a few brusque questions – her name, her age, her education, queries about her experience with the Shovelton family, whom Louisa had named in her letter of application. Louisa was able to answer honestly about the names and ages of the daughters, having heard the talk in the kitchens, but rather less honestly about how she had taken them to Kensington Gardens for their daily walk and mended their dresses.

'I should write to Mrs Shovelton for a reference,' said Lady Redesdale and Louisa heard the clang of an alarm bell in her head. 'But Mrs Roper's daughter-in-law Jennie has vouched for you, so that will do for now. We are in something of a hurry, as you know.'

Louisa nodded, not trusting herself to say anything that wouldn't come out as a squeak.

'Speaking of which, when would you be able to start?' continued Lady Redesdale.

'Today, my lady.'

'Today?' She looked at her sharply. 'Did you bring a suitcase with you? That was rather presumptuous.'

'No, my lady, I haven't brought a case with me.'

'So you have nothing with you?'

'No. That is, I don't need anything.'

'Everyone needs a few things,' said Lady Redesdale.

'Perhaps I could go home to collect them in a week or two,' said Louisa. She didn't want her new employer suspecting she was running away from anything. Though it was probably a bit late for that.

'Yes, I suppose so. I can't deny it would be helpful.' She gestured at her large bump, well disguised by her simple dress. 'We'll give you a week's trial. If Nanny Blor and Mrs Windsor are happy with you, then you'll have every Wednesday off from four o'clock, and every other Sunday at the same time. You must come back by ten o'clock at night or Mrs Windsor will have fits. I shall pay you on the first of every month. One pound.'

'Thank you, my lady,' said Louisa, trying not to grin like a barrow boy. She gave a quick bob.

'There's no need to curtsey,' said Lady Redesdale, pulling the bell. 'I'm not the queen. Mrs Windsor will take you up to Nanny Blor, who will show you around. I expect I'll see you at five o'clock when the children are brought down for tea.' With a small nod, Louisa was dismissed.

So this is it, she thought. Everything is different now.

CHAPTER NINE

The coroner's court at the East Sussex Hospital was a crisp and formal place with whitewashed walls and small, high windows, too reminiscent of those in a prison cell. The coroner, Mr Glenister, sat on a raised platform behind a long desk, with his deputy and the coroner's officer on either side. Eleven men were sworn in as jurors and took their places on benches along one wall, with a clear view of the witness stand. They had just been to inspect Florence Shore's body in the mortuary next door and their pale faces bore testament to the severity of her injuries.

Mr Glenister, a short man with a serious expression, called everyone to attention. News of the brave nurse's untimely and appalling end had caught the public imagination and the gallery was filled with reporters and gawkers.

First, there was an apology from the solicitor of the railway company; they wished, he said, to express their deep regret and sincere sympathy to relatives and friends at the unfortunate lady's end.

The coroner then launched into a lengthy opening speech about the career of Miss Shore: 'She was a lady of philanthropic disposition, a nurse of many years' standing and had devoted herself to tending the sick and people wounded in the war . . . '

Guy, upright between Superintendent Jarvis and Harry, with DI Vine on the same bench, tried to listen to the long list of noble attributes of the poor murdered nurse but his eye had been caught by a wan, petite woman sitting on the front bench, a hospital nurse at her side in starched white. On the other side of her sat a sombre, rake-thin man in a suit that had seen better days. He did not touch the woman but looked to her frequently, as if to check she was still there.

Strands of wispy grey hair had fallen down beneath the woman's unfussy black hat and she clutched a handkerchief, but her eyes were dry; they were open but unseeing and she did not respond to the speech, even as Mr Glenister asked the jurors not to ask questions of 'this poor woman', gesturing to her, until she gave evidence at a second hearing. His speech concluded, Miss Mabel Rogers was sworn in. Guy watched her walk over slowly, the hospital nurse holding her elbow all the while.

The coroner established her residence, her position as matron in charge of the nurses' home and the fact that she had known the deceased for nearly twenty-six years. Mabel explained that her friend had also lived at Carnforth Lodge and had done so for just two months, since her demobilisation from active service. Her relatives, she said, in a voice that neither faltered nor resonated, were a brother in California, and an aunt and cousins in England.

'What was her disposition? Was she reserved?' asked Mr Glenister.

'She was very reserved and very quiet, but cheerful.'

'As far as you know, she had no enemies?'

'No, none at all.'

'As to her physique, was she strong?'

'No, I would not say she was, but she had been stronger in recent years.'

Mr Glenister continued to confirm further facts of the case: 'Did she spend Sunday the eleventh with you?'

'She was with me, but she went down to Tonbridge for the day and returned the same evening to me.'

Yes, said Miss Rogers, she knew Miss Shore had arranged to stay with friends in St Leonards and had assisted her to Victoria station, where she took the 3.20 to Warrior Square. There were detailed questions about the compartment chosen for her friend, the position of the seat and the luggage she had with her. Miss Rogers confirmed she had selected a compartment for her friend, which was empty until a man in a brown tweed suit entered shortly before the train was due to depart.

'Did you get into the compartment as well?' asked the coroner.

'Yes.'

'Did you sit there and talk to her for a while?'

'I am not sure whether I sat or stood but I got in.'

Sunlight suddenly broke through the high row of windows and revealed a cloud of cigar smoke floating above their heads; Detective Inspector Haigh from Scotland Yard had stubbed one out shortly before proceedings began. Guy looked up and gave an involuntary cough. He tried to stifle another and his eyes began to water.

'When the train started, there was nobody else in the compartment but Miss Shore and the man?'

'No.'

'Your friend was in her usual state of health?'

'She was very well.'

He then asked Miss Rogers to confirm her actions on receiving the telegram about her friend: she had been at the theatre so she got it late and caught the 11.20 p.m. train to Tonbridge, continuing on by car. She looked down at her lap and took a shaky breath.

'Did you see the deceased when you arrived?' continued the coroner.

'Yes.'

'I suppose she was in bed?'

'Yes.'

'You stayed at the hospital until the time of her death?'

'Yes,' said Mabel. She spoke a little more faintly with each answer.

'Did she regain consciousness during that time?'

'No.'

'When did she die?'

'On Friday at five minutes to eight in the evening.'

'Was the man who got into the carriage a stranger to you?'

'Yes.'

'And to the deceased?'

'Yes.'

'As far as you know, you had never seen him before.'

'No.'

Mr Glenister gave Miss Rogers a sympathetic smile and said he had finished for the time being. The foreman said the jury had no questions. A newspaper reporter looked as if he wanted to ask something but clearly thought better of it and scribbled his last few notes. The next hearing was set for 4 February at 3 p.m., in Hastings Town Hall. The coroner closed by calling the assault 'a cowardly and dastardly act', before dismissing the court.

The policemen filed out together last of all. Guy and Harry gave each other an excited look as they walked out; it had been their first murder inquest and they felt childishly pleased to have been there. Out in the hall, the various uniforms stood around, holding back until Mabel Rogers had walked out, the thin man holding her firmly by the arm this time.

Haigh took command. 'Vine, we'll head back to your station. We need to co-ordinate our plan before the next inquest.'

Vine stroked his moustache and gave just the slightest pause before replying; Haigh was not his boss and he well knew that the local constabulary were in charge of the case, but Haigh was his superior and, after all, he couldn't contest the fact that his chief had called in the services of Scotland Yard.

'Yes, absolutely. We can use my office.'

At Bexhill police station, the men sat on a variety of wooden chairs pulled into the blank box that was Vine's office. Haigh, asserting his right as detective inspector at Scotland Yard, continued to assume control of the situation.

'This is a troublesome murder, men. We've got no weapon and no real witnesses. I've had the chief of the Brighton railway line on the telephone this morning. They want this case solved fast.' He rolled another cigar between his fingers as he spoke. 'Today's article in the *Mail* on famous railway murders isn't helping matters when it comes to their passengers' sense of wellbeing, it seems.' He decided to light his Havana and held it up, looking on Vine's desk for some matches. There were none.

Guy did not have the nerve to speak; instead he took his glasses off and started to polish them with the corner of his jacket. Harry coughed and tried to catch his friend's eye. They had spoken about this over the weekend, when they met on Saturday evening, ostensibly for a cocktail or two at Harry's usual nightclub but more truthfully because they had both been shocked by the news of Miss Shore's death. What had started as an investigation into a brutal assault – nasty enough in itself and certainly outside their usual

66

routine – was now a murder. There was a confusion in their minds that only the other could understand: shock, awe and *manliness*. Yes, this was something that would make them men at last, like their friends and brothers who had been to war.

They had discussed the scene of the crime, the lack of a weapon despite an army of policemen combing the seventy-odd miles of railway line between Victoria and Bexhill. The only thing that had caused a stir was a blood-stained khaki-coloured handkerchief, but it was the sort of object owned by thousands of former soldiers. Other clues, such as they were, were paltry: the blood on the walls; broken spectacles; an empty purse; stolen jewellery. Guy wondered over and over again if there was something he should have spotted. Miss Shore's train, after all, would have stopped at Lewes. Her attacker must surely have left the train at that first stop. Might he have noticed someone getting off the train who had been engaged in a struggle?

Of course, at the time his mind had been on Miss Cannon ... Guy had told Harry over a Brandy Alexander that he wanted a promotion, if not a move across to Scotland Yard, and he knew this case was his chance. Harry, generally more interested in working out the finger movements of his latest jazz piece, nonetheless wanted his friend to do well too. Staying quiet was not going to help.

He coughed again and this time Guy looked up. 'Say something,' Harry mouthed to him. Guy raised his eyebrows back but knew Harry was right.

'Sir? Perhaps we could ask at pawnbrokers and second-hand shops to see if anyone has tried to sell a brown suit, like the one Miss Rogers said the man was wearing? Or they might have tried to sell off Miss Shore's stolen jewellery?'

'What? All the pawnshops in Sussex?' Haigh chewed on his

unlit cigar. 'Still, you could be right, it's not a bad idea. If we can find a suit to match the description, we can look for bloodstains. With no weapon found, it's all we've got to go on.'

Guy nodded, his colour rising slightly. He pushed his glasses further up his nose. 'Also, sir, I wonder if we might conduct some further interviews. I was thinking of Mr Duck, the train guard – he must have seen something. And Miss Rogers. Perhaps there's more she can tell us about the man who got into the compartment? Wouldn't it be better to talk to her before the next inquest hearing? She might have forgotten things by then.'

'All right, Sullivan, that's enough,' said Superintendent Jarvis. 'I think you're forgetting your place for the moment. We've got it all in hand, haven't we Haigh?' The two superiors exchanged a nod of mutual understanding, which left the rest of the men like gooseberries beside a couple who had just got engaged.

'Absolutely, sir,' stammered Guy. 'Sorry, sir.'

'You and Sergeant Conlon can start with the pawnshops in Lewes. Manning can drive you down there now. Report back and we'll take it from there. You're lucky you were on the scene at the time, lads. Make the most of this chance,' said Jarvis.

Haigh looked slightly put out that he had not issued these directions, but with only a little grumble he nodded to show his assent. 'We'll meet back here on Friday to discuss what, if anything, has been found. Off you go, then. Vine – can you tell me of a decent restaurant around here . . . ?'

And with that Guy and Harry were on their way, officially investigators of a notorious murder.

CHAPTER TEN

O n her second night at Asthall Manor, when she had been given the job, Louisa had been shown around by Nancy. She had begun in the entrance hall, which had two fireplaces and dark wood panelling. 'It looks grand,' said Nancy, 'but it's all been salvaged by Farve.' There was a large central staircase, which ran all the way up to the attic, where the linen cupboard was, and on the last landing Louisa spotted a row of cupboards, all painted in indigo blue. 'It's the Mitford livery,' said Nancy, as if Louisa would know what that meant.

The nursery wing consisted of a single floor which acted as Nanny Blor's sitting room, as well as playroom for the little ones and their bedrooms. While the rest of the house was intimidatingly large to Louisa's eyes, her new domain was cosy, sitting almost by itself on top of the library, which Nancy told her had been converted by Lord Redesdale from a tithe barn. There was a walkway to it from the front door, which he had also created, called The Cloisters. Nancy said she spent most of her time in the library – 'Grandpa was a collector of books; he even wrote one or two himself' – and when Tom was home, he would play the big piano in there.

While the main house had over a dozen bedrooms, in the nursery wing there were just four, but they had their own bathroom and hot water supply. One bedroom was shared by Nanny Blor and the youngest babies, next door to the room in which Louisa was to sleep with Pamela and Diana. One more was due to arrive in two months and Louisa had fallen in with everyone's assumption that the seventh and final child would be a boy called Paul. Blue knitted jumpers and bootees were already filling a drawer.

Nancy led Louisa to her own room, its name, *Lintrathen*, painted above the door. Tom, away at school, had a room of his own too – 'Because he's a boy, even though he's only eleven,' Nancy explained. She brought Louisa over to the window in her room. 'Look,' she said, and Louisa saw the gravestones of the churchyard next door. 'When it's full moon, it's easy to frighten the others about ghosts in the house,' she tittered.

Nancy shut the door and sat cross-legged on her bed. Louisa had the sensation that she was about to get a second interview, more probing than the one with Lady Redesdale. But perhaps she just wanted to talk to someone. Louisa suspected Tom was everyone's best ally when home; they all seemed to miss him a great deal, speculating endlessly about what he would be doing at school or what food he would be eating ('Sausages,' said Nancy, envy lacing her voice). Louisa imagined it must be something of a welcome breather for Tom to escape the cluster of sisters and their constant noise of chatter, teasing and whines. It would certainly take some getting used to for her.

Despite Nancy's entreaty, Louisa had stayed hovering near the door, unsure that sitting on the bed would be the right thing to do. The fib she had told about looking after the Shovelton daughters had seemed quite innocuous at the time but it was dawning on her in those first hours just how little she knew about what to do.

'Come on,' said Nancy, 'do sit down. I want to know all about you.'

Louisa blanched. 'I think perhaps I had better be getting back to Nanny Dicks, to see what she needs me to do.'

'Call her Nanny Blor,' said Nancy. 'Everyone does – even Muv.'

'Back to Nanny Blor, then.'

'Just a few minutes, please. Won't you tell me at least where you grew up? I do so want to know about you. We can be friends and friends know all about each other, don't they?' said Nancy. 'You have no idea what it's like for me here. I've been sobbing with boredom, stuck up in this attic with the same silly little girls day in and out.'

Louisa looked about herself, feeling trapped. 'There's not much to tell,' she said. 'I grew up in London, with my mother and father.' Then she hesitated. It seemed a rather mealy-mouthed answer and she would like a friend, too. But could she really be friends with someone so different? Nancy had poise and an air of confidence that no friend of hers had ever had as a schoolgirl. Not even Jennie.

'Yes, but why did you want to leave London? I can't imagine *leaving* there – it all sounds like glorious fun to me. My aunt says there are unmarried women who live quite alone, going to night-clubs and drinking Champagne.'

Louisa wasn't sure what to say to this. 'Maybe, but I wasn't one of them.' She moved over to the window. 'It's beautiful out here. I shan't ever want to leave the countryside.' She had gaped at the beauty of the frost in the garden that morning, with silvered blades of grass and a spider's web that looked like a giant snowflake.

'When will you go home to pick up your things?' asked Nancy abruptly.

'I don't know, in a week or two. I don't need much,' said Louisa carefully.

'No, I should think not. You've come with nothing at all!' laughed Nancy, and though there was a hint of a teasing tone, Louisa knew she wasn't being deliberately mean.

Ada, in fact, had offered to lend her some things until her first payday, and she would go and buy whatever she needed then. But she had no desire to take the conversation any further and made her excuses, leaving the room to find Nanny Blor.

Soon, Louisa and Nanny had settled into a sort of routine once the youngest children were abed, sitting together in the room that led directly off the stairs – a playroom, dining room and sitting room in one that was Nanny's room more than anybody's, with her own carriage clock on the mantelpiece. In chairs by the fire they would listen to the clock ticking and do the crossword in the *Daily Mirror*. A rocking horse stood in one corner, and in the other was the round table around which they sat for breakfast, luncheon and tea. A mahogany sideboard housed the nursery silver and china with red roses on it, Lord Redesdale not seeing any reason why the children should 'eat like savages' away from the dining room.

Quite aside from her duties in cleaning, laying the fires and bringing things from the kitchens, Louisa had found that the division of labour between her and Nanny had fallen quite naturally. Louisa was more concerned with the older children, while Nanny was quite proprietorial with the babies. Nanny would sit with Unity and Decca in the nursery, reading them books or patiently building towers of blocks for them to knock down. When she had a moment with them, Louisa found their soft cheeks irresistible for kisses and their babyish chatter endeared her to them quickly. Diana and Pamela occupied themselves for hours at a time playing 'house' with their dolls when not in the schoolroom.

Twice a day Nanny insisted on a brisk walk around the garden, which all of the children complained about at various times, except for Pamela. Even when the weather was awful, Pamela was happy to be outside and always enjoyed her daily ride. She was strictly forbidden from riding her elder sister's beloved mare, Rachel, on whom Nancy went hunting, much to Nanny's terror. When not riding, Nancy could always be found in the library, head deep in a book.

That first day, after her interview with Nancy, Louisa found Nanny in the linen cupboard. Although referred to as a cupboard, it was really a room, with a small high window that was always tightly shut, and wooden slatted shelves from floor to ceiling. She had stepped in to be hit by a fug of warm, damp air, a sharp contrast to the nursery floor where Lady Redesdale had decreed all windows were to be kept open at least six inches the year round.

'Oh, there you are! I wanted to show you in here,' said Nanny. 'It's far too hot for me, I can't bear it, makes me feel faint. I'd like you to be in charge of the linen. All our sheets and towels are here, as well as the girls' petticoats and vests . . . ' Nanny went on to explain how the linen needed to be rotated to avoid any one sheet or towel wearing out. 'There are no napkins,' she continued. 'Lady Redesdale thought the cost of laundering them was too expensive when they lived in London and everything had to be sent out. The habit seems to have stuck.' She gave a faint disapproving look. 'You'll need to do mending, too, but you can manage that, can't you?'

Louisa nodded. If she could, she would move in a wooden chair on which to sit as she darned, and breathe in the smell of the soapflakes to feel a little closer to home, though she had no desire to leave. Here, she felt safe. In this house she was cocooned from the harsh truth of what she could only think of as her real life in London. Nobody could get her here.

CHAPTER ELEVEN

~~~~~

'**R**ichly yet quietly dressed in a morning suit of grey tweed, a natty pearl tiepin stuck airily into his chocolate tie, the man presented a prepossessing exterior . . .'

'No decent man would wear a pearl tiepin! And what is a chocolate tie? What utter rot,' Lord Redesdale called out across the library as he rose from his armchair.

The scene would have looked odd to anyone passing by as there was evidently nobody else in the room. But under a table, hidden from view by a starched white tablecloth, were huddled the five Mitford girls and their new nursery maid. Nancy was reading aloud to her adoring audience from the latest edition of *The Boiler*. She had whispered to Louisa earlier that morning that the stories in it by W. R. Grue were, in fact, written by her. Grue's speciality was tales of horror – 'All the better to frighten them with,' Nancy had sniggered.

Her father, perhaps, was not so appreciative a listener, but Louisa had come to learn in just a few days that Lord Redesdale's bark was invariably worse than his bite.

Nancy stuck out a bright pink tongue, safe in the knowledge that he wouldn't see her misdemeanour.

'And don't let me catch you pulling a face at me. Sewers, the lot of you.' Lord Redesdale chuckled and walked out of the room.

It was nearly lunchtime and Louisa thought she probably should get everyone up to the nursery but Nancy was almost at the end of her story. She had come down with the girls to keep an eye on them and allow Nanny to put her feet up.

The first days at Asthall Manor hadn't been easy; Louisa felt out of place in such a big house and was shy of the children, especially when they were all banded together. Yet under the table, hidden from view, she felt like one of them as they listened to Nancy reading in her best dramatic voice.

Now and then, after a particularly scary bit, Diana would let out a quick shriek, but she otherwise looked as if she was quite happy to be frightened. Her face already contained brush strokes of the beauty that would surely later dazzle anyone she met. Pamela – 'The soppiest of us all,' Nancy said – seemed always to hold her breath, waiting for the next cruel tease, which her older sister was only too quick to provide. Nancy had told Louisa that her three happiest years had been those when she was alone as the child of the house, until Pamela had arrived and spoiled it all, never to be forgiven.

The sisters were getting fidgety, their stomachs beginning to growl with hunger. Unity had already complained of pins and needles. Decca was pulling on Louisa's buttons. Nancy waved the torch she had stolen from her father's coat pocket.

'Will you just *listen*?' she instructed, then continued in a low, slow voice: 'Suddenly his appearance of noble languor vanished and he sat upright, fork in hand with all the air of one who sees his end approaching. A foreign-looking individual of unprepossessing countenance and claw-like hands drew near—'

'That's quite enough of that, Miss Nancy!' The tablecloth was lifted to reveal the highly polished black-laced boots and woollen stockings of Nanny Blor. 'Come out, all of you, and get yourselves upstairs. I want scrubbed hands and faces for luncheon, and if I find a single dirty fingernail I'll tell Mrs Scobie no pudding for any of you.'

Louisa crawled out first and started apologising to Nanny, who motioned her to be quiet with a flap of her hands. 'Don't you be the one to say sorry. Miss Nancy knows it's her that needs to say it. You go and fetch our tray from Mrs Stobie.'

Louisa nodded and gratefully ran off to the kitchens, with a lurching feeling that she had had a near miss. The week's notice was not yet up and she needed to keep this job. There had been no word from Stephen and she was beginning to breathe out at last, allowing herself to believe that he was not able to find her.

Behind her, the children scrambled out in reverse order of age: Decca, on her wobbly, fat legs, holding on to Unity, then Diana, followed by a pink-faced Pamela and, finally, reluctantly, and with a show of making it look as if she meant to be coming out now anyway, Nancy.

Once she was up in the nursery with a chafing dish of roast lamb and potatoes, Louisa began to put out the plates for her and Nanny; they would eat alone together. As there were no guests that day, the children were having *luncheon* with their parents. Louisa rolled the peculiar word around her head. Before coming to the Mitfords, she had only ever had *dinner* in the middle of the day. The Mitfords had dinner in the evening. There seemed to be a never-ending list of words and ways of doing things that were different to the way she'd always done it at home.

Louisa heard the quick footsteps of the girls coming up the stairs, just as she noticed that Ada had thoughtfully put the *Daily*

News on the tray. Yesterday's, of course, passed along up to the nursery after Lady Redesdale and then Mrs Windsor had finished with it.

'Get their hands washed, Louisa,' said Nanny, walking across to inspect the plates. 'Hmm. No bread today. How are we supposed to mop up the juices? Does Mrs Stobie expect us to eat gravy with a *spoon*?'

In a chain that linked pudgy fists and small, dry hands, Louisa pulled along the three smallest girls to the bathroom. Nanny went to the bedroom to find the Mason Pearson hairbrush; both Pamela and Unity's thick tresses were slipping out of the silk ribbons they'd been tied in that morning.

Nancy went to the sideboard and picked up the newspaper, turning to the announcements page. When Louisa came back into the room, she started reading out loud: 'The engagement is announced between Rupert, son of Lord and Lady Pawsey of Shimpling Park, Suffolk, and Lucy, daughter of Mr Anthony O'Malley and the late Mrs O'Malley of North Kensington, London. Oh dear,' she giggled, 'that must have put the cat amongst the pigeons at Shimpling.'

'Do you know them?' asked Louisa.

'No,' said Nancy, 'but you can see that's a mismatch. I don't expect Miss Lucy O'Malley met her beloved Rupert while she was being presented at court.'

'While she was what?'

'Presented at court,' said Nancy. 'You know, when the debs are presented to the King. Mind you, it hasn't happened for a few years because of the war – this summer will be the first in ages. I wish it was my summer!'

'When will you do it, then?' asked Louisa.

'When I'm eighteen. Ages.' She turned back to the paper, and

Louisa fussed around the girls, straightening out their dresses and smoothing down their hair. Nancy looked up again. 'You know, Muv says we might all go to London this year, after the baby is born. Perhaps Farve will let me go to a dance. I *am* sixteen and I think if I put my hair up I could look much older.'

Nanny heard this last bit as she came back with the hairbrush. 'His Lordship will think no such thing,' she said firmly and pulled Pamela over to her, undoing the pale pink ribbon that pulled her hair back.

Nancy gave a pout and closed the paper, reading the headlines on the front page. 'Here's a rather grim story,' she said.

'What's the Beastly Scale?' asked Pamela, turning her head and causing Nanny to pull her ponytail more firmly. 'Ow!'

'I'd say about ten,' said Nancy. 'Maximum Beastly. A nurse was brutally assaulted on the Brighton line last Monday, somewhere between London and Lewes—'

'The Brighton line? But we've been on that train. Nanny! Listen to this.' Pamela's eyes were wide.

Pleased to have an audience, Nancy continued: 'She was discovered unconscious by three railway workers on Monday and died last night. The police are looking for a man in a brown suit.'

'Stop that, Miss Nancy,' said Nanny. 'It's not right for small ears. They've had quite enough to put up with this morning already.'

But Pamela had picked up the trail of the story like a hound. 'Nanny, that's the train we've been on to see your sister. We only went there last summer! Does it say which compartment it happened in? I wonder if it's the same one we were in?'

Louisa caught Nancy's eye and an understanding passed between them, but still Nancy pressed on – the thrill of the tease was too great to let go.

'Closer investigation showed that she had received a severe injury to the left side of her head . . . there was a ghastly wound in the head, and blood on her clothing—'

'Miss Nancy Mitford! You're not too old to be put across my knee and spanked with a hairbrush if you don't stop *this minute*,' threatened Nanny, going red with the effort of her crossness.

'But Nanny, it's so sad,' said Nancy, trying to put on a tone of great concern and woe. 'She was a nurse – Miss Florence Nightingale Shore. Do you think she could have been related to the famous one? Oh yes, it says here, her father was a cousin. She'd only just got back from five years' war service in France with the Queen Alexandra's Imperial Nursing Reserve—'

'Did you say Florence Shore?' asked Nanny quietly.

'Yes, Nightingale Shore. Why?'

'She was a friend of Rosa's. Oh dear.' Nanny put a hand out to steady herself and Louisa rushed to her, walking her to the armchair.

'Who is Rosa?' asked Louisa.

'She's Nanny's twin sister,' said Pamela. 'She and her husband have a teashop at St Leonards-on-Sea and we've been down there to stay with her. It's complete heaven. She sells these cakes with custard in the middle and if you don't bite carefully, it all comes oozing out and runs down your chin—'

'Yes, yes, dear,' said Nanny, shushing her. 'Oh, poor Rosa. Supposing Florence was on her way to see her? You know, Florence was a nurse at Ypres, when His Lordship was out there, and it was her letters to Rosa that let us know he was safe and well. She knew, you see, that I worked for his family. It was a great comfort to Her Ladyship at the time. And now she's been murdered! Oh, it's too awful. She was a good woman. All those soldiers she nursed . . . What an end. I don't know what the world is coming to, I really don't.' Nanny Blor sank back into her armchair and started fishing for a handkerchief.

Louisa, who hadn't been listening closely at first, gave a start. 'What station did you say she was discovered at?'

Nancy gave her a quizzical look but went back to the paper. 'It says that men raised the alarm at Bexhill and she was taken off the train at Hastings, but they think the attack must have happened somewhere between London and Lewes. Why?'

'Oh, no reason,' said Louisa. 'I just wondered.' But a thousand thoughts flashed through her mind. She had got off at Lewes. And then Guy Sullivan had suddenly been called to trouble at a station – had that been Hastings? She couldn't exactly remember but she thought it probably was.

Nancy folded the paper and put it back down on the side. 'I think if we do go to London this summer I might ask Muv for a new dress. If I do go to a dance, I need to make the right impression,' she said, but nobody responded. Nanny was staring into the fireplace and Louisa was brushing Diana's hair.

'I said, I might ask for a new dress. Perhaps I could even get something that could be used for my season? I won't grow all that much between now and when I'm eighteen, will I?' Nancy continued, in a voice slightly louder than before. Still, there was no response.

'That poor woman,' muttered Nanny. 'She deserved much better than that. I must write to Rosa. Louisa, dear, could you find me some writing paper?'

'Yes, Nanny,' said Louisa, wondering if she could bear to read the article when the children had gone. She wasn't sure what this all meant but she felt certain it meant something. 'Miss Nancy, could you take the girls downstairs, please?'

Nancy looked sulky but she held out her hand for Decca, who wobbled over to clasp it, and slowly the two of them led the rest down the stairs to join the grown-ups for roast lamb.

My dearest love,

Forgive me for not writing these last two weeks but I have
had not a single moment to myself – not one, at least, where
I am able to do something other than eat or sleep when
relieved from work. Not long after my last letter to you, we
were told we would be moving to Ypres, where I am now. It's
a few hours north of the Somme, yet in many ways it is, for
me and my nurses, as if we have not moved at all. We are
confined to our work in the Casualty Hospital for almost
all our waking hours. In the short distance outside between
the canvas canopy of the hospital and that of our dormitory,
a few yards away, there is little to see that we haven't seen
before.

The earth is beaten down by the tramping of the army
boots, no flowers can emerge and all we know of the sunshine
is that it makes our hospitals hot and uncomfortable for us
and the men. Of course, the sound of gunfire is constant and
the shells explode with a ferocity that never fails to make one
jump. There's a thunder that rumbles around one's head and
never rolls out. It is so unlike our experience in the Boer War
that I feel ashamed when the younger nurses come to me

expecting words of reassurance or an explanation as to how it will all turn out – I feel as naive as they do.

Somehow, of all the war so far, Ypres has been especially unnerving. I arrived here with eight experienced nurses from our encampment, as part of a drive to pull in as many capable hands as possible. The nine of us are working in a hospital with seven hundred beds. Every day we send men out, patched up as best we can, but we receive a constant intake of wounded men, and we must make do with finding them places to lie on the floor when the beds run out, as they always do.

For once we are not having to deal quite so much with the harrowing tragedies of limb amputation, which the newer recruits always find particularly distressing. These still go on, of course, but most of our wounded are from a sudden and appalling use of poison gas against our men. They tell us it floats across the trenches as a foul yellow cloud and before they know it, it has burned their skin and they have breathed it into their lungs.

These poor men! Our hearts break for them, if we have but a moment to sit and think about it. It is just as well, then, that we do not. We must be in our hospital all through the days and nights, which bring no distinction when it comes to duty, appetite or routine. One snatches sleep where one can, but fitfully.

The doctors have worked some minor miracles this war but they are almost inert with frustration in the face of this vile gas. There is nothing they can do. They can barely even relieve the pain and we must watch the men die slowly, each breath a razor slice inside their chest. Most terrible of all, somehow, has been the discovery that far from every case is fatal, but you can never tell which way it's going to go. Even the apparently worst afflicted may make a recovery. But for what? To be sent back to the front line? It is hardly what any of us could wish for.

Stories are our sustenance in these straitened times, whether it's the men telling us of their lives back home or extraordinary tales of courage that somehow emerge from this terrible war. So you may imagine that I was particularly thrilled to hear one of someone whom I do not exactly know but do have a link with: Mr David Mitford. I'm sure you will remember that Rosa's twin sister, Laura, is nanny to his children.

All his family must be in a state of anxiety since DM's older brother was killed at Loos very recently, leaving behind a pregnant wife. If she has a boy, then he, the baby, will be the heir to the family title, but if she has a girl then it will fall to DM (who will become Lord Redesdale). Meanwhile, DM has insisted on returning to war despite having only one lung – he's been invalided once already – and, my dearest, you can only imagine how I felt on realising he has been stationed here at Ypres!

That's not the half of it. He arrived in April, shortly before the battle broke out, and was given what was probably supposed to be a straightforward commission as transport officer, keeping the battalion supplied with ammunition. But this battle has been like no other, the demand for the ammunition has been exceptionally high and the danger has been great. Someone in his battalion told one of the men in the hospital about his courage and the story has been whispered between us for days.

As we were told it, it was clear to DM that the

ammunition would have to be moved at night so as to remain under cover of darkness, but the battle never lets up and the goods must be taken right across the town in the line of fire. There is no other route to take that would be quick enough. The constant need for munitions means the trip must be done not only every night but twice a night. DM decided that the method he would take would be to load the horses up, then ride them through the town at high speed – in the darkness, through the streets, as shells are thrown and guns are fired.

There is more.

Each night, to spread the risk, DM has decreed that a different soldier will take a load each time. But he, himself – father of five children, possible heir to the barony, an older brother already dead, missing a lung himself – will go every time. It sends shivers all through me to think of it. Every night, twice a night, he and his men ride their horses across town. So far he has been successful and not yet lost a single man. But how long will this battle last? We do not know and I fear for him each night, as we all do. The men say he is a good man.

That said, they are almost all good men. None of them deserve the terrible fates that they have been given.

I must stop here. I have a few hours of leave and am planning to take a walk in the bluebell woods not far from here. I'll be alone and will enjoy the time in a place of beauty to sit and think of you. Remember our picnic in the bluebells three years ago? I hope you are keeping yourself as safe as you can. I know my tales of woe are as nothing to yours and you are the bravest one I ever knew.

Most tender love,
Flo

CHAPTER TWELVE

～～～

Guy and Harry began their search for the brown suit and stolen jewellery in the pawnshops and second-hand clothiers of Lewes. Guy was ebullient; he felt like a proper policeman at last. In the second pawnshop, the seedy man behind the counter who hadn't bothered to wash his shirt since Christmas, if the stains under his arms were anything to go by, laughed in their faces. 'Why,' he wheezed, 'would someone who'd made off with diamonds and cash pawn a suit? He wouldn't even get two shillings for it if he came in here.' Guy had blustered that it was one way to get rid of the evidence but the man just carried on wheezing and laughing, thumping himself in the chest, and the two of them had walked out fast. In one second-hand shop, they were shown a huge pile of men's clothes that had been handed in since the date of the attack, and holding their noses they had sorted through what was unquestionably a dead man's wardrobe – including, presumably, the pyjamas he had died in – that had not yet been laundered despite the evidence of a heavy Woodbines habit.

Still, Guy encouraged Harry to press on. When they had run out of places to check in Lewes, they called it a day. They would get the train back to London, then come back down again in the morning to try places in Bexhill and Polegate.

'It's unlikely the man will have got off at Polegate, seeing as the railway workers got on there,' said Guy, 'but we've got to try.'

Harry was less enthusiastic, but at least it was a day off from the usual routine, he said.

Guy did his best to rally him round. 'If we solve this,' he reminded him, 'we'll get promoted. Maybe even Scotland Yard.'

Nevertheless, in spite of their efforts, the next few days proved just as hopeless for Harry and Guy, and no suit or jewels that matched the description turned up anywhere. DI Vine had decided to make a tour of the seaside boarding houses and found an abandoned brown suit but analysis by the investigation's pathologist found no bloodstains. There was a commotion when a soldier turned himself in and confessed to murdering a woman on a train, but a brief interview at Scotland Yard was enough for them to ascertain that he had nothing to do with it. He was handed back to the army as a deserter.

At least the second inquest came around fast after that. Everyone was present as before: the coroner; the deputy; police from all three forces; their solicitors and the eleven jurors. This time, more witnesses were to be interviewed, as well as Dr Spilsbury, which was thrilling to Guy.

'He's the one who identified the decaying dead body in Dr Crippen's basement as his wife,' he said to Harry, who in return told him to calm down.

First to be interviewed was Mabel Rogers, still dressed in deepest black. Guy noticed that this time she was not accompanied by a nurse, though the man was with her again, looking no less shabby than before. She wore no wedding ring, so he could not have been her husband, but he was clearly providing her with comfort. They looked to each other frequently and when she hesitated on the stand, she seemed to gain confidence in her voice after a reassuring nod from him. She was asked by the coroner to repeat some of the points she had made last time concerning the man who had come into the carriage.

'I've already said everything I can remember,' said Miss Rogers. 'He was wearing a brownish tweed suit of mixed and light material. I did not notice the kind of hat he wore but he had no overcoat. I do not think he had any luggage, but he might have had a small bag. He must have been about twenty-eight or thirty years old and he was clean-shaven.'

'What class of person was he, do you think?'

'A clerk, or something like that,' she replied.

'How much money do you think Miss Shore had with her on the journey?' asked the coroner.

'About three pounds, I think,' said Miss Rogers. 'We had been shopping together that morning and she had said that she must not spend any more or she would not have enough for the journey.'

'Can you tell us any more about her appearance? What jewellery was she wearing?'

'She was wearing a new fur coat and looked nicely dressed. I expect that the assailant thought she was well-off. She usually wore two rings with diamonds set in them and a gold wristlet watch.'

Guy was rapt. He had been at two or three coroners' inquests when someone had jumped before a train, but he had never heard a murder inquiry before. Not just any murder, either. This was sensational: a woman on a train, no weapon found, no suspect arrested. The court was packed with reporters again, scribbling furiously in their notebooks.

After Miss Rogers was dismissed, an engineer was called up to show the plans for Lewes station, with an explanation as to why those passengers sitting in the rear two carriages would have either to wait for the train to move up for them to disembark or jump on to the tracks, as those frequently did who had failed to ask the guard or were too impatient to wait.

Then Harry nudged Guy in the ribs. The coroner had just called George Clout, the first of the railway men who had discovered Florence Shore and raised the alarm at Bexhill station. Harry and Guy had been present during the interviews with the men immediately after the discovery but perhaps the coroner would prompt a confession. It had been known to happen – the presence of a jury and the severity of the court could frighten anyone into the truth. At the moment, these men were their only suspects.

Clout confirmed that on that day he had been working at Hampden Park Railway. He had joined two men he knew, William Ransom and Ernest Thomas, to catch the 5 p.m. train from Polegate Junction to Bexhill. They had boarded the last compartment; he and Thomas sat with their backs to the engine, while Ransom sat on the same side as Miss Shore.

The coroner began his questions: 'Did you notice a lady there?'

'I saw someone there in the further right-hand corner facing the engine,' said Clout, taking his hands out of his pocket when he started speaking.

'Was it dark when you got into the compartment?'

'Nearly.'

'How was it lighted?'

'Poorly lighted.'

'Incandescent gas, I suppose?'

'Yes.'

'After you sat down you saw somebody?'

'After about ten minutes, after we had gone about a mile, I noticed the person was a lady.'

'How was she sitting?'

'Leaning back, with her head on the padded back.'

'Did you notice her hands?'

'I could not see her hands, they were under the corner of her coat.'

'Were her feet on the floor?'

'Yes.'

'When did you next look at her?'

'About halfway between Polegate and Pevensey.'

'What did you see?'

'I saw there was something wrong with her.'

'Why?'

'From the position she was in.'

'What next?'

'I could see blood on her face.'

'Fresh blood?'

'I could not say.'

'Was there much?'

'There was a lot.'

'Was it running down?'

'I could not say.'

'What did you do?'

'I said to Ransom that something is wrong with that lady in the corner. I think I said, "She has had a nasty knock of some kind". He did not seem to hear what I said. He had a cold.'

'Did you speak to Thomas?'

'No.' Clout shifted on his feet. He did not seem comfortable in such a formal setting, to say the least.

'Why didn't you?'

'I didn't say anything further about it until we got to Bexhill.'

'Did you do anything?'

'No, sir. Not until we got to Bexhill.'

'Why didn't you?'

'I did not think it was so serious.'

'Did you notice whether the lady was breathing?'

'Yes, she was, and she appeared to be reading.'

'Were her eyes open?'

'They kept opening and closing.'

'Spasmodically?'

'Yes.'

Guy noticed Miss Rogers looking upset during this exchange, bending her head to fidget with the bag on her lap and pulling at loose threads on her coat. She may have been an experienced nurse but it couldn't have been pleasant to hear about her friend's injuries, and to realise that she had tried but failed to raise an alarm for help. It was also rather extraordinary that these men did not appear to have been more concerned at the time. Clout said he had noticed no blood in the compartment, nor did he mention any other signs of a disturbance. The other two men merely corroborated what Clout had said.

The train guards were called to give evidence and George Walters was sworn in. If Clout's testimony had been disturbing, Walters' was worse.

'She was sitting in a sloping position facing the engine,' he began. 'Her head was back on the padding and her legs were pushed forwards and showing to the knees, because she had slipped down. Her hands were in front of her and her fingers kept moving. She put one hand up several times, her fingers moved, and she appeared to be looking at her hands.'

A second train guard, Henry Duck, also spoke. He had been on the train from Victoria and was alerted to the trouble by Clout at Bexhill. It was Duck who had decided that she needed to be taken to the nearest hospital in Hastings. A phone call was made from Bexhill to arrange an ambulance at the next station. Mr Duck also remembered seeing a man jump down from the end of the carriage at Lewes on that fateful Monday afternoon and make his way along the platform, but it was dark and he had not caught much sight of him. As it had been a dark night and there were no lights at the station, he had only seen him by the light of his lamp.

Could this have been the attacker? There were two compartments at the back, one of which had carried the nearly dead Miss Shore, and the man might have jumped out of either of them. Where did he go afterwards? None of the staff at the station had noticed him but there was no reason to, especially if the man had a train ticket and could exit through the barrier in the normal way.

Guy felt Harry shift impatiently beside him; it was almost teatime. Harry was ruled by his stomach and looked forward to his daily slice of cake. Guy felt not a single hunger pang, not when he knew Dr Spilsbury was the next witness.

The coroner called the doctor to the stand. He was a good-looking man and his eyes were clear and bright. He wore a suit of a sharp cut with a flower in the buttonhole, his hair neatly parted and combed absolutely flat. In precise tones he described Miss Shore's injuries, inspected the day after her death. Guy did not understand the biological details but he knew enough to grasp that there were three wounds on her head, which had caused extensive bleeding all over the brain.

'Cause of death?' asked the coroner.

'Coma due to the fracture of the skull and injury to the brain,' said Dr Spilsbury.

'What do you consider the cause?'

'They were caused by very severe blows by a heavy instrument having a fairly large striking surface.'

'Would a revolver cause it?'

'Yes, the butt end of a revolver of an ordinary size.'

'Can you form any idea how many blows were struck?'

'At least three, there might have been more.'

'Would any of them cause unconsciousness?'

'Yes.'

'Do you think after one of these blows, the lady could have seated herself in the position she was found?'

'No. She must have been struck sitting down or placed in the position by her assailant. She could not have placed herself in that position had she been standing up.'

This was very interesting, thought Guy: whomever had hit her had subsequently sat her up and placed the newspaper on her lap, though they forgot the broken specs on the floor, unless they had slid off when the train moved. For whatever reason, the attacker wanted it to take a while for anyone who got into the carriage later to notice that something was wrong with Miss Shore. Why would this be? Guy wanted to think about this more but pulled himself back to the inquest.

Dr Spilsbury continued to answer more questions in his calm, methodical voice. He confirmed that the weapon had penetrated the brain and that this weapon could not have been an ordinary walking stick, nor could she have been injured by being struck while leaning her head out of the window. He believed she had been attacked while sitting down. He had seen, he said, no signs of a struggle apart from bruising on the tip of her tongue. There was one final question.

'Was there any indication of an attempt to ravish the deceased?' asked the coroner, even more sombrely than before.

'No, sir,' said Dr Spilsbury.

Miss Rogers must have been relieved to hear this. The inquest was almost over, bar brief interviews with local doctors. The coroner summed up the position and the jury returned their verdict a few minutes later. Despite all efforts by the police to find the attacker, Florence Nightingale Shore had been murdered by a person unknown.

Afterwards, in a bar a few doors down from the court, Jarvis, Haigh and Vine sank their disappointment along with a few beers. Guy and Harry, keenly aware they were still on duty and sitting with their superiors, nursed glasses of ginger ale. They barely spoke but listened in on the conversation, which touched on the case very little, much to Guy's disappointment. At one point, Vine muttered something about it being a random robbery, she was in the wrong place at the wrong time, it was most likely some desperate former soldier, to which Haigh and Jarvis nodded agreement and drank another large draught.

Guy's knee was jiggling up and down in frustration. He waited a minute, then couldn't help himself and spoke up: 'If it was a robbery, why did he attack her with such force? She was an old lady, or as good as. He could have just grabbed her jewels and money and made off.'

The three senior police officers exchanged a knowing look with wry smiles and Vine replied in a tone that made Guy want to rip his moustache off. 'He might not have meant to kill her, just knock her out. Some of these soldiers forget how strong they are, don't they? He left her alive, didn't he? Didn't make sure he'd finished the job. No, it wasn't a planned murder. Sorry to disappoint you.'

Guy said nothing to this. It still didn't sound quite right to him but he didn't have the courage to question a detective inspector.

Not long after that, Haigh stood up and shrugged on his coat. 'I'm off, lads. Best of luck. Don't suppose we'll be seeing each other again for some time.'

'What do you mean? What happens now?' said Guy, ignoring a glare from Jarvis.

Haigh tipped his hat up. 'Nothing, sonny. Unless someone comes forward, we've pursued all the avenues. Case closed as far as you're concerned. I'd look for something else to shine your torch on if I was you.' With that, he chuckled, pushed open the door and was gone.

CHAPTER THIRTEEN

N ancy stepped out of a cab and started to walk towards the entrance to Victoria station. Louisa backed out of the car next, holding on to Decca, who had her fat arms tight around her neck. She tried to crane her head around to the striding figure. 'Miss Nancy! Wait!'

Nancy stopped and threw her hands up in the air. 'We're going to miss it!'

Louisa said nothing as she held out a hand for Unity, who was next out, her face at its most serious. Diana, her blond hair shining in the midday sun, was last, much to Nancy's clear irritation. She asked Diana if she was a tortoise and mimicked a head drawing into a shell, which Diana simply ignored.

A second taxi had pulled up close behind them and soon disgorged Nanny Blor with Pamela and Tom. Although they had left behind the thrilling signs of spring in the country – lambs leaping in the fields, daffodils pooling at the edges, like broken egg yolks – there was a sharpness to the air in deepest London. Green leaves were budding on the trees and there was enough blue sky to make a sailor's suit. A gust of wind blew up suddenly, almost knocking Louisa's hat off.

This was not a journey she had wanted to make, the return to London, to Victoria station and then the Brighton line. She had slept fitfully for the last week, drifting in and out of dreams where she was being chased, feeling Stephen close enough for his hot breath on her neck, only to find Unity had crept into bed with her and was snuggled into her back, sighing deeply.

Otherwise, she had settled into the Mitford routine, such as it was, very well. There had been no attempt from her uncle to find her and she had, until the last few nights, managed to push him from her mind for the most part, concentrating on folding the linens or walking Decca slowly around the garden, counting snowdrops.

But with Lady Redesdale on bed rest for the next few weeks, as she had been for the last month – the baby was due any day now – and the children irritable with their Lenten sacrifices, it had been decided that a few days by the sea, staying with Nanny's twin, Rosa, was just what was needed. Louisa had asked if she might not be more useful staying at Asthall, to look after Lady Redesdale and the expected newborn, but Nanny Blor determined that she needed her more. The maternity nurse would be more than enough for Her Ladyship, who was, after all, practised at the business of birth.

The trip had been inevitable, whatever Louisa felt about it. From the second the idea had been mooted, Nancy had campaigned for its fruition. The others were just as enchanted at the thought of Rosa's teashop with its scones and steamed-up windows, the sea that was too cold to swim in but just about bearable for paddling, the caws of the seagulls and the exotic taste of salt in the air.

Nancy was taken with the notion of playing detective on the train. She had realised early on that they would be taking the same fated journey as Nurse Shore, if not the very same train. Lord Redesdale, believing his daughter to have taken a sudden, if surprising, interest in household economy, had readily agreed to their travelling third class.

Alongside cuttings from the reports on the attack and subsequent inquests, Nancy had put a notebook and pencil in her pocket, together with a magnifying glass she had snuck out of her father's desk. It had an ivory handle, delicately carved, with a satisfyingly heavy silver rim around the glass itself. She knew he would be furious when he realised it was missing but had already told Ada that it would be returned. She didn't want the maid to get into trouble.

Tom, taking seriously the instruction from his father that as the only male in the party he needed to keep an eye on things, had hurried ahead to Nancy. She linked her arm through his – despite the five years between them he was only a head shorter than her – and they led their merry band past the enormous station clock and on to platform nine, where a train was waiting for them, as sleek and glossy as a sleeping seal.

Nanny Blor huffed up at the rear of their gang, signalling to Louisa, who was struggling slightly with the sinking weight of Decca and rat-a-tat walking step of Unity.

'I need to spend a penny,' Nanny whispered. 'Give me Miss Decca. You can settle everyone on to the train.'

Louisa handed over the child and, catching the eye of the young porter who was wheeling along their luggage, hurried to catch up with Nancy and her brother. She had met Tom for the first time only a few days before, when he arrived home for the holidays, and had liked him instantly for his cool-headed nature and polite manners. Although still only eleven years old, the fact of his being away at school gave him an independence his sisters could never claim and it was clear they found his other life as exotic as that of a man who came from Timbuctoo. He took the teasing of his siblings in good nature, too, and rarely seemed to nip back, though Louisa had found in his room a homemade badge that declared: 'Leag Against Nancy, head Tom'.

Nancy was telling her brother the sad story of Nurse Shore's demise. It was a tale with which he was by now very well acquainted, but each re-telling featured a further polish. Nancy told the story as if presenting a brilliantly cut diamond, examining it at different angles to see which side caught the light best.

'Slow down, please, Miss Nancy,' said Louisa, pulling Unity along, aware of Diana trailing behind and that Pamela, liable to be distracted by the sight of someone with a dog or even just a pigeon pecking at crumbs on the platform, could easily be left behind altogether.

'We've got to get the last compartment,' said Nancy. 'I don't want anyone else sitting in there.'

'Run ahead then and save our seats,' said Louisa, allowing herself to slow down slightly. She hoped Nanny wouldn't take too long.

When Louisa arrived a few minutes later, she saw that only Nancy and Tom were in there, much to Nancy's delight.

'This could be the one, Louisa!' said Nancy, beaming. 'The very compartment that saw the final moments of Nurse Florence Nightingale Shore.'

Louisa paled slightly and looked around. There weren't, thankfully, any signs of the nurse's *final moments*. Nancy had taken the magnifying glass out of her pocket and was inspecting the seats closely, with something of a theatrical flourish.

'Hmmm, no sign of any blood,' she said. 'In the paper it said she had received three severe blows to the left side of the head,' she continued, oblivious to Tom's stony reaction. He looked, in fact, distinctly queasy. 'So there must have been some blood some-where. Ah – what's that?'

She leapt upon something small and shiny lying far beneath the seat. A sweet wrapper. 'Well, you never know, it might have been the very last thing she ate,' said Nancy, and put the square of waxy paper in her pocket.

'I think this is where she sat,' she went on, choosing the seat in the corner, furthest from the open door, facing the engine. 'So this is the last time she ever saw Victoria station—'

'Miss Nancy!' said Louisa. 'Not in front of the children, please.' She climbed on board with Decca and Diana; Pamela had been given instructions to wait on the platform so that Nanny Blor would find them. With the children deposited, the porter brought the luggage on and there were a busy few minutes stashing it on the racks and beneath the seats.

Nancy suddenly spoke. 'I say, porter.'

The young man, his thin arms heaving a case up, was caught mid-swing. He looked at Nancy.

'Did you carry the bags for Nurse Shore? You know, the one who was murdered on the train?'

'No, miss,' he said. He nodded to Louisa and left without even waiting for a tip.

Nancy just looked out of the window again. 'Oh, that's a shame,' she said. 'I bet he *had* met Nurse Shore, though.'

Louisa knew this would now be woven into Nancy's anecdotes about the day's trip.

Nanny Blor appeared at the door and looked in nervously. When Miss Nancy had suggested they go third-class, she'd been comfortable enough with the idea at first. She had told Louisa that the task of keeping the children quiet in first class meant she could never enjoy herself, but she wasn't at all sure about sitting where a woman had been killed. She had never met Florence Shore but she knew a great deal about her from Rosa and had even written to her once, to thank her for the news of Lord Redesdale during the war, as it had been so reassuring for all the family and servants.

There was no time to hesitate. The guard's whistle blew and Nanny scrambled to get in and sit down before the jolt of the moving train could take her unawares. Unity had already crept in before her, inspected all the available places and chosen one by a window, quite alone.

Louisa watched Nancy taking notes in her little schoolbook and though she looked quite comical – her nose crinkled in concentration, her girlish pigtail of dark hair betraying her childishness – she was, after all, trying to find clues for a real murder that had happened. Yet Louisa could not bring herself to feel afraid of their being attacked by a stranger, even one who had killed before. She was much more frightened of seeing Stephen. If he was staying on the coast nearby, it would all be over for her.

CHAPTER FOURTEEN

◀━━━◆

While Nancy and Tom sat together, notebook and pencil out, Pamela and Diana were opposite, looking out of the window, in the perfect position to eavesdrop Nancy's whispers to their brother. Louisa sat beside them with Decca; she knew she looked washed out and anxious but she tried to keep her mind off the last time she'd made this journey by singing snatches of 'Pack Up Your Troubles' in the baby's ear and jiggling her on her knee. Nanny Blor sat by the opposite window, straightening her skirts and catching her breath; she started rummaging in her bag, looking for some mints.

For the next hour, the children, their nanny and their nursery maid were uncharacteristically quiet. Decca was soon soothed by the rocking motion of the train and leaned against Louisa, sleeping. Unity watched every passing tree and building, looking enraptured to be moving further and further away from home with every turn of the wheels. Diana read her book, dozing occasionally and leaning against Pamela, who pointed out horses galloping across the hills or cows chewing the cud. Tom sucked toffees that he had found in his pocket. Louisa caught his eye as he did so and when he tried to hide the bulge in his cheeks, she guessed he had no wish to share – the tyranny of children who have siblings – so kept silent.

All the while, Nancy continued to write careful notes on the three tunnels they passed through, noting when they occurred in the journey, guessing the timing as best she could without a watch, and how long they lasted (she counted in potatoes). She looked at houses and wondered aloud if anyone in them could have seen what was happening in the carriage as it sped past; she wondered where you might throw a weapon away. So absorbed was she in her detective work, that she failed to see the tears slowly running down Louisa's cheeks; at least, she made no comment. Nanny Blor had her chin on her chest and was lightly snoring.

Louisa rubbed her face and dug in her pockets for a biscuit for Decca. An hour had almost passed and she wanted to look out of the window at Lewes station, to see if Guy was there.

She'd often thought about writing to him but other than posting him the money she had borrowed – which she'd sent with a short note to say thank you but adding no address where he could find her – she had not dared. She couldn't see how he'd ever want anything to do with her. What if he suspected she had tried to steal that man's wallet? The memory of that day flooded through her in waves as if it could sink her.

'Lou-Lou?' Nancy looked at Louisa. 'What is it?'

'Nothing.' She gave a watery smile. 'Something came to mind, that's all. I'm fine.'

The two of them had begun to forge a tentative friendship, one that was rooted in their sex and age but obstructed by the fact that Louisa was a servant and Nancy, if not quite a mistress, was certainly closer to that end of the spectrum. Louisa felt their hands almost reaching out to each other but not able to touch, like the painting of God and Man on the Sistine Chapel ceiling that she'd seen in a book.

'You look as if someone's walked on your grave,' said Nancy. 'Have you been here before?'

Louisa hadn't told any of them that she had been at Lewes station the day that Nurse Shore had been attacked. It was, after all, the same day that her uncle tried to force her to Hastings; she didn't want her employers to know that she was running away from anything, let alone such a person as Stephen. The less she talked about her life before the Mitfords, the better.

'No,' said Louisa. 'Not really.'

Nancy gave her a questioning look but Louisa started to fuss with Decca, so she was forced to resume looking out of the window again. The train was just pulling into Lewes station and as the guard had warned, the final two carriages, including theirs, had no platform beside them. Nancy had walked across to the window and opened it, letting in the cool spring air, and leaning her head out.

'Careful, Miss Nancy,' said Nanny, woken by the breeze.

'I'm just looking to see how far down it is,' said Nancy. 'It is quite far. You'd have to jump a bit, I think. And then climb up on to the platform.'

'What are you bothering your head with all this for?' said Nanny, though this sounded like less of a question than a statement intended to close the matter. 'Shut the window, please, it's too cold.'

Reluctantly, Nancy pushed up the window and sat back down with a soft thump, just in time to reveal the view to Louisa, as the train started up again. They rolled slowly through Lewes station and Louisa looked carefully but she couldn't see the tall, navy silhouette of Guy Sullivan. Whether she felt relieved or disappointed, she wasn't quite sure.

'It's a funny thing, though, isn't it?' said Nancy suddenly.

Her sisters and Tom, immune to her wonderings and teasings, remained absorbed in their books or musings of their own. With no one else responding, Louisa felt obliged.

'What's funny?'

'Well, it's occurred to me that you can't open these doors from the inside,' said Nancy. 'You have to open the window, lean out and then turn the handle. Don't you think it's odd that if the man in the brown suit had attacked the nurse, then fled the scene at Lewes station, dropping down on to the tracks, that he would turn back to reach up and close the window? I mean, there's no reason for him to do that.'

'How do you know that?' asked Louisa, interested, despite herself.

'It said in the report in the paper on the inquest – when the railway workers got on the train, both the windows were closed.'

'Ah,' said Louisa. She didn't really know what conclusion to reach with this. Nancy shrugged her shoulders and turned back to her notebook. The fields and hedges went on flashing past their window.

'Are we there yet?' asked Pamela, bored with trying to count animals.

'Not long now,' said Nanny Blor. 'Polegate next, then Bexhill, and finally St Leonards and we'll be there. If you all keep nice and quiet until we arrive, I'll ask Rosa to get you all a cream bun each for tea.'

CHAPTER FIFTEEN

~~~~~~~

For the next few days, Nanny Blor and Louisa happily oversaw their charges as they stayed by the sea. In woollen jumpers and cotton dresses, the children walked along the beach every morning, Decca and Unity stopping frequently to inspect underneath stones, Diana and Tom marching ahead like soldiers. Pamela spent many agonising minutes watching mysterious creatures in rock pools squirm away from Nancy's net as she fished hopelessly.

Louisa watched her own pale, thin face take on a healthy colour from the wind and sun, not to mention the brandy snaps that Rosa took great pleasure in handing out. Nanny and Rosa, pleasingly, were recognisably twins, each with their long hair pinned up, and Rosa's comforting figure a clear match for Nanny's stout middle.

Where Nanny saw her duty in a firm but fair hand with the children, Rosa delighted in a stream of affectionate sentiment, kissing each one as they came in, their damp jumpers steaming in the warmth of the café, which was constantly full and yet somehow there was always a table to be found for them, a teapot of scalding hot tea brought instantly. It was clear that Rosa was missing her two daughters, Elsie and Doris, only a little older than Nancy, who had both gone to work as maids in a big house near Weston-super-Mare.

Away from the strictures of Asthall Manor, Louisa found it easier to talk to Nancy and there were a few occasions when the two of them would find an excuse for a walk together, whether to post a letter or buy a button to replace one that had fallen off Diana's coat. Louisa indulged herself that, although Nancy's coat was of a finer wool and better cut than hers, they were of a similar height and shape, and any passer-by might assume it was two young women walking out as friends together.

Nancy linked her arm through Louisa's. 'Thank you for taking me with you,' she said, uncharacteristically polite. 'I had to get out for a bit. The girls were driving me around the bend.'

The phrase sounded too grown-up for her rosebud face, and Louisa couldn't help smiling. 'That's all right, Miss Nancy,' she said.

'Oh, don't call me "Miss", Lou-Lou. It sounds so formal. Call me Nancy, please.'

'I'd better not let Nanny Blor catch me doing that.'

'Very well, then, just when it's the two of us out together. Now which way are we going?'

Louisa hesitated. She hadn't had any intention of going to the post office at all; all she'd wanted was to get some air. Thoughts of the past had been encroaching on her lately, a general dark fear of Stephen. Being near to Hastings hadn't helped, what with his connections in the town, though she was fairly certain he would have returned to London, where he could be sure of a free bed under her mother's roof. And there was nothing to let him know that she was in St Leonards now. More than that, as she got comfortable with the Mitfords, particularly with Nancy, she found she wanted to tell her more. It was just a question of how much she could tell.

That morning Louisa had overheard Rosa and Nanny Blor talking about their mother and it had made her feel homesick to the point of nausea. She had been struck with a sharp pain of longing for her ma and the knowledge that she was too afraid of going home to see her, in case Stephen was there, had pushed her to ask Nanny if she might go to the post office as a matter of some urgency.

'Um, yes. This way. I think the post office is down here,' she said, and paused. 'Nancy.'

Nancy giggled. Louisa regarded the girl beside her, nominally her charge but she had a sharp wit that was far from girlish. Her clothes were not fashionable and some were visibly homemade – Lord Redesdale was not a man about to pay a dressmaker's bill for his *daughters* – but nobody who saw her could think she was anything less than upper class.

Louisa straightened her back and lifted her chin. But as she did so, her lip wobbled and, before she knew it, the ache behind her eyes had given way and tears were flooding down her cheeks.

'Lou-Lou?' said Nancy. 'What is it? Tell me, what's the matter?'

'I can't tell you,' said Louisa, hiccupping and wiping her face. 'It's too many things. I miss my ma,' she continued as a fresh tide swept over her.

'I think you are lucky. I *long* to get away from mine,' said Nancy.

'Yes,' said Louisa and tried to smile, to chase away the dark shadow of fear that was threatening to close over her. The sun was out but spring had not yet completely banished winter from its seaside holiday. They didn't have long before Nanny would start to wonder where they were. Not that Nancy seemed concerned about any timekeeping.

'There's something else,' said Louisa, tentatively.

'What is it?'

'I get frightened now and then that someone will come to the house and try to fetch me away,' said Louisa, wondering as she said it just how much she could reveal.

'Goodness, that sounds rather thrilling,' said Nancy. 'Who is it?'

'It's my uncle, my father's brother. You see, when I arrived that day at your house, the reason I looked so awful and had no things was because I'd run away from him. He had my letter from Mrs Windsor and had tried to hide it from me.'

Nancy raised her eyebrow. 'I suppose that does rather explain things.'

'The thing is, I can't quite shake the feeling that he'll try to find me.'

'Is there any way he could find out the address?'

'I don't think so. I haven't told Ma exactly where I am, and nobody else knows.'

'Then I don't think you have anything to worry about,' said Nancy, with the simple faith of a child.

'No, perhaps not,' said Louisa, and though she knew Nancy couldn't really understand, she still felt lighter and less alone.

They walked along in silence for a few more minutes.

'Do you have a sweetheart, Lou-Lou?' said Nancy, out of the blue.

'What?' said Louisa. 'No, of course not.' Though she thought of Guy as she said it and wondered if that wasn't a flip in her stomach.

Nancy sighed. 'No, nor do I. Except for Mr Chopper, of course.'

'Mr Chopper?'

'He's Mr Bateman's assistant, Farve's architect. He's *deeply* serious and couldn't be moved to look at me even if I danced a jig by the fireplace. He comes around for tea to show the plans and refuses any distraction. It must be love, don't you think?' Nancy rolled her eyes and Louisa rolled hers back, which made them both laugh.

'Farve says there's a shortage of men, anyhow. Perhaps we shan't ever marry and we'll be the "surplus women" they're always worrying about in the newspapers. We shall wear thick worsted stockings and glasses, and grow our own vegetables. We could read books all day long and never dress for dinner, like the O'Malley sisters.'

'Perhaps,' said Louisa, smiling. It really didn't sound so bad.

CHAPTER SIXTEEN

O n their fourth afternoon the Mitford party had made a hurried dash back to the café from the beach when the sky had turned black and a thunderstorm threatened. By the time the first fat drops splashed on the pavement, the girls and Tom, together with Nanny and Louisa, were huddled around a table, squashed in the corner by the window, bickering gently over the choice of cake. Louisa chanced to look up and saw Guy Sullivan walking into the café.

She panicked. What was he doing there? Before she could stare any more, she realised that Nancy had followed her eye and was also looking at the smartly turned-out policeman, his hat tucked under his left arm. She could see that behind his thick glasses he was squinting slightly as he walked towards Rosa, who was wiping her hands on her apron and smiling as she stood behind the counter that displayed the best of the day's cakes.

'Can I help you, sir?' she asked.

'Good afternoon, ma'am,' he said politely. 'I'm looking for Rosa Peal.'

'Then look no further,' she said, still smiling. 'That's me.'

'Ah,' said Guy. 'I need to talk to you about Miss Florence Shore.'

The smile vanished from Rosa's face. 'That poor woman,' she said. 'I still pray for her every night. That was a terrible thing that happened to her. But I don't see how I can help you.'

Guy looked around. 'Perhaps it would be better to talk somewhere privately?' he suggested, taking in the craned necks and paused conversation of the squeezed tables around them.

'There isn't anywhere,' said Rosa. 'And besides, I've got nothing to worry about. Tell me what you think I can do. But first, let me get you a cup of tea and a bite to eat.'

Guy tried to protest but she dismissed him, and before he was quite sure what had happened, he was sitting at a table and had eaten most of a scone that had arrived with the sweetest raspberry jam and thickest clotted cream he could dream of. Absorbed in the task of eating this as quickly as possible, while also wanting to prolong the pleasure, he failed to see Louisa, who was in a state of high panic.

What if he mentioned something about how he had found her, in a dishevelled heap on the tracks? That she'd had no money to get to her job interview? None of it would put her in a good light. She was trapped. So long as he was in the café, she had to stay in her chair, thankfully in the far corner, where she was pretty sure he couldn't see her.

'What do you want to know, then?' said Rosa, sitting down in the chair opposite and setting her own cup of tea down.

Guy, mid-mouthful, crumbs on the corners of his lips, hurriedly tried to resume a professional pose. He pulled out his notebook and pencil. 'Thank you, Mrs Peal,' he said. 'You see, the investigation has reached a bit of a dead end, so I thought I'd try to find out a bit more about Miss Shore. I understand she was on her way to stay with you, on the twelfth of January this year.'

'Yes, she was,' said Rosa. 'It was a terrible shock. She was on the three-twenty from London, so I knew she'd be arriving about half past five. I had got to St Leonards station in good time to meet her, only to be told the train had been stopped at Hastings. There was another woman who was supposed to meet someone off the same train and she said she would get a taxi there and kindly agreed for me to share it. When we arrived, there was such a commotion, I didn't know what was going on, but I certainly didn't think it was anything to do with Flo.' She paused and took a breath, visibly moved by the memory.

'Go on,' said Guy.

'I saw a woman being carried off on a stretcher and suddenly realised it was Flo. I couldn't do anything as she was put in an ambulance and taken straight off to the hospital.'

'Did you go to the hospital?'

'No, I couldn't. I'd walked down and was a bit out of puff, and they took her off very fast. I knew her good friend Mabel would be there as soon as she could be so I just went home. I didn't really think there was anything I could do for her then.'

'No, you were right,' said Guy sympathetically.

'I went to see her in the hospital a day or two later but, of course, it was no good; she never revived. The wake was here, of course, before they took her body to London for the funeral. Oh, but it was terribly sad. All the good things that woman had done, to have her life ended like that ...' Rosa brought a slightly grubby handkerchief out of her apron pocket and started to dab at her eyes.

'How did you know Miss Shore?' Guy asked, pencil still poised.

'We were nurses together, before the war. We worked in St Thomas's. I was a few years younger than her and she looked out for me. She was a very good nurse and so brave, too. Did you know she went to China when she was a young woman? Not many can say that. Never been further than Dieppe myself and that was enough for me. Can't get a proper cup of tea on the Continent.'

She gave a sniff, exactly like her twin. 'I think they have funny water.'

Guy brought her back on track. 'How long did you work together?'

'About a year, I think. I wasn't very good at nursing. I was happy to chat and tuck them up in bed, but sometimes it got a bit harder than that and I'm not too good with blood, you know. Makes me a bit faint. Anyway, I met my husband and that was that. We moved down here and opened up this place.'

'You kept in touch with your friend?'

'Oh yes, she was a terrific letter writer. And sometimes she liked to come and stay down here. She'd walk up and down the beach for miles.'

'Did she always come alone?'

'Yes,' said Rosa. 'Apart from one time, she came with her friend Mabel. A nice lady but it was difficult for me to put them both up, so it didn't happen again.'

'Do you know, did she have a gentleman friend?'

'She kept herself to herself, did Florence,' said Rosa. 'There was someone she was fond of, I think. She never really spoke to me about him but occasionally mentioned someone of an artistic nature that she thought very highly of. I'm not sure if he was a gentleman friend or not. Is this really helping?'

'Yes, Mrs Peal, it's very helpful indeed,' Guy said, trying to convince himself. Now that he was here, he wasn't at all sure what he'd thought he'd find.

'Humph, well. The funny thing is, during the war she wrote me letters about where she was stationed. One time, she was in Ypres and she noticed that the transport officer there was David Mitford – he's Lord Redesdale now – and she remembered that my twin sister worked for the Mitfords, as their nanny. Flo wrote to me so that I could let them know that he was safe and well. That was such a kind thing to do. Anyway, what's funny is that my sister's down here for a few days. Isn't that a coincidence?'

'Yes,' said Guy, baffled. He wasn't sure what the connection was, if any. But the name she had mentioned rang a bell and he couldn't think why. Then he saw that Rosa was waving to a table in the corner with a large group of assorted children and another woman who closely resembled Rosa.

There was also another young woman who looked familiar in some way. He peered at her, although it was difficult, she was looking out of the window, refusing to take her eyes off whatever it was out there – the lamppost? He couldn't see anything.

Then she lifted her head, almost as if she had felt him looking at her, and his heart thudded as he realised who it was: Miss Louisa Cannon. She must have got the job, then. Redesdale! That was the name in the letter. Lady Redesdale. Guy allowed himself a small moment of congratulations for remembering this detail; it seemed like a very *policeman* sort of thing to do.

Before he could stop her, Rosa had got up and was walking over to the table to talk to her sister. He could see Louisa first try to busy herself with one of the younger children and then, perhaps, she saw that her attempts to hide were futile. She looked up, turned her head and her brown eyes caught his. Guy gave her a smile and when she had read it and was sure of it, she gave him a smile back. At least, he hoped it was a smile, he couldn't always be sure. He took his glasses off and gave them a rub.

Rosa was at the table now, talking to her sister, explaining that the young policeman was here to ask about Flo, though goodness knows why, she didn't know anything. Nanny Blor clucked sympathetically in return.

'What?' said Nancy. 'This policeman is investigating the murder? I want to talk to him, Nanny. Let me talk to him.'

'Whatever for, dear?' said Nanny.

'All the evidence I collected on the train, I ought to tell him about it.'

'I hardly think you had better do that. He's got far more important things to think about, I'm sure.'

'Perhaps Miss Nancy should talk to him, Nanny,' said Louisa. Nanny looked at her in wonderment. 'It's just that, well, don't policemen have to look at everything? Perhaps Miss Nancy spotted something he missed out.'

'I don't agree, but if you want to talk to him, you go ahead.' Nanny huffed a little and started rubbing Unity's face with her handkerchief, much to her displeasure.

Rosa had already beckoned Guy Sullivan to the table. 'This is Miss Nancy Mitford,' she said as he approached. 'She'd like to talk to you. I'd better get back to my customers, if you don't mind.'

Nanny got up from the table and gave him a cursory glance. 'I'm going to take the others upstairs,' she said. 'Mind you both come along soon. It's time for their baths.' This last was directed at Louisa, who blushed.

'Hello, Miss Cannon,' said Guy. 'Do you mind if I sit down here?'

Flustered, Louisa said nothing but motioned at a chair. Nancy had the good grace not to watch this scene with her mouth open. Louisa tried to give Nancy a look that would seal her sympathy and discretion; it did.

Nancy spoke up first. 'How do you know each other?'

Louisa made sure she answered before Guy. 'We don't, not really. Mr Sullivan helped me when I was trying to find the right train on my way to my interview with Lady Redesdale. We talked for a little bit.'

She turned to Guy with what she hoped was a calm expression, though she felt far from calm inside. It was as if her entire future depended upon his answer. 'What can we do for you, Mr Sullivan?'

Guy understood immediately. In fact, Louisa had not needed to worry a jot. He pulled his chair into the table a little closer. 'It's good to see you, Miss Cannon,' he smiled. 'Please, tell me how you are.'

CHAPTER SEVENTEEN

~~~~~

Louisa and Guy sat down on a bench overlooking the seafront. Between them was a bag of hot chips, each one covered in salt and the sharp tang of brown vinegar. Louisa thought that the combination of these and the cold air that whipped her face was a perfect sensation, and she briefly allowed herself a moment to think of nothing else as she licked the salt off her fingertips.

For just one hour, Louisa had been excused from her duties with the girls. She had intended to walk alone along the beach but when she came out of Rosa's teashop, she had been gratified to see Guy waiting for her outside. He wasn't in uniform, so she almost hadn't recognised him in his long brown overcoat, a cap pulled down low over his forehead. His hands were stuffed in his pockets, trying to get warm. He had been standing outside for some time.

'I thought you had to come out eventually,' he confessed. 'Though I hadn't dared to hope that you would be by yourself. Will you come for a walk with me?'

Taken unawares, Louisa couldn't think of enough of an excuse not to, and nodded her assent. 'But I only have an hour,' she said. 'And I'm hungry, even though I shouldn't be. I think it's the sea air.'

'Chips it is, then,' said Guy, laughing, and they walked side by side, braced against the stiff sea breeze, to Wharton's Fish & Chips, which he assured her his informants had declared the best in town. Guy felt his chest swell as he walked. He watched Louisa hold on to her hat with a gloved hand, saw her quick steps in her neatly laced boots and wished he could offer her his arm to hold on to but knew that moment hadn't arrived yet. Patience, he told himself, a little more patience.

Once they were on the bench, looking out at the steel-grey sea, the swell visible and terrifying, the waves rhythmically crashing on to the stones, he started to tell her about Florence Shore. The day before, in his pleasure at seeing Louisa, Guy hadn't discussed the case at all, much to Nancy's disappointment. Relieved not to have to talk about herself, Louisa now prodded him with questions.

'What do you think she was like?' asked Louisa, after he told her that the investigation had ground to a halt for lack of a murder weapon and witnesses. The 'man in the brown suit' had apparently vanished into thin air – the train guard had seen someone alight at Lewes from the rear carriages but he couldn't be sure he came from the murdered woman's compartment and it had been too dark to catch anything of his clothes or face.

'That's what I'm trying to find out now,' said Guy. 'I don't know if it will help but I thought if I could talk to people who knew her, I might discover a reason that someone would murder her.'

'Perhaps there was no reason. Maybe it was just terrible luck that she was in that compartment and a robber got in.'

'But if someone just wanted to rob her, they could have done that easily and run away at the next stop, they didn't need to be so savage. She was almost an old lady; she couldn't have fought back if someone had snatched her jewellery and money from her. And

Dr Spilsbury, the pathologist, said there were no signs of a struggle. I think that means she knew her attacker.'

Louisa sat and thought for a minute. Having the physical strength to fight back didn't always mean you could. Fear or shame held hands down tighter than any rope. Even when – perhaps especially when – you knew the person who was threatening you.

'What about the men who found her on the train – might it not have been one of them?'

'Possibly,' said Guy, 'but none of them had any blood on their clothes. It doesn't seem possible to have hit her that hard and not get blood somewhere. After all, it was on the floor and wall of the compartment. And they alerted the guards as soon as they got to Bexhill instead of getting out and running away. There's something else, too. When they got on, they didn't notice she was dying because whoever had attacked her had sat her up, to make it look as if she was reading. Why would a robber do that? I've gone over and over it.'

'What if,' she said, 'they intended it to be a murder and they ran out of time. They might've wanted to make sure that her injuries weren't discovered too soon, so they could be sure she would be dead before anyone could get her to a hospital.'

Guy leaned back to look at Louisa in admiration. 'I think you're right. Someone meant her to be killed and that someone was someone she knew.'

They both took this in quietly.

'But why are you talking to Mrs Peal? She couldn't have done it,' said Louisa.

'No, but Miss Shore was on her way to see her. Mrs Peal knew she was on the train, for one thing. And she knew her well.'

'It couldn't have been her. She wouldn't hurt a fly,' said Louisa.

'I'm not accusing Mrs Peal,' said Guy, his policeman's hat

mentally back on, cautious of making litigious statements. 'I just thought she might shed some light on Miss Shore, that's all.'

From the investigation so far, Guy had built up a picture of Miss Florence Nightingale Shore that felt quite definite in his mind: an educated, middle-class woman who was brave, serious and diligent. She had been a respected nurse during the war, full of compassion for the soldiers in her care, often staying behind to nurse them in the makeshift hospitals when the shelling outside would send others running for more solid shelter. She had earned a certain renown for looking after the Indian and black soldiers from the colonies and treating them with equal priority and respect as she did for the English officers. She had never married, although Mrs Peal had made those allusions to an artistic man, possibly a gentleman friend, but there was no identity for him as yet.

In the last few years, thanks to the war, Miss Shore had rarely come back to England on leave. Friendships had been held together thanks to her apparently indefatigable letter-writing. There was the aunt, a baroness, that she had spent the day with, just before she died. The aunt had given an interview but Guy thought he might try and see her himself, though it was, he admitted, getting harder to get permission from his super to do so. As far as Jarvis was concerned, the case was closed and spending time on it was a waste when he could be put to better use checking signal boxes.

'She thought of others more than herself, didn't she?' said Louisa. 'Those letters she wrote about Lord Redesdale from Ypres, she didn't need to do that and Nanny Blor told me that they were of great comfort to Lady Redesdale.'

'Did she write to Lady Redesdale directly?'

'Not so far as I know,' said Louisa. 'I think she only wrote to Mrs Peal, who passed the news along.'

A seagull cried overhead and woke Louisa from the reverie,

making her suddenly sit up in alarm. The hour must have passed; she had to get back to work or Nanny Blor would fret.

Guy, without thinking, took one of her hands in both of his. 'Can I see you again?' he asked. 'Might we walk again tomorrow?'

Louisa withdrew her hand. 'I don't know. I'm not sure if I'll have any time off tomorrow. I must go.' She stood up and took a step away. 'Thank you for the chips,' she said and gave him a brief smile before turning around and walking away from him along the promenade, the seagull still cawing its cry that sounded like a warning.

CHAPTER EIGHTEEN

⟜⟜⟜⟜

Before heading back to London, Guy decided to go to East Sussex Hospital, only a short walk away from the beach, where Florence had been admitted and then died. The house surgeon and doctor who had attended to her had been only very briefly interviewed at the inquest and he wondered if they had any more to say.

However, when he arrived at White Rock Road, where the Victorian hospital stood, vast and clearly in need of repair, the house surgeon was off duty and the doctor was attending to patients. Fortunately, he was in his uniform and the nurse he spoke to was eager to help him with his enquiries. She sent a porter around to Dr Bertha Beattie's lodgings and the message came back that she would meet him at a café across the road.

The appointment was 4 p.m. and the sea blew in damp air every time someone opened the door, so Guy was alerted to the formidable entrance of the doctor as soon as she walked in. She was a handsome woman, with an efficient look, as if she had a white coat on beneath her fur wrap. Spotting Guy's police helmet on the table, she came directly to him.

'Mr Sullivan?' she checked before she sat down.

Guy stood awkwardly as she lowered herself on to the chair, which appeared rather spindly now. 'Yes. Thank you, Mrs Beattie, for coming in.'

'*Dr* Beattie.'

'Ah, yes, absolutely,' Guy stammered.

Dr Beattie ordered herself a pot of tea and a bun, then turned to face him. 'What can I do for you? As you know, I spoke at the inquest.'

Guy explained that sometimes a small detail that may have been thought insignificant before could turn out to be very important. He was determined to solve this case, so could they at least try? The doctor nodded, as if to say, 'Go on'. Most of all, he continued, without witnesses or a weapon, he was trying to find a motive for the attack. Although some money and jewellery had been stolen, these items did not seem to warrant a violent assault that could not have been intended to result in anything but death. Would she mind, he asked, going over the details of Miss Shore's state when she was first admitted to the hospital? After all, Dr Beattie had been the first person to check her condition.

'She was semi-conscious when she arrived,' said the doctor in reverberating tones. It was not hard to imagine a scalpel in her hand. 'I spoke to her but she did not reply.'

'Did her condition change quickly?'

'Very. She was deeply unconscious by the evening. She had arrived with us before six o'clock and never recovered from that state.'

'What about her appearance when she arrived?'

'Of things that were out of the ordinary, I noticed that her dress was torn, and there was a tear on the left leg of her underclothes, as well as on her scarf.'

'Could those have happened when she was being carried out of the train and on to the stretcher?' asked Guy.

'I don't think so. And we were naturally careful – we understood that her clothes would be part of the evidence. But as to how to explain them – I can't help you there.'

'Might they have been torn in a struggle?'

'Possibly, but it could simply be that they were torn before she even got on the train. One can't say with any certainty.'

'Were there any bruises on her person?' asked Guy, embarrassed even to allude to an inspection of Miss Shore beneath her clothes.

'No.'

'Which you think means she wasn't in a struggle?' hedged Guy.

'I don't think anything at all, Mr Sullivan. I am not a pathologist but a house surgeon.'

As there was little point in trying to draw her into any kind of speculation, Guy tried another tack. 'During the time she was still alive in the hospital, did she have many visitors?'

'I wasn't there the whole time but I understand her friend Miss Rogers never left her side. Some local friends came by, I believe. Not a great many but she was not as abandoned as some I have seen.'

'Doctor, I'm sure you have seen most things in your career,' said Guy carefully.

She nodded.

'Do you think she knew her attacker?'

Dr Beattie took the time to consider Guy's question, but when she replied it was without hesitation. 'I wish I could give you a definite answer, but the fact is that we just don't know. There doesn't seem to have been much of a struggle, but whether that was because the assailant attacked her quickly or because she knew who he was, I am completely unable to tell you.'

'He?' said Guy. 'The attacker was definitely a man?'

'I would not like to be absolute on this point. However, it seems highly unlikely that a woman could inflict those injuries with such force.' Dr Beattie ate the last of her bun and neatly patted her lips with a handkerchief from her pocket.

'Thank you,' said Guy. 'I do appreciate your coming to see me now. I know it's your day off.'

His inquiries were over here.

CHAPTER NINETEEN

~~~~~~

'It's another girl.' Lord Redesdale dully related the news to Nanny Blor over the telephone.

'Oh, very funny, my lord!' said Nanny, bursting into laughter.

'What do you mean?' he asked crossly. 'It's a girl! A girl, dammit!'

Nanny was silenced at once. 'Beg pardon, my lord. I thought it was an April Fool,' she said. 'Of course that's wonderful news. What's the tiny one's name?'

'We don't know. We hadn't thought of any. For God's sake, we've used up all the girls' names.'

'Yes, my lord,' said Nanny, always the eye in the storm. 'And how is Her Ladyship?'

'She's fine. She has to lie down for two weeks: doctor's orders. I rather think you might all head back now. It's Easter on Sunday. I think it would cheer her up to have the children back.'

'Absolutely, my lord. We'll get the train this afternoon. I'll telegram ahead so Mr Hooper can meet us.'

'Righto.' The phone clicked.

Nanny was standing in the teashop; the telephone was in pride of place by the till. This meant there was no such thing as a private telephone conversation because Rosa didn't believe in secrets – not when it came to her customers, at any rate, and she could charge them half a bob to use it. Not that she made much money; few customers knew anyone with a telephone they could ring.

The rest of the morning was spent in a blur of packing and tidying. The girls and Tom made a show of fury to be leaving Mrs Peal and her cream cakes, but it was lacklustre. They loved Easter at home, with the bells of the church ringing out all morning and an egg hunt that took them over every inch of the garden and even into the churchyard over the wall.

News of the baby, now they knew it was only another girl, failed to raise any kind of comment. Even Nancy couldn't do much more than let out a dramatic sigh, earning her a reproachful look from Nanny.

Guy had returned to London after his interview with the doctor and had sent Louisa a short note saying he didn't wish to intrude upon her time but he wanted to let her know that he was to be easily found at his home address, should she possibly want to write ... He suggested that perhaps she might hear something else of Miss Florence Shore from Rosa or Nanny Blor that could be of importance, as he had no intention of giving up on the case. Reading it, Louisa thought: So that's that, then, and put the note in the back of her book.

Arriving back at Asthall Manor after dark, tummies still full from the enormous parcel of buttered bread and teacakes that Rosa had tearfully sent them all off with, they changed the atmosphere of the place in minutes. There was commotion and shouting as the girls and Tom fell upon Mrs Windsor and Ada, their favourite maid. Hooper, Ada and Louisa lugged the cases up the stairs to the nursery, to the sounds of Lord Redesdale admonishing his children to be quiet, though they could hear it was done in quite a sanguine manner.

Lady Redesdale lay prone on her bed, attended to by a maid. Nobody went to look at the baby except for Nanny Blor, who whispered to her a welcome to the world.

The nursery had only been shut up for a week but Louisa enjoyed the feeling of unpacking and knowing where things went. A return to somewhere that had started to feel like home had given her a burst of energy, even after such a long day of travelling.

In the library, the girls, Tom and their father were warming themselves in front of the fire. After the first day of April, the radiators were switched off and fires were not to be lit before 3 p.m., except in Lady Redesdale's bedroom. Not that anybody complained or even thought to change the rule, even if it snowed: this was the law of the house.

It wasn't long before Nancy was regaling her father with stories of their week in St Leonards: the squashing up in beds in Mrs Peal's flat above the teashop; the freezing sea; the murder inquisition . . .

'Murder inquisition?' said her father sharply. 'Explain yourself, Koko.'

'The murder of Florence Shore on the train,' said Nancy. 'The same train we took! The policeman on the case came to St Leonards. And I'll tell you something else you won't have thought to remember, poor, dear old dunce. Florence Shore was the nurse who wrote to Nanny's twin from Ypres, to let us know that you were alive.'

Lord Redesdale looked at his eldest daughter. 'My word. She certainly did write those letters. I had no idea at the time, of course, but your mother told me when I got home that she'd had the news that all was well. Goddammit, she knew I'd been mentioned in dispatches before I did.' The shadow of those dark days fleetingly passed over his face. 'You're right. I hadn't put those letters together with the murdered woman's name. Never met her myself, though she had a reputation for being very good with the men. An attentive listener and kind, they said. Of course, the doctors preferred the nurses not to get too involved with the men.'

'Why not?' asked Nancy.

'It was a war,' he said abruptly. He drifted into silence briefly, then snapped himself back. 'What was the policeman doing there then?'

'Well, he knew that Miss Shore was on her way to stay with Mrs Peal when she got on that train – you know, the one where she was murdered—'

'There's no need to be so bloodthirsty.'

'I'm not. He was asking Mrs Peal if there was anything she could think of that might help him solve the case. He was awfully nice, Farve, terribly tall and good-looking—'

'That's enough of that. You shouldn't be noticing that sort of thing.'

'And also,' Nancy carried on, 'he knows Lou-Lou. They met when she was on the way here.'

'Who the blast is Lou-Lou?'

'Lou-Lou! Our nursery maid.'

'Oh, her,' said Farve, losing interest.

Louisa had been hovering by the door while this conversation was going on, waiting to interrupt at the right moment to tell the children it was time to go up to bed. She noticed Lord Redesdale barely register her existence but did not allow herself any self-pity: it was more important that Nancy be stopped in her tracks.

She stepped across the threshold, into the room that was no more used to welcoming her sort than she was comfortable being in it. 'Apologies, my lord, but it's time for the children to go upstairs,' she said.

Lord Redesdale looked at her and coughed. He had the grace to look a little shamefaced. The children cried out in protest but Louisa was unusually firm, and inside a minute, they'd all been got up and pushed up the stairs.

Nancy went out last and walked beside Louisa. 'I wasn't going to say anything, you know,' she pleaded.

'About what?' said Louisa, wondering if Nancy realised that she'd been about to reveal something of her life as if she was no more than a chapter in a bedtime story. Was that all they thought of her? A cipher, a character to be goggled at?

Whatever the truth of it, she was not about to let Nancy know that she'd almost pierced a very fragile and soft part of her; she knew enough of the eldest daughter to know that it was better not to hand her that sort of power. She used it mercilessly against her sisters in spite of her fundamentally loyal spirit.

'Oh, I was just talking nonsense . . .' said Nancy, trailing off.

Louisa said nothing but walked on ahead to the nursery to catch up with Diana and Decca. She had hoped that she and Nancy were more alike than different, but perhaps she was alone after all.

CHAPTER TWENTY

B ed-prone and fed up in the weeks after Debo's arrival (it had taken some time to furnish the baby with a name), Lady Redesdale had done little. So by the time the month of May came around, she appeared to feel quite herself again and decided she would like to get to London for some of the Season.

Lord Redesdale, ever keen to see his adored wife happy, rented a house in Gloucester Road and the whole family, including Mrs Windsor and Mrs Stobie, the cook, decamped to be in the city just in time for the Chelsea Flower Show, heralding two months of fashionable parties.

Still, the promised summer weather had not yet shown itself; the air was warm but it rained almost every day. Even the brightest of frocks struck a desultory note when overshadowed by a large black umbrella. Nancy, stubborn as ever, refused to feel disappointed. Although Farve had reminded his daughter sternly that she was not yet of an age to go to a dance of any sort, she felt sure that the combined forces of a new decade, the first proper, joyful season since the war had ended, and her own sheer willpower would overcome this paternal hurdle.

Disappointingly, on arriving at Gloucester Road, Lady Redesdale had set about organising herself to attend only a few parties and made it clear that they would not be staying there for longer than three weeks. Although she had missed seeing certain friends in the last few months of her pregnancy, she was not naturally a very social animal, and her husband, of course, could not be trusted out in public for long. It only took one 'sewer' to make a misplaced comment about Germans or hunting and the whole thing would be off.

Dances were the last thing on Louisa's mind. She had been very reluctant to return to London for fear of coming across Stephen. This meant that going to see her mother was still something she wasn't sure she could do, though she longed to, desperately. On the other hand, Guy was in London and perhaps she might see him.

Correspondence between the two of them had been non-existent since St Leonards, and while she knew she had to work, at the same time she could not help remembering the kindness in his face and the warm clasp of his hands on hers.

In London there was a slight change in the working pattern, at least. Nanny Blor took charge of the youngest babies – Debo, Unity and Decca; Diana and Pamela were happy to tag along on the twice-daily walk around the park and entertain themselves in the Gloucester Road nursery, which had the novelty of borrowed toys, including a darling doll-sized blue and white China tea set. Diana would take the role of Great Lady while Pamela fussed around her as the maid, pouring endless cups of tea as her sister criticised her skills.

Louisa had been given the role of chaperone to Nancy. Not that there was a great deal to guard against; there had been two or three tea parties with cousins and a walk around the Natural History Museum in South Kensington with an old neighbour of

Nancy's from the days when the family used to live off Kensington High Street.

Nancy was hugely envious of her friend Marjorie Murray for attending a school in Queen's Gate. 'A proper school, Lou-Lou, can you imagine? Where their brains are fed information of use.'

'I'm not so sure about that,' laughed Marjorie as they stooped to look at the stuffed sloth in the glass cabinet. 'There's plenty of conversational French and fierce instructions on the correct way to waltz. And besides, all the other girls don't stop talking about which men are the most eligible and who they'd like to marry. I wouldn't exactly call them bluestockings.'

'What's the point anyway?' said Nancy. 'One isn't allowed to do anything fun for simply years yet. I shall be combing my grey hairs before Farve lets me out of the house.'

'No,' conceded Marjorie, 'though there is the occasional thing in London. There's a ball this Thursday, actually, that I'm going to. It's a charity thing, I think. Red Cross, you know. For the soldiers.'

Marjorie was wearing a blush-rose dress with dark red piping and tiny buttons all down the front. While it couldn't be described as a flapper dress, it had a looseness to the fit that showed it didn't rely on a corset. With white stockings and shoes with small heels, Marjorie may have been only seventeen years old but her sophistication was there for all the world to see. Louisa knew that Nancy's plain yellow cotton skirt could not say the same, though she had been pleased that morning with the cheeriness of its colour.

'Well, your parents are progressives is all I can say,' said Nancy.

'Let's go upstairs and look at the shells,' said Louisa, keen to divert Nancy's attention, but she wouldn't be dissuaded.

'Can anyone buy a ticket to this dance, then?' asked Nancy, as they followed Louisa up the enormous staircase.

'I suppose so,' said Marjorie. 'Seeing as the money is all in a good cause. My godmother is organising it. That's really the only reason I'm allowed. My father won't be letting me go to anything else.'

Nancy slowed down to let Louisa go ahead a little further and then she whispered to her friend, 'Can you get me two tickets? I'll get you the money. I've got some saved from my last birthday.'

Marjorie was doubtful. 'How will you explain to your parents where you are?'

'Don't worry about that, I'll find a way. Will you do it? Will you get me the tickets?'

'Fine, then. But don't tell anyone I did it for you. I'll be in a whole heap of trouble otherwise.'

'Promise,' said Nancy. 'Oh, Marjorie! Just think – it could change our whole future!'

'I wouldn't put quite so much on a few dances with some stiff old men and wounded soldiers. There's almost no one left to come to a ball, you know,' said her friend, though Nancy's smile was contagious, and the two girls skipped up the stairs to catch up with Louisa.

CHAPTER TWENTY-ONE

A few mornings before the dance, Louisa was up early as usual, woken by baby Debo's mewling, though the placid mite was easily quietened with a bottle. They could hear the trundling of cars outside, the alien sounds of a city coming to life, and the sun had warmed the cushions by the window by the time the children's porridge had cooled enough to eat. Decca had resisted a brush through her thick tangle of blond curls and had roped Unity into a climbing game around the nursery in their nightdresses, while Pamela and Diana got themselves dressed. Nancy slept on and probably could have carried on until midday, had Louisa not learned to give her a shake.

Lord Redesdale expected his oldest daughters to be dressed and ready for breakfast by 7.55 a.m., when he would sit at the table staring at his pocket watch, counting down the seconds until the maid came in with the toast. With his short dark-grey hair and trim moustache, he maintained a military atmosphere of punctiliousness even when surrounded by children. After breakfast – a prompt ten-minute affair if the children did not poke their fingers into the butter or spill milk on to the tablecloth, causing more fireworks – Lord Redesdale would retire to the study. The day before, Nancy had burst in and was delighted to discover him exactly as she had suspected: in the armchair, his newspaper having fallen across his face, a loud snore vibrating the pages. Entering without knocking was now strictly *verboten*.

On this morning, as on every other, he would emerge shortly before noon to go to his club, where he would have a light lunch and a heavy snooze by the fire, then return home for tea and a final nap before changing for dinner. Where the urban made him soporific, in the country Lord Redesdale would walk for hours in the winter, his dogs at his side, and in the summer could happily spend whole days fishing in the River Windrush that ran through their garden.

Nancy told Louisa that her father had remarked loudly at tea two days before that, as far as he was concerned, the parties in London were full of the most ghastly reprobates with whom he could not find a single scrap of conversation he wished to have. Lord Redesdale did not like London.

Nor did Nanny Blor. Louisa had become increasingly fond of this solidly built woman, a reassuring presence that she truthfully had not had before. Though wrinkles creased Nanny's forehead, her red hair still flamed and her zest for the children never waned. She bustled about the nursery distributing both kisses and firm instructions in equal measure. It was quite clear to Louisa that the children loved her, perhaps more than their mother, around whom they were reticent. In London, Nanny grumbled that the air was filthy from the motor cars, the rented house meant she was constantly worrying about the children's sticky fingers making marks on the furniture and the garden was too small for the necessary daily perambulations. So every morning and afternoon, the children were rounded up and taken off for a quick-march stroll around

Kensington Gardens. Louisa suspected that, for all her bluster, Nanny Blor secretly rather enjoyed pushing baby Debo in her huge Silver Cross pram, knowing she could well hold her own against the snobbish Norland nannies. Their uniform held less water than her status as a nanny in charge of a baron's brood. Of course, the nanny who revealed that she worked for an earl or a duke would provoke a large sniff and the comment that she really had to be getting on as she had better things to do than standing around chatting all day.

It was on one such walk, taking their usual route past the Peter Pan statue that Pamela was particularly fond of – 'Those dear little rabbits,' she would sigh each time, and Nancy would grimace on cue – that they started discussing again the Florence Shore case. Nanny had had a letter from Rosa that morning, which had prompted it.

'There's been nothing in the news lately, has there?' asked Nancy.

'Not so far as I know,' said Nanny, 'and Rosa hasn't mentioned anything for a while. She keeps an eye out and tells me.'

'To think that the man who did it is still out there,' said Nancy in deliberately dramatic tones, pretending to peer behind a tree. 'He could be lurking around any corner . . . '

'That's enough of that, Miss Nancy,' said Nanny, pulling Unity to her a little closer.

'Sorry, Nanny,' said Nancy. She never said sorry to anybody but Nanny. 'The policeman thinks it was someone she knew anyway. Doesn't he, Louisa?' Nancy went on.

Louisa, who'd been thinking that she would rather like to see Guy again, nodded. He must be in London, she supposed, but she hadn't the nerve to let him know that she was there too.

'I think it must be about money. It's always about money,' Nancy said with conviction.

'She had a bit of money,' said Nanny Blor.

'Did she?' said Nancy. 'How do you know?'

'Rosa told me. She might've been a nurse but she came from a good family,' said Nanny. 'I'm not saying any more, I'm not a gossip.' Nanny set her face forwards in a way that was supposed to mean the subject was closed.

'How would Rosa know?' persisted Nancy.

Nanny hesitated, then said, 'I think our lawyer might've mentioned it to Rosa.'

'Your *lawyer*?' Nancy's voice was incredulous.

'Yes, our lawyer,' said Nanny sharply. 'I've got interests, you know, outside of you. Flo recommended him to me and Rosa when our father died.'

'Where is he? Is he still your lawyer?'

'What's it to you, Miss Nancy?' said Nanny, but she could never resist for too long. 'Yes, he is still our lawyer. He's in London; he has an office in Baker Street.'

After that, it was small beer for Nancy to get his name (Mr Michael Johnsen) and his office address (98b Baker Street). When they got home, Nancy grabbed Louisa and stole them into the study, safely free of Lord Redesdale until teatime.

'Let's telephone this Mr Johnsen and arrange to see him tomorrow morning,' said Nancy, her eyes shining. 'We might find something out that could really be of use.'

'I don't know,' said Louisa. 'I'm not sure we should be interfering like this.'

'I'm sure he'll only tell us what we're allowed to know. It's not against the law. And if we do find anything out, then you've got a good excuse to get in touch with Mr Sullivan, haven't you?'

'Who says I want an excuse?' said Louisa, but she couldn't stop herself from smiling.

*

140

The following morning, having promised Lady Redesdale and Nanny Blor that Nancy needed Louisa with her to go to the Army & Navy store to buy some more white gloves, the two of them stole off to Baker Street on the underground train. By 11 a.m. promptly, they were sitting in Mr Johnsen's office on leather chairs that felt rather too big, across from his desk that couldn't be seen for stacks of papers and folders, most of which threatened to topple over.

'My piling system,' said Mr Johnsen with a nervous giggle, smoothing his hair back with the flat of his palm. His suit had shiny patches at the elbows and his stomach betrayed a habit of long lunches. 'It's not often I see a peer's daughter in here,' he said and looked as if he might giggle again but stifled it. 'What can I do for you?'

Nancy had drawn herself up to her fullest height, crossed her legs elegantly at the ankle, as Louisa knew her mother had asked her to do a thousand times, and laid her gloves neatly across her lap. She looked up at the solicitor coquettishly.

'You see, it's like this Mr Johnsen,' she began, and Louisa realised, both aghast and admiring, that Nancy was flirting with him. 'It's rather unorthodox, I know, but the late Miss Florence Shore was a dear friend of our nanny's twin sister and she thought she'd be mentioned in the will. A Mrs Rosa Peal. She lives in St Leonards so couldn't possibly come all this way to London to ask you, and seeing as we are here, we thought we could do the favour, do you see?'

Mr Johnsen nodded and smiled nervously, showing small, grey teeth poking out from beneath fleshy pink lips.

'I gather the will was read last month, so – ' Nancy gave her most winning smile here and Louisa swore she could see beads of sweat breaking out on Mr Johnsen's forehead – 'could you let us know if our friend is in it? I assume you managed to look it out for me?'

Mr Johnsen's hand went straight to a pile just on his left. 'Yes, I did, Miss Mitford. It's a public record now. Strictly speaking you should apply to the probate registry, but seeing as you're here . . . If you don't tell anyone, I won't.' Here he gave an attempt at a wink, which failed. He looked as if he was trying to blink smut out of his eye.

Nancy put a hand on the desk and leaned forwards. 'We won't say anything, Mr Johnsen, you can be sure of that,' she said reassuringly. Then she sat back and held her hand out for the paper.

Louisa, who had been almost entirely ignored by the two of them up to this point, drew her chair up to Nancy's a little closer and they read through it.

The nurse's estate was indeed an impressive sum for somebody who spent her years working in public service and living modestly in a nursing lodge: £14,279. Her brother, Offley, was executor, in charge of distributing what looked like a rather long list of small gifts to various godchildren and friends – twenty-five pounds here, one hundred pounds there. A carriage clock that had been given to her by her godmother and namesake, the famous nurse Florence Nightingale, was left to a cousin's daughter. As they'd expected, there was no mention of Rosa Peal.

'Look, here,' said Louisa, 'an instruction for a residuary estate of three thousand six hundred pounds to be invested into a trust fund for her cousin, Stuart Hobkirk. That's a generous sum, isn't it?' She looked up but the solicitor wasn't listening; he was taking a pinch of snuff as discreetly as he could.

'Yes,' said Nancy, 'after her brother, he's been left the most. And look, she left him a diamond pendant. That's quite a bizarre thing to leave a man.'

'Not, perhaps, if it was something that she often wore and wanted him to remember her by,' said Louisa.

'You mean, it might have been a love token?' said Nancy, and the two of them raised their eyebrows at each other. Curiouser and curiouser.

Then Louisa noticed the date besides the dead Miss Shore's signature: 29 December 1919. She pointed to it and whispered to Nancy, 'Don't you think that's rather close to the day she was attacked?'

Nancy clamped her lips together, as if to stop herself from squealing, and nodded excitedly. Then she changed her composure again and turned to the solicitor, who had sat back down behind his desk and was watching the two young women. 'Thank you, Mr Johnsen. You've been most kind. It's rather strange but Mrs Peal does not appear to be mentioned here. Might she have been in an earlier will?'

'Perhaps, but only the last will is the one that counts, I'm afraid,' he replied. 'I might have a copy of an earlier will but it doesn't make any difference what she wrote before if she changed it sound of mind.'

'Yes, of course,' said Nancy, sounding uncannily like her mother. Her ability to assume an adult's pose of confidence was never less than impressive. 'Well, then, we had better be on our way. Thank you so much for your time.' She stood, and Louisa did too, as Mr Johnsen, attempting to button his suit jacket over his straining stomach, ran out from behind his desk to get to the door before them and open it.

'Not at all, Miss Mitford,' he said, almost bowing at the waist. 'It was a pleasure. Anything you need, please don't hesitate to ask.'

CHAPTER TWENTY-TWO

‿‿‿‿‿

In the far corner of the Tea Room in Victoria station, Guy sat alone at a table, drinking a cup of tea as slowly as he could. Harry was not at work that day, though he didn't know why, and he was staying out of Jarvis's eyeline before he could be sent off to one of the duller, more solitary tasks meted out to his rank. As usual, Guy was returning his thoughts to the murder of Florence Shore, turning over the facts as he knew them, wondering where there was a chink of light, something that the police or the coroner might have missed. He could not stand the thought that a man who had killed a war nurse, in turn someone who had saved the lives of so many men, should go unpunished.

Idly watching the queue of men and women as they went to pay for their tea, Guy's eye landed on a man in railway livery; a large white moustache lay beneath his nose, like a polar bear stretched out.

He knew that man.

Guy pushed his chair back with a shove and leapt up. 'Duck!'

The waitress behind the counter suddenly disappeared behind the till and several people in the queue looked around, puzzled, their heads lowered.

'*Mr* Duck,' said Guy and the waitress went bright red. The queue laughed but Henry Duck turned around slowly as Guy braked in front of him. 'Yes?' he said.

'My apologies, Mr Duck,' said Guy, conscious now of having brought the entire café to his attention, 'it's just that . . .' He lowered his voice and leaned in closer. 'You were on the train when Florence Nightingale Shore was attacked, weren't you?'

Henry Duck looked flustered. 'What of it? I've already given my statement to the inquest.'

'I know,' said Guy, 'it's just that, well, the case has been sort of closed but I know the murderer has to be out there somewhere. I think I can find him. Would you mind answering a few more questions?'

Henry pulled out his watch chain and looked at it. 'I've got a few minutes,' he said. 'I suppose it wouldn't do any harm.'

'Thank you,' said Guy. 'I've got a table in the corner; no one can overhear us there.'

'I hope I don't get into trouble for this,' said Henry, but he followed Guy nonetheless. They summoned the waitress over and asked for two more cups of tea. They talked a little while she fetched a teapot and more milk – the usual station workers' gossip about passengers that delayed trains – and once she was out of earshot, Guy took his notebook out and adjusted his glasses.

'I heard you at speak at the inquest,' said Guy. 'But I wondered if I might ask you again about the man you saw at Lewes station.'

Henry nodded.

'From my notes here, it says you were in charge of the train from Victoria, and when it arrived at Lewes, two minutes late, you got down on to the platform.'

'That's right,' said Henry. 'It was a dark and dirty night and there were no lamps at the station, so I walked along the platform holding my own lamp.'

'I know this is repeating your statement but could you tell me again – when you walked down, did you see anybody get out of the train?'

'Yes, a man got out of a compartment behind my van. He got out on the foot-board, shut the door, stretched along to the next compartment and swung off.'

'Did he pass you? Did you see him?'

'Just momentarily. He got down just as I got to him.'

Guy looked again at his notes. 'You said you spoke to him, to ask him if he hadn't been told to get into the front portion of the train, but he didn't answer you. Was he in a hurry, do you think?'

'No, not 'specially,' said Henry.

'Can you recall how he was dressed?'

Henry took a sip of his tea and Guy noticed with distaste that he ran his tongue over the bottom of his moustache as he put his cup back down. 'It's getting harder to remember but he had a dark, drab mackintosh coat on, and I think he wore a cap. Both his hands were in his coat so I don't think he had either a stick or an umbrella.'

'What about his build?'

'I should describe him as of athletic build,' said Henry.

'Athletic?'

'Broad shoulders, I suppose. Look, sonny, I'm going to have to go soon, my train leaves in a few minutes.'

'I won't keep you much longer,' said Guy. This description did not match that given by Mabel Rogers: her man was thin with no overcoat. 'We know it's usual for people to get out like that. There was nothing to call special attention to him?'

'Nothing at all,' said Henry.

'Have you seen him since?'

'No,' said Henry. 'Not so far as I know. But as I said, it was dark and I saw him only briefly. At the time I thought there was nothing in it.'

'But you are certain that the man got out of the compartment in which Florence Shore was found?'

'No, I can't be absolutely certain,' said Henry. 'That's the shame of it. I wish I was. I'd better go. I'm sorry not to have been of more help.'

'You've been very helpful,' said Guy. 'Thank you.'

When he arrived back at work, the constable on the desk handed him a letter. 'Getting love notes, are you, Sully?'

Guy snorted and told him to be quiet, but his heart jumped when he saw the familiar handwriting on the envelope. Miss Louisa Cannon – and she had something of great interest to tell him.

CHAPTER TWENTY-THREE

~~~~~

The following week Louisa and Nancy stood in the doorway of the Savoy, shivering in their dresses. After a hot, close day the rain was coming down in big drops, bouncing off the pavement like rubber balls. Their carefully combed and pinned hair had been flattened, their feet were soaking wet and their spirits thoroughly dampened.

'All that planning,' whined Nancy, 'and now we look like two drowned rats. Shall we pack it in and go home?'

'We can't,' Louisa reminded her. 'We've told Lady Redesdale that we're having supper with Marjorie Murray and her godmother, and they're not to expect us home before eleven o'clock.' She was regretting having been talked into the scheme.

'At least it's almost the truth,' said Nancy.

After Nancy had procured the precious tickets from Marjorie – they had been almost disappointed they weren't delivered by pumpkin coach, such was the fantasy they had built around the dance – she had set about securing Louisa as a chaperone for the evening.

Louisa had resisted as far as she could but, in the end, she too was a young woman who wanted to wear a pretty dress and go dancing, like any other. Nancy persuaded Louisa that, seeing as she was going to go whatever Louisa said, at least as chaperone she could keep an eye on her. When Louisa protested that she had nothing to wear, Nancy said she would lend her a frock. She didn't have too many ballgowns in her wardrobe and they'd both have to fudge it somehow, but with their hair up and some lipstick . . .

'No lipstick,' Louisa had said. 'I draw the line there.'

Then it was just a question of asking Lady Redesdale at the right moment – that is, when she was too distracted to think properly. 'Which is most of the time,' pointed out Nancy.

When her mother was writing her letters, Nancy appeared at her shoulder and said that Marjorie Murray's godmother was taking her out to supper at the Savoy for her birthday and had very kindly asked if she could come too, seeing as she was in London. And Lou-Lou could chaperone her.

'Is it Marjorie's birthday?' asked Lady Redesdale, barely halting the scratching of her pen.

'No, her godmother's,' said Nancy.

'Oh?' She looked up. 'That seems an unusual way to do it.'

'Yes, funny, isn't it?' said Nancy, forcing out a small laugh. 'So, can we go, please? We won't be home late.'

'Mmm?' said Lady Redesdale, her head bent back to her task again. 'Yes, you can go. No later than eleven o'clock, please.'

'Yes, of course,' said Nancy, and said to Louisa later, 'She'll be asleep anyway; she won't know what time we get back.' Although she was crossing her fingers behind her back.

And now here they were, hovering in the doorway.

'We'd better go in,' said Louisa. She was feeling a little unsure of herself – responsible for Nancy and, at the same time, sharing very much in her girlish anticipation for the night ahead. All of which was tinged with nerves that they were doing yet another thing they really shouldn't. The visit to the lawyer had unsettled her and she couldn't stop returning to it in her mind. At least she had passed something of it along to Guy. Perhaps he would make sense of it. She shook her head and tried to tell herself to enjoy the party. It was not, after all, a usual sort of an evening for her.

They could hear strains of music over the milling of the crowd. Women of all ages were crowding in, shaking off the rain and laughing, even as they despaired over their sodden shoes and hair. Their dresses were a riotous indulgence of colour and cloth, from palest pinks to deepest blues, from satin to tulle, with hand-stitched embroidered flowers, flashing brooches and daring prints overlaid on top. Tiaras shone and lips looked bitten, dark red and parted, breathless with joy.

It had been so long since happiness was allowed to ride unbridled over the night; tonight, grief was banished and the thoughts were of the hours ahead that promised to repair broken lives.

Not many men, though, Louisa noticed. Here and there, one saw a sliver of an officer's uniform as he stood, crowded by women, his walking stick discreetly tucked close to his leg. Other men stood alone awkwardly, conscious that they were outnumbered and that even this glitter could not chase away the dark shadows in their minds. The waiters, at least, were men too young to have fought, and they had a jaunty look as they wheeled around with their silver trays of Champagne.

After they had given their coats in and collected their dance cards, Nancy and Louisa dived into the crowd, Nancy both looking for, and fearing, seeing someone she knew. Thankfully, it was Marjorie they saw first, dutifully posted beside her godmother, who greeted the guests at the ballroom entrance. The band had just struck up a waltz and those that already had their dance card marked were walking on to the floor with their partner, a trace of smugness belied by their dropped heads as they looked backwards to the friends they had arrived with.

'Hello, Nancy,' said Marjorie, bending away from her god-mother, unsure of whether Lady Walden knew Lady Redesdale, but erring on the side of caution.

Nancy was wide-eyed, very young and very grown-up all at once. 'Hello, Moo,' she said. 'Who else is here?'

The classic question. In a crowded room, 'no one' was there unless you knew them and, for all her bravado, Nancy wouldn't talk to anyone to whom she hadn't been introduced. Marjorie pointed to a dark-haired girl in sky-blue tulle and long white gloves drinking a glass of Champagne. Close behind her against the wall sat a woman who resembled her but looked thirty years older and rather grumpy.

'Lucinda Mason,' said Marjorie. 'Her aunt's in a frightful gloom. It's her third season and no husband yet. They went to Molyneux this year for her dresses in the hope of upping her chances.'

Lucinda was the older sister of Constance, who was Nancy's age and therefore not at the ball, but the two sisters had played with Nancy in Kensington Gardens when they were small.

'Let's go and cheer her up,' said Nancy, pulling Louisa by the arm.

'I've got to stay here,' said Marjorie. 'I'll catch up with you later.'

Before Nancy could reach Lucinda, a lean man in officer's uni-form approached her and they started talking. The aunt's eyebrows unfurled and she pulled out a bag of knitting in happy anticipation.

As Nancy came up behind, she saw Lucinda open up her dance card, which was completely blank, and say to the young man, 'Yes, I believe I can have the next dance with you ... Oh, hello, Nancy. I didn't expect to see you here.'

Nancy wasn't perturbed. 'No,' she said archly. 'I've come with Marjorie Murray. How are you?'

Louisa remained a few steps behind and caught the aunt's eye. She realised, her heart sinking, that she was more aligned with the ferocious chaperone than the other young girls. Even in a borrowed dress of grey silk she could not pass herself off as 'one of them'. She cast about for a waiter; some wine would be good.

'Very well,' Lucinda replied. 'Oh, er, Mr Lucknor, this is Miss Mitford.'

The two shook hands. He had dark eyes and perfect posture, but his cheekbones made him look as if he had lived off stale bread and gruel for some years. Perhaps he had. This had the effect of making him look both vulnerable and rakishly good-looking – a dangerous combination – and Louisa watched Nancy's reaction to him warily.

'Please, call me Roland,' he said. 'Good evening, Miss Mitford. Perhaps I might have the pleasure of a dance with you, too?'

Lucinda tried, and failed, to hide her miffed feelings. But she knew, as they all did, that one had to share the men about.

'Perhaps,' said Nancy. 'I've only just arrived. One doesn't like to mark one's card too early, does one?' She cocked her head to one side and Louisa could not but admire her insouciance.

'I shall return,' said Roland, then gave her a bow before offering his arm to Lucinda. The two walked on to the dance floor as the next waltz began.

Nancy turned to Louisa excitedly. 'See! Oh, Lou-Lou, it's as easy as that.'

Louisa did not share in Nancy's glee. 'Be careful. It's *not* as easy as that,' she said.

'Don't be a spoilsport. Let's have a drink ...' said Nancy, touching the arm of a passing waiter and grabbing two glasses. But Louisa gave her a stern look and she put them back with a pout.

'I'm not taking you home with wine on your breath,' said Louisa, conscious of her responsibility. Now that she was here, she wondered how she had ever thought she was going to join in. The girls here were beautiful, confident, fragrant: a world away from her and everything she had ever known.

CHAPTER TWENTY-FOUR

Nancy and Louisa stood side by side, their tenuous friendship feeling as fragile as a brandy snap in that moment as they watched Lucinda and Roland wheeling in and out of the dancers. Louisa was reminded of working with her mother in the laundry, the hours she would spend in a daydream, watching the women turn the mangles with their sinewy, strong arms, sleeves rolled up high. Those days felt a million miles away from the room she was in.

Her reverie was broken by the appearance of two men before them in officer uniforms. One of them was badly scarred on his left cheek, the other looked as if he may have had a little too much wine already.

'May we have the next dance, ladies?' said the one who had to adjust his stance slightly to avoid swaying.

Nancy had a glint in her eye. She said nothing but stepped forwards and took the tipsy soldier's arm; a new waltz had begun. Louisa looked at the scarred man who was holding his arm out for her.

'Why not?' he said, pre-empting her reluctance. 'Give a man a whirl around the floor.'

Louisa hesitated and the man jerked his chin towards her. 'It's my face, isn't it?' he said. 'You can't *bear* to look at it.'

She could hear he was repeating a phrase that had been said to him in the past. 'No, it's not that,' she said.

'Got a sweetheart already, have you?'

Louisa nodded, as small a nod as it was possible to make.

'I'm only asking for a dance.'

He held his arm out again and she took it. They started dancing and she followed his lead, the waltz not exactly being a dance she had done often in the past. All she knew of it was her father giving her a turn or two around the parlour on Christmas Day, after he'd had a couple of glasses of porter. She just about kept up and only trod on his toes once or twice, to which he said, 'If you stopped looking down at the floor and looked at me, you'd do better.' So she looked up, though not at his face but over his shoulder. It was true, once she stopped trying to think about what she was doing and relaxed herself into his lead, her feet seemed to make the right steps.

She thought about Guy, imagining that she was dancing with him, and before she knew it, the band was playing a different tune. Louisa opened her eyes and looked at her partner's face; he had cold, grey eyes and his grip around her waist was getting uncomfortably tight.

'I think that's enough,' she said. 'I'd like to get a glass of water.'

He didn't say anything but jerked his arm, pulling her in even closer. He bent his face into her neck.

'Stop it,' whispered Louisa, terrified that someone might notice.

The soldier pulled away. 'I'll get you a drink,' he said, and let go of her waist, only to wrap her arm around his stiff woollen sleeve so that he could lead her away.

Held firm, Louisa had no choice but to follow him. She looked around for Nancy but couldn't see her. She realised she didn't know how long it had been since she'd last seen her. The room was feeling warm and the constant jerking notes of the music were closing in on her mind, preventing her from thinking clearly. The soldier let go of her arm and took two glasses from a tray, instructing the waiter to bring him back a whisky.

'I don't want wine,' she said to him.

'Drink it,' he said gruffly. 'You'll feel better.'

She took a sip. 'I have to find my friend,' she said.

'You don't need to worry about her,' he said. 'My name's Mickey Mallory, by the way.'

Louisa did not offer her name in return, but continued to move her head around, looking for Nancy. As she did so, she noticed that the men, unaccustomed to wearing their woollen uniforms in a crowded ballroom rather than in the freezing trenches of France, had drops of sweat running down their necks that were beginning to dampen their collars. Poor things. The dance was meant to be a benefit for soldiers, not an endurance test. There was a theory that if the women could see the men in uniform, they'd remember better what they had been through and give more generously.

She spotted Nancy, now dancing with Roland, the officer they had briefly been introduced to. Nancy looked smugly around her, no doubt trying to catch the eye of girls she knew so that they might see her dancing with a handsome soldier. As Louisa watched, she saw Nancy yelp and almost immediately the officer was leading her over to the side as she limped. Nancy caught Louisa's eye with a look that clearly said she didn't want her coming over, so Louisa turned her back.

Mickey looked pleased. He smiled at her and said something but she wasn't listening.

'I think I'd like to sit down,' said Louisa.

He assented with a surly reply and, as discreetly as she could, she led them to chairs close to Nancy and Roland, but out of their sight. She was just near enough to be able to catch their conversation. It was stilted and she missed some things thanks to the band and Mickey's prodding – he was asking her to dance again and she got the impression he was not a patient man. Dismissing his suggestion, Louisa leaned back and turned her head towards Nancy.

'How's your ankle? Is it feeling better?' said Roland.

'Oh, yes,' came Nancy's reply.

'Good-o. In that case—'

'But I don't think I should stand up just yet,' she broke in. 'Could you sit with me a while?'

Louisa stole a look and saw Roland looking uncomfortably about him as he sat on the very edge of the chair, as ready to leap up as a frog on a lily pad. He had the look of a poet about him, for all his clean-shaven stiff upper lip. His eyes were thrown into shadow by his thick lashes and he held his back ramrod straight, but his left foot was jiggling. He took out a gold cigarette case and offered one to Nancy, who shook her head, much to Louisa's relief. After he had exhaled his first puff, he seemed to relax a little and looked at Nancy. Louisa strained her ears even more.

'Did you say your name was Mitford?' he asked. 'Are you anything to do with David Mitford?'

'That's Farve!' said Nancy. 'I mean, my father. He's Lord Redesdale now.'

'Is he, indeed? He was very brave, your father.'

'You knew him in the war?'

'He wouldn't remember me,' Roland said. 'But I was in his battalion at Ypres and we all knew who he was.'

Something in this statement jolted Louisa, though she couldn't think exactly why. She took another small peek and saw him finish his cigarette, then stub it out beneath his black boots. An elderly chaperone saw it too and looked at him crossly.

'Did you know Nurse Florence Shore?' asked Nancy.

That was it, thought Louisa: the Ypres connection.

'No,' was the curt reply.

'She was a nurse at Ypres, that's all. I know there would have been lots of nurses there, so you probably didn't know her. But she was murdered on a train, on the Brighton line. It was so awful. I've been on that train lots of times . . .'

Louisa tried to keep listening but she didn't think anything of consequence was being said. The band leader began singing the chorus of 'Roses of Picardy' – 'Roses are flowering in Picardy / But there's never a rose like you . . . ' She thought that it would have been nicer to be dancing to this song than sitting on a wobbly chair, trying to avoid Mickey's gaze. Then she heard Nancy apologising for bringing up the subject of the war. She declared her ankle better and Louisa saw the two of them walk back on to the dance floor. Roland looked back as they walked away and saw Louisa watching them. The intensity of his gaze made her shrink.

Louisa was aware of Mickey glaring at her. 'Prefer the look of that other chap, do you?' he said accusingly.

She shook her head. 'I don't want to dance any more,' she said. 'Please, go and find someone else.'

He didn't move. 'I like the look of you,' he said in a way that did not feel flattering. 'In fact, there's something about you . . . Have I seen you dancing in Soho?'

Louisa sat up straighter. 'No, you haven't.' She was feeling uncomfortable and shifted on her chair, trying to move further away, but as she did so, his arm shot out and grabbed her.

'Don't move,' he said in a quiet voice. 'I think I've just realised where I've seen you before.'

'It's not possible,' she said.

'I think it is,' he growled. 'The Cross Keys, isn't it? I think your uncle might owe me a bob or two.'

Frightened, Louisa tried to stand and as she attempted to pull away from him, another man appeared like lightning. She didn't recognise him but she guessed he knew Mickey.

'I've had enough of you here tonight. Let go of her arm or—'

'Or *what*?' said Mickey.

There were no words spoken but a punch was thrown, and as Mickey let go, Louisa sprang away and rushed on to the dance floor, looking frantically for Nancy.

The band had taken a short break between songs and the girls peered hopefully at their cards, as if the blank spaces might have been filled in magically since they last looked. The men shuffled, trying to find the ones they had lined up for the next dance. Now, a noisy chatter sprang up around the two men as more punches were thrown and others joined in, trying to pull them apart. The band struck up a gay new tune as waiters urged people to disperse.

With relief, Louisa saw Nancy standing alone and pulled her arm. 'We've got to go,' she said.

'Why? What's happened?'

'I'll tell you later. *Please*, Nancy. Let's go.'

'But I'm just waiting for Roland – he only went to get a drink,' said Nancy stubbornly.

'I mean it, we have to leave now.'

Louisa pulled Nancy by the hand and out into the hall, where the cooler night air had been let in through the front door of the hotel as men and women came and went. It brought them both back to their senses and they gloomily fetched their coats from the cloakroom and headed out into the street. The rain had stopped but the pavements were slick, glowing with the reflection of the bright streetlights. They turned left out of the Savoy, heading towards Trafalgar Square, with Louisa leading them at a fast pace, looking back over her shoulder frequently.

'Why do you keep doing that?' asked Nancy. 'Just tell me what's going on. Is someone following us?'

Louisa looked again. The people on the pavement were moving slowly, sidestepping puddles, the women holding up their long dresses, the men attending to them. London at night seemed hardly less full than during the day. Then she saw Mickey shoulder forwards, pushing his way through, his face grim. Louisa pushed Nancy into a shop doorway, silencing her protests with a finger to her lips. Nancy's face was screwed up in disgust and Louisa realised that the corner they were in had provided relief for either man or dog not long before.

She edged forwards a tiny bit and looked back. Mickey had been stopped by another man and there was an argument going on between them, though she couldn't hear anything they were saying. The second man looked lean but strong, his arms were folded and his demeanour was firm but calm, even at a distance. It wasn't long before she saw Mickey storm off, angry but no longer spoiling for a fight. The other man walked back towards the Savoy after looking around. Who was he hoping to see? It was only then that she realised with a start that it was the officer that had been dancing with Nancy.

She took Nancy's arm and started walking them both towards Trafalgar Square again, away from the party.

'Honestly, I wish you would tell me what's going on. Is someone following us or what?' said Nancy.

'They might be.'

'Who are *they*, Louisa?'

'Someone who thought they knew me. Someone who might . . .'

'Might *what*?' Nancy's composure had vanished.

'Might tell my uncle I'm in London.'

CHAPTER TWENTY-FIVE

Louisa slowed down, then stopped, taking in deep breaths of air. Everything about her seemed to be shaking.

'Come on,' said Nancy, 'let's go and sit by the lions. They always used to cheer me up when I was little.' They walked together, arm in arm, towards the great cats of London, guarding Nelson's column. Louisa felt an uncomfortable familiarity in her sensations – the fear, the running away. It made her think again of Florence Shore, attacked on the train that same day. Had she been running from a man, too? The mysterious man in the brown suit that got on the train at Victoria – was he the attacker? Despite Nancy's combing of the newspapers, there didn't seem to have been any progress on the case reported.

How long ago it seemed, she thought, and yet here she was, running again.

At least now the city was warmer, the trees were thick with leaves and nothing seemed so menacing as it had in the depths of winter. They walked together to a bench, Louisa's trembling subdued now, Nancy taking the mantle of responsibility, steering her gently.

'What happened?' she asked again, the fury gone.

'It was . . .' Louisa hesitated. How much to tell her? She needed a friend, but more than that she needed to hold on to her job. 'Two men started fighting, and I was caught up in it,' she said.

'My goodness! That's rather exciting,' said Nancy.

'It wasn't exciting at all, it was horrible,' said Louisa sharply.

'I think if two men started fighting over me, I should be thrilled. Now, as it is, I don't even have one man interested. If you hadn't made us leave like that, I might have made an arrangement with him.'

'I'm sorry your night was ruined but I wouldn't have allowed you to make such an arrangement in any case.'

'*Allowed* me? You will neither allow nor disallow me to do anything! You are a *nursery maid*, not my mother.' Nancy stood up, in a rage that had caught fire in seconds. She looked like her father.

Louisa stood up, too. 'I'm glad you have made your feelings clear. I think we should return home now.'

'No,' said Nancy. 'I shan't go home with you. I'm going back to the dance. It's not even ten o'clock yet. You can do what you like.'

She started to walk back in the direction of the Savoy. With a big sigh, Louisa walked after her, until the two of them were half-running, half-stalking in a fashion that might have been comical if it wasn't so absurd, when Nancy turned a corner and slammed into a policeman.

'You need to watch where you're going, miss,' he said, wheezing from the body blow.

Louisa came around shortly after to find a flustered Nancy helping the policeman pick up his hat and babbling apologies. His hat pulled firmly back on his head, the strap stretched below his chin, the policeman recovered his equilibrium. He looked at Louisa. 'Are you with this young lady?'

She nodded.

'Right ho, then. You'd better be on your way.'

Louisa took Nancy firmly by the arm and pulled her back, away from the Savoy. She made a slight show of resistance but must have known that Louisa was right. They walked in silence for a few minutes, Louisa uncertain of how they would get home and when would be a good time to do so. It may not have been raining any more but the wet pavements had wrecked their shoes and stockings, not to mention the hems of their coats. Nanny Blor would be furious and almost certainly guess that they had not spent the evening having a quiet birthday supper with Marjorie and her godmother. If only Nanny didn't sit up until midnight reading penny dreadfuls, they might sneak in without her seeing. By now they had almost reached the wide avenue of the Mall, with Buckingham Palace dormant at the end. As Louisa was wondering what to do to get out of this scrape, they heard Nancy's name being called from across the street.

Roland.

He was waving at them both and calling out her name. 'Miss Mitford! Wait!' Holding on to his hat, neatly sidestepping the puddles, he ran over to them, concern on his face, his mackintosh billowing behind him.

Louisa stood stock-still, watching him. She didn't let go of Nancy's arm, though Nancy was waving to him, calling back, 'Hello!'

Then he stood before them, panting slightly, eyes shining like a cat's in the dark. 'I've been looking for you,' he said. 'You disappeared so suddenly. There was that fight; I wanted to be sure you hadn't got caught up in it.'

'Yes,' said Nancy, 'he was dancing with Louisa—'

'I see,' he said, cutting her off. 'I recognised one of those men. You're better off staying away from the likes of them. What are you doing now? It's late to be out.'

'We're walking home,' said Nancy.

'I think I'd better see you back safely, in that case,' said Roland. 'Where are you staying?'

'There's no need,' said Louisa. 'We can manage.'

'We're on the Gloucester Road,' said Nancy.

'It's a long walk,' said Roland. 'Let me. I know the way.'

And so the three of them walked along together, a close trium-virate, often talking but sometimes quiet, taking in the streets by night, the different people that walked beside them.

At one moment, in Chelsea, a crowd of beautiful young people spilled out on to the pavement, laughing and squealing, a blur of silks, tassels and top hats, nearly all of them smoking, one woman with bobbed hair clutching a cocktail glass, stumbling slightly. They moved as a single, amorphous entity before dividing seam-lessly into two cars, which screeched as they tore up the road. Nancy whispered to her companions that she thought she might have recognised one or two of them – an older brother of a London friend, a distant cousin. How she longed to be one of them, she lamented, and Roland laughed at this.

At last they arrived at the house and the sight of the front door silenced Louisa. She realised she had no idea what time it was and she was the one who was supposed to be chaperoning Nancy safely. The house was in darkness except for a light in the hall, waiting for them to come in and turn it off.

'We're here,' said Louisa to Roland. 'Thank you for seeing us back safely.'

'Yes, thank you so much,' said Nancy gaily. She tripped up the steps and gave a light knock on the glossy black door. At once – had she been waiting? – it was opened by Ada, who let Nancy in and caught sight of Louisa, still standing on the pavement with Roland.

'Goodbye,' said Roland, who gave a small bow to Louisa, but

she didn't respond. She had heard the sudden halt of footsteps and then the sound of someone running away. The street was barely lit but she caught a flash of something at the corner, the glow of a cigarette in the black.

Roland turned and walked away, and Louisa went into the house. It was probably nothing, but she crossed her fingers as she thought it.

CHAPTER TWENTY-SIX

~~~~~

Guy stood on the doorstep of 53 Hadlow Road in Tonbridge, a modest red-brick, semi-detached house. He took a handkerchief out of his pocket and wiped his forehead under the rim of his hat. It was 10.59 a.m. and he had had to run down the last three streets after he had taken a wrong turning. Apart from the gentle clicking of a pair of shears as a man trimmed his hedge, there was no sound. He checked his notebook: *Baroness Farina, aunt of victim. Spent the Sunday with FNS. Son, Stuart Hobkirk, left money in a trust by FNS.*

After the note from Louisa, in which she revealed to him that she and Nancy had been to see Miss Shore's lawyer, he had been shocked at their daring but also deeply interested in the information they had gathered. It had spurred him to arrange this meeting with haste.

Guy rang the doorbell and a young maid with a mobcap on opened the door. She looked at him quizzically but didn't say anything.

'Ah, hello. I'm Mr Sullivan from the London, Brighton and South Coast Railway Police, here to see Baroness Farina,' said Guy, an apologetic note in his voice.

'You don't look like a policeman,' said the maid.

Guy tried out a short laugh. 'Oh, no. Well, I'm off-duty, as it were.'

'Is the baroness expecting you?'

'Yes, I think so. I sent a note.' He coughed and shuffled his feet a bit. 'May I come in?'

'I suppose so.' The maid shrugged and walked away from the front door, leaving Guy to close it. 'She's out in the garden. Follow me.'

They walked across a small hall and through a drawing room that made up in style what it lacked in space, with its deep-red walls, crowds of paintings hung close together and Moroccan rugs overlapping each other on the floor. Guy almost tripped over a large white Persian cat, fast asleep on top of a pile of books, just as he approached the French windows, which opened on to the garden.

Guy could smell the roses before he stepped out and saw an old lady in a long white dress with a high collar, several strands of pearls hanging from her neck. She was sitting at a painted-white iron table, holding a pair of opera glasses up to her face as she frowned at a newspaper article.

'Ma'am,' said the maid abruptly. 'Gentleman here to see you. Says he's expected.' Without waiting to hear what her mistress had to say, she walked off.

'Wretched girl,' said the baroness to her retreating back. 'Are you Constable Sullivan? Come over here. Forgive me, it's too much for me to stand up.'

Guy walked over, shook her hand and stood awkwardly, aware that he was blocking her light.

'Sit down, sit down. I don't expect you want a cup of tea, do you? It's too hot,' she said.

Guy swallowed with difficulty and felt beads of sweat threaten to run down his face as he sat down on a matching iron chair, its hard curlicues offering little in the way of comfort. 'No, I'm fine, thank you, Baroness. I appreciate you seeing me.'

The baroness put her paper and opera glasses down. 'Anything for my poor niece,' she said. Her emphasis betrayed a soft Edinburgh accent.

The case was officially closed but there was an answer out there and, if he found it, a promotion to Scotland Yard would be his, along with a pay rise that would mean he could afford to leave home and get married. A picture of Louisa, sitting beside him on the bench at St Leonards, came into his mind, her face wincing then laughing as she put a too-hot chip in her mouth.

He sat up straighter, stiffening his resolve, and shifted the chair a little further in, though this was clumsily done – he hadn't realised it would be quite so heavy. He took a pencil from his pocket and laid the notebook on the table.

'Goodness, so formal,' said the baroness, and gave a short, high-pitched laugh.

'I believe Miss Shore came to see you on Sunday the eleventh of January of this year?'

The baroness looked at him. This was going to be a proper police interview after all, then. 'Yes, she got the train down from London and arrived here shortly before lunch. We were celebrating her birthday. I gave her a gold necklace with two amethyst pendants hanging from it, which the robber must have taken . . . ' She broke off. 'You are aware I've told all this to the police already?'

'Yes, ma'am,' said Guy, taking notes. 'Did she tell you of her plans for the following week?'

'A little. She was planning to go and stay with her friend in St Leonards, I believe.'

'Can you tell me anything of her mood that day?'

'She was subdued, you could say. But Flo was never one for being very excitable.'

Guy nodded and jotted down a note or two. 'Did she mention if she had anything on her mind?'

The baroness drew herself up and looked at Guy coolly. 'She was an Englishwoman; she did not often speak of her *mind*,' she said. Then she seemed to soften slightly. 'But, now that I think about it, I think she was concerned about the future. She had only been out of her war work for a few weeks and was thinking of retirement. She had worked very hard for most of her life, and she wasn't sure what was going to happen next. She had money, so at least she didn't have that to worry about.'

Guy chose not to reveal what he knew here and to see instead what the baroness would volunteer.

'Yes, in spite of the fact she worked as a nurse, Florence came from a respectable family. Her mother was my sister.' The baroness eyeballed Guy, daring him to suggest her appearance was anything less than absolute respectability. At that moment, another white cat jumped up on his mistress's lap, padding his paws over her white dress and leaving faintly grubby marks. She continued as if she hadn't noticed. 'A few years ago, she was left a considerable sum by her own sister and set up a trust for my son, so that he might receive the income from it in the event of her death. We're very grateful for it, but we hadn't expected it to happen so soon.' She cast her eyes downwards and groped for a handkerchief, without success. 'My poor niece,' she said again.

'I take it you mean Stuart Hobkirk?' said Guy.

Pride flushed the baroness' face, brightening the eyes that had started to fade to a pale blue. 'Yes, Stuart, from my first husband. He's an artist. He's doing terribly well – he has a painting in this year's Summer Exhibition. He's part of the St Ives artists group in Cornwall.'

Guy looked blank.

The baroness exhaled sharply. 'One always forgets how those outside of an artistic life know so little.'

Guy felt reproved, though he didn't know quite what for. 'Your son and Miss Shore – they were cousins?'

'Yes, not that that had to stop ...' There was a pause. The cat licking its paws was the only sound.

'Stop what?' prompted Guy.

'They were very close,' said the baroness. 'But there were certain members of the family who simply didn't understand. Flo *understood* Stuart. She knew that he had to be an artist; he couldn't be anything else. And she knew that her money would make certain of that.'

'I see,' said Guy, not at all sure that he did.

The baroness leaned forwards. 'I'm afraid some of those not in the artistic world might be shocked,' she said. 'But sometimes, well, let's just say, one cannot always wait for marriage ...'

Guy paled. This was not at all his world, one where old ladies insinuated sinful behaviour. He looked away and focused intently on a rose in the garden, a butterfly busy in the stamens. With a start, he realised there was a connection to be made here. Rosa Peal had mentioned an artist as a gentleman friend of Miss Shore's. Her cousin, the man who inherited a substantial trust fund from the nurse, was also this lover? Before he could ask more about this, the baroness had carried on speaking in firm tones that brooked no interruption.

'Offley was absurdly angry about it all,' she continued. 'But quite honestly, the man lives in California now; he can't be expected to understand anything.'

'Mr Offley Shore – Miss Shore's brother?'

'Yes, my nephew,' said the baroness. 'Even as a child I found him hard to get on with. He's been writing me furious letters. He thinks that all the money should have gone to him. Such a greedy man. He's had the lion's share. Frankly, Stuart could have done more with that money than *he* will, lying about in America, eating oranges.'

Florence Shore's brother was angry about the will. This was news indeed and meant another suspect Guy was certain nobody else from any of the police forces had considered. He wanted to ask more but the baroness pushed the cat off her lap with a grunt and picked up her opera glasses. The interview was over.

'Thank you, Baroness,' said Guy. 'You've been very helpful.'

'Are you going to catch the man that did it?'

'I sincerely hope so,' said Guy. 'I'm doing all I can.'

'But you're doing it alone, I take it? The case has been closed, as I understand it?'

Caught, Guy could only nod. 'Officially, yes. But that doesn't mean he's not out there. *Someone* did it, and I mean to find him.'

The baroness nodded and returned to her article. She said not another word.

Guy stood awkwardly and tipped his hat, which he hadn't dared to remove throughout the interview. 'Goodbye, Baroness. Thank you for your time.'

He departed through the French windows, sidestepping the sleeping cat, and let himself out through the front door.

CHAPTER TWENTY-SEVEN

❧

B ack at work, Guy asked Jarvis if he might have a day tidying the papers in the vast filing cabinet that sat in the corner of the office. When anyone opened one of the drawers, it moaned and clanked like Frankenstein's monster awakening for the first time. Jarvis appeared rather baffled by this request but said he didn't see why not, there was nothing else urgent to attend to and it probably had to be done.

This bought Guy time to sit and think through the matter of the Shore case as he sifted and straightened the notes that had been variously jammed into the metal beast. Not to mention that copies of the Shore case statements were in there, too. It wasn't long before he found a telephone number for Stuart Hobkirk in Cornwall – not for a home address but for an artists' studio that it seemed he worked in daily. There was a short statement that someone had taken from him in which he stated he was in the studio on the day of Shore's murder.

At 4 p.m., there were few people around and Guy took the opportunity to telephone Mr Hobkirk. He decided to do it now, denying to himself that Jarvis would not be pleased if he knew.

The telephone was answered after a few rings and the voice at the other end said he would fetch Stuart. Guy could hear disembodied shouts, a clatter like a door with a loose glass pane shutting and then heavy footsteps on a wooden floor.

'Stuart Hobkirk speaking. Who is this?' The voice was deep and then there was a long bout of coughing, followed by a thump of the chest. 'Sorry,' said Stuart. 'Bloody smokes.'

'This is Mr Sullivan,' said Guy. 'I'm from the London, Brighton and South Coast Railway Police. I was wondering if I might ask you a few questions?'

'What?' said Stuart. 'About my poor cousin, I suppose? I've already spoken to you lot.'

'Yes, I appreciate that, sir. But other lines of enquiry have opened and we need to follow them up. It's simply a matter of confirming one or two things.' Guy hoped he sounded more assured than he felt.

'Are we really going to have to go over it all again? I'm sure everything I've got to say must be written down somewhere.'

'Could you confirm for me that you are Florence Shore's cousin?' said Guy, ignoring his protests.

'Yes,' sighed Stuart.

'Could you tell me where you were on the twelfth of January of this year?'

Guy could hear a match being struck and Stuart inhaling on a cigarette before he answered. 'I was here at the studio, painting, as I always am practically every day.'

'Were others in the studio that day?'

'Yes,' snapped Stuart. 'Have you got what you need now?'

'Not quite,' said Guy. 'May I have some names of the other people who were there?'

'What on earth for?'

'Only to ask them to corroborate your statement, sir.'

Stuart exhaled and Guy imagined the grey smoke snaking down the telephone line. He did his best not to cough at the thought of it.

'Well, the thing is, I'm not entirely sure I *was* at the studio that day. I think I may have been at home alone. I sometimes work there, when the light is good.'

'I see,' said Guy. 'Would anyone have seen you there that day? A postman, perhaps? Or a daily?'

'Look, man, how would anyone remember? It was another ordinary day. No postman would write in his diary: "Saw Mr Hobkirk today".'

'No, sir,' said Guy. Stuart's temper was going to get the better of him, he could tell.

'So the fact is, no one can confirm where I was. But I was in Cornwall. Whatever I was doing, I was hundreds of miles away when my dear cousin was so brutally—' He interrupted himself with another bout of coughing.

'Yes, sir,' said Guy.

'I'm going to hang up now,' said Stuart, carefully and slowly, as if he was talking to a stupid child. 'And I don't expect to be contacted again by any of you. As far as I'm concerned, every time you talk to me you waste a chance to find the person who did it. Leave me alone to get on with my work and my sorrow.'

'Yes—' said Guy, but the telephone had already clicked silent at the other end.

CHAPTER TWENTY-EIGHT

Three days after the ball, when the girls had been put to bed, Louisa asked Nanny if she might go out for the rest of the evening to visit her mother. Nanny said she thought that would be a very nice thing to do. Lord and Lady Redesdale were out at a dinner, and besides, Ada was about if she should need anything. Then Nancy asked if she might go along with Lou-Lou.

'Whatever for?' said Nanny.

'No reason, really. Just to keep her company, and so I can get out of the house for a bit. It's a lovely warm night, Nanny,' pleaded Nancy.

'Seems to me you've been out gallivanting all too much this week. So long as you are both back before half past nine,' said Nanny, glancing at her book on the table, *The Noble Highwayman and the Miser's Daughter*. The bookmark was quite near the end.

'It's not gallivanting. We're going to Chelsea, to see an ill woman,' said Nancy.

'Oh! Poor dear. Perhaps you'd better take her something.' Nanny rooted around in her apron pockets and pulled out a paper bag with a few red-and-white-striped mints inside. She picked a bit of fluff out before proffering them to Louisa. 'Here,' she said.

'Thank you, Nanny,' said Louisa, 'but you keep those for yourself. We'll be back soon.'

The walk from Gloucester Road to Lawrence Street was only half an hour, and with the warmth of the setting sun on their faces, it was pleasant, if not quite enough to chase away her fears. Louisa took Nancy down back streets she had never seen before, weaving them out of the way of the ambling couples and tourists. In Elm Park Gardens, Louisa pointed out a handsome grey-brick block to her young charge.

'That building is entirely flats for women,' she said.

'Only women live there?' asked Nancy, looking up at the windows, blank but for their tied-back curtains.

'Most of them have left home to come to London to work,' said Louisa. 'We used to do a bit of washing for some of them – bed sheets and so on. They wash their smalls in the little sinks in their rooms.'

'That sounds terribly sad,' said Nancy.

'I don't think it is,' said Louisa. 'I became quite friendly with a couple of the women there and they used to have parties and things. Some of them were pleased to be working instead of being married, not being chained to the kitchen sink, as they put it. But it's a hard life – they don't have much money.'

'I thought you said they were working?'

'Yes, but women don't get paid as much, do they? No dependents, you see. It's just pin money.'

'Except it's not, is it?' said Nancy thoughtfully. 'They're buying their own food and rent.'

They walked in companionable silence after that, until they reached the Peabody Estate. Although only around the corner from the neat terraced houses of Old Church Street, with its smartly painted front doors and well-tended window boxes, Lawrence Street had four-storey high blocks, with grey net curtains visible in the long rows of small windows. The Cross Keys on the corner had a few men gathered outside in the warm evening, drinking beers and pulling on their cigarettes but saying little.

Nancy took Louisa's arm. 'Are we quite safe here, Lou-Lou?' she whispered.

Louisa looked at Nancy, then at the men outside the pub. She thought she recognised something of the profile of the man from Christmas and flinched, which Nancy noticed.

'They're harmless,' Louisa said. 'It's inside my mother's home I'm worried about. What if Stephen is there?'

'That's why I'm here,' said Nancy. 'He won't do anything if I'm with you.'

Louisa nodded and they gave each other's arms a reassuring squeeze before turning into the large archway that led to the open space in the middle of the Peabody Estate. Children ran criss-cross at speed, chasing and pinching each other. Two young mothers sat together on a patch of grass, their voices chattering like a pair of budgerigars as their babies suckled peacefully. The sun was setting and in the orange light, on the ground below her old bedroom window, Louisa spotted a cat, stretching its paws as it appeared to consider the adventures for the night that was coming. She let go of Nancy and ran over to him, scooping him up in her arms and nestling her face in his warm neck. The cat purred and wriggled gently beneath her grasp.

'It's Kipper,' she said to Nancy. 'He's not ours, he lives four doors down, but he was my friend here when I was little. He's so old now, poor thing.'

'I like his name,' said Nancy, smiling.

Still holding on to the cat, not minding his ginger hairs slowly shedding themselves over her blue jacket, Louisa walked up the stairs to her old home, Nancy following. The front door was unlocked and Louisa breathed in the comforting smells of soap flakes and boiled cabbage. She noted that Stephen's jacket and hat were not hanging on the coathooks.

Putting the cat down, who ran off down the hall, she called out, 'Ma! It's me. Where are you?'

'Oh, Louisa! Is it really you? Just in here,' her mother called back from the front room.

The two girls stepped inside the warm fug, where Winnie was sitting in an armchair by the unlit fire, a thick woollen blanket over her knees and a shawl around her shoulders, a gaunt figure in the dusk. Louisa was reminded anew of how much older her own ma was than any of her friends' mothers. She caught sight of Nancy and started to pat down her hair, tucking the stray wisps behind her ear.

'Louisa, dear, you should have told me you were coming and bringing a friend.'

'Hello, Mrs Cannon,' said Nancy, putting out her right hand. 'I'm Nancy Mitford. How do you do?'

Winnie gave a chuckle. 'Oh, I'm doing very well, just a little cold,' she said before she gave way to a short coughing fit, leaving Nancy to put her hand back down. When she had recovered, she looked up at her daughter and her friend. 'Don't look so serious. I'm right as rain. That is, as much as I ever am.'

'Oh, Ma!' said Louisa. 'I've missed you so much.' She bent down to embrace her mother, kissing her on the forehead before Winnie pushed her off.

'Don't fuss. Let me introduce myself to Miss Mitford,' she

said, putting her hand out, which Nancy retrieved and shook gently. 'Now, it's very nice to see you but what are you doing here?'

'We're in London for a few days. I wanted to see how you were. I've brought a bit of money for you, too.'

'What I need is to see you settled down, my girl,' Winnie said. 'When I was your age, I—'

'Had a husband to cook and clean for. I know,' said Louisa. 'But it's not quite as simple as that for me, is it?'

Winnie put her nose in the air. 'I don't see why not,' she said. 'It was quite simple for me. I saw your father delivering the coal at Mrs Haversham's and that was that.'

Louisa looked at Nancy and rolled her eyes. The room was dark and though their eyes had adjusted, it seemed that shadows engulfed the room. She moved to turn on the lamp beside her mother but Winnie put out her hand.

'It won't come on, dear. I haven't quite managed to get out to pay the meter. I'll do it tomorrow,' she said and tried to stifle another cough.

'Have you not been getting the money from the post office?' said Louisa. 'I've been putting in most of my wages every month.'

'Oh, I have, dear. Thank you. It's only in the last little while I've not been getting out of the house ... ' She looked uncomfortably at Nancy and adjusted her skirts.

'Why hasn't Stephen paid, then?' said Louisa.

'Oh, you know what your uncle's like ... He's not been here for a few days. I don't know where he is.'

'Staying somewhere with free gas, no doubt,' said Louisa.

'There's no point in getting cross. I'm perfectly well. It's not cold and I'm so tired by the time it gets dark, I'm quite ready to get to bed and go to sleep. Your father and I lived like this before the war, you know. We just had candles and life was a lot simpler and easier, if you ask me.'

Nancy plucked at Louisa's sleeve. 'Perhaps we ought to be getting back? Nanny might be worried.' She seemed ill at ease.

'Wait here,' said Louisa. She darted upstairs and felt underneath the bed she and her mother had shared. Yes, it was still there, in the far corner, dusty and undiscovered. She came back down, wiping it with her sleeve, and handed it to her mother.

'What's all this?' said Winnie.

'Coins I saved,' said Louisa. 'There should be enough there for you to pay the gas meter.'

'Where did this money come from?' Winnie asked suspiciously.

'It's just odds and ends I put away, Ma,' said Louisa. 'Please, take it.' She bent down to kiss her mother on the cheek, feeling her papery skin beneath her lips and smelling her stale breath. She whispered, 'I'll send you more money soon, Ma.'

'Thank you,' said her mother. Louisa could hardly hear her, though her face was right next to hers. 'But don't worry about me. You look after yourself, my girl, then I won't have to worry about you. I just want to see you married and in a nice situation.' She stopped and took a couple of deep breaths – it was more than she'd said in one go for a long time – then spoke more firmly. 'You could have this flat, you see, as my next of kin. The Peabody Trust people, that's how they do it. You'd be nicely set up. And all my old jobs, I know my women would take you on.'

Louisa tried to blink back the tears that threatened to fall on to her mother's face. 'Yes, Ma,' she said. 'I will. Goodbye. I'll write soon. I'm sorry I didn't before but I couldn't let Stephen—'

'I know,' said Winnie hoarsely. 'Goodbye, my dear.'

As Louisa stood up, she saw her mother pull the blanket a little higher and turn her face to the wall, closing her eyes. Louisa and

Nancy walked out of the flat, closing the front door gently behind them.

As they were crossing the grass, Louisa was just turning to say something to Nancy – she had been upset to see her mother looking so frail – when she heard a dog barking. She looked over and saw Socks run in through the archway, ears up. He'd probably seen Kipper, his old foe. Stephen wouldn't be far behind. Before his heavy footsteps could approach too closely, Louisa grabbed Nancy's hand, a finger to her lips to make sure she stayed quiet, and pulled her out through a side door into the dark streets. A narrow escape – but how many more times would she get away with it?

CHAPTER TWENTY-NINE

⌀

After the phone call with Hobkirk, Guy's mind was racing. Before he could draw his conclusions absolutely, he knew he needed to rule Florence Shore's brother out. Back at the police station, he telephoned the transatlantic liners that had arrived in England from America in the three months before January 1920 and asked them to send their passenger lists. They took only a few days to arrive and, as he suspected, the name Offley Shore was not anywhere to be seen. So far as Guy knew, Mr Shore had not even been able to make it to his sister's funeral service.

This meant one thing: Stuart Hobkirk was the chief suspect. The only suspect.

What Guy needed was to bring Mr Hobkirk in for questioning, but he could not do this without Jarvis's permission. Guy left a message with his super's secretary, requesting an appointment. Then he went and sat at a desk, chewing his pencil and twitching his feet.

'Put a sock in it, will ya?' said Harry. 'Some of us are trying to read a newspaper over here.'

'Sorry,' said Guy. 'I can't concentrate on anything.'

'Nor can I but it's never worried me,' said Harry with a snort and went back to checking the racing tips.

When there was nothing left of his pencil, Guy was summoned to Jarvis's office. It was stuffy in there – he never opened a window – and although it was not yet 5 p.m., Guy saw that Jarvis had poured himself a large whisky. The day's work was done.

'Sullivan.' Jarvis was in an affable mood. 'What can you do for me?' He guffawed at his own joke.

Guy stood before the desk. A clock ticked loudly and he felt sweat trickle behind his ears. If he didn't hurry, his glasses would steam up.

'It's about the Florence Shore case, sir. I think there may be an important development.'

Jarvis sat up straighter. 'Do you? How's that, then? I'm not aware of having sent you on anything to do with the Shore case. The Met are looking after it, if at all. Case is closed so far as we're concerned. Has someone come forward?'

'Not exactly, sir.' Guy concentrated hard on keeping his hands clamped behind his back, though he longed to wipe his brow.

Jarvis said nothing but waited for him to go on.

'There was a cousin, sir. A Mr Stuart Hobkirk. He stood to benefit from her will.'

'So did others, if I remember rightly.'

'Yes, but her last will and testament was made at the very end of 1919, shortly before she died, in his favour.'

Jarvis raised an eyebrow slightly. 'How do you know this?'

Guy hesitated. He couldn't tell quite the whole truth. 'I was informed by Miss Shore's lawyer.'

'Go on.' The tone was less of an invitation than a challenge.

'It seems that other members of the family were not very happy about his receiving this inheritance. Miss Shore's brother, for instance. This suggests that it was something of an unexpected aberration in Miss Shore's affairs.'

'Not necessarily,' said Jarvis. 'People are always surprised by the contents of a will – usually when they discover they have been left less than they were hoping for.'

'Yes, quite, sir. However, his alibi is weak, too, sir. He changed his story. At first he said he was working in his studio but when asked to give names of people who were there, he said he was at home alone, painting.'

'I see,' said Jarvis, closing his fingers around the glass.

'The other thing is that there have been . . . suggestions that Mr Hobkirk and Miss Shore were romantically involved.'

'Get to the point, Sullivan.'

'I don't think it was a random robbery and attack on Miss Shore, sir. I think it was someone she knew. If you remember at the inquest, the pathologist said there was no sign of a struggle.'

'I remember.'

'It occurred to me that if Miss Shore knew her attacker, she wouldn't have struggled. She might have been talking to them and then been taken completely unawares when they struck her. If they were involved, sir, it might have been a crime of passion.'

Jarvis was silent for a minute. Guy gave in and pulled at his damp collar with his fingers.

'I see. So because you *think* that Miss Shore *may* have known her attacker, and because somebody has *suggested* that she and Mr Hobkirk were romantically involved, and because he was left a bit of extra money in the will, you think he is chief suspect for a premeditated murder. You don't appear to have trusted your seniors to have checked out his alibi, either. I suppose you want my say-so to bring him in for further questioning?'

The familiar shadow of humiliation fell on Guy. 'Yes, sir.' A mouse in the corner chewing its fingernails would have made more noise than his reply.

'I don't even want to discuss the fact that you have been prying in corners without permission.' Jarvis took a slow swallow of whisky. 'Get out of here, Sullivan. I don't have time to waste on nonsense like this. I suggest you stick to your usual duties. I believe you're down to do an inventory on the lost property at Polegate Junction tomorrow?'

'Yes, sir.'

'Don't keep saying "Yes, sir".'

'Yes, sir. I mean, no, sir. I mean, thank you, sir.' Guy gave a nod, though the super wasn't looking at him, and walked away, his hand almost slipping on the handle, but he made it out, pulling the door quietly behind him.

Guy arrived home that night in the nick of time before his mother started to serve supper. As he walked into the front room, his brothers and father were already at the table, a construction that had survived three generations of cutlery and elbows. The straight lines of polished mahogany had been sanded down by Guy's grandfather, a carpenter of some fame in his circles and the story of how he had been commissioned to build an armoire for Queen Victoria's chief lady-in-waiting was well known by his living descendants.

Mrs Sullivan had laid out all six places in the usual way: six white plates, six polished forks, six bone-handled knives, six thick china mugs. Guy could see his mother's back in the kitchen, bent as she sliced the bread. On the hob the dripping was spitting despite the gas having been turned off a minute before. Her whole body was focused on the task, feet set apart on the floor, her hand on the knife as it sawed slowly down the loaf, each slice of even thickness, as straight down the sides as the table legs. Her sons knew her ears would have been listening intently for the muffled push of the front door, hoping to hear it before the clock struck on the hour. Late arrivals got no supper.

Guy hurried to his chair, at the corner by his mother's, his back to the window, where a tiny crack that nobody had ever been able to close blew a cool breeze across his shoulders.

Mrs Sullivan, still in the kitchen, barely raised her head, said nothing, carved the sixth slice and then brought the bread out to the table. A large dish of hot fried potatoes was already there. The brothers were noisy, not missing an opportunity, even one as regular as this, to josh their sibling. There was a clamour as each vied to get his tease in louder than the others.

'What happened tonight, eh? Was the signal stuck on a red light?'

'The army'd have got you in shape, boy!'

'You can't be late in the army; you'd be shot for it!'

Guy said nothing. He knew there was no defence he could give that anyone would listen to. He waved them off with a shake of his head and a wry smile, to show he didn't care.

'What's for supper, Mother?' he asked.

'Potatoes, as you can see. Bread and dripping, no sugar tonight,' she said, pulling her chair in, and her tone was stern but her face was open and there was just the faintest trace of a smile.

Mr Sullivan called everyone to order with a wave of his hand and they bent their heads for grace. 'For what we are about to receive may the Lord make us truly thankful. Amen.'

Six heads sprang up at once, four pairs of hands reached out and greedily grabbed their bread and potatoes in perfectly synchronised motion before Mother and Father took theirs, then the jug of hot dripping was passed around. Mrs Sullivan splashed milk in each mug, then poured in the tea.

There was silence for a while as everyone ate and drank, before the spell was broken by Walter, the oldest and biggest brother. Walter and Ernest were Irish twins, joked Father, born ten months apart, and it looked as if Walter had taken all of Mother's strength to build him up and left none for Ernest. The younger 'twin' had been a small baby, dangerously so, and stayed the skinny one ever since. The brothers worked together on a building site on the Vauxhall Road, Ernest able to haul a hod of bricks as easily as Walter, much to their foreman's surprise.

'What was it this time, Guy? Sheep on the line?' Walter snickered into his tea.

'No sheep at Victoria station,' said Ernest, pretending to correct Walter. 'But I heard there was a tomcat prowling on the tracks. Gave the police *paws* for thought.'

Walter slapped his brother on the back and bared his teeth in a single, silent *Ha*.

'That's enough, now,' said Mrs Sullivan.

'S'all right, Mother,' said Guy, pushing his glasses up. 'The super kept me back. Wanted a word.' He sat up a little straighter, to try to fool them into thinking it had been a good word, but to no effect. The brothers fell about laughing like cartoons, though their parents kept straight faces, eyeing each other across the spoils of supper.

'You going to be in charge of the hanging baskets? Make sure no one runs off with the petunias on platform seven?' This last came from Bertie, the youngest brother, repositioned since Tom was killed.

Guy pinched a corner of bread and wiped it around the plate, pushing the last of his dripping in ever-decreasing circles. The jug had worked its way clockwise around the table and, with his mother after him, he never liked to take too much. As he circled the bread and sweet fat, the sounds of his family faded out. If he looked at his plate for long enough, he'd cease to hear them altogether.

He knew he was right about Stuart Hobkirk. He'd show them.

CHAPTER THIRTY

'**L**ou-Lou! Where are you? I need you *now*!'
Louisa heard Nancy shouting on every step as she ran up the stairs from dining room to nursery, until she found Louisa in the linen cupboard, slowly folding pillowcases, not wishing to be discovered.

'I've been looking for you everywhere!'

Louisa snapped out of her reverie. 'Sorry,' she said. 'What is it?'

Nancy stood before her, her green eyes like torch lamps. 'It's today. He comes today. I thought it was tomorrow but it's not, it's today. Muv just reminded Farve and I'm not at all ready. I wanted to wear my blue dress and I don't think it's been pressed . . .'

The Mitford clan had returned to Asthall Manor from London and Louisa hadn't realised she would be so grateful to see the sight of the house. It may have been her place of work but it was beginning to feel like home, too. Reassured that her mother was surviving, as much as she ever had, at any rate, and knowing that Stephen could not get to her here added to her calm – a novel and enjoyable sensation.

June in the Cotswolds continued to astonish her with its

unfolding beauty. After the exploding colours and scents of May, intoxicating with its blossom and the constant singing of birds, June's long, still days, with bees diving into the bowed heads of the heavy roses, made her feel as if she could lie down in the grass and disappear like Alice into Wonderland.

On this day, Lady Redesdale, in her capacity as founder and chair of the Asthall & Swinbrook WI, was hosting one of her frequent committee lunches, an occurrence that merited no comment from any but Mrs Stobie, who complained loudly that they might all talk of charitable work but it was her, putting in all the extra hours God sent to make a trifle, who was in need of charity.

'Louisa!' Nancy shook out her skirts pettishly.

'Sorry,' said Louisa, putting down the pillowcases. 'What time is he coming?'

'Hooper's picking him up from the station at twelve. Do you think I should go to meet him too? Or do you think I should wait until he's here? It's just, I don't want Farve getting in the way too much. I mean, it is me he wants to see.'

'We don't know that for certain.'

'But he wrote to Farve after the ball. I don't see what other reason he could be coming here for.'

'One thing at a time,' said Louisa. 'I don't think you should go to the station to collect him, no.'

'He might think me unfriendly for not meeting him,' replied Nancy. Louisa could almost see the heat rising in her like Mrs Stobie's dough.

'His Lordship will not allow it,' said Louisa with conviction. She had learned the ways of her master in these last few months.

'No,' Nancy muttered. 'I don't suppose he will. Farve probably won't even let me sit next to him at luncheon. If only I could tell him that we met at the ball, then he would know—'

Louisa interrupted. 'You mustn't tell His Lordship about the ball. That would be the very worst idea. The only thing we have to make sure of is that Mr Lucknor doesn't mention the ball and meeting you there. Perhaps you could be at the front door as he arrives – you could ask him for his discretion, then?'

'But Muv will be there, and probably all the others, the brutes,' said Nancy, crestfallen.

'Right. In that case, I will ask to go to the station with Hooper. I'll say I need to stop at the village for something, some castor oil or something,' said Louisa. 'And I'll get the blue dress; I can press it for you now.'

'Oh, thank you,' said Nancy. 'I don't know what I would do without you, darling thing.'

When Louisa and Hooper arrived at the station just before noon, Hooper silently chewing tobacco as he pulled on the reins of the trap, she saw the puff of smoke in the distance that heralded the arrival of the train and its eagerly awaited passenger, Roland Lucknor.

Louisa walked on to the station platform as the train arrived, the doors opening before it had come to a stop. She saw the various passengers alight, and remembered herself arriving at the station only five months before, bedraggled and frightened, yet hopeful. When she spotted Roland, she thought she saw something of those things in him, too. He was a handsome man with broad shoulders, but though his brown shoes gleamed with polish, his suit looked a size too large for his sinewy frame.

She waved and he came over. 'Hello, Mr Lucknor,' she said. 'I came to meet you as I had an errand to run in the village. It's such a beautiful day, His Lordship sent the horse and trap to take you back to the house. I'm afraid with petrol rationing after the war, they prefer not to use the car too often. Still, it shan't take too long.'

'Thank you,' said Roland. 'It was kind of them to send anyone to meet me at all.'

Louisa smiled at him and turned, indicating he should follow her. On the trap, Louisa sat on the back bench, looking out to the road behind them, leaving Roland to sit beside Hooper, who merely grunted to acknowledge his new passenger. With Hooper there, the easy informality they had had on that long walk through London at night had vanished.

Hooper yanked at the reins and they set off at a smart trot through Shipton-under-Wychwood, the creamy Cotswold stone of the houses appearing at their most handsome in the June sunshine. Gardeners could be seen on the other side of low walls, tending the finishing touches to the displays that were the culmination of their year-round labours; young girls in white embroidered frocks walked around the village hand in hand, admiring each other; and mothers took a rest from cooking their Sunday lunch, red-faced in their floury aprons as they stood in the cool of their doorways and waved to neighbours.

When they reached the wider road that would take them to Asthall Manor, with Queen Anne's lace and its bursts of white flowers, thickly clustered along the sides, no sound but the clip-clopping of the horse's hooves, Louisa turned around and tapped Roland on the shoulder.

'Excuse me, Mr Lucknor, there's something I need to tell you.'

Alert, he looked at Louisa with concern. His eyes were blacker than ever in the sunshine. 'What is it?' he asked.

Leaning over to check that Hooper wasn't listening in, Louisa whispered, 'Well, it's just that when you met Miss Mitford and me ...'

'Yes?'

'We weren't supposed to be at that ball. Lord and Lady Redesdale don't know.'

'I see,' said Roland with a disapproving look, but he wasn't old enough to carry it off. She wasn't afraid of him.

'So perhaps when you see Miss Mitford today, you could . . .' She looked over at Hooper again, but he was chewing slowly, his eyes on the horse. 'Perhaps you could pretend it was the first time you'd met. The point is, if you say you met Miss Mitford there, she'll be in the most awful trouble and I will probably lose my job. Please, sir. I know it's an imposition.'

Roland looked at Louisa levelly. Then all at once he smiled and said, 'Of course. You don't need to worry about a thing.' Then he turned around to face forwards and they didn't speak again for the rest of the journey.

CHAPTER THIRTY-ONE

As the trap came around the immense oak tree on the drive, Louisa spotted Nancy walking along the garden path, clearly doing her best to look nonchalant, bending down to smell the recently bloomed roses, not something Louisa could remember ever having seen her do before. She couldn't help but be amused by the signs of infatuation showing in Nancy: hair that had been brushed and re-brushed, coaxed into shape against its will, and a flush of red between her collarbones.

Roland did not appear to see her, looking instead at Lord Redesdale as he stood at the front door, a gun hooked over his arm, calling out to the new arrival: 'Hello, there! Sorry about the gun. Damn rabbits, you know. How was your train journey? Good, good.' This last said without waiting for any reply.

Pamela was standing by her father, watching the guest arrive. She looked placid and unkempt as she usually did, always set slightly apart from her sisters, yet not at all standoffish. If it wasn't for Nancy, Pamela would easily have been Louisa's favourite. She stopped that thought in its tracks – Nanny had told her often that one had no favourites when it came to the children.

Louisa saw Lord Redesdale motion to Nancy, who had tried to pick a pink tea rose, only for the petals to scatter at her feet and leave her with a stem she couldn't twist off without yanking. It wasn't quite the picture of summer elegance she must have been going for.

'That's my eldest daughter, Nancy,' he said, offhand. Nancy tried to turn and wave hello but she was mid-yank and didn't manage it. Lord Redesdale observed her briefly before harrumphing, 'Come in, come in. We've got just enough time for a snifter before luncheon. Twelve minutes. Bloody Mary? Good, good.'

Nancy leapt to Louisa, clutching at her arms. 'Did you say anything to him? He didn't even look at me.'

'Yes, I don't think he'll give us away. I've got to get back to the nursery. Try and stay calm,' said Louisa, rattled by Nancy's reaction. It was most unlike her.

'I will,' said Nancy, 'it's just that . . . Did you see how handsome he is? He looks like a French pianist. All sort of sad eyes and long, delicate fingers.'

Louisa laughed, then forced a serious expression on her face. 'I think Nanny would say you've been reading too many novels.' To which Nancy gave a big sigh. 'You really must calm down. If they find out about the ball . . .'

'They won't, don't worry. I'd better go in. I'll come and find you after luncheon, tell you how it went,' said Nancy as she started to run into the house, before remembering herself and braking suddenly on her heels, smoothing down her skirt and hair as her mother did, then walking slowly, chin up, to the drawing room.

Louisa went into the house through the kitchen door at the back to find Mrs Stobie in a flustered state. 'That wretched Ada is in bed snivelling with a cold,' she said. 'Mrs Windsor has washed her hands of her, which is all very well for Mrs High and Mighty, but I've got soup for the first course, which is going to send Her Ladyship into a spin as it is . . .'

'Why?' said Louisa.

'Oh, don't ask me,' scoffed Mrs Stobie. 'Apparently you should never have soup for luncheon, though I don't see why not. And this is vichyssoise anyway – nice and cold on a day like this.'

'Why don't I help you?' said Louisa.

'That would be handy, I admit, but you'd better check with Nanny. I don't need her on my back as well as Mrs Windsor too.'

So it was, slightly to everyone's bewilderment, that Louisa was in the dining room ladling out the vichyssoise as Mrs Windsor poured the Sancerre. Lady Redesdale raised an eyebrow but said nothing. She was, in any case, clearly much absorbed by their guest, seated on her left.

'Tell me, Mr Lucknor,' she said, 'what have you been doing since the war?'

Roland took a sip of wine and cleared his throat before answering. 'To tell you the truth, Lady Redesdale, it's been a little tricky. I'm not long out. I was only demobilised at the end of last year. But there have been one or two business ventures—'

'Don't bother my head with those,' said Lady Redesdale sharply.

Nancy, watching from the other side of the table, showed a pained expression at her mother's abruptness. She looked at Mrs Windsor hopefully as she came around with the wine, only to receive a tight-lipped shake of the head in reply. Destined to remain a child at the dining table.

'What I mean is,' Lady Redesdale continued, more softly this time, 'what are you interested in?'

'Aside from business, politics, I think,' said Roland carefully. 'These are interesting times for us, aren't they? A new decade, no more war . . .'

A man with a young face but grey hair parted severely in the middle lifted his head up from sniffing the soup and said brightly, 'That's heartening to hear. Lady Redesdale is kindly hosting the Conservative Party fundraiser this summer. I'm the candidate hopeful.' Nodding to himself, as if to assert the truth of what he had just said, he tucked the bottom of his tie into his shirt and lifted the soup spoon.

'Hopeful?' roared Lord Redesdale from the other end of the table. 'If this isn't a safe seat then my name's Lloyd George!'

Mrs Goad, a familiar stalwart of the WI committee, spluttered on her wine at this, which prompted Lord Redesdale to laugh even more. He was silenced by a sharp look from his wife. Nancy, Louisa could see, was for once rather intimidated by the situation. None of her sisters were at the luncheon and she had only secured a place at the table by promising that she would help at the fundraising party, but she knew that the slightest foot wrong would mean an instant chucking out.

Ignoring the kerfuffle, Lady Redesdale turned back to Roland, who had started to eat delicately. Louisa fiddled with the soup dish and ladles on the service board – she had to be sure that he didn't say anything that would give her away.

'I agree,' Lady Redesdale said, as if nothing had intervened. 'These are very interesting times. Do you hope to go into politics yourself?'

'Never say never, Lady Redesdale. But I do sometimes wonder if more good isn't done on the ground, as it were?'

Lady Redesdale was responsive to the young man's modest manner and good looks – no one could deny those. 'Yes, you're quite right. We can't all get involved in running the country.' She gave a tinkling laugh and Lord Redesdale looked up at her from the other end of the table, nonplussed.

Louisa couldn't delay any longer; Mrs Windsor was giving her strange looks. So she went back downstairs to the kitchen, where Mrs Stobie was fussing over the roast beef, which was sure to be overdone before the potatoes were ready. While they wrapped the beef in a square of linen to rest, Louisa hopped from foot to foot, prompting Mrs Stobie to ask her tetchily if she needed to be excused to go to the bathroom.

Back in the dining room, as she cleared the soup dishes, then handed around the carved slices of beef with potatoes dauphinoise and buttered carrots, Louisa could hear that the conversation was flowing easily. Roland had clearly perfected the art of drawing giggles from Lady Redesdale, the sound of which no one at Asthall Manor could surely quite recall having heard before.

Mrs Goad steadily worked her way through each platter, readily accepting seconds and saying little until after the raspberries and clotted cream were put down before her, at which she emitted a happy wheeze and said, 'You do such good luncheon, Lady Redesdale.'

Lady Redesdale had had as much to do with the preparation of the food as she had had to do with the tiling of the roof, but she was nonetheless content to receive the compliment.

At the end of dessert she stood up, at which cue Nancy and Mrs Goad stood, too, and then she said, 'I need Mr Coulson to join us for coffee in the drawing room. Strictly speaking, it's a committee meeting today. Please forgive me, Mr Lucknor. I hope we see you again soon.'

Roland stood and nodded. 'Of course, Lady Redesdale. It's been a pleasure.'

Smiling, Mr Coulson took his tie out of his shirt and gave a little nod to Lord Redesdale and Roland, before following the ladies out.

'There's no port, old chap,' said Lord Redesdale amiably. 'Shall we go to my study? We can discuss this business proposition of yours. I'm most interested . . .'

An hour or so later, Louisa was walking down the hall, Decca holding tightly on to one hand, Unity trailing sullenly behind, on their way for a walk around the garden, when she spotted Nancy, completely still, her ear firmly pressed at Lord Redesdale's study door. Before Louisa could say anything, Nancy put her finger to her lips. She stood up straight and came over to her.

'I've been listening for ages,' she whispered. 'I keep waiting to hear my name being mentioned, but no, there's absolutely nothing. Oh, Lou. Do you think he might not feel the same as I do? I shall pine!' She made a show of clutching at her throat, but it was playful.

Louisa tried to look cross but she couldn't help it, Nancy made her laugh more than anyone. 'No mention of the ball either, then?'

'No, they've been talking about the war and golf, as far as I can make out. It couldn't be more dull.'

'Are you sure that was all?' Louisa knew she shouldn't ask. It wasn't any more her business what was going on behind that door than it was for her to sit under the prime minister's chair, but she couldn't help herself.

'Yes, I think so. It was hard to hear, though. They do mumble so.'

'Well, whatever their conversation is, it's not for us to guess. Come away from that door now.'

'Yes, yes, I will,' said Nancy. 'I only—'

She was startled by the door handle turning and almost leapt into Louisa's arms, were it not for Decca still holding fast. Unity flattened herself against the wall at the sound of her father's child-proof door opening. Roland was saying goodbye to Lord Redesdale, who asked him to see himself out. Louisa knew the next thing they would hear would be the gramophone playing a record and faint snores between each song.

Frozen by the appearance of Roland, Louisa and Nancy said nothing, but fortunately he broke the spell first.

'Miss Mitford, I was hoping to see you again.'

'Oh,' said Nancy loftily. 'Were you?'

'I see you're about to take the little ones out for a walk,' he said as Unity stuck out her head from behind Louisa, displaying a rather skew-whiff white cotton sunhat. 'Perhaps I might join you all? My lift to the station is not for another half hour or so.'

Louisa spoke for Nancy. 'Yes, that would be fine, sir,' she said. 'We're just going once around the garden.'

As they walked out into the warm haze of the afternoon, Louisa heard Roland say to Nancy, 'Miss Mitford, could it possibly be that I've seen you somewhere before?' and Nancy arched an eyebrow in reply.

CHAPTER THIRTY-TWO

Louisa had a letter from Guy asking her if she would like to accompany him on a trip to Cornwall. 'There's some police work I need to do there,' she read out.

Nancy had been unleashing her poetic feelings about Roland and something about the warm sun had encouraged Louisa to do the same about Guy. It felt harmless enough as they sat there together on the lawn, Debo lying on a rug beside them, Nanny Blor on the bench beneath the tree, knitting a tiny lemon-yellow cardigan.

'Police work?' said Nancy. 'The Florence Shore case? You lucky thing.'

'Don't be silly,' said Louisa, already feeling uncomfortable about reading it out loud. 'He goes on to say: "I was planning to go during my holiday week later this month. There's a train from Paddington to St Ives, where my aunt runs a small bed and breakfast. I wonder if you might care to accompany me? It's very pretty there and you might enjoy watching the fishermen bringing their catch in."'

'An aunt's bed and breakfast,' said Nancy. 'Does that mean it's all above board, then? It sounds terribly racy to me.'

'Guy would never suggest anything that was racy,' said Louisa, trying and failing to look indignant. 'Besides, I am my own woman now. Who is to tell me whether I can go with a man to Cornwall or not?'

'I suppose so,' said Nancy. 'I'm jealous, is all. Look at my eyes – greener than ever!' She flashed them wickedly at Louisa and laughed. This summer was her last as a child, somehow; she told Louisa she could feel herself getting near to being the adult she so longed to be.

'The thing is, I don't think I do want to go,' said Louisa sadly, reaching over to grab Debo, who was trying to roll over on to her tummy, without much success. She propped the baby up against her and gently stroked her soft head. 'It's not as if he knows me. Not really.'

'He knows as much as he needs to, to know that he likes you,' said Nancy.

'Well, that's not enough,' said Louisa in a tone she hoped would make Nancy change the subject. While she liked Guy, the idea of spending time with a policeman was impossible. Around her way, the police were the enemy and she'd had one or two close encounters that had left her afraid and ashamed. Nor could she trust that someone he worked with might not recognise her.

No. It couldn't happen.

Nancy, however, had not registered Louisa's discomfort and was still babbling on. 'I mean, we are helping him with the Shore case anyway, aren't we? Speaking of which, the more I think about it, the more I'm certain it's that cousin of hers, the artist. He needed the money, didn't he? I tell you, it's always about the money.'

'What about the brother? He was inheriting money, too, and was angry that his cousin had a big share of it,' pointed out Louisa.

'Offley was in America; it must be Stuart,' said Nancy, who rarely came unstuck from her guns.

'What if her brother asked someone to do it for him?' said Louisa.

Nancy dismissed this as too far-fetched.

'Well, whatever it was, we don't know,' said Louisa and stood up. 'I'm taking Miss Debo inside now; she needs a change.'

Louisa wrote back to Guy and told him that she wouldn't be travelling to Cornwall with him. She felt a pang of regret as she wrote it but she knew it was the right thing to do. It wasn't long before she received a despondent reply. Guy wasn't sure he would go either, writing:

It's hard to know whether or not to go on with this case at all. I've been making what investigations I can but my super won't let me off duties to pursue leads any more – not that there have been any new leads to speak of. If he hears of my going to Cornwall, I think he might have something to say about it. All we know is that a man in a brown suit got on the train at Victoria and probably got off at Lewes. I've recently interviewed the train guard and his description of the man who got off doesn't match that of Miss Shore's friend – it might not have been the same man at all.

No weapon has been found, which is the real problem. Dr Spilsbury said she was hit with a large, blunt instrument, which could have been a revolver or an umbrella handle. And as for who that man in the brown suit is – assuming it was someone she knew, as we believe – the only suspects I've come up with are Stuart Hobkirk, her cousin, on the grounds that he stood to inherit some money and his alibi is weak, and her brother Offley Shore, who contested the will. But he lives in California and wasn't even in England at the time. It's not enough.

Louisa pictured Guy's gentle face bent intently over the letter, frowning a little as he mustered the courage to tell her of his disappointment and frustration.

All at once she remembered something Nancy had said when they were on the train to stay with Rosa: that the doors didn't open from the inside. To get out, a person had to open the window and lean out to turn the door handle on the outside. The train guard saw a man get down from the train at Lewes but there was no mention of him reaching back to close the window. Yet the railway workers said that when they got on at the next stop both the windows were closed.

What this added up to, she wasn't sure. All she was certain of was that she didn't like Guy feeling unhappy and wondered what she could do to help.

In the evening, when the little ones were tucked up in bed, Louisa and Nanny Blor were having a late supper together in the nursery sitting room – cocoa and slices of bread, thickly spread with salted butter.

'Did you ever meet Florence Shore?' Louisa asked in the silence as they sipped their hot drink.

'Good heavens, my love. Whatever's made you think of poor Miss Shore again?' said Nanny Blor, putting her cocoa down and fidgeting in her apron for a spoon. All sorts of things seemed to emerge from her deep pockets. Louisa had seen her pull out a pair of false teeth once, to which Nanny had simply said, 'Oh, how useful,' and put them back. Nanny had never worn false teeth.

'I don't know,' Louisa lied, 'she just popped into my mind. Did you, though – meet her?'

'No,' said Nanny. 'She was Rosa's friend and our visits never coincided. I'd heard about her from Rosa for so many years, ever since they met at nursing school. Her name, you know, the Nightingale bit, made her something of a curiosity from the start.'

'What was she like?' asked Louisa, tucking her legs up beneath her on the armchair, as if settling in for a bedtime story.

'Oh, I don't know that I could presume to say,' said Nanny, a sniff threatening to come on, but she coughed instead. 'I think she was like most of her kind – war nurses, that is. They don't say much; they just get on with the job. Rosa was fond of her, though. I think she was a loyal sort, friendly enough. She kept herself to herself.'

'She never married?'

'Oh no, she was married to the job. There was a man, of sorts, I believe. A cousin of hers – an artist. But there was some reason why it couldn't happen between them. Besides, she was very attached to her friend Mabel. Flo might have worried about her being alone if she went off to live with a husband. Poor Mabel, she will have taken the death very hard.'

'What did she do when she wasn't working, then?'

'You should be careful – you remember what curiosity did to the cat,' said Nanny sharply, but Louisa knew she liked a gossip; it was just a show of resistance. 'She stayed with friends; she was always popular. And she had a bit of money – she came from a smart family and she'd inherited quite a bit – so I think she could always look after herself.'

'Until the end,' said Louisa.

'Yes,' said Nanny sadly, 'until the end. Who knows what happened there? It seems a very mean ending for a life that was lived for others. She'll have got her reward in heaven, I suppose. Now, there'll be no reward for me if I stay up talking like this at all hours. I'm off to Bedfordshire. Will you turn off the lights?'

'Of course,' said Louisa. 'Good night, Nanny.'

'Good night, child.'

CHAPTER THIRTY-THREE

~~~~~

It wasn't many days after that Nancy shyly took a letter out of her pocket to show Louisa. 'He's written to me,' she said, triumph on her face.

And so he had. Roland – who signed off 'your obedient servant, Roland Lucknor' – had written a short note to Nancy, thanking her for the 'most pleasant' walk around the garden, and hoping that they might meet again in London. He knew they weren't to speak of it but he was glad of their chance introduction at the ball, as it had meant he was able to find Lord Redesdale. *Those of us who were at Ypres find it hard to talk about those years*, he wrote, *so it means a great deal to find another who understands, even if the shared memories remain unspoken.*

'He's a poet, isn't he?' said Nancy, dramatically pinning the note to her breast with both hands. 'Oh, why must you look like that? Don't spoil my fun.'

Louisa had paused her sewing and sat very still. Sunlight streamed on to the green-and-white-striped baby's dress covering her lap. 'I want to be happy for you,' she said. 'I just think you should be careful. He's a lot older than you. You're still a young girl.'

'Catherine of Aragon was sixteen years old when she married Prince Arthur,' said Nancy, defiant.

'I don't think that argument will wash with His Lordship,' said Louisa. 'And besides, I don't think we should be leaping to the conclusion of marriage just yet.'

'Why must you sound so suspicious? I can't see that he's done anything wrong except be completely charming.'

'Perhaps that's why I'm suspicious,' said Louisa, and she lifted her hand holding the needle to indicate that she meant to get on with her work.

'So you admit it,' said Nancy. 'Well, I shall prove you wrong. And I shall write to him now and suggest we meet in London. You shan't stop me.'

'Meet whom in London?'

Louisa stood immediately and Nancy turned around, startled to see Lady Redesdale in the doorway.

'I've just come up to see Debo,' she said. 'Whom are you planning to meet, Koko?'

Nancy composed herself. 'Marjorie Murray,' she answered. 'She's suggesting I go to the Summer Exhibition with her.'

'I hardly think you are going to go to London unaccompanied,' said her mother severely. 'Is that letter from her? May I see it, please?'

'Muv! It's my letter.'

'I'm perfectly aware of that. Hand it over to me, please.'

Louisa froze, unable to say anything. She knew what this meant and watched Nancy hand the letter to Lady Redesdale in slow motion. She thought: This must be how drowning feels. Guy flitted into her mind, the letter she had meant to write, and just as quickly faded away. Everything evaporated but the scene unfolding before her.

Lady Redesdale read the signature at the end first. 'Why is Mr Lucknor writing to you?'

Nancy spoke to the Persian rug. She appeared to be focusing on a blackberry juice stain that was pretending to be a part of the pattern. 'I don't really know.'

Lady Redesdale turned over and read the letter from the beginning. 'What does he mean – he's sorry you and Miss Cannon had to leave the ball so suddenly? What ball? Louisa, you can speak up, too.'

'Your ladyship, I'm so sorry—'

'Muv, please don't blame Lou-Lou; it's not her fault, I made her do it,' interrupted Nancy, looking directly at her mother now, all but on her knees, hands clasped in prayer.

'Do *what*?'

'Go to a ball. We went to a ball. I made Louisa come with me as my chaperone.'

'When did this happen?' Lady Redesdale's expression, thought Louisa, helped her understand for the first time the phrase: 'a face like thunder'.

'It was the night we said we were having supper with Marjorie Murray and her godmother. They were there, and it was at the Savoy, but it was a ball. Muv, you can't be too furious. Lou-Lou was there; I wasn't alone.' Nancy's eyes were growing bigger, filling with tears. 'Please don't tell Farve.'

'We are going to tell your father straight away,' said Lady Redesdale, her voice glacial enough to cancel summer. 'As for you, Louisa, we shall be discussing that, too. I suggest you go and talk to Nanny Blor and explain to her exactly what you've done. I'm very disappointed.' There was a weary sigh. 'Very disappointed indeed.'

She turned on her heels and walked downstairs, Nancy

following close behind, looking back at Louisa and mouthing, 'I'm so sorry.'

Shaking, Louisa went to find Nanny Blor, who she knew would be fussing over Decca and Unity, coaxing them to wear sunhats before they went into the garden.

'Oh, there you are!' said Nanny. 'Do give me a hand, would you, dear? I can't bend down low enough to tie the hats on the little mites, and they are wriggling so. Decca, darling, do be still.'

'I don't want it on!' squealed Decca. 'It looks stupid!'

'No one's looking at you, dear,' said Nanny as she placed her hands on her lower back and let out a small 'oof'.

Louisa bent down and swiftly tied the little girls' hats on, then said to Nanny, 'I'm so sorry, Nanny Blor, but I think I'm going to be asked to leave.' She clenched her jaw and pressed her tongue to the roof of her mouth, desperate not to cry.

'Whatever for?' said Nanny, confusion registering on every feature of her face. Perhaps decades of reading children their bedtime stories had simplified Nanny's emotions to a picture-book quality. If she felt it, you saw it.

'I went with Nan—, Miss Nancy, to a ball in London that she didn't have permission to attend.'

'Didn't have permission . . .' Nanny repeated, stupefied. The idea of doing something not explicitly permitted by her employers was as remote to her as a man on the moon. Natural laws simply didn't permit it.

'Her Ladyship has just discovered it and taken Miss Nancy down to see her father. She said I had to come and tell you. Oh, Nanny, I'm so sorry.' If she was drowning before, she'd sunk to the bottom of the seabed now.

'Dear girl,' said Nanny. 'I don't really know what to say. Oh dear, oh dear. I do hope they don't ask you to leave. I don't really know what I'll do without you. And the thought of having to train some-one else . . . ' She found a chair and sank into it, her face collapsing like a punctured beach ball. 'But you really shouldn't have done it. What possessed you?'

'Miss Nancy asked me. Her friend Marjorie Murray was going and she wanted to go with her. She knew His Lordship would never give permission but said she'd go anyway. We thought at least if I was with her that would be a little less bad. And now I know that it wasn't. And it was an awful evening anyway.'

'Why was it so awful? Do I want to know?' Nanny had started to recover herself.

'I . . . well, I saw someone I didn't want to see and we had to leave in a hurry,' said Louisa, tripping over her words. 'Please don't let them sack me. I can't go back home.'

Nanny looked at her sympathetically. 'I do know something of what you're feeling,' she said. 'I've met plenty of girls in my time who had high hopes of bettering themselves with a job in service. I should know. I made that decision myself, all those years ago. I'll see what I can do, though I can't make any promises. His Lordship's ever so strict when it comes to his daughters. But come on, there, there.'

Louisa bent down into Nanny's arms, accepting her embrace, inhaling the comforting fragrance of pear drops. She gulped her sobs down and stood up, embarrassed, feeling Decca tugging on her skirt. Unity was still standing on the rug, watching them, her hat on but untied again.

The next few days were agony for all in the house as Lord Redesdale variously shouted at the dogs for lying down in the wrong places, Ada for coming into the dining room at the wrong minute and, for quite a protracted amount of time, at a stuck needle on his gramophone player. Nancy, whom her sisters had been told not to talk to, was also completely ignored by both parents – 'Sent to Coventry,' as she called it, a fate far worse for her than a constant stream of fury.

Louisa tiptoed about in the nursery, hardly daring to go downstairs, so Nanny had to be the one to take the girls to the drawing room for tea, huffing and puffing her way back up.

Eventually, after three days of this, Lady Redesdale summoned both Louisa and Nancy to the morning room after breakfast. The two girls stood before her as she sat at her writing desk.

'Louisa, His Lordship and I have decided that although this was a serious misdemeanour,' she gave a fierce look as she said this, 'we are under no illusions as to the persuasive powers of our eldest daughter. Also, Nanny Blor needs you. So you will stay but we will be keeping a close eye on you from now on.'

Louisa nodded. 'Yes, my lady. I understand. Thank you.'

Lady Redesdale turned to her daughter, whose face carried a sullen pout. 'As for you, Nancy, we have decided that it would be best if you went away to school. You will go to Hatherop Castle, an hour from here. We can only hope that they manage to teach you the good behaviour and manners required for you to get on in life, in a way that we have clearly utterly failed to do. You've been saying for years that you wanted to go to school. Well, now you've got what you wished for.'

'But, Muv, I—'

'Whatever it is you're going to say, I don't want to hear it. You will begin at Hatherop after the summer,' said Lady Redesdale, before turning away. 'You can both go back upstairs now.'

Louisa's heart was still hammering from the state she had wound herself into as they'd stood before Lady Redesdale. The relief she felt that she would not, after all, be banished back to London, where her only options were a life as a washerwoman or as a— No, she wouldn't even *think* the word . . . She was safe, for now.

For Nancy, however, whatever she was feeling, it was not relief. She wailed as they climbed the back stairs. '*Your father and I*,' she mimicked. 'This was all Muv's doing, I know it! Farve would never stand for any of us to go to school – all hairy bluestockings playing hockey, he says. This is Muv. She can't stand it that I finally have a friend in the house, so she has to send me away.' They reached the landing and Nancy grabbed Louisa's arms. 'What shall I do? Roland is never going to be able to write to me there. You'll have to write to him for me, Lou.'

'I can't,' said Louisa. 'You heard what Her Ladyship said. If I do one more thing wrong, I'll be out. I can't risk it. I'm sorry.'

'I know,' said Nancy, relenting at once, knowing the gravity of Louisa's words. 'And I need you here. So we won't do that. I shall think of something. Oh! She's so infuriating! It's true that I wanted to go to school, but that was because it was such hell to be here, learning nothing, with no one to talk to. It's not been like that since you got here.'

'You shall have to make the best of it,' said Louisa. Calm had at long last returned to her. 'It won't be for long. And I will still be here. Now, let's go up and tell Nanny the news. She's been in a state for days.'

CHAPTER THIRTY-FOUR

~~~~~

Mrs Windsor burst into the nursery, her face black with fury. Nanny and Louisa had just finished getting the younger girls ready to go down to the library for tea.

'Good afternoon, Mrs Windsor,' said Nanny Blor equably, completely ignoring the sudden *froideur* in the room.

Mrs Windsor glared at Louisa. 'Telephone for you,' she said with her jaw still clenched. 'A Mr Sullivan. Don't let it happen again.' She stalked out.

Louisa flushed and ran downstairs to the telephone cupboard, off the hall. Thankfully the housekeeper had gone elsewhere to work off her temper.

'Mr Sullivan?' Louisa whispered into the telephone. The handle felt heavy and she wasn't entirely sure how to know if it was working.

'Miss Cannon,' said Guy, his voice echoing slightly, 'I'm sorry to telephone but, well ... I thought I might as well try.'

'Try what?' said Louisa, looking about her in case Mrs Windsor should suddenly appear like a pantomime witch. If she arrived in a room in a puff of smoke above a trapdoor it wouldn't be in the least surprising.

'You remember I told you about the suspect, Stuart Hobkirk? I went to look at his painting in the Summer Exhibition at the Royal Academy and it seems there is a gallery in London showing some more of his work. It opens in a few days' time. Is there any chance you could come with me?'

'Why?' said Louisa.

Guy was taken aback. That wasn't the question he'd been expecting. 'I'm not supposed to be questioning him. If you were there, it might look better.'

'You could put the blame on me, you mean?' She shouldn't really tease, but it was irresistible.

'I didn't mean it quite like that, but I suppose so. And, also . . .' He hesitated, but not for too long. 'I'd like to see you. I know it's a long shot but I had to ask.'

Louisa could hear Guy breathing at the other end. Not for the first time, she thought what an extraordinary thing the telephone was. He was *miles* away.

'We're going to be in London for a few days soon, as it happens,' she replied, sounding as casual as she could. 'But I'd have to talk to Nanny Blor to get the time off.'

'Yes, of course. I understand. But you really think you might?'

Louisa laughed. 'Yes, I do.'

'It's next Thursday, in St James's. We could meet outside Green Park station at six o'clock?'

'I'll do my best to be there. Goodbye, Mr Sullivan.' Louisa hung up the telephone and wiped her hand on her skirt. It was sweaty but she told herself it was caused by nothing more than the warmth of the room.

Their stay in London was only ever intended to be a short one, largely for the purpose of buying the things Nancy needed for

Hatherop Castle. She had been placated in the last few weeks by the idea of the friends she would make at the school and the new library of books she would have at her disposal. A long list of items had been drawn up to fill the trunk and Louisa was to accompany Nancy and Lord Redesdale to his favourite shop in London, the Army & Navy, where they would find everything they needed.

On the first night, Louisa and Nancy were in the kitchen, making themselves a hot chocolate to take upstairs to bed, when they heard a commotion at the front door. They peered out into the hallway and saw Lord Redesdale remonstrating with a young man in his twenties, with tousled hair and unfocused eyes. He was stumbling and slurring his words in anger.

'It's Bill,' said Nancy.

'Who's Bill?'

'Aunt Natty's boy. The one who lives in France, though I think he lives here now.'

Louisa watched Lord Redesdale try to push Bill out of the front door, but he was resisting, becoming increasingly agitated. 'I think he's drunk,' said Louisa. 'We'd better leave them to it.'

The two of them crept up the back stairs to their rooms and nothing was said of it again, until some months later.

CHAPTER THIRTY-FIVE

The following Thursday found Guy standing, rather nervously, outside Green Park station. The air was warm and there was a hopeful jaunt to the steps of the commuters, a feeling of summer in the air. The birds and the bees, thought Guy. After a few minutes, as he was beginning to wonder whether Louisa would show up and how long he should wait, he saw someone running down the road, her hand holding her hat down, her skirt flapping behind. She kept up the pace until she was almost beside him and he realised it was Louisa.

'Mr Sullivan!' she panted. 'It's me.' She laughed at his squinting eyes behind his glasses, a friendly, familiar sight now.

'Gosh, yes, so it is you,' said Guy, and felt a wave of pleasure rush through him. 'I'm so pleased you came.'

'Oh, they owed me some time off, it was easy,' said Louisa, only lying a little bit. Nancy had kicked up a fuss, wanting to come out with her, but Louisa had wanted to do this one by herself.

They walked towards St James's, the pavements teeming with busy men hurrying along in their suits and hats despite the heat, umbrellas wielded with the self-importance of silver-topped canes. Guy started to tell her about the exhibition they were going to.

'It's a show of artists from St Ives in Cornwall, and he's one of them. It's the opening night tonight. I'm sure he'll have to be there.' He was a little afraid that Louisa might think he had got her out on false pretences.

'Yes,' said Louisa, 'I expect you're right. I've never been to an opening party before. Do I look smart enough?' She stopped in the middle of the pavement and stood before him, inviting judgement.

Guy took in her brown eyes, rosebud mouth and slim figure in a blue cotton jacket, her narrow ankles and small feet in polished shoes that had heels to lift her just an inch. He thought she was perfect.

'Well?' prompted Louisa.

Guy said nothing but held out his arm for her to take and together they walked the last few hundred yards to the party.

There was already a crowd of young people gathered inside, drinking wine and chattering loudly amongst themselves. He accepted a glass for himself from a waiter, Louisa refused, and the two of them stood about trying to look as if they were meant to be there, but feeling like potatoes in a bowl of roses. Louisa was agog at some of the dresses, which seemed to be made of the tracing paper that the children used to copy pictures in Lord Redesdale's book of Renaissance art. In the corner was a man she was sure was wearing lipstick.

After ten minutes, Louisa beckoned Guy to bend his ear towards her.

'We're not going to recognise Mr Hobkirk by magic,' she whispered. 'We had better ask someone where he is.' She giggled and Guy hoped he wasn't blushing.

He asked a couple standing close by and the woman, wearing a black chiffon dress with red roses printed alarmingly over her breasts, pointed the artist out for him with her long cigarette holder.

Stuart Hobkirk was a man in his fifties but looked younger. He had the appearance of someone who had spent plenty of years as a starving artist even if he was well fed now. Thick blond hair was swept off his face and his velvet jacket fitted him neatly. He was smoking, surrounded by five or six similarly dressed, rather louche types, all hanging on his every word. Guy saw he was going to have to choose his moment carefully.

Eventually, Stuart finished his anecdote and started to walk away from the knot of fans towards a waiter. Guy stepped forwards and interrupted him just as he was exchanging his empty glass for a full one.

'Mr Hobkirk?' said Guy, hand outstretched.

'Yes?' said Stuart, with the air of a man who was summoning the patience to listen benignly to someone tell him again how marvellous he was.

'My name is Mr Sullivan,' said Guy, 'from the London, Brighton and South Coast Railway Police. We spoke on the telephone before, about your cousin Florence Shore.'

Stuart's expression changed to one of displeasure. 'I don't think this is the time or place.'

'Please, sir,' said Guy, 'just a minute of your time. I know it's not very convenient and I apologise, but it's important that we talk now.'

Louisa had been standing close by, choosing to remain quiet, but she smiled at Mr Hobkirk encouragingly.

'Very well, then,' said Stuart, stamping out his cigarette on the floor and taking a gulp of wine. 'We'd better sit down; I can't stand for long, as you can see.'

Guy and Louisa now noticed he held a walking stick, and as

Stuart moved towards a small sofa at the side of the room, he had a distinctive limp in his left leg.

Louisa's stomach sank. He couldn't possibly be the man who had jumped down from the train. He couldn't jump down from anywhere.

Guy and Stuart sat, with Louisa standing next to the sofa. She felt like a guard dog.

'You mentioned before that you were at home alone, painting,' said Guy.

'Yes,' said Stuart, clearing his throat.

'I know you said there was no one to corroborate this but it is rather important that you try to think of someone,' said Guy.

'Why? Am I a suspect?'

Guy wasn't sure how to respond to this, but his silence was all that was needed to encourage Stuart.

'Look, the thing is, I couldn't say anything because I was at a party. Yes, before you ask, it *was* during the day. It had started at the weekend and carried on.'

'I don't understand,' said Guy. 'If you were at a party then there will be plenty of people who can say you were there.'

'Ye-es, there are. In fact, two or three of them are here tonight. I couldn't say anything before because, you see . . . Well, the truth of it is, I had taken a lot of cocaine and smoked opium, and I was quite out of it. Off my head, in fact. I didn't want my mother finding out.' Now that he had confessed, Stuart's attitude was more devil-may-care than humble pie.

'In short,' said Guy, not wanting to get into a discussion about the drugs, which though shocking were not against the law, 'there *are* people I can talk to tonight, who will confirm that you were in Cornwall on the twelfth of January this year?'

'Yes,' said Stuart, mollified. 'This whole thing has been so ghastly, you know. What with Offley being so angry about the will.' He turned and looked Guy right in the eye. 'I loved Florence. She understood me when so few did.'

Guy shuffled in his seat. 'Yes, I, um, I understand that you and Miss Shore were . . . close.'

Stuart suddenly roared with laughter. 'Do you mean you thought we were lovers?'

Guy went bright red and couldn't quite manage an affirmative reply.

'My dear boy, of course we weren't. Darling Flo was not that way inclined, shall we say. No, her lover was Mabel Rogers.'

CHAPTER THIRTY-SIX

A fter Guy had spoken briefly to the two people that Stuart
mentioned and they had given statements to the effect that
he was at the party, although nobody could remember too much
of what went on or on which day it was, he and Louisa left the
gallery.

Their walk along St James's was quiet. Guy had been shocked
into silence at the final revelation but Louisa's mind was more on
Stuart's hobble and his walking stick. They had talked it over for
a few minutes then said goodbye at Green Park in low spirits. Guy
had so hoped to impress Louisa with his police skills and instead
he'd appeared an even bigger fool than before. At least, that was
how it felt to him. Now he had no suspects, no leads and if Jarvis
found out what he had done, his job would be on the line. Louisa
was bitterly disappointed for him.

That night, back in the house the Mitfords were renting, Louisa
had found Nancy awake and waiting for her.

'Well?' said Nancy, creeping into Louisa's room. 'What
happened?'

Louisa sat on her bed. 'Nothing. That is, it can't be Stuart

Hobkirk. He has a walking stick and a limp. There's no chance he was the man seen jumping down at Lewes station.'

'Couldn't the walking stick have been the weapon?' said Nancy.

'Possibly, but even with the motive of the inheritance, it doesn't work. His hobble is too noticeable. Supposing he had somehow managed to jump down, the guard who saw him at Lewes would have noticed him walking with that limp.'

'What about it being a crime of passion? And his weak alibi?'

'He introduced Guy to two people who were able to say they were with him that day, and he said that he and Florence weren't lovers. He said her only lover was her friend, Mabel Rogers.'

'Gosh,' said Nancy. She thought about that for a minute. 'I didn't really know that went on.'

'Well, yes, it sort of does,' said Louisa.

'Like pashes, I suppose . . . So, that's it, then?' said Nancy. 'We don't have a suspect any more?'

'No,' said Louisa, feeling sad for Guy as she said it. 'We don't have a suspect any more.'

Nancy said goodnight and Louisa got into bed but couldn't sleep. She lay there in the dark, thinking. Then, spurred on by an idea, she got up, turned on her lamp and took out a sheet of paper and a pen to write a letter.

Dear Guy,

Please don't give up on the investigation. I think you can do it and I want to help you. What's more, I think I might be able to.

It's something Nancy said some time ago and I didn't think anything of it then. It was when we were travelling on the train from Victoria to St Leonards, the same line on which

Miss Shore was attacked. Nancy noticed that the doors do not open from the inside. Anyone who gets out of the train by themselves has to open the window and lean out to turn the handle. The railway workers who got on at the next stop said both the windows were closed. But the train guard said the man he saw get out at Lewes did not turn back to close the window.

Don't you see what this means? Someone else must have closed the window for him. It wasn't one person that killed Miss Shore: it was two.

PART TWO

1921

CHAPTER THIRTY-SEVEN

~~~~~

Louisa stood on the beach at Dieppe, inhaling great lungfuls of warm sea air. She knew the seagulls flying overhead were no different from those that flew in England, but it seemed as if their cries had a slight French accent to them. To her delight, everything in France felt different, whether it was the hazy heat from the sun, the fine sand on the beach or the buttery deliciousness of the croissant at breakfast. Even the sunburn she got on her nose the first day seemed nothing less than excitingly exotic. Of course, each thing that thrilled Louisa sent Nanny Blor into paroxysms of despair and frustration: the loos were filthy, the tea revolting and the men both suspicious and smelling strongly of garlic.

The house Lord and Lady Redesdale had taken for these weeks was close to the infamous Aunt Natty, of whom Nancy had breathlessly given Louisa a fulsome biography.

'She's had strings of lovers,' she said, 'at least two different fathers for her four children, not including her husband, and she's mad for gambling, even though Farve says she has no money at all.'

'Are you sure?' whispered Louisa, this picture being entirely at odds with Lady Blanche's white-haired appearance, albeit one which was never less than crisply stylish. Not to mention that her son-in-law was Secretary of State for the Colonies, Winston Churchill, of whom everybody said great things were destined.

Nancy and Louisa had been sent out to buy baguettes for luncheon and decided to stop and sit at a café close by the beach for a few minutes to watch the holidaying Parisians walk past, women in long white skirts with matching jackets, their ivory skin protected by parasols and their lips slashed with red lipstick, even at midday. No trace of sticky sand or melting ice-creams besmirched their carefully put-together looks, which was more than Louisa could say for herself, furiously rubbing at the splodges of *glace à la framboise* on her skirt.

'I've written to Roland,' said Nancy suddenly. 'I couldn't tell you before, I had to get you away from everyone, so I'm telling you now. I've told him we're here, in case he could come.'

'What? Why have you done that?' said Louisa.

'I want to see him again,' said Nancy, 'and I think he wants to see me, too. We've been writing to each other.'

'But what about what happened after the dance? Lady Redesdale can't possibly approve.'

'The thing is, Farve likes him. I know they've met up and had luncheon in London. And Muv likes him too, really. She was all for recruiting him to help with the Conservative fete before that business about the party. And she doesn't blame him for that, only me. Don't worry, he won't just turn up; I told him to write to Farve and ask. We've got plenty of room. Oh, Louisa, do be excited for me. It will make it much more fun if he's here.'

'I suppose so,' said Louisa, though she felt far from sure of that. The narrow escape she had had from losing her job was not something she wished to risk again. 'We'd better get back or Nanny Blor will be worried we've been kidnapped by the white slave traders,' she said.

'If only!' joked Nancy, but she stood and they went on with their task, Nancy happily showing off the French she had learned at school. 'Not,' she had said to Louisa, 'that they have taught me anything more than that and a bit of dancing.' She had had a good time there, despite the cloud under which she had arrived, making friends with other girls and even finding an enthusiasm for the Girl Guides, though Louisa suspected this was preferred as a device for torturing her sisters with endless tasks than for the practical joys of knots.

Back at the house, they rushed into the hallway with the bread still warm from the bakery and were instantly subdued by Nanny Blor rushing up and telling them to be quiet.

'What's happened?' said Nancy.

'I'm not quite sure but it's bad news. A telegram arrived and your parents have been shut up in the *salon* for the last hour,' said Nanny Blor, all but wringing her hands. 'Quick, you had better get the bread to *madame* in the kitchen; luncheon's almost ready.'

When Lord and Lady Redesdale were sitting down in the garden under the shade of the covered porch, Louisa was helping the cook to serve, as she had done each day of the trip. She didn't mind as she enjoyed hearing the children chatter with their parents and was able to give a stern look if any of them misbehaved. Not that they usually did; the worst culprit was Unity, who occasionally slid right under the table and stayed there until luncheon was over, her parents choosing to ignore this oddity of behaviour altogether.

Today the mood was low, the children taking their cue from a white-faced Lady Redesdale and their father, who barely spoke louder than a mutter when asking someone to pass the salt. It was Nancy who forced them to explain what was going on.

'It's Aunt Natty's son, Bill,' said Lady Redesdale to Nancy. 'He's dead. And I've got to tell her.'

'What?' said Nancy. 'Bill? But how? Was he ill? I didn't know he was ill.'

There was silence from both her parents. Louisa was pouring out the fresh lemonade for the children and even the sound of the liquid splashing felt invasively loud. Nancy understood that this was not a time to pursue an answer and the rest of the luncheon was eaten in a muted tone, with only the younger children talking, and even then, not much.

Shortly after the table had been cleared away, Lady Redesdale departed alone, dressed completely in black. As she pulled on her gloves, she said that she could only hope Lady Blanche had not yet left her house for the casino. At this Lord Redesdale moaned and sat down heavily on to a chair that was too French to be comfortable.

Nancy kneeled down on the floor beside him and leaned her head against his knees. 'Poor old man,' she said as he wept quietly. He had only cried in front of his children once before, when he had heard the news of his older brother's death at Loos in the war.

'He was delirious today, I think,' said Nancy, as she and Louisa sat drinking hot chocolate in the garden when the cool of the evening had settled. Everyone else had gone to bed, exhausted by the emotion of the day, even though little had been said by anybody about the reason for it.

Nancy and Louisa had discussed over and over again the episode in London when Bill had turned up in the night.

'Farve said that Bill had asked him for money and he had refused him, because he had none to lend. And then he cried that Bill killed himself over gambling debts. I mean, it can't be true, can it?' said Nancy.

'Which bit?' asked Louisa. It was all rather a lot to take in.

'Well, all of it. Does Farve have no money? That can't be right.

I know we're not rich but I didn't think that meant we had nothing at all.'

Louisa thought of Asthall Manor, the garden divided in two by a lane, a stream bursting with trout on one side, a garden full of vegetables and trees overhanging with fruit on the other. It wasn't her idea of nothing at all. But perhaps he didn't have much money in the bank. Her father used to tell her about toffs that had titles but lived off fried potatoes. Perhaps that was the Mitfords. It didn't seem too likely but truth was often stranger than fiction, wasn't that the saying?

'Could Bill really have killed himself?' continued Nancy. 'How could he do that? Why would he do it?'

'You mustn't judge a man for that,' said Louisa, 'not until you've been in his shoes. He must have felt desperate, if that is what he did. He can't have thought there was any other way out.'

Nancy drank the last of her cocoa and stood up. 'Well, I don't know what it's all about but I'm going to bed. I hope Roland writes to Farve soon. We could do with some cheering up around here. Come on, Lou-Lou, let's get our beauty sleep.'

With that, the day was over for Nancy, and she would think no more of Bill again, while his mother lay sobbing into her pillow less than a mile away.

CHAPTER THIRTY-EIGHT

～～

Five days later, Roland arrived at the house in Dieppe. The atmosphere was still depressed. Though the manner of Bill's death had not been widely discussed, there was the matter of the autopsy, which meant the funeral would not take place as soon as might have been hoped by the family, who wanted the matter over. Lady Redesdale decided that they would remain in Dieppe for the time being, to protect her sister-in-law from harmful gossip and intrusive visitors, as far as they were able.

Lord Redesdale had not yet recovered his usual bark, but his bite, decided Nancy, was consequently far worse. Pamela, most unusually, was the suffering recipient of Rat Week – each daughter, for no apparent reason, would be chosen by His Lordship at different times to be the bearer of his brunt. This time he refused to even countenance Pamela's face at the breakfast table, which only drew her into further quiet sobs. Louisa tried to comfort her by sneaking out almond biscuits from the kitchen.

Not quite fourteen years old, Pamela's figure was starting to fill out in awkward places and Nancy delighted in calling her 'Woman', which Louisa judged sadistic, but nothing would stop her. Despite her distress, Pamela would never rise to Nancy's teasing but would only walk away or stare into her lap, fat tears splashing down. Yet the second sister was far from being the passive lump Nancy made her out to be. Louisa had discovered that Pamela had a jolly outlook on things and her love of animals far outweighed any concern she had over what stupid humans might be doing. A walk with the dogs through the fields was enough to put her right. It added up to making her an attractive person to spend time with, and when Nancy was being at her meanest, Louisa was inclined to do just that.

So Louisa was taken aback, having not talked to Nancy much in the last few days, when she saw Roland in the garden before dinner, enjoying a gin and tonic that had been prepared for him by Lord Redesdale. He looked paler than before, though not so thin, and his eyes were still dark shadows in his handsome face. He wore a fashionable linen suit with a pale pink handkerchief in his top pocket, which gave him the air of a dandy. As he raised the glass to his lips, she noticed that his hands were trembling slightly, and wondered what he was nervous about. The two men were alone in the garden and their faces were serious, their voices low. Perhaps Lord Redesdale was telling him about Bill.

'What are you doing, Louisa?'

She jumped. How long had Lady Redesdale been standing in the hall as Louisa looked through the window?

'Nothing, my lady,' she said hastily. 'Beg pardon.' She scuttled off back to the kitchen, where she had been headed to fetch some warm milk for Debo.

That night, Louisa was woken from her sleep by Nancy shaking her shoulder. 'Lou-Lou, get up, please. It's Roland – he's making terrible noises.'

Louisa sat up, then felt the blood rush from her head. 'What do you mean?'

'I can hear him crying or something. I don't know. I can't go in there. No one else will either, I know. Please, Lou. It sounds so ghastly.' Nancy's face was stricken. 'I don't understand it. We had a lovely evening, we all had supper and even Aunt Natty seemed a bit better. I was reading in bed when I heard these noises . . .'

Louisa got up and pulled on a jumper over her nightdress. 'You'd better go back to your room,' she said. 'It wouldn't look right if you were found with him. It'll only be a bad dream or something.'

Nancy nodded and returned to her bed, while Louisa padded down the hallway. It wasn't a large house, nowhere near as big as Asthall, and the bedrooms were all relatively close together. Though Lord and Lady Redesdale occupied a large room on the floor below, all the children's bedrooms and guest rooms were on the top floor. As Louisa got closer to what she knew must be Roland's, she heard sounds like a dying animal. Taking a deep breath, she turned the handle and went in.

There was a single iron bedstead in the corner and a wooden painted chest of drawers in the other, though Roland's clothes were neatly folded over the back of a chair. He was lying on the top of the bed, the sheets flung to the floor, the pillow by his feet. Though the night was chilly, he was sweating profusely, his hair slick, dark patches showing under the arms of his pyjamas. His eyes were wide open but unseeing and he tore at his face, his knees tucked up to his chest.

Louisa didn't think as she went over and instinctively wrapped her arms around him, making soothing noises. She was unsure whether to try and wake him out of his dream, if it was a dream. His open eyes were disturbing. He was calling out his own name, as if he was trying to warn himself of something, then would suddenly subside into a fresh round of choking sobs. Louisa had left the door to his room open but the hallway remained dark and nobody else came. There was no light on in his room but the moon shone through the thin white curtains, so Louisa could see his forehead smooth as he calmed beneath her embrace. As she stroked his head, she heard him say, 'Thank you, Nurse Shore, I feel much better now.'

Louisa's heart stopped, or so it felt like, but she remained where she was and, after only the slightest hesitation, resumed her rhythmic strokes. His breathing was almost steady now and his eyes had long closed. The nightmare had ended but the dream was still there. Once or twice more he thanked 'Nurse Shore'.

Slowly, carefully, she moved away from him, moved the pillow back beneath his head, put the sheet and a blanket across him, then stole out of the room, closing the door behind her. Roland would never know she had been there.

My dearest love,

I'm very tired today, as I am every day, it seems, but also exhilarated by the finish of the last terrible battle. It's the not knowing, I suppose, of when it will end. And exhaustion seems to eat the very marrow of my bones when I remember that we have won this battle but not the war (– yet).

During those weeks, there was a near-constant flow of men arriving on stretchers, crying out in pain, crying for their mothers, crying for their friends. Each one had to be cleaned and dressed with bandages as best we could. More often than not we had to hope that the holding of their hands helped as much as morphine. The doctors could never get around the men fast enough to administer the drugs.

But! You mustn't worry about me, my dear. At my time of life, I know that I'm lucky to have had the years I've had, and I've seen enough not to be too shocked. I do feel terribly sad for the young; these sights and sounds cannot but make them cynical, and that's if they live.

Perhaps it's me that's the cynic, as the men show such bravery and courage, despite everything. You get to know some of them really quite well, the business of nursing being

*such an intimate one. I don't mean physically, though there
is that, of course. It's more that one knows what they are
thinking because they tell you; the truth of their thoughts
burst spontaneously out of their mouths. The officers may
be good at small talk in the drawing rooms of Mayfair, but
here they get to the point. There is no time to waste when
it comes to letting one know what they need. We even read
their letters to their mothers and their own dearest loves, not
because we are snooping but because we're writing the letters
for them. Their stories make your heart break.*

*There is a lad here that we've all become rather fond of,
Roland Lucknor, an officer, who is very gentle. He has had gas
poisoning and the initial effects were terrible, but we're hoping
he's improving enough now to recover fully in a few weeks. Of
course, he has been cast very low by it all. He's a sensitive man
and not at all suited to the war (as if anyone was). We talked
for a long time when he first came in. Roland told me that he
signed up almost as soon as war broke out, determined to do
something good for his country and make his father proud.
He told me he hasn't seen his father since he was fourteen
years old, and then only for a single evening (his father is a
missionary in Africa). His mother died when he was nine years
old and he hadn't seen her for four years before that, so has
no memory of her. He has a godmother in England he adores,
who he stayed with in the school holidays, but she has lost her
mind and no longer knows who he is. So I'm very much afraid
that he feels there is little to live for. Sister Mary and I spend
our time telling him to cheer up and reminding him of good
old Blighty and all the marvellous things waiting for us when
we get home: cauliflower cheese, long walks in the hills, a pint
of ale. The trouble is, it starts to make us feel homesick.*

For all the men, the shock and terror of the fighting here
is overwhelming: the constant noise of the shelling; the
sleep deprivation night after night; the cold and wet of the
mud, despite the summer; the painful reminders of home
when letters and parcels arrive; the sickness; the loss of their
friends ... There is nothing normal, nothing reassuring about
daily life here.

And yet, one carries on, putting one foot in front of the
other, moving forwards. I think only about the things that
need to be done, the mechanics of the nursing, the organising
of the sisters' rotas and so on. We are lucky because we are
rewarded by the men who do get better. Just the sheer fact of
their being alive is enough to make us happy, though they
give us plenty of gratitude, too.

I'd better end here, my dearest. Please write and let me
know you are well. I expect I shall be at this address for a
few more weeks yet. I do not know when I will manage some
home leave.

Most tender love,
Flo

CHAPTER THIRTY-NINE

~~~~~

The next morning Louisa and Nancy had time for only the briefest exchange of words, in which Louisa said little but that she had calmed Roland from his bad dream. She urged Nancy not to say anything to him. It would only shame Roland to know, she said, and Nancy agreed.

As it turned out, there was little opportunity for Nancy to talk to Roland in any case. She told Louisa later that over breakfast he had said to her that he was on his way to Paris as he had a desire to see some of his old friends from before the war. He didn't know, he confessed to Nancy, if they would still be there but he had a longing for the streets of the Left Bank, the smells of the Seine and a glass of absinthe. When Nancy had asked what that was, he had laughed knowingly, and she complained to Louisa that it was yet another question to which she was considered too childish to know the answer. Yet Louisa felt sure she had seen him watch Nancy affectionately, when he thought that she could not see him.

After breakfast, he and Lord Redesdale had gone to sit out on the terrace that overlooked the sea for a cup of coffee and a cigarette. Louisa was down at the far end of the garden, pinning out some washing to dry in the balmy sea air when she heard the most terrific shouting. This was not an unusual sound when coming from her master, but to her astonishment, this time it was Roland who appeared to be standing up and agitated, shouting and waving his hands about, while Nancy's father remained in his chair, looking deeply apologetic and upset. Before she had had time to gather up her basket and get out of sight, Roland had vanished and was not seen again. Lord Redesdale remained under a cloud for the rest of the day.

There were only a few days remaining of their time in Dieppe and there was a rush to do favourite things 'for the last time' – the final mouth-watering croissant, the final paddle in the sea, the final exotically bitter cup of coffee – so it was not until they had reached London, where the Mitfords had decided to stay for a couple of nights on their way home to make further arrangements for Bill's funeral, that Louisa thought to telephone Guy about what she had now determined was a new development in the Shore case.

She had not discussed it with Nancy, feeling that the girl's propensity for stories was not an advantage in a situation like this. Instead, she went off alone to find one of the new telephone call boxes in Piccadilly and, pennies in hand, dialled the operator and asked for the London, Brighton and South Coast Railway Police at Victoria station, crossing her fingers as she did so that Guy would be there.

Thankfully, he was soon summoned, but the conversation was stiff, largely due to the fact that he was far from alone as he stood by the telephone at the reception desk.

'Miss Cannon,' he said formally after taking the telephone from the smirking police officer who had picked up the call, 'I hope there is no trouble?'

Louisa sensed his discomfort and sought to reassure him. 'No,

none,' she said. 'I'm sorry to call but I thought I must because . . .
I think I may have discovered something important in the Shore
case.'

There was a pause and Louisa thought she could hear a slight
quickening of his breath. 'What is it?' he said.

'It's someone called Roland Lucknor. He's an officer that Nancy
met at a dance. We knew that he was at Ypres when Lord Redesdale
was there; they were in the same battalion, in fact, though he said
that he didn't know Lord Redesdale at the time, only knew of him.'
She stopped and took a breath. It was important to get this right.

'Yes,' said Guy, 'go on.' He was impatient, aware of others trying
to listen in.

'Well, Nancy asked him once if he knew Florence Shore, as a
nurse in the war, and he said no. But a few days ago, he came to
stay with the Mitfords in Dieppe, on his way to Paris, and he woke
in the night screaming. Nancy heard him and got me to go into
his room—'

'You went into his room in the night?' said Guy before he could
stop himself. He heard someone stifle a laugh in the background.
'Sorry, what happened then?'

'He was sweating and crying; it was awful. I don't know if it was
a dream or that thing soldiers got in the war . . . '

'Shellshock?' said Guy.

'Yes, something like that. It was awful because his eyes were
open but I don't think he was aware of what he was saying or even
that I was there. I calmed him down and then he said, more than
once, "Thank you, Nurse Shore".'

'Nurse Shore?' said Guy. 'Are you certain?'

'Quite certain,' said Louisa, and then heard the pips go.
Hurriedly, she put more coins in. 'Are you still there, Guy?'

'Yes,' he said.

'Why did he deny knowing her if he *did* know her?' said Louisa.

'I don't know,' said Guy, 'but I agree, it doesn't look good for him. Can you find out anything more?'

'I don't know,' said Louisa. 'He comes to the house now and then. I think he's doing some sort of business deal with Lord Redesdale. Perhaps we should ask him if he knows Stuart Hobkirk? Supposing he was the accomplice?'

'I think we need to be careful about making those kind of connections before we've spoken to him,' said Guy, as much trying to tell himself not to get too hopeful at this turn. 'Nurse Shore will have tended to many men and we can't suspect each one.'

Feeling dismissed by Guy, Louisa decided she would investigate Roland herself. If he was a danger to either Nancy or Lord Redesdale, she'd want to know first and protect them from him. The only question now was one of opportunity.

CHAPTER FORTY

❧

Troubled by Louisa's telephone call, the case had come rushing back to Guy. He'd put it to one side for a time, not knowing how to go any further, and now this chink of light made him wonder if he could pursue it again.

Talking it over with his mother one night on the front steps, he had even told her the shocking revelation from Stuart Hobkirk. At this, she persuaded him that he should go and see Mabel Rogers.

'That poor woman,' she said, as they enjoyed the last of the day's sunshine and drank tea, while his brothers were in the pub. 'Those war nurses were a rare breed, as brave as any soldier, and no one ever talks about them. You don't see them in the parades, do you? And after all that, she lost the only thing she had – the promise of a comfortable future with her friend.'

'You don't know that,' said Guy. 'She might have lots of friends. Lots of other things to do.'

His mother shook her head sadly. 'I do know,' she said. 'Trust me, she was away at war for years. There's not many'd understand her and what she's been through. She'll have little money and be lonely. You ought to go and see her. She'd most likely appreciate a hand of friendship.'

Guy knew Mabel lived at Carnforth Lodge on Queen Street in Hammersmith as the matron there, as it had been stated during the inquest and he still had the notes in his little book. Not long after the conversation with his mother he realised the address was only a short bus ride from work he'd been sent to do at Paddington station, so he decided on the spur of the moment that he would go to see the nurse.

At once he saw that his mother had been right. Carnforth Lodge was a dilapidated, depressed building on the side of a busy road. The windows and net curtains were clean, a sign of its proud inhabitants, but the columns on the side of the front door were black from smoke. Its poverty was painted across the front in large letters, like a newspaper headline: Hammersmith & Fulham District Nursing Association Supported by Voluntary Contributions. The last two words had been painted smaller to squeeze them on to the frontage. Bang next door was the Six Bells pub – as unlikely a pairing as a nunnery and a butcher's. How strange that Florence Shore, who had money, had chosen to live here.

Guy pushed open the front door and found himself in a dim hall. There was a sign for a porter's office on an open door and Guy knocked on it gently.

'Yes?' called out a man's voice.

Guy stepped in. The man was sitting in a wooden chair beside a rickety table, drinking out of a mug. He didn't stand when Guy came in but merely looked up.

'What can I do for you?'

He looked familiar, though it took Guy a minute to work out

why. He was the man who had been holding Mabel Rogers' arm at the first inquest.

'I'm looking for the matron, Miss Mabel Rogers,' said Guy.

The porter put his mug down. 'On what business?' he asked.

'It's personal,' said Guy.

The porter took in Guy's uniform and raised his eyebrows. 'Is she expecting you?'

Guy thought this rather impertinent of a porter, but if he had been the man at the inquest, he was probably a good friend of Miss Rogers. Perhaps after Miss Shore's death there had been a few unwanted people calling in, the type that liked to clutch at the edges of morbid events.

'No,' he admitted, 'but I won't stay more than a few minutes.'

'Right, I'll show you in,' said the porter.

He led Guy down the hall and gave a firm knock on a door. They heard, 'Come in, come in.' When they entered, Mabel was behind a desk, bent down, looking through one of the drawers.

Muffled, she said, 'Be with you in a moment. Can't find my— Oh, there they are.' She sat up, holding a pair of fabric scissors triumphantly. Her face soon changed. 'Who are you?'

'Apologies for startling you, Miss Rogers,' said Guy. 'I'm Guy Sullivan. I'm with the London, Brighton and South Coast Railway Police.'

The room was unfussy and clean. There was a small pot of fuchsias on the mantelpiece and a faded rug on the floor. Mabel herself was something of a stark contrast to her surroundings; her dress hung limply on her frame, her long face bore not a trace of having ever expressed a pleasantry in its life and her wispy hair was pulled back in a severe bun.

'You can go, Jim,' she said to the porter, who nodded but looked reluctant to leave. He left the door open slightly. 'What can I do for you?'

Guy sat on the chair that faced her desk. Was it his imagination or was it measured a little lower than was standard? He felt himself distinctly beneath Miss Rogers' gaze. 'Oh, well, nothing, actually, Miss Rogers,' said Guy. Not for the first time, he hadn't quite thought through a decision. 'I came to offer my condolences to you about Florence Shore. I know it has been some time but . . .' He trailed away, aware that it sounded rather inadequate.

Mabel gazed out of the French windows to the garden beyond. Two hens were pecking at the grass. 'I think of Flo every day,' she said. 'We will not be at our ease until we know what happened.'

'Yes,' said Guy. He took a pause, thinking through how to do this as tactfully as possible. 'I know the two of you were old friends—'

'For more than a quarter of a century,' said Mabel.

'I wanted to let you know that although things appear to have come to a stop, I am still working on the case.'

'Are you? If you've come to interview me, I must say, I really don't—'

'No, no,' Guy was anxious to reassure her. 'Not at all. I know you have given statements in court. Though I did wonder if perhaps you had heard of someone called Roland Lucknor?'

'I don't mind telling you, Mr Sullivan, that I have lived through two wars but I found the death of my dear friend far more distressing than anything I saw in Africa or France,' said Mabel, standing up from behind her desk. 'Please, I must ask you to leave now.'

Guy was horrified to realise that Mabel was on the verge of tears. 'I only wanted to give you my sympathy,' he said, 'a hand of friendship. To let you know that Miss Shore hasn't been forgotten. I'm determined to find the man that did it.'

Mabel closed her eyes briefly. 'That man didn't only kill Flo; he killed me, too. I have nothing to look forward to any more. Thank you, Mr Sullivan, for your kindness. It means a lot to an old lady like me.'

CHAPTER FORTY-ONE

L ouisa's chance to investigate Roland came rather sooner than she had expected, as it turned out. Not long after their return from France, Lady Redesdale's father died. Even Nancy had been moved by the death of Tap Bowles.

'We didn't see him much but he was awfully funny,' she said. 'And now he's died in Morocco he's going to be buried there, so no funeral for us.'

Lady Redesdale had worn mourning for the appropriate time but there was little question that the family's circumstances had improved somewhat.

'I'll say there was a generous inheritance,' said Mrs Stobie gleefully. 'I've been asked to order all the good cuts from the butcher's and some special delicacies to be sent up from Harrods.'

Even Mrs Windsor went about with something that approached a smile on her face, which Nanny put down to the new linens that had arrived.

It wasn't much longer after the money had made itself noticed that news reached Louisa that Roland was coming down to stay for a night as part of a house party. Further evidence, said Mrs Stobie, that there were fruits to be enjoyed. Louisa was more concerned that Roland's acceptance of the invitation was rather more directly connected to the family fortune. If he meant to have some of it, she would have to stop him. Not that she had any idea how she was going to do this.

Nancy, meanwhile, was as thrilled as ever at the idea of seeing him. 'Whatever that row with Farve was about, it must be over,' she said. 'Neither of them would say anything to me, of course.'

'Yes, I suppose,' said Louisa, though she worried it was either money – wasn't it always, as Nancy herself had said – or something more sinister, somehow connected with Florence Shore. Surely Lord Redesdale didn't have anything to do with it? She shook the idea out of her mind.

Naturally, when Roland arrived, she saw little of him, as he was with Lord and Lady Redesdale and the rest of the guests in the drawing room, before changing for dinner and joining them. Nancy had been asked to the dinner too, which she took as an encouraging sign that her parents must not only suspect something of a romantic nature between the two of them but even supported the idea.

'Childhood might really almost be over, Lou,' she said breathlessly.

'Or you could just be making up the numbers,' said Louisa, and then felt guilty at Nancy's crestfallen face.

There were, however, bigger things on her mind. Finally, when the dinner gong had sounded and the younger children were in bed, Louisa snuck across to where the guest bedrooms lay. She didn't know for certain which room Roland would have been put in, but there were only ever three or four made up at any one time. As she hesitated on the landing, Louisa heard the voice of Mrs Windsor talking to Ada. In haste, she opened the first door on the left and ran in, surprising both herself and a woman who was sitting before the dressing table, trying to do up the clasp on her necklace.

'Yes?' said the woman. She looked to be a contemporary of Lady Redesdale's and was a striking beauty. Her lips had been painted dark red and Louisa was awestruck by the daring of it.

'Beg pardon, ma'am,' said Louisa, giving a little bob. 'Mrs Windsor sent me up to see if I might be of assistance. Everyone else is at dinner. Might I help you with your necklace?' She stepped forwards and did the clasp with efficiency. 'Would you like anything else, ma'am?'

'Well, I—' the woman began, but Louisa had already started to back away to the door.

'Glad to be of assistance, ma'am. Good evening.' And she darted out into the hall again, leaving the woman staring at herself in the mirror as if she'd been had.

Directly opposite was a guest room with only a single bed in it, the walls simply painted in dark green; it was the room usually given to bachelors in a shooting party. Louisa took a chance this would be Roland's and stepped inside. A lamp on the table had been left on, the bedspread was crumpled, as if someone had lain upon it for a nap, and there was a book left open upon it – *The Turn of the Screw*. In the flyleaf, Louisa could see in faint pencil: *R Lucknor*. This was the right room.

His clothes had been neatly folded and his jacket was hanging on the back of the door. Louisa thought she recognised it with its slightly worn look to the cuffs and a button re-stitched with mismatching thread. There was a leather bag on the floor. Louisa kneeled down and put her hand inside, feeling the soft wool of pairs of socks. She didn't know what she was looking for, except that she wanted to find anything that he might have deliberately hidden.

There were footsteps in the hall. She paused and listened, though it was hard to hear over the blood rushing in her ears, but they walked on past. Louisa felt around the edges of the bag and then the loose, silk-covered strip of cardboard that lay on the bottom came away and beneath it ... Yes. There were two slim bank books with hard covers. Inside were the usual notations of money in and money out. It didn't really mean anything to her, but what was puzzling was that one book was in the name of Roland Lucknor and the other was in the name of someone called Alexander Waring. Why would he have someone else's bank book?

In the hall, a door banged shut and Louisa's heart jumped with it. She stashed the books into her pocket and crept out of the room.

Back in the nursery, where Nanny Blor was dozing by the fire, her knitting on her lap, Louisa couldn't believe what she'd done. But it was too late now. All she knew was that she'd do her very best to stop Nancy from getting any further involved with Roland.

CHAPTER FORTY-TWO

I t was 4 p.m. and Louisa was sitting in a booth at the Swan Inn with Ada, the two of them enjoying the rare coincidence of having an afternoon off at the same time. They'd enjoyed wasting an hour at the chemist looking at ribbons and bottles of eau de toilette that they could never afford, then gone for a glass of sherry at the pub. It would be supremely frowned upon by Mrs Windsor, but Louisa had had her arm easily twisted. Time with Ada was always a pleasure; she was never less than a sight that cheered, with her perfect white teeth and freckles on her nose that didn't fade, even in the bleakest midwinter.

'To be honest, I was hoping we might see Jonny in here,' said Ada, when they were halfway through their drinks.

'Jonny? The boy from the blacksmith?'

'He's not a boy, he's a man of twenty-three,' said Ada. 'And he's ever so nice.'

'Just don't let Lady Redesdale catch you,' said Louisa. 'All hell broke out when their last nursery maid ran off with the butcher's boy. I got her job, so I'm not crying into my soup for her, but ... Go on, then.' She nudged Ada with her elbow, feeling jocular. 'What's happened?'

'Nice girls don't tell,' said Ada, but she snickered into her drink.

Louisa was about to drop another tease when something flashed in the corner of her eye. She looked down and saw a black-and-white dog run around the corner of the bar. She shrank back into her seat.

'What is it?' said Ada.

Louisa shook her head. She heard a short, sharp whistle and then she knew. Stephen.

'I've got to go,' she said.

Louisa ran to a side door of the bar, taking the risk that Stephen would be coming in behind Socks. She pushed the door open and kept on running, hardly daring to look behind her. No one shouted after her and she didn't stop until she was out on the road back to Asthall Manor, panting from the heat and the fear.

What was Stephen doing here? It could only mean one thing. He meant to ruin her.

CHAPTER FORTY-THREE

~~~~~

The next morning, having had a night without a wink of sleep, Louisa rose early. There was no sound except for the prattle of birds on the roof. Even the children were still sleeping, their chests rising and falling almost in unison, their breathing steady. She went down to the kitchen, where thankfully Mrs Stobie wasn't yet at work. With a cup of tea at her side, she wrote to Jennie – she needed to know if Stephen had said anything to her mother, though she thought it pretty unlikely, and in any case it would take Jennie a week to reply at least. In the meantime, she had to confront this situation sooner rather than later.

After all this time, why would he come looking for her again? And why would he stay in a pub nearby and not come to find her at Asthall Manor? Most likely he was intimidated by the house and the people he guessed would live there.

This line of questioning had no sooner calmed her than the answers she came up with unnerved her all over again: because he had run out of money or luck, or both; because he had discovered at last where she was and, after looking for so long, he was angry.

When – there was no 'if' – he got desperate, he'd be at the front door and her job would be gone. No one wanted a nursery maid who brought violence to the house, and Stephen meant violence.

Well before that happened, she had to get a grip on it. Ada had had a glimpse of Louisa's distinctly murky past, for Louisa had to explain why she ran out so suddenly, and though she knew Ada was a loyal friend, she also knew gossip was as good as gold for a trade in the village. It wouldn't be long before she would hardly be able to go to the post office without people giving her looks and whispering. Everything she had achieved since she'd got to Asthall – gone, undone in an instant. She wanted to howl with rage and fury.

She couldn't go to the Swan herself to ask if he was staying there. If he saw her, she'd be defenceless. There was nothing else to do but to ask someone to help her. As to who that could be, however, Louisa was completely stuck. She needed brute strength, but there were no male servants in the house and she was on no more than nodding terms with any man in the village.

Believing her uncle to be close by threw Louisa completely off-course and over the next few days Nanny Blor commented several times on Louisa's absence of mind.

'You'd lose your own head if it wasn't screwed on,' she said after Louisa went into the nursery to fetch a pair of socks for Diana and came out with a vest.

Not to mention that Louisa found excuses not to go to the village if an errand were required, though at least she could rely on Ada to cover for her a little. Lady Redesdale, too, showed impatience when Louisa brought the children down for tea but failed to notice that Decca was wiping her hands on the sofa cushions after eating cake.

All the while, no matter what task she had in hand, Louisa worried away at what Stephen was doing, what he was saying to the villagers about her and whether he might suddenly turn up at the door, like one of Nanny's proverbial bad pennies. She didn't want to alarm anyone so kept this to herself, burrowing into the darker recesses of her mind like the moles that were ruining the lawn tennis court.

'Oh my goodness, Elinor Glyn here, lying on a tiger skin. Better not let Muv see this . . . ' Nancy giggled as she idly flicked through the pages of *Vogue* in the nursery before dinner. 'Louisa? Don't you think?'

Louisa still failed to respond.

'Oh, honestly, Lou! What is going on with you?'

Louisa looked stricken. She couldn't live alone with the worry and decided to tell Nancy what had happened.

'Well, he won't come here,' said Nancy. 'He'd be far too frightened of Farve.'

'I think you're probably right,' said Louisa, 'but I've got to do something about it. I've been too afraid to go to the village for days. Nanny Blor already thinks something's up and Lady Redesdale has had a sharp word with me twice in the last week.'

'Yes, you can't have Muv getting too cross. She's liable to sack you on a trifling. When she was my age she ran her father's house and had to stand up to some grumpy footman or other, which is why we've never had a male servant. She won't stand for any—' Nancy saw Louisa's face. 'Oh, don't fret, Lou. You're safe here, I know it. Look, I'm sure there's something we could do. What about Roland? He's coming to luncheon the day after tomorrow. He was in the war; he's probably got a gun.'

'A gun! I don't want anything like that. I just need Stephen scared off,' said Louisa. The almost certain knowledge – for that is what it had become in her mind now – that Roland had something to do with Florence Shore meant he had started to assume almost monstrous proportions. She felt the old, but well-worn feeling of fear clothe her in its black rags.

'I'm not saying he has to use it. I just mean he probably has one. Tom's always going on about the Webley revolvers that officers were issued. He could wave it about a bit or something.'

'But why would he do anything like that for me?' said Louisa. Nancy wasn't helping her feel any calmer.

'I don't know,' said Nancy, exasperated. 'You may as well ask him. If he says no, we'll have to think of something else.' She picked up her magazine again. 'I'm so looking forward to seeing him. Now that I've been on the Continent, I'm sure I impress him as a *femme du monde*, don't you think, Lou? Shall I wear my hair-slide?'

So that was that, then, thought Louisa. Roland Lucknor was her solution. She had to hope he wouldn't be her problem, too.

CHAPTER FORTY-FOUR

Guy and Harry were taking a desultory walk at the tail end of Victoria station, far enough away from the noisy commuters with their incessant, pointless questions – 'Is this platform six?' asked while standing underneath the sign – yet close enough to smell the heavy, black oil that coated the huge wheels of dormant trains, waiting for the whistle that would spring them into life.

They were on their usual daily round, a dull job that was barely relieved by the sight of a tramp trying to catch a kip in an empty carriage. The three of them went into their routine, each accusation met by a polished protestation, and completed in the exact same unheeded way.

'Be off with you,' said Harry, though he found it hard to put a note of spontaneity into it any more, he had repeated the line so many times, 'and don't come back.'

The tramp shook his fist at them and disappeared around the corner, where they knew he'd wait five minutes until he could safely put himself back in the carriage for a couple of hours. Guy failed to resist looking back to see the old man peer around the pillar, his filthy white beard hanging over his donkey jacket, making sure the two policemen walked out of sight.

'I think he just stuck his tongue out at me,' he said to Harry.

Harry laughed. Nothing could put him out of his good mood. Later that evening he'd be on the stage of the Blue Nightingale club, his saxophone firmly gripped, his eyes tight shut, his hips swaying to the intoxicating sounds of ragtime.

'Why don't you come along tonight?' he asked. 'Mae will be there and she's sure to have a pal along . . .'

Guy sighed and looked down at his diminutive friend, but not without a smile. 'Thanks but it's not really for me.' They walked on a few paces more, their eyes adjusting to the fading light and only just spotted a grey mouse darting along the platform ahead of them. 'You see, the thing is, I can't—'

'If you say you can't forget Miss Cannon, I'll lamp you one,' interrupted Harry. 'What are you waiting for, man? She'll be off with someone else if you don't look out, and then what will you do? I can't listen to your pining for the rest of my days.'

Guy went pink. 'I wasn't going to say that,' he fibbed. 'But it *is* hopeless. I can't marry anyone on my wages, and Mother still needs the few bob I give her. I know you're right, but I'm stuck.'

'Do you know if she's got anyone else?' said Harry, a little more sympathetically this time.

'No,' said Guy. 'I mean, I don't think so. I write to her, now and then. When I've got something to say. But there's not been much lately.'

'Does she write you back?'

'Yes, and she's friendly enough. I can't really tell what she means by it, though. I thought she liked me but I'm not so sure now . . .'

Harry stopped and put his hand on Guy's arm. 'Hang on – is that someone calling you down there?'

Guy pushed his hat back and squinted. They had turned about and were walking towards the main concourse, where men and women were swarming beneath the noticeboard, but a young man in the distinctive railway policeman's livery was waving at them as he walked, almost ran, down the long platform.

'Sully!' he called out. 'The super wants to see you.' Guy and Harry broke out into a brisk near-run and caught up with him as he stopped to catch his breath. 'Now. In his office.'

'Thanks,' said Guy. 'I'll see you later,' he said to Harry.

'What's it about?' shouted Harry after him.

'No idea,' Guy called back as he ran off.

At the office, Guy knocked on the door and had almost stepped in before Jarvis had time to tell him to enter. He stood to attention and pushed his glasses back up to the top of his nose.

'Reporting, sir,' he said. 'You wanted to see me?'

The super was sitting at his desk, holding a letter in his hand. He looked at Guy seriously but said nothing. Guy shifted on his feet a little and gave a nervous cough.

Jarvis leaned forwards, both elbows on his blotter pad, and put the letter down before him. He gave a sigh, then said, 'The Met have been in touch. They're on my back, Sullivan. And I wonder if you're to blame.'

'Me, sir?' said Guy, looking confused. 'What for, sir?'

'For carrying out investigations not under orders, Sullivan.'

Guy looked at him blankly. Then he realised. 'The Florence Shore murder, sir?'

'Yes, the Florence Shore murder. Have you been sticking your nose where it isn't wanted, Sullivan?'

'Well, sir, the thing is, in a way. But it was a long time ago.'

Jarvis banged the table and Guy jumped. 'Don't make this any worse than it has to be. I like you, Sullivan. You show promise. But if you lie to me—'

'I'm not, sir,' said Guy. 'I swear I'm not. I went to see Baroness Farina in Tonbridge, sir. In April, I think, last year. But she didn't have much to say and nothing really came of it, sir.'

'Nothing?' This, accompanied by a stern look.

'Well . . . she mentioned . . . she mentioned her son, a Mr Stuart Hobkirk. He's an artist, living in St Ives, and he stood to receive an inheritance on Miss Shore's death, sir, as I'd mentioned to you.' He paused and realised that he had better finish what he'd started. 'Last summer, I saw that Mr Hobkirk had an exhibition in London, so I went to see him there. It was by chance, sir. A lady friend of mine wanted to go and I happened to see him.' Guy wished he could cross his fingers as he said this.

Jarvis said nothing but his lips had gone thinner.

Guy went on. 'He didn't say much, sir. Only that he had been very fond of his cousin. I observed that he had a hobble and used a walking stick, so was unlikely to be the man the train guard observed jumping down from the train at Lewes. His alibi also stood up and I was able to talk to two of the guests there who said they were with him on the day of the attack on Miss Shore.'

There was a deathly pause.

'I see,' said Jarvis. 'So not only did you go to see the Baroness Farina, somehow believing you would find out more from her than the combined efforts of three police forces and two inquests, but after I told you there was nothing to investigate when it came to Stuart Hobkirk, you chose to disregard my orders altogether. I am staggered, Sullivan. What's more, you are still lying to me!' He thumped the desk again, harder this time.

Guy took a deep breath. 'No, sir, I'm not. I saw Mabel Rogers, sir, but not on police business.'

Jarvis looked as if he had a fish bone stuck in this throat. His eyes goggled and he made a rasping sound.

'I wanted to offer my condolences, sir. We didn't discuss the case.'

'Then why has Stuart Hobkirk written to the Met, asking them to cease and desist with their inquiries, as he found the last interview – I quote – "deeply upsetting"?'

'That wasn't me, sir. On my honour.'

'I can't bear to hear any more, Sullivan. Every single thing you say is making this worse. As if the Met wasn't always looking down their noses at us as it is, it looks as if I can't control my own men.'

'I know, sir. I'm sorry, sir.' Guy looked at the floor. He didn't know what to do. He could only tell the truth of it, pathetic though it seemed. Which begged the question: who the hell *had* been to see Stuart Hobkirk?

'I had high hopes for you, Sullivan,' Jarvis said. 'High hopes. But I can't do anything more. Talking to witnesses on this case, in whatever capacity, but especially without my permission, means instant dismissal. Get out of my office and leave your badge at the front desk. You won't be needing it again.'

CHAPTER FORTY-FIVE

O n the second – and last – day of the house party, luncheon
would be served promptly at a quarter to one, and afterwards
Nancy was to invite Mr Lucknor for a walk around the garden,
chaperoned by Louisa. All Louisa had to do was prepare for that
walk and the request they were going to make of him. She was as
jumpy as a grasshopper but she knew it had to be done: she had to
put an end to her fear of Stephen. He was a weak man; a fright, a
threat from a real man would be enough to see him off, she was
sure of that. She just had to trust in Nancy to play her part.

Louisa bent down, kissed Decca on the head and took her hand
to take her up to the nursery for their own luncheon. Funny how
she called it that now without even thinking about it. Her old
friends back home would think her a changed person. She hoped
she was.

At half past two, the sun glaring, Louisa was summoned to the
drawing room by Lady Redesdale, as she hoped she would be.
Louisa and Nancy planned that she would encourage her mother
to send for the children. Approaching the room, she could hear
the murmurs of womanly chatter, which fell silent as she entered.

There were three female houseguests – including the beauty Louisa had startled in her room – each one perched on the very edge of their chairs, tiny coffee cups balanced on saucers they held uncomfortably in the air. Nancy was on the rug, arranging her skirt prettily around her.

'Ah, there you are,' said Lady Redesdale, as if she had been waiting some time for Louisa's arrival, when in fact she had come down the stairs seconds after the bell had rung. 'I'd like you to bring the children in to meet everyone. They've been learning poems. Then when you've done that, fetch Mr Lucknor from Lord Redesdale's study.'

This last instruction was unexpected. Louisa went back up the stairs and hurried with Nanny to get the children presentable, Decca squirming away from the blue flannel dress that Nanny was trying to jam over her head.

Tom was hopping about with excitement at the prospect of meeting an officer. 'Will he have his revolver with him?' he asked Louisa. 'I'd like to see a real soldier's gun. Officers were issued Webley revolvers, so he probably has a Mark Six—'

'Don't talk such nonsense, darling,' she interrupted, having learned some of Nanny's idioms. 'Go and find your jacket, please.'

When all of them were as ready as they could be – Pamela nervous, Tom eager, Diana butter-meltingly beautiful, Unity scowling, Decca excited (Debo too tiny to join them) – they were led downstairs by Nanny and Louisa into the drawing room, where all the women, except Nancy and Lady Redesdale, exclaimed coos of pleasure at their arrival. Nanny stayed with them, while Louisa went to fetch Mr Lucknor from Lord Redesdale's study, on the other side of the house.

As Louisa approached the door, she heard raised voices: the strident tones of Lord Redesdale were booming, while Roland's were quieter but with enough of a timbre to be distinctly heard through a solid oak door. She couldn't make out the words but it seemed that while Lord Redesdale was hitting his stride, there was something defensive in his voice; he was interrupting himself in order to hear Roland, who was speaking much more calmly, although assertively.

Louisa hesitated to interrupt but knew if she didn't, someone else would. Lady Redesdale would be waiting impatiently as the charms of the children started to wear off for the guests. And Louisa still needed to ask Roland for the favour. Nervously, she knocked and, without thinking, turned the handle.

Almost at once, she realised her mistake. As the door opened, she heard Lord Redesdale before she saw his face, contorted by anger: 'For God's sake, I'm not going to give you any more money!' Then he eyeballed Louisa and looked on the point of actually exploding. Roland, whose back was to the door, turned and she could have sworn he looked as if he was about to give her a wink he was so unruffled.

She hesitated for a fraction of a second before she said, 'Excuse me, my lord. Her Ladyship has asked if Mr Lucknor could come to the drawing room to hear the children recite their poems.'

She gave a tiny bob and then shut the door behind her. She went back down the hall, pausing to lean into the shadows and steady her breathing. A few seconds later, she heard the door open and close again, then the footsteps of Roland as he caught up with her.

'Miss Cannon,' he said. 'Can I have a word?'

CHAPTER FORTY-SIX

L ouisa halted and turned to face him. That he wanted to talk to her had thrown her off-guard. And then there was the simple, blinding fact that to be so close to him made her hold her breath. His nearly-black eyes looked down straight into hers and his mouth was set in a straight line. He was near enough that she could feel his warm breath. One hand was on her shoulder, the other loose at his side, his long fingers less than an inch from touching hers.

'I hear you're suffering,' he said. 'Your uncle Stephen.'

The shock of hearing Roland say his name made Louise stumble two steps back, though he had crowded her against the wall. 'How did you know?' she said.

'Nancy whispered something to me before lunch. Don't worry – I want to help you.'

Goddamn Nancy.

'I know men like that,' he continued. 'They're all bark and no bite.'

'I'm not sure that's true in his case,' said Louisa, but she remembered how Roland had seen that man off after the ball in London.

'He might be able to bully and frighten *you*,' he continued, 'but if I talk to him, he'll go, I know it. Give me something I can use against him.'

'What are you going to do?' Louisa was whispering now.

'I'll find him. He's staying nearby, isn't he? I'll let him know that if he comes back, he'll worry for his life.'

'I don't understand – why would you do this for me?'

Roland looked behind him, checking that Lord Redesdale's study door was shut. It was, and his gramophone was playing a soprano by his adored Amelita Galli-Curci at high volume.

'Because I need your help here in the house. There are things you can do for me. Let's just say, we're both in need of a little assistance right now. What do you say?'

What? she thought. What did she say?

She shivered, whether from the cold of the passage or Roland's nearness, Louisa couldn't be sure. There was just one lamp lit on a small console table, throwing them both into shadow.

'It's probably wrong of me to ask you but I think we can help each other,' he continued. 'Tell me something about this Mr Stephen Cannon that I can use.'

'Tell him that you were sent by Mr Liam Mahoney in Hastings,' she said. She had had time to think this through in the last few days and she was glad of it now. 'But I don't understand – will you really do this for me?'

'Yes,' said Roland, bending close to her. 'I'll do it. But I need a little something from you first.'

'What?' she breathed.

'I need you to be my champion in the house. I'm having some ... difficulties with Lord Redesdale. He's a little reluctant to invest further in my golf business. Nothing I can't handle, you understand. But I don't want to be cut off from Miss Mitford.'

'What do you mean?'

Roland's face softened. 'She's a dear thing. And she's nearly eighteen ...'

'You want ... what? Not *marriage*, surely?' said Louisa. This threw a spoke in the wheels.

Roland didn't reply to this but looked away. There was a momentary silence. She had to get him to the drawing room soon, otherwise Lady Redesdale would wonder what had happened and Nancy would start getting agitated. But she had to ask him about Nurse Shore. Only ... she wanted him to get rid of Stephen first.

'Please. You have to trust me. Do you trust me, Louisa?'

'I don't know,' she said quietly.

'Tell me what to do and I'll do it. I'll prove myself to you. Then you can talk to Nancy for me.'

Shakily, Louisa outlined their plan: after coffee, Nancy would suggest a walk around the garden with Roland and Louisa, saying it would be good for him to have some fresh air before his train back to London. That would give him time to go and see Stephen at the Swan Inn. Earlier, Nancy had propped up a bicycle by the door in the garden wall that led straight out on to the road, so he could get out without being seen by anyone at the house. She didn't say the word exactly, but it was understood that should anything happen to Stephen, she and Nancy would be Roland's alibis.

This had all seemed like a good plan earlier, when she and Nancy were cooking it up, but now, confronted with the reality of it, it seemed hopeless at best, reckless and dangerous at worst. The memory of Roland calling out Nurse Shore's name had also returned with heightened clarity; any doubts she had had in the last few months that he had said it disappeared. Not to mention those bank books, stuffed at the back of her wardrobe. Appalled at what she had done, she hadn't looked at them since she'd taken them.

'Fine,' he said. 'Let's go. But remember: I know the power of servants in a house like this. I need you to tell Nancy that I'm the one for her. You will owe me that.'

Louisa said yes. What else could she do?

CHAPTER FORTY-SEVEN

In the bottom garden, Louisa and Nancy sat in the summer house by the bathing pool, surrounded by a copse of trees. Even if Nanny Blor took the other girls out for a walk, they wouldn't be seen. The summer house was wooden and shabby, with no glass in the window frames, letting the wind and the early golden leaves blow right through. Louisa looked up at the dusty eaves, every corner thick with old spiderwebs, the paint peeling like bark on a rotting tree. She shivered and wondered, again, if she had done the right thing.

Roland had left behind his overcoat, a snappy trench, together with a pale blue cashmere scarf and a homburg hat. He had snuck out wearing a tweed cap, which Nancy had snatched out of the boot room, and a dark-green wax jacket. They huddled together on the bench, an old rug on their knees. Louisa hoped they wouldn't have to wait too long. It wasn't yet unbearably cold but the frightened silence made time stop still. They watched a wood beetle cross the floor and almost lost patience with its ambling insouciance – didn't it *want* to get to the other side?

'It'll be tea soon. Let's just go back inside and wait for him there,' said Nancy.

'We can't do that. Please, just a little longer,' said Louisa, with more surety than she felt, alongside frustration that Nancy didn't appear to understand the seriousness of what was happening. How, exactly, would Roland see Stephen off? Would Stephen even take any notice? Fear gripped her. What if her uncle attacked Roland and he came back injured? What if he didn't come back at all?

Nancy stood up and stretched her arms. 'I'm bored.'

Louisa looked about her helplessly. 'We could play a game?'

'What? I spy? No, thank you.' Nancy walked over to Roland's coat and picked it up. 'I like his coat. It's completely wrong for a day in the country, of course, but very stylish in London.' She held it up to her nose. 'It smells of him, sort of woody and nice.'

'Put it down, Nancy,' said Louisa. 'We can play Botticelli.'

Nancy ignored her and instead started to put the coat on, wrapping it tightly around herself and burying her face in the collar. It was far too long for her and the hem was brushing in the twigs and dusty leaves on the floor.

'You'll make it filthy – take it off!' Louisa was panicked, she wasn't sure why, but it felt intrusive to wear his coat.

Nancy peeped over the collar and wiggled her eyebrows playfully. 'Don't be a silly.' She stuck her hands in the pockets and started to pull things out. 'One handkerchief – clean. That's a good sign. No one likes a man with a snotty nose. Two keys on a ring. That suggests a flat – a shared front door and then his door. One key would be a house, which would be preferable, but one can't have everything, can one?' She was smiling, enjoying the naughtiness.

Louisa was not. 'Please, stop it. Supposing he comes back?'

'He won't, and why should he mind, anyway? One wallet – ooh, what's in here? Two pounds and an ID card. Look at this, Lou-Lou! Roland Oliver Lucknor. I didn't know his middle name was Oliver.'

Louisa was afraid of what Nancy might find. She didn't want her to discover that she had done a deal with the devil and she knew that nobody who snooped ever found anything that made them feel better.

'I don't want any part of this, Nancy.'

'Spoilsport.' But she put the card back in the wallet and the wallet back in the pocket. As Nancy took the coat off, her attention was caught by something else. 'What's this? An inside pocket.'

Louisa buried her face in her hands, but she couldn't deny her attention was caught, too.

'A book – *Les Illuminations* by Rimbaud. French poetry,' said Nancy, turning the pages. 'That's rather romantic. There's an inscription in here: "For Xander, *Tu es mon autre*, R."' She paused, thinking. 'Why would you have someone else's book? I suppose he must have borrowed it from someone.'

Louisa was watching her carefully now. 'Nancy, don't. It's not any of your business.'

Nancy shrugged. 'It might be. I'm only looking in a book, I'm not opening any letters.' But she put it back, folded the coat on the bench and sat down next to Louisa to wait a little longer.

It was still light when Roland returned and the temperature had dropped noticeably, but when he took off the wax jacket, Louisa caught a glimpse of dark patches of sweat on his shirt. He had entered the summer house quietly; they'd not noticed him until he was standing there before them, his face set in stone.

'It's done,' he said grimly. 'He won't be bothering you again.'

'Did you—' Louisa started to say but Roland cut her off.

'I'm not discussing it. I just came to let you know. Will you please send my apologies to Lady Redesdale? Tell her I had to leave to catch my train. Perhaps you might be so good as to ask the driver if he could take me to the station now?'

'Yes,' said Louisa, hardly able to speak. She still felt worried, despite Roland's assurance that Stephen would be leaving her alone from now on. She knew Stephen, she knew what it would take to make him go away, and she couldn't bring herself to admit that Roland might have been capable of it. She thought she could see tiny flecks of blood on his shirt collar and shut her eyes, like a child. If you can't see it, it's not there.

He turned to Nancy. 'I'll write to you soon. Think well of me, won't you?'

Nancy nodded, stupefied by the intensity of the atmosphere.

In less than quarter of an hour, Roland was in the car, out of the gate and on to the road. Louisa, back in the house, watched with Nancy from her bedroom window, their arms linked, their faces pale. They had brought something about, Louisa thought, and they didn't yet know what. She hoped they never truly would.

My dearest love,

One night we were warned in advance that the shelling would be very bad – usually it is hard to know what is going on unless one runs outside and grabs someone to ask – so we were all moved into the cellars of a building close by. It was a hideous, exhausting operation, carried out by the nurses and one or two soldiers who are not so badly wounded and can walk. There were just two candles, so we sat in the near-dark, listening to the shells – four a minute – waiting to see if one had landed on us, hearing it crash elsewhere and then waiting for the next.

Roland Lucknor, who has always been resilient and charming, despite the constant pain he is in from an early gas attack, became hysterical in the middle of it. He started laughing absurdly, then this turned into a kind of screaming sob, which he would not quieten. I tried being alternately sympathetic and firm, but nothing worked. Eventually his batman came over, a sweet fellow called Xander, and started singing French love songs in his ear – at least, that's what they sounded like to me – which calmed him down. The two of them knew each other before the war, in Paris, I gather, in rather a louche atmosphere of writers and artists.

Roland, by now in a sort of hallucinatory hysteria, started calling for his mother and curled right into Xander's chest, who held him tightly in his arms. As it was so dark, no one else could see, and I know others would be affronted by this but, poor fellows, who is anyone to judge if the only comfort they are to get is from each other? If they believe those arms belong to their mothers, I, for one, am not going to deny them.

Rather sadly, the next day when we were back above ground again, Roland and Xander had a terrible row, shouting at each other in the ward. I hurried over to them, to try and calm them down, but seemed to make it worse. I don't know what it was about; perhaps Roland had realised what had happened and was humiliated.

It's been so many months now, I hardly dare hope that you are still waiting for me, but a little hope is what pulls us through, so I cling on to it nonetheless. Think kindly of your poor, pathetic friend, please.

Most tender love,
Flo

CHAPTER FORTY-EIGHT

❧

Guy walked along the side of the road towards what he hoped was Asthall Manor. He'd been walking for two hours from the station and he could feel the sharp air with each intake of breath. Gusts of wind blew meagre heaps of yellowing leaves ahead of him, as if someone had torn the pages out of an old book in a temper.

Dismissed from work, he had got through the first week by doing odd jobs around the house for his mother and the weekend passed as usual, but when the second Monday came around, he didn't think he could stomach another whole week at home. His brothers wouldn't let up their teasing for a second, and the pitying looks of his parents were almost worse.

Thankfully, each week he paid his mother money towards the housekeeping and saved the rest in the bank, bar a pound or two to see him through for the odd beer. All the change went in a jar and there was enough in there for a third-class return train ticket to Shipton, as well as a night or two at a local inn. Once he'd realised this, he'd left the house before he could change his mind.

Now, having walked on the road with nothing but his own thoughts for company, he worried whether his hasty plan had been such a good one. He didn't even know for sure that Louisa would be there – they might have gone to London, or Paris, or wherever toffs might go, and she would have had to go with them.

Nor was he absolutely certain that she would be pleased to see him. Her last letter had been, as usual, friendly but distant. Guy was definite about how he felt – he wanted to take her in his arms, pull her into his chest and protect her from any storm. But whether she would so much as want to share an umbrella in the rain ... well, he would try to find out now.

As he came up to the gate, hope rose in his heart as he saw smoke curling from the chimneys. They must be at home. He had a note in his pocket to leave for her if she was out or busy. On the driveway, Guy saw the handsome oak tree and decided against knocking on the front door but looked instead to see if there was any kind of back entrance where he might find a servant to pass along the note.

A stone wall, high and handsome, lined the limits of the house's grounds and Guy noticed a door in the wall, in a bend close to the building, the wood painted the same colour as the stone – an unobtrusive place one might exit the garden and into the road, he thought. He'd leave that way too; he hadn't enjoyed walking into the drive, a place more suited and used to the sweeping entrance of a smart motorcar, he was sure. His dusty shoes and thin brown suit were shabby, and as he was wondering again if this was a bad idea and he should turn around, he saw a young girl in a dress and apron, a cap on her head. She was carrying an empty laundry basket in one hand and raised the other in greeting.

'Hello,' she called. 'Can I help you?'

Her smile was friendly and Guy felt encouraged. He quick-stepped towards her, definitely at the back of the house now, with herbs growing in huge pots grouped together, the scented leaves tumbling up and over the earthenware. He caught rosemary and it stuck in his throat, sending up a sudden memory of his mother as she served up roast lamb one Easter, a rare treat before the war, when all her sons were alive and around one table.

'Hello,' he said as he got nearer, not wishing to shout out. 'I was wondering if I might leave a note for Miss Louisa Cannon?'

Ada – for Ada it was, as he would later discover – gave a broad grin. '*Miss* Louisa, eh?'

Guy stood stock-still, his bag dropped at his feet, the note in both hands. He looked at her stupidly. 'Er, yes. Is she here? May I give you the note?'

'You may as well see her yourself,' said Ada, enjoying his discomfort. 'Come along – you look in need of a cup of tea. Mrs Stobie'll fetch you one up in the kitchen.'

When Louisa was summoned into the kitchen from the linen cupboard – where she'd been folding and re-folding the children's bedsheets and blankets, a task she'd taken to repeating daily, just to get some time to herself, away from Nanny Blor's good-hearted but increasingly frustrated enquiries as to whether she was 'quite herself' – she found, sitting at the scrubbed pine table, Guy Sullivan. This was not what she had expected, and Ada, mischievously, had not given her fair warning. She took a sharp breath as he stood and found herself rooted to the spot, not knowing what to do or say. Mrs Stobie pretended to busy herself at the stove, brushing the pastry top of a pie with beaten egg. Ada looked on, unabashed. She gave Louisa a small shove in the back.

'Say hello to the poor chap. Look at 'im – he's been walking for days to see you.'

'Not quite days, Miss Cannon,' said Guy, who sensed he needed to take charge of the situation. 'I just got the train up. It's a nice day for a walk. Anyway,' he continued, as Louisa looked at him – was that pleasure in her face? Or anger? – 'I didn't mean to disturb; I just wanted to leave you a note. Let you know I was staying nearby.'

Louisa recovered herself. 'Hello, Mr Sullivan,' she said. 'It's very nice to see you. Forgive me, I ... well, I wasn't expecting it.' She turned to Ada and gave her a meaningful look. 'Thank you, Ada. Hadn't you better be getting on?'

Ada chuckled, tipped her friend a wink and went out of the kitchen. Mrs Stobie turned away from the stove and, wiping her hands on her apron, said she'd better be off, too. She had the week's menu to plan before she met Lady Redesdale next morning. Mrs Windsor, she added, was on an errand in Burford and wasn't expected back until teatime. In other words, the coast was clear.

Louisa fetched herself a cup and sat down at the table, opposite Guy. The mild shock of his arrival had brought colour to her cheeks, and her hair, though neatly pinned up in a style that closely resembled a daring bob, had a few flyaway strands that softened the edges. Just looking at her made Guy's fingers tap nervously and he hid his hands on his lap, beneath the table. His cap was laid beside the teapot and jug of milk that Mrs Stobie had put out.

Louisa poured herself a cup of tea without saying a word until she had had her first sip, making him feel even more nervous. Her voice was softer than when the others had been around; it gave him hope if she had a tone just for him.

'Why are you here?' she asked. Had Stephen been reported missing?

'I wanted to see you,' he said.

Balm was poured on her troubled waters. 'That's very nice,' she said. 'But it's not the whole story, is it?'

'I've been sacked from the force. I didn't really know what else to do. I just knew that I wanted to see you.'

'Sacked! Why?'

'For conducting inquiries into the murder of Miss Florence Shore off my own bat.'

'What inquiries?' said Louisa. 'The visit you made to Stuart Hobkirk?'

'Not exactly. That is, someone has been to see him since we did. I don't know who it was, though I'd like to find out. I admitted to seeing Mabel Rogers, too, so I didn't help myself. I shouldn't have mentioned it. I hadn't even discussed the case with her, though I did ask her about Roland Lucknor.'

'Did you say that to them?' Louisa went white. Those bank books ... She should give them to Guy but the last thing she needed was the police investigating Roland more closely. Supposing they found out about Stephen, and her part in it?

'No,' said Guy, 'I said I'd gone to see her out of sympathy, not as a policeman, which was sort of true. At any rate, she didn't even respond to his name when I said it. It's all over for me, Louisa. What shall I do?'

Louisa looked at her untouched tea, grey and cold. She could hear the faint chimes of the grandfather clock in the hall striking three. 'I don't know,' she whispered. 'Look, you'd better go now.'

'Is there an inn nearby? Somewhere I can stay for the night?'

Louisa knew there was only one and if he asked anyone else, that's where he would be sent: the Swan Inn. But Stephen had stayed there until his sudden disappearance and the place was still full of the story. Every other man in the village, it seemed, had money owed them by him and they were all in the bar escaping the wrath of their wives. A stranger was sure to get his ear bent by

282

those keen to share their woes. And thanks to Ada's man, Jonny, quite a few of them knew she was Stephen's niece. Louisa had been staying inside the house as much as possible lately; when she went to the village a couple of days ago she had been accosted by one angry man wanting to know where Stephen was. She didn't want Guy to know about her past. If she was to have a future, then all her yesterdays had to stay there.

'No,' she said, 'if you stay nearby, there'll be gossip about us. You've been here now and you'll get spotted in the village. You don't know what it's like in the country. Everyone knows everyone's business.' This wasn't quite as true as Londoners liked to believe but it would serve her purpose for now.

'Must I go back tonight?' said Guy, thinking of the long walk back the station.

'Yes,' said Louisa, her heart still beating fast.

'I suppose you're right.' Guy leaned towards her. 'The truth is, Louisa . . . ' He paused, daring himself to go on. 'The truth is, I'll do anything you say, you know. Anything.'

Louisa smiled at him but said nothing. She liked Guy but it couldn't happen. She stood up. 'I'm sorry I can't see you out but I'd better get back up to the nursery; they'll be wondering where I am. I'll write to you as soon as I can.'

Guy stood and before she could do anything, he had moved around to her side of the table. She leaned slightly back and he put a hand up, a signal to let her know not to be alarmed.

'It's all right,' he said. 'I just wanted to say goodbye. Will you at least shake my hand?'

She laughed a little at this – his manner was so unassuming, she knew she could never be afraid of him. 'Of course,' she said. 'Goodbye, Guy.' They shook hands, a little self-consciously. 'I'll write.'

When Mrs Stobie came back into the kitchen a minute or two later, all she could see were the cups and teapot placed neatly by the sink and empty chairs at the table, a feeling of absence in the room.

CHAPTER FORTY-NINE

⁓

In November, it would be Nancy's eighteenth birthday and her mother had promised her a ball in the library. Louisa knew that Nancy felt adult life approaching at last and was impatient for it to start. In the meantime, there was much to be done for the planning: the list of guests, the dresses, the flowers . . . In just a few steps in a single night, Nancy would walk from the schoolroom to the ballroom and her childhood would be over. It was not so much a party, Nancy had said, as it was an initiation rite. If she could have added African drums and smoke signals, she'd have done it. A quartet and a log fire would have to do.

All of this was exciting, and Louisa was happy for her, but for one thing: Nancy had told Louisa that she intended to ask Roland to the dance, and she was sure her mother would approve.

After a sleepless night, Louisa told Nanny Blor that she needed to speak to Lady Redesdale about something, and asked permission to go down and see her after breakfast.

'Of course, ducks,' said Nanny Blor, 'but it sounds a bit serious. Is it something I should be worrying about?'

Louisa shook her head and said no, she didn't think so, it was just something she needed to run by Her Ladyship; it wouldn't take long.

At 9 a.m., in her best plain frock and having given her shoes an extra polish, her hair as neatly in place as she could manage, Louisa went down the stairs to the morning room, the place Lady Redesdale went to after breakfast to write her letters. An early autumn sunshine lit the pale furniture beautifully, and Lady Redesdale's head was already bent to her daily task at her bureau, her pen flying rapidly across the thick cream paper, the Mitford crest embossed at the top.

When so little seemed to happen at Asthall Manor, nobody could quite guess at what Lady Redesdale's endless letters contained. She was not a particularly keen gardener so it seemed unlikely she was swapping helpful tips on how to prune petunias with one of her sisters-in-law. The children were never any real cause for concern and her husband stuck rigidly to a routine that prompted little news, unless she was to disclose his tallies at shoots. Nancy speculated that her mother was lost in a fantasy, which was relayed to distant friends and relatives, writing about make-believe balls and parties attended by the Prince of Wales, with her daughters courted by European princes. This seemed to her the only possibility when 'our lives here are so dull there is nothing to say about any of it'.

Louisa thought Lady Redesdale was more caught up in her children, in fact, than any of them recognised. There were many and frequent diktats on their reading, the food in the nursery, the number of inches each window should be opened by to allow for continuous fresh air in all weathers, and so on. Not to mention that she taught all of them their lessons in their early years. Louisa suspected that Lady Redesdale was not so much uninterested as easily distracted from engaging with her children.

Standing just inside the doorway, Louisa coughed and Lady Redesdale looked up. If she was bemused to see the nursery maid in the morning room without the children, she didn't show it.

'Yes, Louisa?' she said, as usual still holding her pen, ready to resume her writing in a moment.

'I'm sorry to bother you, my lady,' said Louisa timidly. 'It's just that . . .'

'Come a little nearer, I can hardly hear you.'

'Sorry.' Louisa stepped forwards but kept her distance, as if she was by the lion's cage at the zoo. 'I just needed to talk to you about something.'

'Yes?' Lady Redesdale looked impatient but she put her pen down and her hands in her lap. 'What is it?'

She was about to break her promise to Roland but she was afraid of him now. If he was banished from Asthall, she'd be safe. 'Forgive me, my lady. I know what I'm about to say will seem rather insolent, so please believe me that I say it only because I have yours and Lord Redesdale's best interests at heart.'

'Goodness. How intriguing. Do go on.'

'It's about Mr Lucknor. I know Miss Nancy wants to invite him to her dance but I think it's very important that she doesn't. In fact, I don't think he should come here again at all.'

'That's quite something for *you* to say. Why ever not?'

'I believe that His Lordship may be giving him money for reasons that are . . . not quite right.'

'I don't quite think I can be hearing this correctly. Are you presuming to tell me that the business my husband is conducting is something you don't agree with?' Fury had passed its palm over Lady Redesdale's face.

Louisa stammered but she knew she had to press on. 'I'm sorry, my lady. I know it's not for me to say—'

'You're certainly right about that!'

'But I don't think Mr Lucknor is quite what he seems. I think if he comes back here, he could be a danger to you.'

'Is this something we should tell the police about?'

'No, my lady.'

'Because it's not serious enough or because you don't actually have any real reason for these things you are saying?'

Louisa hesitated. None of this was coming out right but how to explain it without telling her about Stephen and the blood on his collar? Or that she had gone into his room in the night and heard him call out a murdered nurse's name, one he'd denied knowing? That she couldn't believe that any business proposition he put to Lord Redesdale could be honest, when he had a bank book belonging to somebody else?

Lady Redesdale knew exactly how to read Louisa's silence. 'I cannot have a nursery maid interfering in my husband's business. I'm sure you understand.' Lady Redesdale spoke calmly. 'You are dismissed from your position as of today. I will give you a reference and the rest of the month's wages, but that is all. Hooper can take you to the station this afternoon.'

'I'm to be dismissed, my lady?' said Louisa, floored by this reaction.

'Yes.' She exhaled impatiently. 'It's very disappointing but when servants interfere in the matters of their masters, they reveal their ambitions to be above their station and that's no good for anyone. Please go now.' She bent her head again and picked up her pen. There were to be no last words, no chance of a reprieve.

Louisa said no more and walked out of the room.

CHAPTER FIFTY

U pstairs in the nursery, news of Louisa's imminent departure caused a great hue and cry. Nanny Blor sat in her armchair like a bag of flour, watching Louisa as she gathered together the few mementoes she had acquired in her time there, not quite two years yet. There were shells from St Leonards-on-Sea and a stick of rock that she had bought, intending to give her mother, but it had seemed too silly when they'd got back so she'd held on to it. Two or three more tiny shells from the beach at Dieppe, and a metre or so of mint-green velvet ribbon that Nancy had bought her in London.

Out of her wages Louisa had bought two cotton dresses, a jacket and a new pair of boots, but she still had her old green felt coat and brown cloche hat. There was little else besides, and it was the sight of her whole life being packed into a cloth bag that made her want to cry more than anything. She had convinced herself that she was building a new life here but it had turned out to be as collapsible as a soufflé.

Pamela and Diana were weeping quietly but Louisa guessed this was more in despair at the tension than at her departure. They were used to changes of servants and governesses, and had long learned not to become too attached, apart from Nanny Blor, of course, but she was different, she was practically family. Tom was at school and the babies, Decca and Debo, were too young to understand what was going on. Unity scowled alone in a corner of the nursery, though whether at Louisa's going or because today was a day for scowling, one couldn't be sure.

Nancy, however, was stalking around the nursery in a rage, tears streaming down her face. Nobody seemed able to give her a satisfactory answer as to why Louisa was going and she didn't believe her nursery maid and her friend – yes, her *friend*, her only friend in the house – when she tried to protest that she wanted to go. Why was it happening so suddenly? Her mother, of course, was completely impassive in the face of Nancy's pleading, telling her to go upstairs and wash her face. Farve was oblivious to all the drama, out all hours now it was the shooting season. Her parents were so thoughtless, she continued, it was weeks until her eighteenth birthday ball and who could take her to London now to find a dress? (Not, thought Louisa, that her mother had promised her a London dressmaker.)

In any case, Nancy's anger was so big, filling every room, that it left no space for explanations; she wasn't capable of hearing anything even if anyone tried to speak. Louisa kept herself calm, hugging all the children goodbye and telling Nancy brightly that they could still write to each other.

'But what will your address be?' said Nancy, following Louisa into her room.

'I will go home,' said Louisa. 'It'll be easy enough to write to me there.'

'Yes, but what about your uncle?' Nancy hissed dramatically. Louisa had not mentioned the spots of blood.

'It's all right, I don't think he'll be bothering me again,' said Louisa, affecting indifference.

'But he must have gone back to London after Roland went to see him,' said Nancy, not letting it drop.

'Shhh,' said Louisa. 'Please don't worry about me. I'll be fine, I always am. And so will you.'

With that, Nancy saw there was no more to be said.

Ada, upset, was in the nursery too, summoned to replace Louisa immediately. She gave Louisa a book, a new Agatha Christie, with a flower from the garden hastily pressed inside it.

'It's all I had to hand,' Ada said, swallowing a sob. 'I'm so sorry you're going. Who shall I have to gossip with now? I'm surrounded by old ladies.'

Louisa smiled. 'Thank you,' she said. 'I have nothing to give you but I will write. Thank you for the book; I know I'll enjoy it.'

At last, everything packed, there was nothing else to do but walk around to the stables to find Hooper and ask him to take her to the station. He grunted in his usual way and showed no alarm at the request; the toings and froings were none of his business so far as he was concerned. Louisa had pleaded with Nanny Blor and the children to stay in the nursery when she left. She didn't want to cause a scene, certainly not one that Lady Redesdale could view from her window.

So she left with no fanfare, not even a wave, sitting alongside Hooper and keeping her back to the yellow-grey stone and gabled roof of Asthall Manor.

PART THREE

1921

CHAPTER FIFTY-ONE

O n the journey to London, Louisa realised that she couldn't
go home. She felt like an outcast. Even if she could return
to Peabody Estate, she would be reminded all too often with jibes
and pointed comments that she had failed at her work in a posh
house. She'd be accused of hoity-toity airs if she mistakenly used
a Mitford-ism instead of the common-or-garden words she'd been
brought up with. All of that, perhaps, she could stand, but there
would be no one who would understand what she had had to leave
behind or why. She missed her ma and wanted her reassurance
more than ever, but if she asked any questions about Stephen, what
could she say?

Roland Lucknor. If she could nail him to the Shore murder,
she'd be absolved and she'd get her job back, as well as clear her
conscience over Stephen. It was the only answer.

The police seemed to have closed the file on Florence Shore's
murder. *Could* she solve this? She had a way in, if she could find
out more about Roland. She needed to do something; everything
else was failing at her touch, it seemed.

Louisa had taken down Roland's address before she left and had it written down on a slip of paper in her pocket. It had been easy to find, as Nancy had a dozen unfinished letters to him stuffed underneath her mattress. At the time, she hadn't been quite sure what she was writing it down for, but now she knew. She would go there and see him for herself. Perhaps she could talk to him, persuade him that he must leave Nancy alone. She felt afraid but her worry for Nancy was greater. There was no time like the present and she had nothing else to do, so she went straight to the address in Baron's Court from Paddington station.

The mansion block that Louisa found herself standing in front of only a short while later was built in handsome red brick. It looked like a comfortable, affluent sort of place, able to ignore the seedier elements of London more or less around the corner. There was a wide front door for Roland's block, which was open, and Louisa could see a porter inside, wearing a cap that was probably intended to pass as a sort of livery but looked rather too scruffy for that. He was sweeping the hall with a broom that was almost the same height as him. Louisa hesitated at the threshold.

'What can I do for you, miss?' said the porter with a friendly smile.

Louisa saw that she'd got so far, she'd better get to the end of it now.

'I'm looking for a Mr Roland Lucknor, flat nine, I think.'

'You won't find him there today, miss,' said the porter, leaning against the broom. 'Nor any day; he hasn't been here for months.'

'Oh,' said Louisa. 'But what about his post? I know he's been receiving letters.'

'Nothing's come here, miss.'

Yet Nancy had written to him here. Perhaps he had arranged to have his letters sent on. He could easily have asked the local postmistress for the favour.

'When was the last time you saw him here?' said Louisa.

'I don't know, a while ago. A lady turned up in a fur coat to see him and there was a row. Terrific shouting, it was. After that, we never saw him again.'

'What did the lady look like?' said Louisa. A fur coat? Was that Florence Shore? She'd been wearing one on that fatal train journey.

But this question seemed to make the porter realise he'd overstepped the mark, sharing information about one of the tenants with a complete stranger.

'I couldn't presume as to tell you that, miss.'

'Sorry,' said Louisa, 'I didn't mean to pry. It's just that he's a friend of mine and I'm trying to find him.'

The porter looked sympathetic. 'Course you are. I just have to be careful. Discretion, that's the name of my game. People think being a porter's an easy job but you see things and you have to keep them to yourself.'

'Yes, I do see,' said Louisa. 'I don't want to get you into trouble.'

'If he comes back, would you like me to give him a message?'

'Oh, no. No, thank you,' she said and left, as if Roland might suddenly appear out of the shadows.

Back out on the street, Louisa realised where she could go. She was feeling tired and hungry now, having left before lunch, but she felt better for knowing what she was going to do next. She would take a train to St Leonards-on-Sea. With luck, Rosa might give her some work as a waitress in her café, at least until she had a plan for what to do next. But first, she needed to post a short note to Guy.

The sight of the steamed-up windows of Rosa's café on Bohemia Road quelled Louisa's panic and when she was only a few steps across the threshold, she found herself enveloped in the comforting bosom of its proprietor, her floury apron leaving marks on Louisa's coat.

'Oh, I'm so sorry,' flustered Rosa, brushing Louisa down. 'Come along now, take a pew. You look like you need a good cup of tea and I've got a batch of scones just out of the oven. Millie!'

Rosa beckoned to a waitress, dishwater blond hair falling out from under her sagging cap – she looked like she could do with the sustenance more, thought Louisa – but she sank gratefully on to a chair, kicking her cloth bag under the table.

Once she'd drunk three cups of tea and eaten as many scones as she could, piled high with thick clotted cream and raspberry jam with seeds that lodged themselves in between all her teeth, things felt not quite so bad as they had done before. Thanks to Lady Redesdale's promise to pay out the rest of the month, she even had a bit of money in her pocket.

Rosa had had to leave her while she dealt with some customers, but there was a lull and she now came to sit by Louisa. 'So, my love, what is this all about? I'm very happy to see you, you know that. But I can't help thinking it's not a holiday,' she said sympathetically.

If she closed her eyes, the voice and the warmth that resonated from Rosa could have been Nanny Blor. Louisa felt a wave of homesickness, and not for her mother.

'No,' said Louisa, 'it's not a holiday. It's just that I had to leave and I didn't really know where else to go. May I stay a few nights? I can pay for my board, and if you have any work for me to do in the café, I'd like to do it. Please.'

Rosa folded her arms and shifted her bosom slightly as she looked at Louisa and then at the café behind her, where she could see Millie struggling to stack cups and plates, teaspoons falling on the floor like pick-up sticks. 'Yes,' she said, 'I can give you some work to get you on your feet and of course you can stay here. It worries me, though. I'm going to have to tell Laura that you're here.'

'That's all right,' said Louisa. 'I'm not asking you to keep any secrets from your sister. And Nanny Blor – I mean, Laura – doesn't have to keep it secret from Lady Redesdale, though I don't expect she'll ask anything.'

'Are you in trouble? You know you can tell me,' said Rosa in a clandestine whisper, which might have made Louisa laugh at any other time. 'I'm a woman of the world, even though I might be down here, by the sea in a teashop. I've seen some troubles and I know when someone is afraid.'

'It's fine, honestly. There was someone but he's gone now, I think. He won't bother me here. I only need a bit of time to work out what happens next. I said something to Lady Redesdale that I shouldn't have, that was all. She didn't like it and I had to go.'

'Ah, well,' said Rosa, 'and they can sack you just like that, can't they? It's a terrible thing. I hope that Lloyd George sees that lot off, I really do.'

Louisa smiled. She was grateful, but she was also tired. She asked if she might go up to the flat and see herself to bed. She needed, more than anything, a night of dreamless sleep.

CHAPTER FIFTY-TWO

G uy sat in a greasy spoon, contemplating a late breakfast of congealing bacon and eggs with thick slices of fried bread and black pudding. Louisa's note lay open before him, explaining that she had tried to find Roland but he wasn't there and hadn't been seen since an argument with 'a lady in a fur coat. Could it have been Florence Shore?'

What he needed was to find Roland, but if he wasn't at the address Louisa had found for him, there was no clue as to where he could be. In any case, if he apprehended Roland, what could he say? That he'd once had an argument with a lady in a fur coat and it sounded suspicious? That he'd muttered 'Nurse Shore' when he was asleep? It was ridiculous and yet there was something sinister about Roland that Guy could not shake off. What he needed was a better picture of the man.

Leaving his food uneaten, Guy paid the bill and headed out into the damp London day. He would start with Roland's army colleagues and try to build up a picture of him from there.

From the Army List at Hammersmith library, it was fast work for Guy to look up the names of those serving in the same battalion as

Lord Redesdale and Roland Lucknor. He took down the names of the four officers and eight sergeants. He had to hope at least one of their fellow soldiers had survived to be able to tell him something of Roland. In the phone book, he found three matching names in London. Guy looked at his watch: midday. There was no time like the present; he might as well set off now.

Two of the addresses were in Fulham, fairly close to each other. The first yielded no answer to his knock at the door but the second, Mr Timothy Malone of 98c Lilyville Road, was answered by a man with a face that looked not much more than thirty but his hair was as white as clouds. He opened the door and with a lop-sided smile turned an empty pocket inside out.

'If you've come collecting money,' he said, 'I have nothing, as you can see.'

'No,' said Guy, rather taken aback, 'I haven't come about money. I've come—' At this, he stopped. What reason could he give for asking questions about Roland Lucknor? He wasn't on official police business and he wasn't wearing a uniform. He was going to have to lie. 'I'm a private detective trying to find out information about a man called Roland Lucknor. I believe you served in the same battalion as him during the war.'

Timothy's smile widened. 'Why, yes, old chap. I did. Come in, come in. I'll put the kettle on.' Before Guy could reply, Timothy had started walking into the hallway, then turned off into a room. When Guy followed behind, he saw the unmistakeable signs of a bachelor's lonely existence. The wallpaper was curling at the edges, damp having turned it dark brown at the top corners, and the windows let in little light thanks to the grey smut on the outside. There was an unmade single bed in the corner, which Timothy was discreetly trying to straighten out as he asked Guy whether he'd like sugar with his tea. Guy sat down at one of two chairs in front of the window by a scruffy table with a newspaper, reading glasses and, touchingly, an old jam jar with three Michaelmas daisies in it.

'Excuse the mess,' said Timothy. 'I'm still not quite used to doing it all for myself, and with no work, I can't pay for a daily, you see ...' He gestured to his left arm, which ended before the elbow. 'No one wants to employ a crippled soldier.' He tried to do a little laugh, as if he had made a joke, but the sound trailed away to nothing. Timothy clicked his fingers as if summoning an invisible waiter. 'Tea! One moment, coming right up.'

There was some clattering in the corner and Guy could see an old rag being used to clean out two cups and a saucer. Timothy brought it all over and sat down.

'Private detective, you say? That must be interesting work.'

'Er, yes.' Guy coughed. 'So, you knew Roland Lucknor, then?'

'Yes, I did,' said Timothy, 'but who wants to know?'

Guy tried to keep his breathing steady. 'His family,' he said. 'They don't know where he is and they're trying to find him.'

Timothy sat back in his chair and crossed his long legs. Despite his surroundings and the frayed edges of his collar, he exuded an elegance that some men couldn't achieve with an entire wardrobe of Savile Row tailoring.

'Well, it's no wonder they can't find him. From what I remember of his sorry tale, it had been some time since he had had anything to do with them.'

Guy leaned forwards. 'What is it that you remember?'

Timothy had not had company for some time; he was eager to talk and by the time he had finished, he had replenished Guy's cup three times. Roland had been a voluntary officer when Timothy was a CO and for quite some time they had been stationed together not long after war had broken out, when the battalion was at Arras.

Conditions had been ghastly. They soon learned that was the norm, but at the start it had been a shock, and despite Roland's gung-ho attitude, Timothy noticed that it wasn't long before he started to show the strain. One night, he sat up with Roland and his batman – 'Can't remember his name but he was another handsome fellow' – and they had got drunk on a bottle of whisky that the batman had managed to smuggle from somewhere. 'You soon learned not to ask too many questions but just enjoy the stuff if you could get it,' said Timothy.

With the sound of shelling rumbling throughout, Roland had told his story: his mother dead before he was nine, when he hadn't seen her for five years; his father remaining in Africa as a missionary but for one stilted meeting shortly before Roland left school. With no family except for a godmother, he had run away to Paris as soon as he left school, which was where he had met the batman. 'Waring! That was it,' Timothy slapped his leg. 'Thought the old mind was starting to go, there. Those two had some adventures, by the sound of it, all those bohemian types, you know. Lots of parties and women. Sort of thing old Eddie was a bit partial to.'

'Eddie?' asked Guy, bewildered.

'King Edward. He used to love all that stuff.'

'Ah, yes,' said Guy, nodding as sagely as he could. Calling kings by casual names was not really the sort of thing he did.

'Anyway, seems that for all the fun they were having out there, they were dirt poor. They were trying to make a living as writers, I think, but obviously not getting anywhere with it. When war broke out, they saw their chance for a bit of regular food and a roof over their heads. Poor chaps.' He shook his head. 'We were all fools. We all thought we'd be doing our bit for King and country. We weren't to know.' In a moment of melancholy, he gestured to his pathetic room. '*This* is what we were fighting for.'

Guy did his best to give him a sympathetic look. These were the worst moments for him, when he might be forced to admit that he was not one of the band of courageous men who fought for King and country, nor even for a down-at-heel bedsit.

Timothy shook his head. 'I was telling you about Roland, wasn't I? Well, perhaps he did know. He was a man ruined by the war. Screaming in his sleep at night, sometimes crying openly in the day. The gas attack was the worst thing that could have happened to him; he should have been finished off by a bullet. I'm sorry, I know that's a terrible thing to say, but for some of those men, living with the memory of the war was worse than dying. Waring seemed to cope with it rather better but perhaps he was just better at hiding it. I must say I was surprised when I heard it was Waring who killed himself.'

'Sorry, what was that?' asked Guy.

'Oh, didn't you know? Waring was found in some sort of out-house, having shot himself through the head. They had both just been signed off by the doctors. Roland was to be sent back to England on leave, Waring was to go back to the front line. So I never saw either of them again.'

'I see,' said Guy, though he wasn't sure he did quite. 'And why were you surprised to hear that it was Waring?'

'I don't know. No one can know what must be going through the mind of someone driven to do that, but somehow I would have expected it of Roland more than of Waring. Everyone knew that Roland's being sent home meant the doctors thought he had shellshock but they didn't like to call it that. Waring had been signed to go back into battle. Perhaps he just couldn't face it.'

'And you never heard from Roland again?'

'No,' said Timothy. 'Not that that was unusual. I lost touch with quite a few of the men. Most wanted to forget about those days.

There have been one or two reunion events, but if someone doesn't show up, you just assume they want no part of it any more.'

'You mentioned a godmother he liked,' said Guy. 'Did he say anything else about her?'

'Nothing, old boy. Except that her mind had gone, so he hadn't even her any more, really.'

There was a pause. 'Did you know the nurse Florence Shore?' asked Guy.

'Wasn't she the one who was killed on the train?'

Guy nodded.

'Yes, I've heard some of the men talk about her. I know she was stationed out in Ypres when we were there. She nursed one or two of my compatriots. But I never met her myself,' said Timothy.

'Do you know if she knew Roland?' Guy pressed.

'No, I don't.' Timothy looked askance. 'Are you implying you think Roland did it?'

'I don't know, sir,' said Guy. He decided to risk a final question. 'Do you think Roland is capable of killing someone? In cold blood, I mean.'

'Good God, man! What sort of a question is that? What do his family think of him?'

'Sorry, sir,' stammered Guy. 'It was something I needed to ask but you needn't answer.'

'We fought a war,' said Timothy sombrely. 'We were all killers.'

Guy looked at the floor, feeling ashamed of himself. 'Yes, of course,' he said. 'Thank you for talking to me. It's most appreciated.'

Timothy turned away from him, his hand slack in his lap, his eyes staring out to the middle distance at something Guy hoped he'd never see.

CHAPTER FIFTY-THREE

G uy and Harry met on the corner of Bridge Place and Wilton Road, not far from the police station but not too close, either. Harry had sent a note to Guy's house to say he had something important to tell him.

'What is it? You're behaving like a spy,' said Guy, though he couldn't deny that he felt pretty thrilled at the cloak-and-dagger atmosphere.

Harry was in uniform and had skulked along the road to the pre-arranged meeting spot, though it had made Guy laugh. Harry's smallness, his uniform and his good looks did not allow for an incognito assignment.

'I feel like one,' said Harry, looking from side to side like a pantomime villain. 'If Jarvis caught me, I'd be done for treason, I'm sure of it.'

'Go on, then. Tell me.'

'Mabel Rogers telephoned. She said she'd been burgled and wanted you to go and see her. She said it was connected to the death of her friend, Florence Shore. Obviously you couldn't go, so Jarvis sent around Bob and Lance, and they said it was just like

Mr Marchant when they turned up. She was crying and that but said nothing was missing after all. They put it down to her being an old lady and going a bit funny.'

Guy rubbed his nose. The air had started to take on a distinct chill in the evenings and he hadn't put a vest on that morning. 'Do you think I should go around there?'

'What are you asking me for?' said Harry. 'I thought I'd pass it on because you keep on about that case. If you want to get yourself in further trouble, that's your call. I only thought you'd like to know about it, that's all.'

'I do. Thank you. I'll have a think. This was this morning, you say?'

'Yes,' said Harry, his eyes following a pretty girl walking down the street, her lilac dress swinging just below her knees. 'Anyway, I'd better go. For God's sake, you didn't hear it from me.'

'Scout's honour,' said Guy and they both walked away at the same time in opposite directions.

There was only one thing to do. Guy headed straight for Carnforth Lodge. As before, the building looked grey and uninviting. The front door was firmly shut this time, however, and when Guy rang the bell, it was opened by the same porter. Now that he was standing, Guy could see he was a tall man, almost two inches taller than Guy, and thin, underfed, even. He did not look as if he had shaved that morning.

'I've come to see Miss Rogers,' said Guy. He had no uniform on this time and wondered if the porter would recognise him. He did.

'Follow me,' said the porter.

As before, Mabel was behind the desk. She sat, statue still, looking out of the French windows that led to the garden. At the porter's gentle knock, she jumped out of her skin.

'What is it, Jim?' she said, and then, at the sight of Guy behind him, 'Mr Sullivan.'

Jim withdrew and closed the door behind him.

'Miss Rogers,' began Guy, 'I know this is—' He stopped. The office was in chaos. Flowerpots had been knocked over, papers were loose on the carpet, drawers had been pulled out and upturned. 'Someone at the station told me what had happened. I thought I'd better come and see how you were.'

'Thank you,' she said, her voice muted, as if she was lying under a blanket. 'I had hoped you would come. I telephoned your station but they sent two other men around. I didn't want to talk to them. It's been so upsetting. I ...' She turned away briefly, composed herself, then continued. 'It's delicate, you see. I didn't want to talk to someone who wouldn't understand.'

'Understand what?' said Guy.

Mabel turned to face him and brought a shaky hand to her face. 'I'm very frightened,' she said. 'The man who did this, he might come back. Supposing he comes back when I'm here? Oh God—' She broke down in a flood of tears, her back shuddering.

Guy was aghast. He didn't dare to touch her so he stood and waited until the wave had subsided. 'Miss Rogers, try to tell me what happened.'

Mabel wiped her face with a handkerchief. 'You see, someone has been in here but I haven't been burgled exactly.'

'You haven't?'

'No, that is, I had money and some jewellery here in the safe and none of it was taken. But they took a bundle of letters that Flo had written to me.'

'Do you think that's what they were after?'

'No, there was another letter, which was always kept separately. It was with Flo's things, in her room, but they didn't go up there because Jim heard them in here and they ran off when they heard him coming.'

'What made you check Flo's room?'

'I thought I'd better see in case anything was missing from there. I've hardly been up there since . . . That's when I found the letter.' Mabel pushed it across the desk to him.

'This?' said Guy. 'What is it?'

'It's a letter that Flo wrote to me from Ypres. The conditions there were particularly bad; it was the first time they'd seen gas attacks. There were men that she got to know well because they required so much care. One of them was an officer, Roland Lucknor—'

'Roland Lucknor,' echoed Guy. His mind started swirling and he tried to shake it off, to focus on what Mabel was saying.

'Yes. This letter is about him. You mentioned his name before, I know, but I'd forgotten it. Now I think he was the one who came here, trying to find it.'

'You think Roland Lucknor was here?' Guy was astonished.

Mabel nodded.

'But why?' said Guy. 'What does this letter say about him?'

'That Roland Lucknor killed Alexander Waring.'

Outside, Guy heard an ambulance siren. 'You're going to have to explain,' he said.

Mabel put her hands on her lap and looked at him steadily. 'Waring was his batman, and he was believed to have committed suicide. But Flo saw Roland that night and she became convinced that that wasn't what happened. She thought Roland killed him.'

Guy was clutching the letter but the words were a blur; he couldn't read it without having to peer very closely. The writing was faint, the letters small. He was impatient. 'Does Roland know she thought this?'

'Yes,' whispered Mabel. 'She discovered not long before her last Christmas that he had been demobilised and was in London. She wanted to go to his flat and give him a chance either to confess or deny. We argued about it – I didn't want her to. I thought . . . ' She stopped and took a deep breath. 'I thought it was too dangerous and she should go straight to the police; let them deal with it. But she said it was a terrible time in the war, he may have had his reasons. What those could have been we couldn't possibly guess at, she said, but she ought to give him a chance. She could never see the bad in anybody, could Flo.'

'Did she go to see him?'

'Yes. There was a row. I don't know what was said because I was so angry with her for going that I wouldn't hear it. I wouldn't hear it!' Mabel's eyes filled with tears. 'And then, a few days later, she was dead.'

'You think Roland Lucknor killed Florence Shore?' said Guy, feeling as if the last piece in the jigsaw had been found, trying not to feel exhilaration at the same time as pity for this afraid woman. 'Why didn't you mention this before? At the inquest?'

Mabel looked to the side. Through the French windows a cold wintry sunlight had started to shine through, piercing the grey mist London had woken up to that morning. 'I didn't make the connection then. Flo didn't recognise the man who got on the train. Surely if it was Roland, she would have. Perhaps he disguised himself in some way. Anyway, I didn't think he'd know about the letter, but she must have mentioned it to him, mustn't she?'

She looked up at Guy, beseeching, her hands pulling at the handkerchief. 'Now this has happened, I'm frightened. Supposing it's me he's after. What if I'm next?'

My dearest love,

I don't know if I should be writing this letter but I feel I must or I shall go mad with the thoughts that are constantly circling my mind. I am in my last days at Ypres now (the battle was won four days ago, if you can call anything in this war 'won') and thank God. Outside the sun beats down relentlessly and the clammy mud that sucks at one's every footstep has worn me down. Inside the hospital is stifling; the stench of burned flesh, blood and septic wounds has infiltrated every pore of my being; every breath inhales the dying and the dead.

There are still hundreds of men here, some of the sickest that we have been afraid to move, or move only slowly, amongst those who are fitter and can help them on the journey to the hospitals in England. I will return home myself for some leave, travelling on the way with the last of the men. We are all tired, we are hungry – the food here is so basic as to be unrecognisable, with only the meanest portions of meat – and some of us are desperate. If a man is on the edge, if he should do something that mere months ago he would have thought impossible of himself or another, one cannot blame him for any desperate act out here. And yet . . .

I have mentioned before in my letters the officer Roland, of whom I have become fond – as fond as one allows oneself to be, knowing they all may die at any moment – as well as of his batman, Xander. They are a pair of young, handsome men and their lively talk and good humour has kept many of us going through the long nights. I know that they, too, have been maddened by this war. So remember this before you read what I must tell you next.

One week ago, when the battle was still raging, I was doing the rounds of the ward – it must have been 3 a.m. or thereabouts. It is very dark in the night; we have low gas lights but few of them. The men lie on creaking beds that barely take their weight, and those that sleep often cry out. As we are stationed only miles from the front line, a week ago the gunfire was still incessant, noisy and somehow always with the threat of coming nearer.

I needed to step outside to fetch something, I forget what now, and I happened to look across at the storage shed outside. Remember that, though it was the dead of night, there was constant movement of people, constant noise of battle, and I was nearly demented with tiredness and sadness, when I heard a shot come from there, though I couldn't be absolutely certain of this, with all the shots sounding off from everywhere. Then I heard a second shot, quite soon after, and there was no doubt where I'd heard it. Almost immediately, I saw Roland come out of the hut – I recognised his officer's hat, I think, something in the shape of him, too. He came out, looked around and saw me looking at him, and he looked startled. As if I had caught

312

him in the act of something terrible. Then he ran deeper into the shadows.

I didn't know what to do. It was probably nothing, I thought. One fights against paranoia every minute here. I went back inside and carried on working. Not long after, we heard the news that Xander Waring had been found dead. The doctor made an instant assessment of suicide and he was brought into our hospital to be prepared for burial. I had been fond of Xander and requested to be the one to clean him and wrap him before he was taken away, although the task was distressing, despite everything I have seen. There was barely anything left of his face.

It breaks one's heart to think that this was a man once loved as a baby by his mother and now to die so alone. I know what our faith decrees about those who take their own lives but I don't think anyone can truly understand what it must feel like to be pushed to that point.

Roland is no longer here. I asked his CO and he said he'd been sent to England. I hadn't known but the day before the doctor had declared Xander fit and well again and assigned him back to duty, Roland was to be sent to a hospital in England. They believe him on the train there, and perhaps he is. I can't ask without raising too many questions.

I think Roland killed Xander. Why else did he look at me like that as he left the hut? I should report this, I know I should, but what if Xander hoped to die? He may have seemed well, as the doctor declared, but the thought of facing more battle, more fighting, more trenches, more cold, more mud . . . He may not have been able to stand it.

I can't say anything about it now. Keep this letter, my

dearest, hold on to it in a safe place, in case I should need it later. Perhaps this war will end, and justice will need to be done then.

Most tender love,
Flo

CHAPTER FIFTY-FOUR

The morning after his meeting with Mabel, Guy woke up after a sleepless night of going around and around in circles about what to do next. He couldn't believe his luck when he got downstairs and found an envelope with a brief note from Louisa, asking if they could meet. She was staying in St Leonards, she wrote, and would explain why when she saw him, but he didn't need to come all the way down there – she could catch a train and perhaps they could go to a café by Victoria station. She put a telephone number on the note. Hastily, Guy got dressed and ran out to the nearest telephone box and left a message with the rather sour-sounding waitress at the other end to say he would be in the Regency Café opposite the entrance to Victoria station from midday and Louisa could arrive any time. He would wait as long as it took.

In the event, he waited only forty-five minutes, long enough to be nervously drumming his teaspoon on the table top, much to the irritation of the man on the next table. He had braced himself for a long time in the café, so it was with a rush of happiness that he saw her come through the door at half past twelve. She was wearing the green felt coat he had come to love on her, old but well looked after, with large tortoiseshell buttons he fancied she had put on herself as a flourish. It was a narrow fit on her figure, and her navy skirt flared out slightly beneath. She had a serious look as she came towards him, but when she sat down she took her hat off and smiled at him.

'It's good to see you,' he said.

'You too,' said Louisa. 'There's something I need to talk to you about.'

'Me too!' said Guy, bursting with his own breakthrough.

'I told Lady Redesdale about Roland Lucknor. That is, I warned her off him, and she sacked me for the impertinence.'

'I'm so sorry. I'm to blame for that,' said Guy sadly. 'The thing is, it was the right thing to do. I know for certain he is dangerous.'

What? Had he discovered something about Stephen?

'I went to see Mabel Rogers yesterday. Harry tipped me off that she had called the police to say that she'd been burgled.'

'Wasn't that rather a great risk?'

'I don't know that I've got anything left to lose,' said Guy. 'At any rate, she talked to me . . . ' Guy told Louisa about the letter and her belief that Roland had killed his batman.

'Would the police see it as definite proof?'

'I don't know. I think so.' Guy wasn't sure of much in that moment but Louisa's face opposite him. He noticed a square of green in her iris that he had never seen before. 'But before I saw her, I'd met someone from Roland's battalion. He seemed to have liked Roland. He told me that his batman was supposed to have committed suicide but he was very surprised to hear that; he thought it was out of character.'

'What was the batman's name?'

'Alexander Waring.' Guy saw her face. 'Why? Does that mean something?'

Louisa pulled the two bank books out of her pocket. 'I took these from Roland's room. I don't know why, I did it without thinking. I thought it was odd of him to have two. One belongs to him and the other to Alexander Waring.'

Guy grabbed them. 'Do they say anything?'

'I don't know, I can't really understand them. I knew they were friends because Nancy found a book in his pocket that had a loving message in it, to "Xander", from Roland. We thought it strange that he should own a book that he'd obviously given to someone else, but I suppose if Xander is dead . . .'

'What do you mean, Nancy found it in his pocket? What's going on – stealing bank books and going through pockets?'

Louisa took a breath. 'I'll explain, but before I do that, there's something I need to tell you about me,' she said.

'What?' said Guy. Louisa seemed to have taken a completely different turn, but then he'd never been terribly good at understanding women. Hadn't Harry told him often enough?

'That day we met, at Lewes station, I was running away from someone.'

Guy was listening.

'My uncle.' Louisa willed herself to go on. 'My father died not long before that Christmas and his brother came to stay with me and Ma after the funeral. He's often been to stay with us and he's . . . he's not a good man. When I was a child he used to persuade me to take the day off school and then he'd take me to a train station and we'd pick pockets.'

'What?' said Guy, astonished.

'I got quite good at it. I liked his praise and the money he'd give me afterwards. So you see, that day we met, when you thought that gentleman had made a coarse suggestion to me . . .'

Guy knew he didn't want to hear what was coming next.

'I'd been about to lift his wallet but you came just in time—'

'I *did* see your hand in his pocket,' said Guy. 'I told myself I must have imagined it.'

'I was desperate,' said Louisa. 'I didn't know what to do. I had to get away but I had no money.'

'Why didn't you just ask for my help?'

'I didn't like to,' said Louisa. 'I've never asked anything of anybody. And we'd only just met. Why should you have lent me money?'

Guy took a shaky breath. 'You said you were running away from your uncle.'

'Yes. He owed money to someone, a gambling debt. And he had told him that he'd repay him with me.'

'What do you mean?' said Guy. 'Were you going to go out thieving for him again?'

'No. He was offering *me*.' She couldn't bear to look Guy in the face. 'He was taking me to Hastings, where this man lived. They said just one night would do it.' She breathed out. She had never felt so filthy, so ashamed.

Guy took it in. He asked, very quietly, 'Had you done that before?'

'No,' said Louisa.

Guy looked relieved.

'That's why I jumped off the train,' said Louisa. 'I knew what he was up to and I couldn't bear it. I couldn't have done it.'

'No,' said Guy. He didn't really know how to respond.

'And it was better, you see, after that. Because of you. I got the job and Stephen didn't find me there. I thought it was all behind me. Until just lately. He turned up in the village and I was frightened.'

Guy stayed quiet.

'I had to stop Stephen. I couldn't have him ruin everything for me. I would have lost my job and gone back to London – to *nothing*. To him, to Ma, to work as a washerwoman. I'd rather be dead. So I asked for Roland's help . . .'

Guy was confused. Who was this woman?

'He said he could get rid of Stephen for me and I wouldn't have to worry about him again.' Louisa searched Guy's face, trying to read what he thought of her now. 'Don't you see? I know Roland is a killer because he *has* killed – he killed Stephen for me.'

Guy tried to absorb this. Louisa looked grey and exhausted. He wanted to reassure her but he didn't know that he could.

'I didn't know he would do that,' said Louisa, trying not to trip over her words. 'I thought he would just scare him off but he hasn't been seen since that day. I didn't mean for Roland to do *that*.' Tears were pouring down her face now and she wiped them with the flat of her hand as Guy sat completely still.

'The point is,' said Louisa, 'I know where Roland is. Or, at least, where he will be.'

'What?' said Guy. 'Where?'

'He's going to be at Nancy's eighteenth birthday party. We've got a few days to make a plan but that's where you can get him. Surely there you can arrest him for the murder of Alexander Waring, on suspicion of the murder of Stephen Cannon, and then question him about Florence Shore.'

'I don't know. I need more evidence,' said Guy.

'You've got the letter and the bank books. We're pretty certain that he was extracting money from Lord Redesdale, probably threatening him about something. Perhaps he would help us. I can ask Nancy, too.'

'How?' Guy felt a little overwhelmed.

'I don't know. I'll go back to the house. I can find a way. I'll do it for you, Guy. The question is, can you do it for me?'

CHAPTER FIFTY-FIVE

~~~~~

Guy and Harry met at the Regency Café, close to Victoria station. Harry had clocked off for the day and ordered ham, eggs and chips with his tea. 'I've got a long night ahead at the club,' he said. 'The band has said I can play along with them for their last two or three songs.'

'That's great, Harry.'

Harry eyed his friend ruefully. 'But we're not here to talk about me, are we?'

'Sorry,' said Guy, 'it's about the Florence—'

'Shore case, I know. Come on, then. Spill the beans. What's happened? Did you go to see the old lady?'

Guy gave Harry the letter. 'She said that someone had been searching for this but hadn't found it. Nothing else was taken.'

'What does it say?'

'It says that Roland Lucknor killed Alexander Waring.'

'What's that got to do with anything?' Harry's order was put before him and he winked at the waitress before squirting brown sauce at the side. He wasted no time in getting the first mouthful in.

'The letter was written by Florence Shore. The old lady, Mabel Rogers, thinks Roland found out she wrote it, and that he killed her.'

'Hang on a minute. He was the man in the brown suit?'

'Possibly. There's more: Roland Lucknor has been friendly with the Mitfords lately, doing business with the father and writing to the eldest daughter.'

Harry looked blank.

'Louisa – she's been working as their nursery maid.'

Harry put down his knife and fork and clasped his hands in prayer. 'Praise be, all roads lead to Louisa.'

'It's not funny, Harry.'

'Yes, it is.' Harry scooped up more egg and sauce, grinning with his mouth full.

'Be serious. I've got a letter here that suspects Roland Lucknor of being a killer. And there's a connection with Florence Shore. They were all in the same place at Ypres.'

'I don't know that that's a connection.'

'And he's denied knowing her. But when he was staying with the Mitfords in France, he called out her name in the middle of the night. He was having some sort of bad dream. Louisa went to see what was going on and heard him say her name, more than once.'

Harry wiped his mouth with a napkin. 'That doesn't look good for him.'

'No, and what's more, he was in possession of a bank book in the name of his batman in the army, who is dead.'

'Which is a bit rum but there might be an explanation.'

'Not when money has been going in and out of his account after he died.' Guy sat back. He'd said it all now. 'What do I do? I can't go to Jarvis; he won't talk to me.'

'What about that other one on the case? DI Haigh, at the Met. I think you should go and see him.'

Guy stared at the letter. 'I can't hold on to this by myself. You're right, I should take it to Haigh. Come with me, Harry. I need a uniform with me.'

'What, now?'

'Yes,' said Guy. 'Now.'

At New Scotland Yard, Guy tried not to be awed by the grandeur of the place even as Harry was suppressing burps. 'Sorry,' he said bashfully. 'You made me rush my tea.'

Harry asked to see Haigh and was told to sit and wait while a message was sent. The place was teeming with police and men not in uniform, perhaps detectives or undercover policemen, with a sense of urgency and purpose nevertheless, all of them striding through the hall where Guy and Harry sat. There were others on the wooden benches beside them: a woman with a small girl in a frilly dress; a young chap with one black eye and a look in the other that suggested several whiskies had been drunk; a white-haired man, who kept rereading the same piece of paper in his hand, then shaking his head and muttering. There were noticeboards with wanted posters, announcements of local meetings and a list of missing persons. Guy wanted to be right in there, amongst them.

All too promptly, the two of them were summoned. There was a long walk down corridors that yawned ahead, but the smell of cigars let them know when they were approaching Haigh's office. The policeman who had shown them the way knocked on the door smartly, then walked off before Haigh had told them to enter. He sat behind a leather desk that seemed larger and more foreboding than a judge's in court. His jacket was off and hanging on the back of his chair, his tie was loose and he had undone his top shirt button. A cigar was smoking in the ashtray and the smoke was floating above them.

Haigh motioned to them both to sit down. He smoothed his palm over his balding head, slicking down the dark hairs at the side. 'Tell me what this is about,' he said, 'and make it quick. I've got to leave in ten minutes.'

Harry kept quiet; Guy had already said he'd be doing all the talking.

'Thank you, sir,' said Guy.

'Who are you?'

'I'm Guy Sullivan, sir.'

Haigh turned to Harry. 'You're the uniform – why aren't you talking to me?'

Harry started to say something but Guy stopped him. 'Sir, I asked him to accompany me. We're from the London, Brighton and South Coast Railway Police, from the Florence Shore case.'

'Ah, yes, so you are. I thought you looked familiar.' Haigh picked up his cigar and sucked on it. 'Hang on a minute. Aren't you the one we had a letter of complaint about? From the victim's cousin?'

'Stuart Hobkirk. Yes, sir,' said Guy. There wasn't much point in denying it.

'Yes, that's it. Was that you?'

'It was. But I can explain, sir.'

'Go on, then.' The cigar went back down in the ashtray. Haigh sat back in his chair and looked evenly at Guy.

'I had discovered that Miss Shore's will had been changed in his favour only a few days before she was killed. I thought he should be investigated and went to see him but was able to rule him out. The thing is, he wrote to you to say he'd been bothered by further police inquiries, but that wasn't me. I think I know now who it was. Because of that and one or two other things –' Guy tried to mutter this bit – 'I was sacked from the force after that, for carrying out investigations without official permission.'

324

'Sacked? That's why you're not in uniform, I suppose.'

Guy's shame glowed.

'Get on with it, then,' said Haigh. 'Tell me why you're here. I'm assuming you think it's going to make a difference to this case and you've got just one minute left to tell me why.'

'Miss Shore's friend, Mabel Rogers, who spoke at the inquest, reported a burglary but then said nothing was missing to the London, Brighton and South Coast Railway sergeants who went around. She had asked to see me, so I went over. She said she had something to show me, because I had worked on the Shore case.' Guy pulled the letter out of his pocket and put it on Haigh's desk. 'It's a letter that Miss Shore wrote to her from Ypres, during the war. It concerns an officer she knew, Roland Lucknor, and his batman, who committed suicide. Only, Miss Shore believed that Mr Lucknor had killed him.'

Haigh picked up the letter and started to read it, as Guy explained the other pieces of evidence that he could: Lucknor's denial that he knew Nurse Shore, then calling her name out in his sleep; the two bank books in his possession, with money going in and out of the dead man's account. He didn't mention Stephen Cannon, as that would have implicated Louisa and he didn't want to do that unless he absolutely had to do so.

At the end of it Haigh folded up the letter and handed it back to Guy. 'It's good, Sullivan, but it's not enough. All we've got here is supposition. What we need is evidence. If you get me evidence, we can do something. I suggest you find it.'

'Does that I mean I have your permission, sir?' said Guy.

'The door is behind you,' said Haigh.

CHAPTER FIFTY-SIX

～～～

Louisa decided not to go back to Rosa's to collect her things but to make her way directly to Asthall Manor. Ada would lend her anything if she needed to stay, but she hoped very much that she could persuade Nancy to help them, then return to London to make further plans with Guy.

Louisa caught sight of herself in a shop window as she walked to the station and thought if someone else saw her, they might think she was someone with a hopeful future.

The train journey was a familiar one now and Louisa allowed herself a snatch of sleep, warmed by the steam pipes in the carriage. By the time she arrived at Shipton station, it was starting to get dark but the moon was almost full and bright. She still had quite a bit of her month's wages with her so decided she would take a taxi to the house but ask the driver to drop her off before the entrance.

The lights in the house were on. They were most likely all in the library for tea. She couldn't let anybody see her but Nancy or Ada, so Louisa decided to head around to the back of the house and hope to catch a glimpse of one or the other before too long.

The similarity between this night and her first arrival at Asthall was not lost on her. Would Nancy come running to her rescue this time? Luckily, she didn't have to wait more than a few minutes before she saw Ada come into the kitchen, thankfully alone, and go to the sink to wash her hands. Louisa crept closer to the window and threw some gravel at the glass.

Ada came outside, drying her hands on her apron. 'Jonny? Is that you? I told you not to come here.'

'No,' whispered Louisa as loudly as she dared. 'It's me.'

Ada broke into a delighted smile. 'Oh, it's good to see you. I've been terribly worried. Where have you been staying? I wrote to your London address but heard nothing back.'

'I've not been home,' said Louisa. 'I can't explain it all now but I really must see Nancy. Can you get her out here? I'll wait for her in the summer house by the bathing pool. But don't let anyone else know.'

Ada grimaced. 'I'll see what I can do but it might be a while before I can see her alone. They're all having tea now. You'll get very cold out there.'

'I'll be all right,' said Louisa, though she could no longer feel her toes.

'Wait a sec,' said Ada. She ran back in and came out again with a flask of tea and some bread and butter. Louisa took it, grateful now she realised that in those short minutes her teeth were on the edge of chattering.

Huddled in the corner of the summer house, the tea long drunk and the bread eaten, Louisa was relieved to see a flashlight heading towards her in the pitch black.

'Lou-Lou?' called Nancy, and Louisa ran out to her.

'I'm over here.'

'Thank goodness for that. You gave me a fright. You know I hate the dark.'

'I'm sorry,' said Louisa, 'but I couldn't risk Lady Redesdale discovering me. And it's important that I talk to you.'

'Goodness, all this mystery. What's it about? Here, have a toffee.' She dug in her pockets and pulled two out, their shiny wrappers glinting.

'Thanks,' said Louisa, saving hers for later. It might be supper. 'I've come here to talk to you about Roland.'

'What about Roland?' Nancy's interest was easily piqued at the sound of his name. 'We've not seen him since he left. Since he ... you know. Your uncle.' She looked at Louisa, concerned. 'Have you heard from him?'

Louisa shook her head. 'Nothing.'

'What do you think Roland did?'

Louisa needed to warn Nancy off Roland but she didn't want to terrify the girl out of her wits. Not until she knew for certain what he had done. 'He scared him off, that's all,' she said. 'Even so, you mustn't have anything more to do with him. We think he might be guilty of murder.' She could practically see Nancy's hackles. 'What's tricky is that we need him to come to the ball. We need your help to arrest him. Guy and I—'

'*Arrest* Roland?' Nancy shouted. 'Did you ask him to do something to your uncle? If you did, then it's *your* fault!'

'Shhh!' Louisa looked around them wildly, though there was nothing to be seen but dense blackness. 'No, it's not about Stephen, it's about Florence Shore.'

Nancy stopped short. 'What? What's he got to do with Florence Shore?'

As calmly as she could, Louisa explained to Nancy: his denial that he knew Florence Shore, then his calling out of her name in the night; the loving inscription in the book to Xander, his batman; that Xander was supposed to have committed suicide but now there was a letter, handed to them by Mabel Rogers, in which Florence Shore suspected Roland of killing Xander; and the argument with a lady in a fur coat, days before Florence Shore was killed. It all added up.

Nancy shook her head. 'I won't believe it. I think you've put two and two together and made five. It simply can't be true.' She caught a sob. 'I *know* him. He's not capable of killing someone. He's *gentle*.'

'It's not just you,' said Louisa. 'I've overheard him arguing with Lord Redesdale about money. Supposing he's blackmailing your father about something? Or extorting money from him in some way? They were all at Ypres together.'

Nancy's tears dried in a flash. 'Are you accusing Farve of something? Be careful.'

'No,' said Louisa, desperate now. 'Of course I'm not. I'm saying that Roland is trouble. He's bad news. Whatever he's done, he's bringing it to you, to your home. You must help us, me and Guy. Guy can get him arrested and then we can discover the truth of it. If there is an explanation then he can tell us and you'll be fine. But I have to protect you and Lord Redesdale.'

Nancy stood up. 'I'm sorry, Louisa. None of it is true. None of it. You cannot count on my help.'

Louisa stood too and faced her. 'I'm going to stay in the village until you change your mind. I'll find a room and leave a message at the post office to tell you where I am.'

'Don't bother,' said Nancy and marched out.

Louisa watched the flashlight bob into the distance until it was extinguished altogether.

CHAPTER FIFTY-SEVEN

O n that night, while Louisa was trying to persuade Nancy to help them trap Roland, Guy was at home. As soon as supper had been cleared, he sat down at the table in the front room and laid open the bank books before him. These had to be clues. He didn't know how or why but if there was something there, he was determined to find it.

Guy rolled up his shirtsleeves and folded his arms on the smooth wood. One book was dark green leather with BANK OF SCOTLAND ESTABLISHED 1695 embossed in gold across the front. Inside, it detailed an account number in the name of Roland O. Lucknor. The second was dark red card, with KENT & CANTERBURY BUILDING SOCIETY in black, which belonged to Alexander Waring.

Inside both books were several pages filled with densely packed details inscribed by various bank tellers, with transactions that dated back to 1910 for the green book, 1907 for the red. Guy noticed that few payments in or out were made during the war years. This was all he could make out. The figures jumped about on the lines and the writing was unintelligible, no matter how frequently he polished his glasses on his shirt.

Guy's mother was sitting by the fire, her apron still on and slippers on her feet. She stared into the flames and was meditatively quiet. The spell was broken by his brothers coming back into the room, on their way out to the pub. Walter had moved out since his marriage a few months previously, and Guy did not miss his overbearing presence. Ernest swaggered in. He'd sloughed the brick dust off and slicked his hair down with water, ready for a few jars at the Dog & Duck. He came over and picked up one of the books.

'Don't,' said Guy, reaching up to grab it back.

Ernest jumped backwards, laughing, holding it in the air and waving it. 'What's this, then? Filthy pictures? You dirty boy.'

'No,' said Guy, going red. 'Just give it back. It's evidence.'

Ernest stopped hopping about and looked at it. 'Evidence of what?'

Guy snatched it back and put it on the table. 'It's for a case I'm working on.'

'But you've been sacked,' said Ernest. 'Hasn't he, Mother?'

Their mother didn't reply, only turned back to the fire. She'd never liked to show any kind of favouritism and never took sides when the brothers fought.

Bertie came in, head swivelling around. 'Has anyone seen my comb?' he said, then saw Ernest's smooth head. 'You. Have you got it? Give it back.'

'Give over,' said Ernest. 'Here, Guy's looking at evidence. Even though he's been sacked. What do you suppose that's all about, then?'

'I am right here,' said Guy. 'I can hear what you're saying.'

Bertie didn't respond but walked to the table and looked over Guy's shoulder. 'Bank books? You laundering money now?' he said and started snorting at his own joke.

Mrs Sullivan stood up. 'I'll make you a mug of cocoa, Guy,' she said and padded out of the room. Perhaps she did allow herself to take sides on occasion.

Guy gave a heavy sigh, polished his glasses one more time and opened both books before him again. He decided to look at the most recent pages of Xander's account. He was looking intently for a few minutes when he became aware of something happening behind him and when he looked up, both Ernest and Bertie were peering over each of his shoulders, hands behind their backs, mock seriousness on their faces.

'Shove off!' said Guy. 'Or make yourself useful. Would you like to look at it for me, Ernest?' He picked up the book and pretended to hand it over.

'Ooh, touchy,' said Ernest, but he walked off and sat in their mother's chair.

'Thought not,' muttered Guy. Ernest could not read.

Bertie had lost interest, too, and wandered off into the kitchen, probably to try and persuade their mother into giving him another slice of ham.

Guy squinted and looked again. He had already seen that although Xander Waring was dead by 1918, there were payments and withdrawals noted in 1919 and 1920. How was that possible if he was dead? Roland Lucknor must have been impersonating him in order to get money out of there. There was something curious, though. There was never very much in the balance; cash was sporadically paid in and only small amounts of cash were paid out now and then. Why would Roland go to the trouble of impersonating someone for one or two pounds here and there?

Guy looked again. His brain ached with the frustration. The different inks and handwriting of the different tellers made it hard to see what patterns there were, but then he saw that there was a regular payment made, on the third of every month, to something annotated as 'BHHI'. The sums varied slightly but were fairly substantial, around twenty pounds or thereabouts. What could that be?

Guy's mother put the mug of cocoa beside the bank books. 'There you go, son,' she said.

'What's the BHHI?' said Guy.

'What's that, dear?' said his mother.

'The BHHI. Have you ever heard of it?'

She stood, her hands on her lower back and looked down. 'Do you know, I think I have. It's the British Home and Hospital for Incurables. Your great-aunt Lucy went there when she lost her mind.'

'Is that where you're off to, Guy?' shouted out Bertie.

'Shut up,' said Guy, and Bertie, discombobulated to hear his brother answer back, pulled a face and carried on eating the ham. 'Do you know where it is?'

'Yes, of course. I used to go and visit her; took you with me once or twice I think, when you were small. It's in Streatham, Crown Lane. How funny I remembered that. I haven't thought of it for years.' Mrs Sullivan walked over to her chair and Ernest leapt out. 'Why are you asking, anyway?'

'It's in this bank book,' said Guy. 'I'm trying to work something out.'

Guy picked up the green leather book. It felt more substantial in every way and the sums were just as hefty. On the first couple of pages there were occasional deposits of cash and then withdrawals made only now and then. But in the more recent pages, there were cheques paid in and the amounts were big. They weren't paid in regularly or even particularly often, but they were large. They seemed to have stopped in April of this year. The writing was difficult to read and Guy picked out the odd letter here and there – then suddenly he filled in the gaps. Baron Redesdale.

Baron Redesdale? Redesdale was the Mitford title. But there wasn't anyone called Baron, was there?

Like a light switching on, Guy understood. Of course, that was his title. It meant Lord Redesdale, Nancy's father. The money they suspected that Roland had been extorting from him was now in black and white.

Guy read it all again clearly. The large deposits were cheques cashed from Lord Redesdale, then there were large cheques written out once those had cleared, annotated by a PO box address. The sums were almost the same as those payments to the British Home and Hospital for Incurables. There had to be some connection, given that Roland had had both the books in his possession.

'I think I've cracked it,' he said out loud.

'What?' said his mother, and his two brothers looked up.

'I've been looking for a connection between two men, and I've found it. It's taken me ages but I got there in the end.' He was beaming.

'Does that mean you'll get your job back, then?' said Ernest.

'I don't know. Maybe. There's more to do, first.'

'Proper police work,' said his mother, an admiring tone in her voice. 'Well done, my boy.'

'Thank you, Mother,' said Guy, and for once, he felt he had earned the acclaim.

CHAPTER FIFTY-EIGHT

Not wanting to stay at the Swan Inn, Louisa had sought out Ada's sweetheart, Jonny at the blacksmith's, to see if he knew anybody who could give her a room for a few nights. He was quick to help her – 'Any friend of Ada's is a friend of mine,' he said kindly – and once settled at his mother's, she left a note for Nancy at the post office as she had said she would, letting her know where she could be found. After that, she could only wait and hope.

Although those hours dragged by, it was, in fact, as soon as the following afternoon, when Louisa was sitting in a somewhat spartan bedroom trying to read her book but finding it hard to concentrate, that she heard a shout coming up the stairs to say she had a visitor.

Louisa ran down, hope billowing in her chest like a sail in the wind. Jonny's mother was standing in the hall, holding on to the bannister.

'They're in there,' she said, pointing to the parlour. 'I've never had the likes of them in my house before. That's our room for Christmas best but I don't know I've dusted it since last week . . .' She trailed off, her face pinched with nerves.

'Don't worry,' said Louisa, 'they won't notice.' She walked towards the door, took a deep breath and pushed it wide. What she saw made her mouth fall open. 'My lord,' she said, 'I beg your pardon. I wasn't expecting to see you.'

Lord Redesdale had been standing in front of the modest mantelpiece, peering at the porcelain ornaments that stood on it. He turned around at Louisa's voice and she saw that his face was just as incredulous as hers, though he covered it up.

He did not address her but instead spoke to Nancy, who had been watching all this with a smile playing at the edges of her mouth. 'Koko? Explain yourself.'

'Can we all sit down?' said Nancy, and she swept her skirt smoothly beneath her and perched on the sofa.

'I'd really rather stand,' said Louisa. A servant never sat down in front of their masters. Nanny Blor had made the point repeatedly when she first arrived and this was certainly not the moment to start breaking protocol.

Lord Redesdale pointedly remained where he was, too.

'Very well,' said Nancy, 'we'll go on like this. Farve, please listen closely and do try not to jump in and start barking.'

Lord Redesdale grumbled and muttered under his breath but waited for Nancy to speak.

'Louisa, I've thought about what you've said and I've realised you're right. We need to explain it now, to Farve, and then the three of us can consider how we will resolve the ... difficulty.'

Louisa was still too amazed to speak.

'Will you just get to the point?' spluttered Lord Redesdale. 'I thought we were here to visit my tenant.'

'Farve, you remember the sad story of the nurse, Florence Shore, who was killed on a train, on the Brighton line?' began Nancy.

'Yes, yes. A friend of Nanny Blor's, wasn't she?'

'A friend of her twin sister,' said Nancy. 'Now supposing I was to tell you that there was an officer out there, at the same time as you, whom you did not know, who was found to have known Florence Shore in Ypres, though he had denied it.'

'Must you be so cryptic?' said Lord Redesdale.

'Yes,' said Nancy. 'Just listen. Florence Shore's friend, Mabel Rogers, telephoned the police a few days ago because she was burgled. Only, when they got there, they discovered nothing had been taken except for a bundle of letters that Florence had written her over the years. However, there was one letter in that bundle they did not have because it had been kept separately with Florence's things, which weren't discovered. In this letter, Florence Shore described a night in which the officer's batman was supposed to have shot himself.'

'At Ypres?' said Lord Redesdale. 'It was so ghastly there,' he added, almost to himself.

'Yes, at Ypres. But Florence saw the officer that night and she had reason to believe that he killed the batman. She wrote this in the letter that Mabel Rogers had.'

Lord Redesdale took a handkerchief out of his pocket and wiped his top lip with it.

'What's more, shortly before the day of the attack on Florence Shore, a lady was seen arguing with this officer at his flat. The lady was wearing a fur coat.' Nancy paused. No story she had told before had ever had such a dramatic effect. 'Florence Shore was wearing a fur coat when she was killed.'

Lord Redesdale put a hand on the mantelpiece. 'I'm still not quite sure where this is going.' But he was pale. He possibly had guessed.

'Keep listening, Farve. I do wish you would sit down, though; I'm getting a crick in my neck,' complained Nancy. Nobody moved. 'The officer has not been seen at his flat since that row. What we do know about him is that he has in his possession two bank books – or rather, *had*.' She stole a look at Louisa, who did not return it. 'One is in his name and the other is in the name of the dead batman. Alexander Waring.'

'I don't see what this has to do with me, or you, for that matter. Louisa, is this your doing?' Lord Redesdale fixed a look on Louisa, who shrank under the fierce gaze.

'Oh, darling old man, don't be dense,' said Nancy. 'It has quite a lot to do with you. It's why we think you can help the police. That officer is Roland Lucknor.'

CHAPTER FIFTY-NINE

～

There was a long walk along Crown Lane from Streatham train station the following morning, but there was no mistaking the British Home and Hospital for Incurables when Guy came upon it. An imposing red-brick building, its name was writ large across the side. The name chilled Guy. Abandon hope all ye who enter here.

There were grounds at the front behind the tall railings but these were empty of people. Inside had the feeling of a large chapel, with a dampness in the air and the kind of quiet that only descends when hundreds of people have their heads bowed in prayer. A young nurse, in a hat that was almost a wimple, sat behind a leather-topped reception desk, a vase of rather forlorn pink carnations beside her, which looked improbable and out of place.

'May I help you?' she said, as Guy approached.

Guy knew what he was about to do was a white lie at best, against the law at worst, but he had to do it if he was going to solve this mystery. 'Good morning,' he said. 'I'm from the London, Brighton and South Coast Railway Police.' He could only hope she did not ask to see his badge; it had been handed in, along with his uniform.

'Goodness,' she said, 'has something happened?'

'No,' he said. 'That is, I'm afraid I can't tell you the details but I need to see your visitor's book. I'm trying to trace the movements of a couple of people – Alexander, or Xander, Waring and Roland Lucknor.'

'Right, I see,' said the nurse. She looked to be barely out of school. 'It's just here. I'm afraid I don't know the names myself.'

Guy saw the book was, in fact, open on the desk before him. He started to rifle through the pages but saw that, like the bank books, he'd have to sit there for some time before he could decipher the hieroglyphs and scribbles.

'I wonder,' he said, pointing to his glasses, 'might you help me? I'm afraid my sight . . .'

She smiled sympathetically. 'Of course,' she said and turned the book around to face her, reading back through the pages. After a few minutes, she gave a small exclamation. 'Ah, here!' she said. 'Not too long ago, last month, the seventeenth. Roland Lucknor. He came to see Violet Temperley. See?' She pointed to the entry.

'Is she here?' he asked. 'May I see her?'

The nurse looked unsure. 'Yes,' she said, 'but you'll have to take your chances as to whether she remembers anything or not. She has her lucid days now and then but her memory is almost gone, except for things that happened a long time ago.'

'I understand,' said Guy, 'but I'd still like to talk to her, if I can.'

The nurse rang a small bell on the desk and another young sister, with a similar look of a noviciate, came hurrying out of a door at the side of the hall. The situation was explained and soon Guy was following her, walking along long, cool passageways and up two flights of stone stairs, his feet clumping awkwardly in the wake of her noiseless steps. She showed him into a large, light room that was dressed like a drawing room, with a mantelpiece above a lit fire and oil paintings of Constable-like landscapes on the walls. The ceilings were high, with dusty chandeliers hanging beneath like relics from a forgotten palace. There was a soft green carpet but no rugs, and the residents sat in either wheelchairs or armchairs, each at some distance from the others, as immobile as statues, their eyes seeing anything but what was in the room.

Violet Temperley was in a wheelchair positioned to face the window, overlooking the empty grounds below. The grey skies outside offered little in the way of a palliative view. She was straight-backed like a paper doll, wrapped in a fine-wool shawl, her cheekbones curiously smooth and her eyes pale cornflower blue. The nurse touched her gently on the shoulder.

'Someone's here to see you, Mrs Temperley.' She gave Guy a little shrug and left the room.

Guy found a wooden chair and put it next to the old woman. She turned to him and whispered, 'Has she gone?'

'Do you mean the nurse?' asked Guy.

Violet gave a nod.

'Yes,' he whispered back.

'Thank goodness. They're very kind here but they do treat one like a child.' She gave him a look of complicity.

'Mrs Temperley,' he said, 'my name's Guy Sullivan. I hope you don't mind but I've come here to ask you if the name Roland Lucknor means anything to you.'

To his consternation, the old lady's eyes immediately filled with tears. 'My darling godson,' she said. 'Such a sweet boy. He had the most golden curls.'

'He's your godson?'

'More like a son. His mother was my greatest friend and she died when he was at school. She had been away for five years even then. She was a Christian missionary.' She wrinkled her nose. 'Her husband's influence. Ghastly man. Put the milk in first. Do you know, even when his wife died, he didn't return to see Roland? He stayed in Africa because, he said, it was too much trouble to come back. One can't blame poor Roly for running away to Paris but I do miss him. He used to stay with me every holiday when he was still at school and I became very fond of him.' She paused and stared at the window. 'I have no children of my own, you see.'

'When did you last see your godson?' he asked. She didn't respond and he repeated the question.

'He's in France, fighting in that ghastly war. I don't even know if he's still alive.' Her eyes went wide and she withdrew into her chair. 'Have you come to tell me something about him? Is he dead?' She peered at Guy. 'Who are you, anyway? Why are you asking me all these questions?'

'I'm sorry if I've upset you,' said Guy, deciding to parry the question for now. 'That's not why I've come. But I am trying to find out where Mr Lucknor might be. I'm not sure that he is still in France.'

'Then where could he be?' She looked afraid.

'I don't know,' admitted Guy. 'Does the name Alexander Waring mean anything to you?'

Violet's pale eyes blinked. 'I'm not sure,' she said.

Guy could see she was starting to flag. 'Might you have a photograph of Mr Lucknor that I could see?'

'Oh, yes, in my room. You'll have to push me there but I can show you the way.' She seemed quite perked up by the prospect and it was only as they were along the hallway that she turned and stage-whispered to him, 'They'd leave me by that window all day if they could. Now they'll have to come and fetch me from my room.' She turned back, giggling into her hand like a little girl.

Violet's room was painted white but there were pretty, thick yellow curtains hung at the window and a number of silver-framed photographs on a dressing table that stood beneath it. Guy pushed her in front of it and she leaned forwards, picking one or two up with her long fingers.

'Here,' she said, 'this is when he was in Paris, with his friend. Such a nice young man.' She smiled. 'He came to see me not long ago and brought me some beautiful flowers, like the ones my mother used to grow in our garden.'

Guy took the photograph, which wasn't in a frame but had been stuck in front of the glass of another. The framed photograph showed a man in an officer's cap – Roland? The loose picture had two men standing side by side, grinning at the camera. Guy couldn't make much out but that they looked relaxed and happy. One of them had a luxuriant moustache.

'Who came to see you?' he asked. 'Can you point to him in the photograph?'

Violet looked up at him and Guy saw her eyes were losing focus. He held up the picture before her. 'Which one is Roland?' he said.

She pointed to the man on the left, with the moustache, but only for the briefest second before her hand fell into her lap.

'The other man came to see you, did you say?'

'Xander,' she said. 'Such a sweet boy. Such lovely flowers.'

Guy was startled. 'Xander Waring, do you mean?'

But Violet had lapsed into a thoughtful silence, holding another photograph in her lap of a Victorian woman. Guy could just make out the long skirts and corseted waist. She turned her head away. 'I'd like to be left alone now, please.'

'Yes,' said Guy, 'of course. Thank you, Mrs Temperley. You've been so helpful.'

Gently, he replaced the framed photograph on the table. The loose photograph he slipped into his pocket.

Two men in the picture. He knew what he had to do next.

CHAPTER SIXTY

~~~~~

Lord Redesdale stared at his daughter. 'Do you know, I think I will sit down,' he said and sat on the armchair by the fire. A small puff of dust blew up as he did so.

Louisa felt calmer now that Nancy had said it all. To hear the story retold by her had only made it seem even more true and real than it had before.

'Are you saying you think Roland killed Florence Shore?' he said quietly after a minute or two.

'I know it seems shocking—' began Nancy.

'Shocking? It's outrageous! You've made a mistake somewhere. And how do you know all of this, anyway?'

Louisa decided she had better speak up now. 'It's because of my friend, my lord – Guy Sullivan. He's a police officer, for the railway police.' She decided that the detail he had been sacked was one she could leave out for now. 'He's been working on the case since it happened. It's only since the burglary was reported that these facts have really come to light.'

'You say *facts*, I say theories,' said Lord Redesdale crossly, but in a tone that sounded very much like his bluster shortly before he gave way to what was always referred to as 'the thin end of the wedge'.

'Is there anything you can think of about Roland that either supports or refutes these facts?' pressed Nancy.

'There's no need to interview me,' said her father. 'You're not a policeman and I'm not a suspect.'

'Nevertheless, can you?' Nancy had her bone.

Lord Redesdale cast a glance at Louisa. 'One doesn't really talk in front of—'

'Louisa's not like a servant,' interrupted Nancy, 'and besides, she's involved in this, too. We've got to talk about this together.'

Louisa dared herself. 'My lord, forgive me for asking, but I did overhear an argument you had with Mr Lucknor in France. That is, I didn't hear what was said exactly but I heard him shouting.'

'The impertinence!' he spluttered.

'Farve, dear,' said Nancy, 'do stop all that. Just *think*, would you?'

'Roland was in some sort of terrible trouble; I don't know what it was. He wanted money . . .' he began. Nancy gave him an encouraging look. Ignoring Louisa, he talked to his daughter. 'I'd already invested in his golf business but I couldn't give any more. Bill had just died and . . . ' He stopped and leaned forwards with his hands clasped. 'I had refused to lend Bill any money. I couldn't give any more to Roland's investment. That's all I'm prepared to say.'

Nancy and Louisa caught each other's eyes.

'Farve, Roland is coming to my birthday dance. We don't know where he is at the moment but I feel sure he'll turn up.'

'Yes, he's already written to ask if he and I might have a private meeting before it starts. I had rather hoped . . . Well, it doesn't matter what I'd hoped.'

'We can arrange for the police to be there, my lord,' said Louisa.

'Does it all really have to happen that night? Lady Redesdale

345

will be very upset. She's put an awful lot of planning into that party. I don't want all those ghastly neighbours gossiping about us for months afterwards.' Lord Redesdale looked stricken.

'I'm sure they will be very discreet,' said Louisa, though she wasn't at all sure they would. 'My lord, this is a very important case that the police have been trying to solve for months. I'm sure that any help you give will be seen as a great public service.'

This was a clever thing to say, Louisa thought.

'Yes, I do see.' He shook his head sadly. 'Still, I do wish it wasn't happening at my house. I know what you say sounds right but I can't help feeling there's something wrong somewhere. I don't believe Roland is a killer. I'm sorry but I don't.'

'I'm going to have to return to London briefly, to see Mr Sullivan,' said Louisa. 'I'll be in touch, to let you know what's happening. I'll see you in a couple of days, I suppose.'

Nancy stood and held out her hand to Louisa. She took it, gratefully, and smiled at her friend, come back to her. 'Thank you, Miss Nancy,' she said. 'I know what it took for you to come here. I won't let you regret it.'

'I know,' said Nancy, with the composure of a worldly adult. 'I trust you, Lou-Lou.'

CHAPTER SIXTY-ONE

~~~~~

At the post office, Louisa sent a telegram to Guy at his house:

> Lord R agrees to help STOP Returning to London
> STOP Meet at Regency Cafe this afternoon 3
> p.m. STOP Louisa Cannon.

When she walked into the café just before the appointed hour, she felt the clouds lift to see Guy already there, waiting for her. She slid into the seat opposite and he looked up, caught unawares. He had been staring at the photograph, trying to make sense of it, though of course he had met neither of the men in it.

'I'm so glad to see you,' he said. 'Such a lot has happened.'

'I know,' said Louisa. 'For me, too.' She ordered a cup of tea and a bacon sandwich, suddenly starving after her journey down.

Guy handed her the photograph, explaining as he did so how he had come by it.

'That's Roland, all right,' said Louisa, 'though it's obviously a few years ago. He looks a bit younger there. A bit happier, too, I'd say. It must have been before the war.'

'Which one did you say was Roland?' said Guy.

'That man,' said Louisa, pointing. 'The one on the right.'

'No,' said Guy. 'Mrs Temperley said her godson was the one on the left. The man with the moustache. Are you sure?'

Louisa looked again. 'Quite sure.'

'Perhaps he's just shaved his moustache off and now he looks like the friend,' said Guy.

'No,' said Louisa. 'I know they are quite similar-looking, but no, that's definitely Roland. Did she say who the other man was?'

'Yes, that's Xander Waring. I mean, she was a little vague but she said the man on the right was the one who had been to see her. She hadn't seen Roland since before the war, she said. Actually, she thought he was still in France, fighting.'

'Hang on, didn't you say it said Roland Lucknor in the visitor's book?'

Guy nodded. 'But she was a muddled old lady. It's quite possible that she thought it was Xander when it was Roland who came to see her.'

'I don't think that's it,' said Louisa, staring again at the picture. She could see a French street sign behind them. Rue Ravignon. They were each wearing cravats instead of ties and their shirt collars were undone. They looked as if they hadn't a care in the world. There was no doubt in her mind: the man on the right was the man she knew – and Nancy knew and Lord Redesdale knew – as Roland Lucknor. But he wasn't Roland Lucknor; he was Xander Waring, if the old lady was right. And why shouldn't she be?

The sandwich was put before Louisa but her appetite had vanished. She pushed the plate to the side. 'Hear me out,' she said. 'What if Xander killed Roland and stole his identity? What if the man we all think is Roland Lucknor is, in fact, Xander Waring? What if Florence Shore discovered this, when she went to the flat and rowed with him, and that was why he killed her?'

Guy's eyes went wide. He thought about it. 'Why would he do that, though? Why go to that trouble?'

'I don't know,' admitted Louisa. 'But it's the only answer I can think of.'

'We don't know,' said Guy, 'but I know a man who might.'

Less than an hour later, Guy and Louisa were ringing Timothy Malone's doorbell. He came to the door and looked pleased to see Guy. 'Ah, hello!' he said. 'To what do I owe this pleasure? And I see you've brought a friend.' He looked behind him. 'I'm afraid the place is rather in a mess . . . '

'Please don't worry about that on my account,' said Louisa. She liked him instantly, with his air of faded grandeur and gentleness. From her time with the Mitfords, she could recognise a well-made shirt when she saw one, even when the collar was soft from years of washing.

'Then the more the merrier, I say. Do come in.'

The two of them were ushered into his room. Louisa took in the single bed, the damp corners and the unwashed cups in the sink. There was a newspaper on the table, the page folded for the cryptic crossword. Timothy saw her eye on it.

'I've been trying to do it all morning,' he said genially. 'Are you any good? You might help me with eleven down.'

Louisa shook her head. 'I'm afraid not,' she said and regretted it. She'd have liked to have sat with this man and given him some company for an hour or two.

'We can't stay long, I'm afraid,' said Guy when Timothy offered tea. 'We need your help with something. Can we sit?'

The three of them went to the table by the window, where the light was good. Guy handed Timothy the photograph. 'Could you tell me who those men are, if you recognise them?'

Timothy took it carefully and studied it, moving aside an empty glass.

'Of course. It's a few years ago, I'd say, but that's Roland Lucknor and Xander Waring. In Paris, by the looks of it.'

Guy and Louisa exchanged a look.

'Could you point and tell us which is which?' asked Guy, almost unable to get the words out for anticipation.

'Yes, that's Roland, on the left, with the moustache. Xander is on the right.'

Guy and Louisa stood on the pavement outside a few minutes later. 'What do we do now?' said Louisa.

'Now we need to identify him as Florence Shore's killer,' said Guy.

'Mabel Rogers would know if he was the man in the brown suit,' said Louisa.

'We need at least one more witness, if we can find them, otherwise it's just her word against his.'

'What about Stuart Hobkirk? He said someone had been to see him and we know it wasn't a policeman. Someone asking him intrusive questions and so on. If that was Roland – or Xander, whoever he is – would that help?'

Guy almost slapped her on the back. 'Yes, that's it. We're going to need Harry's help, though. Come with me.'

Harry ran his hands over his head and gave a low whistle. The three of them were in Victoria station, standing by the newspaper kiosk. Louisa had fetched Harry from the LB&SCR Police office and his curiosity had not been able to stop him from following her out. Guy had been waiting, trying to look anonymous by pretending to inspect the headlines. The owner had just asked him either to buy something or go away when Harry and Louisa arrived.

Harry had given Guy a nudge in the side and whispered, 'I can see what all the fuss is about now,' but Guy had shut him up. Now they had told Harry of the events and shown him the incriminating photograph.

'What are you thinking of doing next?' said Harry. 'I mean, it's all very well but the super's going to blow his top with all this stolen evidence. You're going to have to make it add up to something or get him to confess.'

'I know,' said Guy. 'I thought, if you could get the photograph sent by express to Stuart Hobkirk in Cornwall, then he could telegram to us if he recognises the man in the photograph as the one who went to see him, asking him lots of questions and so on. Because we think whoever that was was probably the killer.'

'How do you work that out?' said Harry.

'Because that person wasn't a policeman, but wanted to know about Florence Shore and the murder case. Who else would it be? If Hobkirk identifies the man in the photograph as the one we call Roland, then that gives us a witness connecting Roland to the murder. That's not all – we're going to go to Nancy's birthday ball on Saturday night. Roland Lucknor—'

'Or Xander,' interrupted Louisa.

'Or Xander,' said Guy, throwing her a grateful look, 'whatever his name is, he will be there.'

Louisa turned towards Harry. 'We're going to ask Mabel Rogers to come to the ball. That way she can get a good look at him, without him noticing, and tell us if he was the man in the brown suit that got on the train.'

Harry noticed the newspaper seller wigging his ears and shuffled the three of them further away. 'And then what?'

'Well, I thought – you could be there,' said Guy, 'to arrest him. We'd have enough to charge him by then.'

Harry looked doubtful. 'I'd have to get permission from Jarvis for all that.'

'I know,' said Guy, 'but you've got enough reason to ask him. I'm only asking for you, another police officer and a car.'

'Haigh said we needed more than the letter,' said Harry.

'I've got it now: I've got the photograph. All we need is for Stuart Hobkirk and Mabel Rogers to say that's the man they saw before and we've got him. We've got Florence Shore's killer.'

CHAPTER SIXTY-TWO

There was only a little over twenty-four hours until the dance for Nancy's eighteenth birthday. The journey back to the room Louisa had taken in the village seemed to be a thousand miles. She wasn't quite sure what to do with herself. She couldn't yet return to Asthall Manor, in spite of Lord Redesdale's assurances that he would be helping, because she didn't know if anything had been said to Lady Redesdale. The other servants, in any case, could not be told any of the details. She did, however, need to let Nancy know what the plan was, so asked a boy in the blacksmith's to cycle around with a message to her, asking if they could meet. There was an hour or so of daylight left.

While she waited, Louisa fidgeted and paced around the room until she thought she may as well go downstairs and ask Jonny's mother if she could help prepare supper or something. But as she was coming down, there was a knock at the front door. Nancy.

'Goodness, I rushed here on my bicycle,' said Nancy, dispensing with the niceties of greetings in all the excitement. 'Blor was in a frightful state about it, saying I need my sleep before tomorrow and what was I doing going out now and, well, you can imagine the rest.'

'Sorry,' said Louisa.

'Don't be!' said Nancy. 'I'm almost a grown-up now. Blor can't tell me what to do.' She peered into the gloom of the hallway, the door of the dusty parlour just beyond. 'Shall we go for a walk around the village?'

Louisa grabbed her coat and hat, and the two young women set off, arm in arm, slightly huddled against the cold. There was a great deal to tell Nancy.

'You're saying that Roland isn't Roland, he's Xander Waring?' said Nancy afterwards, slowly and in shock.

'I know it's a lot to take in,' said Louisa. She explained that the photograph was now on its way to Stuart Hobkirk and that they would wait for confirmation from him that the man they all knew as Roland was the one who had been to see him. And then, as delicately as she could, she explained that Guy Sullivan was going to see Mabel Rogers, to ask her to come to the party, so that she could identify 'Roland' as 'the man in the brown suit'.

'How will we explain her to Mrs Windsor?' asked Nancy.

'We'll have to ask Nanny Blor to say that she'd asked her down, as a friend of her twin sister's,' said Louisa. 'That's the best solution I can think of.'

'It probably is,' said Nancy. 'Also, Farve and I thought we could tell Mrs Windsor that you had been drafted in as an extra lady's maid for me and some of the guests staying over.'

'Thank you,' said Louisa. 'I know you and your parents must be finding this all very hard.'

'Worse things happen at sea,' said Nancy. 'I've had another idea – why don't I telegram to Mr Johnsen and ask him to come, too?'

'Mr Johnsen?'

'You remember, that funny little solicitor we went to see. I just thought that seeing as Muv is scrabbling around trying to find men to come to the dance, she wouldn't think it too odd if I said I had another name. I could ask him to look over Florence Shore's will again, see if anything else comes to light. It might help.'

'Everything is worth a try,' agreed Louisa.

The streets were almost empty bar the odd car driving through, its headlamps sweeping across them. Louisa saw lights come on in the windows of the village cottages, and pictured the cosy hearths glowing, the hot suppers being put down on the tables. Nancy walked silently for a while, absorbing it all. She was so different, thought Louisa, from the girl of only a few months ago, who would have babbled her alarm.

'I must say,' Nancy said at last, squaring her shoulders as she did so, 'I was hoping for drama at my dance but I didn't think it would quite be this.'

'Guy wants it all done with as little fuss as possible. We don't want to ruin your party. It's just that we can't see another time to bring everyone together. Apart from anything else, we don't know where Roland is; we only know that he is coming here tomorrow night.'

'Yes,' said Nancy, 'I know. Will you ask him about your uncle and find out what happened?'

This had crossed Louisa's mind several times in the past few days. She had been thinking about him, perhaps with more sympathy now that he might be dead. Hadn't he been a man driven to desperation by others? Didn't she, after all, know that feeling only too well? He certainly hadn't deserved the ending she'd had meted out to him by Roland, even if that hadn't been her intention in the first place.

'I suppose it will all come out eventually,' she said. 'I can't really say I like thinking about it.'

They walked in front of a window where the lights were on but the curtains hadn't been drawn and Louisa saw Nancy's womanly beauty for what felt like the first time. Her dark hair was tucked underneath, as if in a bob, and her pale face offset her dark eyes and long lashes, and her pink lips that always looked sulky even when she was in a good mood. The loose cut of her coat was more grown-up, too, with stylish pearl buttons and embroidered cuffs. Louisa felt drear by comparison, as if the shabbiness of her own coat had the power to return them to the status of nursery maid and eldest daughter. Yet Louisa knew she understood this emerging woman, who had had to take on such unexpected events in a matter of days and dealt with them with good humour.

'I had better be getting back,' said Nancy. 'Blor will go mad if she thinks I've been bicycling in the dark.' She saw Louisa's look of concern and laughed. 'I've got a lamp, don't worry.'

'I won't,' said Louisa. 'I know you can look after yourself these days.'

Nancy stood before her, her face softening. 'It's funny, I've been longing and longing for this to arrive. To be a grown-up. And now I find myself worrying how I'm going to do without you. We've had some fun, haven't we?'

Louisa felt a pang. How would *she* do without Nancy and her sisters? But she smiled and said, 'Yes, Miss Nancy, we've had some fun.'

CHAPTER SIXTY-THREE

~~~~~

L ouisa had got up when it was still dark, having hardly slept; Roland, Stephen and Guy had walked across her mind throughout the night. She dressed and got herself some bread and butter from the kitchen without even switching any lights on, not wishing to disturb Jonny's parents, before she crept out into the street. By the time she came to the familiar stone wall, the day had dawned with mist covering the fields beyond the gardens, isolating Asthall Manor as if it was an island.

Louisa braced herself and walked in through the back door to the kitchen, surprising, as she knew she would, Mrs Stobie and Ada. Mrs Stobie declared that she had nearly dropped an enormous saucepan of boiling water and Ada came rushing over to give her a hug.

'Whatever are you doing here?' she said. 'Mrs Windsor'll be in here any moment. It's the party tonight, you know. Nancy's eighteenth.'

'I know. I've been asked to come and help out as a sort of lady's maid for some of the guests,' said Louisa, hoping the quaver in her voice wouldn't catch her out in a lie. 'I think Mrs Windsor will have been told.'

Indeed, Mrs Windsor walked in at that moment, saw Louisa and said nothing, but acknowledged her with a curt nod before giving instructions to Mrs Stobie and sweeping out again. The three of them exchanged glances, then Mrs Stobie said she couldn't be standing about all day, didn't they know there was a party on. As it was going to be some time until she could do the real thing she was there to do, Louisa asked for some tasks and soon she found herself in the library with a duster, searching out nooks and crannies that had been missed in the previous days of preparation.

She was just reaching up to some of the higher shelves – tall men might notice the dust up there – when she heard a gasp and, on turning around, saw Pamela standing there, her dark brown hair hanging in thick, messy curls to her shoulders, a scruffy day dress stretched on a figure that was filling out. Perhaps she had never been called pretty but she had a sweetness that radiated.

'Louisa!' she said in happy amazement. 'When ever did you get here? Nobody told me you were coming back. *Are* you back?'

'Just for tonight,' said Louisa, 'to help with the guests and things. I think it was easier to ask somebody who knew their way around a bit.'

'Yes, I suppose so,' said Pamela. 'There do seem to be hundreds of people here, though. The fuss has been going on for weeks.'

'You'll like it when it's your turn.' Louisa smiled but Pamela pulled a pained face.

Two men came in carrying a huge stack of chairs each, obscuring their heads completely, so only their legs were visible beneath. They put them down with grunts and walked out again, only to be replaced by two further men bringing in a narrow table.

'Where have all these people come from?' asked Louisa.

'The neighbours,' said Pamela. 'They've all been lending us their gardeners and footmen; we've even got two butlers, which has put Mrs Windsor's nose out of joint, I can tell you. In return, they've got an invitation to the *party of the year.*' The last was said in an undeniably sarcastic tone, but Pamela couldn't really do meanness and she wrinkled her nose comically as she said it, making Louisa laugh.

'Do you know where Nancy is?' asked Louisa.

'Yes,' said Pamela. 'In her room preening. Shall I fetch her?'

'Could you just let her know I'm here?' said Louisa, and Pamela ran off.

At midday, Mrs Stobie was sweating in the kitchen, pulling out tray after tray of tiny puff pastry vol-au-vents, which borrowed maids were stuffing with prawns in mayonnaise. Louisa was nervously polishing teaspoons and even Ada had snapped twice at Mrs Farley's hallboy for dropping coal in the drawing room. The rush of people criss-crossing in all directions gave the house the atmosphere of Victoria station. Guests had started to arrive and were being shown to their rooms, but a few had wandered down and were in the morning room. The bell had rung several times with requests for cups of tea and plates of sandwiches, so Louisa had installed herself in the kitchen to help with these ad hoc requests. Mrs Stobie looked to be on the point of exploding already and Louisa wondered if she'd survive the night.

In amongst all the bustle, it was amazing that Louisa heard the gentle knock at the back door. Nobody went, so she opened it herself and saw Guy standing there, shivering slightly. The sun was high and the mist had dissolved but the air was still sharp.

'Oh, thank goodness,' he said, on seeing Louisa.

'You'd better come in,' she said. 'There's all sorts of people here today, so they won't notice you.'

Guy nodded. He looked as serious as she'd ever seen him. She took his coat from him and hung it in the porch, then handed him a duster.

'You'd better look busy,' she said, 'then no one will ask anything.'

'I keep thinking about all the things that could go wrong,' he whispered.

'Me too,' she whispered back.

They had just stepped into the kitchen when they saw a young maid in the doorway, asking if anyone had seen Louisa Cannon.

'That's me,' said Louisa.

'His Lordship asks if you could go to his study,' said the maid, dropping a small curtsey, then blushing as she realised she'd done the wrong thing. She scuttled off.

Louisa motioned to Guy to follow her. When they pushed open the heavy door, they saw Lord Redesdale and Nancy inside.

'You sent for me, my lord,' she said. 'Guy Sullivan is here. I thought perhaps he should come, too.'

Lord Redesdale harrumphed in reply. He was standing by his desk in his walking clothes – long spats and a worn tweed suit. Nancy was sitting on the sofa in riding jodhpurs and an old jumper, which Louisa knew to be her most comforting clothes, although she was rarely allowed to get away with wearing them outside the stables.

'We need to know the plan,' said Lord Redesdale.

Guy stepped forwards. 'Absolutely, my lord,' he said. 'Forgive me, I've only just got here.'

'Get on with it.'

Nancy mouthed 'sorry' to Guy but he shook his head; it didn't matter.

'We've had permission from the superintendent of the London, Brighton and South Coast Railway Police to make the arrest, and he has also enlisted Detective Inspector Haigh of the Metropolitan police force. We believe he may be sending down extra cars and men to come here tonight,' began Guy.

Lord Redesdale slammed his hand on the desk. 'I thought this was going to happen with the minimum of fuss? This isn't bloody Scotland Yard!'

'Nobody will enter the party,' said Guy, relieved to hear himself sounding calm and authoritative. More than he felt, at any rate. 'I will meet them and direct them to stay out of the way so that they are unseen by your guests.'

Lord Redesdale grunted again.

'Before that, however, Mabel Rogers is scheduled to arrive on the seven-thirty train. Louisa will go with the driver to collect her from the station. We will then ask her to identify Roland Lucknor.'

'That's all very well,' said Lord Redesdale, 'but where is Roland going to be? How are we going to keep an eye on him? According to you, he might start shooting us all like some crazed murderer!'

'I don't think that, my lord, but we do need to keep him in our sight. Might I suggest that that be Miss Nancy's role? He won't suspect anything then.' Guy looked to Nancy on the sofa.

'Yes,' she said, 'I'll keep him with me.'

'You must act as if all is well but don't leave yourself alone with him at any point,' said Guy. Louisa couldn't help feeling a wave of admiration for the way he was handling all this.

'I understand,' said Nancy.

The door was abruptly pushed open. Tom stood there open-mouthed. 'I say, Louisa!' he exclaimed, 'nobody told me you were here.' He rushed in and wrapped his arms around her waist.

Louisa patted his head and pulled him off her gently. 'I'll come up and see you,' she said quietly. 'You'd better get back to the nursery.'

Tom looked around the room and seemed to feel the seriousness that hung in the air. 'Hello, sir,' he said to his father. 'I just got back from school, you know. Special exeat for the party.'

'Yes, my boy,' said Lord Redesdale. 'I know. We'll go out in a bit, check the traps—' He broke off as he heard his wife calling out Tom's name, then she came into the room. She stopped when she saw who had gathered in there.

'Would somebody like to explain to me what's going on?' she said.

Nancy stood. 'Sorry, Muv, I meant to tell you. I asked Louisa back to help me and some of my friends,' she said. 'And this is Guy Sullivan – he's been lent by Mrs Farley for the day. Farve was just giving him some instructions.'

Lady Redesdale looked as if she was about to object, and in the strongest terms, then saw that there were other battles she was going to have to fight that day. 'Very well,' she said, glaring at Louisa. 'Just for today.' She left the room, dragging Tom with her.

'There's nothing more to say,' said Lord Redesdale. 'You'd better leave and do whatever it is you need to do.'

CHAPTER SIXTY-FOUR

～～～

At seven o'clock, the houseguests had started to assemble in the drawing room, the men in white tie, the women in long dresses and evening gloves, all eager to begin the festivities for the night. Footmen carried trays of filled champagne glasses and candles had been lit, throwing everybody into a soft, flattering light. Ivy had been draped over picture frames and vases of hothouse roses were placed on any exposed flat surface. The chatter was low but anticipation was high.

Lady Redesdale, in a grey silk dress, had joined them and was sitting on the sofa by the fire, her eye on her husband. She still looked rattled by the sight she had seen in the study earlier.

Louisa had peeked around the door, looking for Nancy. She went back out into the hall, where both the fires had been lit, setting off the sheen of the wooden panels, which had been highly polished for the event, and then saw her coming down the stairs. She was wearing a long sheath-like dress of silvery-white satin, revealing her narrow figure. Her hair was glossy and her lips looked as if they had had a dab of reddish colour.

Nanny Blor was standing in the hall, trying to keep control of

Diana and Decca, who were overexcited at all the commotion and running in circles around her legs, while she made exasperated noises. Unity stood quietly, staring into the fire, her blond bob shining from the light of the flames. When Nancy came in, standing in the middle of the hall for what could only have been dramatic effect, Nanny looked up at her and, in a voice heavy with concern, said, 'Miss Nancy, aren't you cold in that dress?'

This made Nancy and Louisa giggle, then Nanny caught it and, before long, so had Pamela, until all four of them were convulsed with laughter, tears rolling down Nancy's face.

'Oh, do stop!' she said. 'I shall mess myself up again.'

Louisa had enjoyed the break in the tension but her heart soon resumed its hammering, like a woodpecker. They didn't know exactly when Roland would arrive and it was this suspense that was putting her on edge. She jumped, then, when the front door was opened, but saw instead her old friend Jennie come in, on the arm of a man who bore the confidence of someone who had had luck and good looks since boyhood. Louisa stayed near the back of the hall, close to Nanny Blor, but Jennie saw her and came running over.

'Louisa,' she exclaimed and clutched her arm, before leaning her head in and whispering, 'I'm so pleased you're here. I still find these things terrifying.'

If only you knew, thought Louisa, but she smiled at her friend. 'You look beautiful,' she said, and she did, her golden hair and creamy skin offset perfectly by rose chiffon with long grey gloves and a tiara – the privilege of married women.

'Come and meet Richard,' said Jennie and pulled her over to her husband, who was talking to Nancy, wishing her a happy birthday.

Nancy seemed almost to have forgotten there was anything to think about than the party ahead of her that night, and was laughing gaily with him. She grabbed a glass of Champagne from a waiter and raised an eyebrow of triumph at her nursery maid as she did so. Louisa exchanged a few words with Richard, though she felt self-consciously aware of the fact that she was there as a maid and not as a guest, and as soon as she politely could, she broke off the conversation, saying she had things to do.

Nancy took Jennie and Richard on either side of her and the three went to the drawing room, the silver threads on Nancy's dress catching the light as she walked.

CHAPTER SIXTY-FIVE

~~~~~~

As Louisa watched Nancy and Jennie leave the room, she was startled by a gentle touch on her shoulder. Guy. 'It's time for you to leave for the station,' he whispered.

'Yes, of course,' stammered Louisa. 'Is there a car ready?'

'Round the back,' said Guy. He winked at her in an attempt at levity. 'You're frightfully posh now.'

Louisa tried to smile back but she was overwhelmed with nerves. It was all going to happen now; there was no turning back. 'Goodbye,' she said. 'Good luck.'

Having grabbed her coat and hat, Louisa stepped outside and saw a driver in livery standing beside Lord Redesdale's car. When Lady Redesdale took the car to London she occasionally paid a man from the village to be her driver, but this wasn't him. 'Are you meeting the seven-thirty train, miss?' he asked.

'Yes,' said Louisa. 'I think we need to get a move on.'

The driver doffed his cap and Louisa had the briefest sensation of what it must be to be rich and have drivers. It wasn't unpleasant.

*

Guy, meanwhile, had to stop himself from running out after her. The truth was, something was itching under his skin. For all that they had their plans in place, something wasn't sitting quite right with him. He walked out of the hallway and tried to find a quiet corner somewhere but it was impossible. Although the party hadn't quite got into the full swing yet, there was an atmosphere of jubilation that was hard to ignore. From the kitchen came a hubbub of heat and crashing pans, and there were still hired hands quick-marching along the passageways, each one carrying something or at least with a look of purposeful intent upon their faces. In the end, he chanced upon what must have been Mrs Stobie's office, a tiny room barely larger than the desk and chair squeezed into it. Cookbooks were piled on the desk and there were scraps of paper with notes that looked like proposed menus. Guy checked that nobody was looking and slipped in. With the door closed, he could almost shut out the noise beyond.

Guy took Florence's letter to Mabel from his pocket and laid it flat on the desk before him. He read it again, trying to see if there was a detail he had missed.

I think Roland killed Xander.

Why didn't she write that Xander killed Roland? Surely she must have recognised that the man leaving the hut wasn't Roland? Unless Xander had started the impersonation immediately, put on his friend's uniform and the officer's hat, and then perhaps the darkness and the shadows had helped him fool her. In the photograph, the two men had had a certain similarity to them; once Roland's moustache had been shaved off, it might have been difficult to tell the difference.

If Florence had gone to Roland's flat to confront him, would she have dared to do so alone if she suspected him of being a killer? When she saw him, she must have immediately realised that he was not, in fact, Roland, but Xander. Had she suspected that beforehand?

Guy took the two bank books out of his pocket and put them on the desk, too. Why was Xander's bank book showing money being paid out for the care of Roland's godmother in the nursing home? Then there were the large cash withdrawals from Roland's account. Some of these sums were very similar to the payments for the British Home and Hospital for Incurables, and Guy could only suppose that Xander was using the money paid in by Lord Redesdale to fund those bills. This in itself did not seem quite like the act of a callous murderer. Then there were those other cheques cashed, annotated by a PO box address. Who could those have been for? Florence Shore? Had he been paying her to keep quiet?

Something still did not add up correctly and Guy was running out of time to work it out.

CHAPTER SIXTY-SIX

At a quarter past seven, Guy was back in the hall, hovering, trying to look as inconspicuous as possible by stoking the fire. He had the sense of being in his own pocket of calm, as the hubbub around him got louder and the lights became brighter while the evening outside grew darker. The guests had come out of the drawing room now and were making their way to the library – the main room for the party – but with new guests constantly arriving in the hall, they became a teeming mass of squeals and twirls as girls showed off their dresses and exclaimed in delight as they saw each other. There were also a number of older men and women – neighbours, presumably. There were very few young men. Two men arrived, leaning heavily on walking sticks, revealing flattened white hair when they removed their top hats. Louisa had told him that Lord Redesdale had been instructed to round up men from the House of Lords to try and swell the numbers. Hardly the stuff of romantic dreams for an eighteen-year-old girl, thought Guy.

Lord and Lady Redesdale were now close to the front door, greeting the guests as they came in, once Mrs Windsor had announced their names. Then, through the front door, walked a lean, well-dressed man Guy recognised instantly from the photograph: the man on the right – Xander Waring.

Lord Redesdale went towards him and shook his hand. 'Dear boy,' he said, 'it's good to see you.'

Guy noticed that the man was less hearty in his response, his eyes shifting over the other guests. Although he knew Roland – he couldn't call him Xander – wouldn't know who he was, Guy kept himself to the edges, making sure he drew no attention to himself.

Nancy overheard her father and broke away from a gaggle of girls, like goslings around a goose. Guy watched as she glided towards Roland, her face tilted up, her greeting effusive. 'Mr Lucknor,' she said, 'now we can begin the party.' She gave him a broad smile and Roland looked back at her as if she had offered him deliverance. 'Walk me into the library,' she said. 'We have to go outside to get there, as you know, but Farve has cleverly had oil stoves lit along the way to keep everyone warm.'

As soon as Roland had handed over his coat and hat to a maid standing by, Nancy took his proffered arm and walked out through the front door, calling out to her friends behind to follow her.

Lord Redesdale turned and caught Guy's eye just before he went out with them. The look was not a friendly one.

So now Roland was here. Where, thought Guy nervously, was Harry and the rest of the police? And when would Mabel and Louisa get here?

CHAPTER SIXTY-SEVEN

A t the station, Louisa stood by the car with the driver, waiting for the train to get in. Aside from their exchange at the house, they hadn't spoken. He had driven fast and they had pulled in almost at the same time as the train had braked at the platform. Only a minute or two later, the passengers started to come out of the station. Louisa realised that although Guy had given her a brief description, she wasn't entirely sure what Mabel Rogers looked like. One old lady walked out and Louisa prepared herself, but then at the last second she was greeted by someone else and the two walked off. Almost one of the last to emerge was a woman, not old but not in her prime either. Before Louisa had moved towards her, the driver had opened the car door in readiness.

'Miss Rogers?' said Louisa, as the woman approached.

'Yes. Have you come from Asthall Manor?' said Mabel, her voice timid. She was swamped by the fur coat she was wearing.

'I have,' said Louisa. 'Please, do get in the car. It's cold out here.'

Mabel took nervous steps towards them. She caught the eye of the driver and handed him her umbrella without saying a word, then climbed into the car, rather awkwardly, keeping a tight grip on her handbag. Louisa got in on the other side, forgetting to wait for the driver to come around and open the door for her. She was not used to drivers opening doors for her. She was not even especially used to cars. Sitting next to Mabel on the back seat, she rather felt the two of them shared the same unease.

After they had exchanged polite comments about the journey, the business of why they were both in the car together raised its head.

'Is the man there?' asked Mabel.

'I'm not sure,' said Louisa. 'He wasn't when I left but he was expected to arrive soon, so he should be by the time we get there. It shouldn't take us more than half an hour at the most.'

'I see,' said Mabel, her mouth a slash, almost invisible.

'Don't be nervous,' said Louisa, kindly. 'He won't be able to do anything to you. There will be plenty of policemen, and Lord Redesdale, all on the lookout.'

Mabel nodded but her face looked no less vexed. Louisa was conscious of what they had asked this poor woman to do – to come on a train journey out of London, to a house and situation that would be very intimidating, and confront the man who had killed her long-term friend and companion. The man who had robbed her of a happy old age and left her instead in penury and loneliness.

'I'm so sorry,' said Louisa, hoping Mabel would understand what she was apologising for. 'If there was another way to do this, we would have done it. But by the end of tonight, it will all be over and justice will be done for your friend.'

Mabel said nothing but looked to the side. Louisa saw the

driver's head angle slightly, as if resisting the urge to turn round. If he was listening, he must have thought it all very curious indeed.

Just twenty minutes and they would be at the party. She crossed her fingers that Guy was ready and waiting for them both.

CHAPTER SIXTY-EIGHT

G uy went outside the front door to see if there was any sign of Harry. Cars were still pulling up and disgorging young women in dresses that seemed to carry their own light, but the rush of arrivals was over. There was a delicious smell from the kitchens and Guy's stomach rumbled; he hadn't eaten much that day. The cigarette smoke and the quick, high notes of music that came up on the air jangled against his nerves, making him feel hollow inside. Mrs Windsor was directing everybody immediately through the Cloisters to the library and they moved like a circus parade through town, all noise and celebration, feathers and triumphant cries. Had someone produced a trumpet and a flag, it would have seemed entirely in keeping.

Guy could see the oil stoves throwing off thick smoke, which, judging by the coughs of some of the guests, was blowing in the wrong direction. There was a lull and then Guy saw Harry come around the large oak tree that stood in the drive, looking particularly diminutive as he led three officers in Metropolitan uniform and, to Guy's shock, Detective Inspector Haigh.

Lord Redesdale had also come out of the library and was

walking towards Guy. 'I say,' he said, 'must everyone be out here? I don't want any talk.'

Haigh stretched an arm out. 'Good evening, Lord Redesdale. We appreciate everything you're doing to help us.'

'Yes, well . . .' said Lord Redesdale, caught off-guard by this. 'I'll show you the way to my study. You can wait in there, though I'm still not entirely clear exactly what we're waiting *for*.'

The men were all standing awkwardly to the side of the front door, when a boy came up on a bicycle. 'Telegram for Sergeant Conlon,' he said. 'I'm guessing that's one of you,' he added cheekily, as he caught sight of the uniforms.

Harry took it from him and the boy zipped off as sharply as he had arrived. 'This will be from Stuart Hobkirk,' he said. 'I told him to send any messages here.'

'Who is Stuart Hobkirk and why is he sending telegrams to other men at my house?' said Lord Redesdale in a voice that threatened to tip into a roar at any moment.

'He's Florence Shore's cousin,' said Guy. 'He told me that someone had been to see him, asking lots of questions about the case, and we know that it wasn't a policeman because none of us had been sent there. We sent him the photograph, to identify Roland in it. It will give us another witness that connects him with the murder.'

'Do you want me to open it or not?' said Harry.

'Give it to me,' said Haigh, and took it. He read it and his face fell.

'What?' said Guy. 'What does it say?' He prayed Haigh wouldn't hand it to him to read; he'd never be able to make it out in the dim light.

'It says that he doesn't recognise either of the men in the photograph.'

There was a deathly pause.

'Well, what does that mean?' said Lord Redesdale. 'Does that mean Roland *isn't* the man you want?'

'Just a moment,' said Harry. 'Perhaps Roland wasn't working alone. We know it had to be two people who were there at the time of the attack. Whoever was working with Roland might be the one who went to see Hobkirk.'

'Maybe,' said Guy, 'but something isn't right. I need to get closer to Roland, see if he says anything else this evening.'

Haigh nodded. 'Good idea.'

'Lord Redesdale, may I have your permission to borrow a footman's outfit?' said Guy, turning to the bewildered baron.

'All I wanted was a nice quiet life,' muttered Lord Redesdale. Without answering the question he wandered off back through the Cloisters.

'Come on. We haven't got a moment to lose,' said Guy, marvelling at his ability to take charge in front of a detective inspector and wondering simultaneously if it would ever happen again in his life. If only his brothers could see him now. 'Mabel Rogers will be arriving any minute.'

CHAPTER SIXTY-NINE

◦────◦

The driver, Louisa noticed, was not haring down the roads at the same breakneck speed they had gone to the station, but as they didn't have a train to meet, perhaps this made more sense. It was safer, at any rate.

When they were still a good ten minutes from the house, Mabel turned towards Louisa slightly, as if her neck was stiff. 'I've been thinking,' she said, 'perhaps it would be better if you asked Roland Lucknor to come out to me, in the car. Rather than me going into the party.'

'You mustn't worry about everybody at the party,' said Louisa. 'They're all very friendly.' She wasn't quite sure this was entirely true but she felt Mabel needed the reassurance.

'I would feel safer in the car,' said Mabel, 'and if we get him on his own, he wouldn't be able to run, would he? Perhaps we should stop the car before we even get to the house, just a little way off, then he could be brought out to me there?'

'I'm not really sure . . .' Louisa began but she saw the worry etched on Mabel's face. 'We'll see. I'll ask G— the policeman in charge, to see what he can arrange. I promise you, you're in completely safe hands, no harm will come to you.'

'Thank you,' said Mabel, and turned back to face the front again. As she did so, her coat fell open slightly and Louisa saw a pretty necklace catch the light. It was a gold chain with two amethysts hanging from it. Anxious to distract Mabel from what lay ahead, Louisa complimented her on it.

'What a lovely necklace,' she said. 'It's rather unusual, isn't it? Two amethysts.' As she said it, she pulled herself up short. She had remembered something.

Something very important.

Back at the house, Guy was in a small room near the kitchen – an old scullery, he supposed – struggling to put on a footman's trousers. Inevitably they were too short and he tried to pull his socks up as high as possible so that the gap wouldn't be visible.

A young man ran in. 'Have you seen a chauffeur's livery in here?' he asked.

'What?' said Guy.

'A chauffeur's livery. I usually have it in here. I come down and drive Lady Redesdale now and then, and they asked me to help tonight with the guests and I can't bloody well find it. I hung it up while I had a cigarette. I'm supposed to be picking up more guests and my jacket and cap have gone completely bloody missing!'

CHAPTER SEVENTY

~~~~~~~~

G uy, uncomfortable but dressed in a footman's costume – he couldn't really bring himself to call it a uniform – walked into the library, which was now full to bursting of party guests. A three-piece orchestra was playing gay tunes from the corner, smoke hung in a blue pall above them and the overwhelming sensation was of riotous colour and noise. Nobody seemed to talk or to listen, but to shout almost incessantly at the person standing opposite them. The older women wore tiaras and understated dresses but the young had feathers, chokers and sequins, tassels that swung from their hips and wore stockings of all colours. They kicked their heels and fiddled with their strings of pearls, flashing white teeth and diamonds in their ears.

Guy felt rather sorry for Harry, missing out on this bit. He stood in a corner, close to Nancy, who had left Roland talking to her next-door neighbour, a safe old chap who was renowned for his endless anecdotes about the Boer war.

'You'd think it was an anagram, the way he goes on,' Guy heard Nancy say to a friend, and the friend laughed just a little too enthusiastically at the joke.

Guy was holding a silver tray with nothing on it. He'd intended to look as if he was collecting empty glasses but soon realised he didn't trust himself not to drop them.

A passing young buck pointed to him and shouted over to his friend, 'I say, do you think that bally waiter can't see he's got no champers on his tray? Have you ever seen such thick glasses?'

'The wrong kind of glasses!' his friend hooted back and Guy flushed in fury but said nothing.

His attention was soon distracted as he saw Nancy approached by a much older man with a stomach that arrived at its destination a good two steps ahead of the feet.

'Mr Johnsen,' said Nancy politely. 'So good of you to come.'

'Jolly good of you to ask me,' said Mr Johnsen. 'Lovely Champagne.'

'So I see,' said Nancy and risked half an eye at her friend, who giggled behind her hand.

'I've been thinking about that case you came to see me about,' he said.

Nancy's attention was caught. She turned her back to her friend with an apologetic smile and bent a little towards the solicitor. 'And what have you thought?' she asked.

'Well, it's just . . . I thought it was funny that you said her brother, Offley Shore, you know, was in such a temper about the will because he was never the original recipient of the estate that Miss Shore established.' He stopped and took another big gulp of wine.

Nancy looked at Guy and he gave her a nod. She needed to find out more.

CHAPTER SEVENTY-ONE

The car drew up and parked by the side of the road, a short distance from the gates of Asthall Manor. Louisa could see the rain falling in the light of the headlamps, quite heavy now.

'We're here,' said Louisa to Mabel, a little pointlessly.

'Bring the man here,' said Mabel, 'but not anybody else. Please.'

The driver handed Louisa the umbrella belonging to Mabel. 'You'll need this, miss,' he said. 'I'm sorry, but I'd better wait here. I can't leave the car and Miss Rogers alone.'

'Yes, of course,' said Louisa. She took the umbrella, which had a long, straight wooden handle, completely plain but for a strange, dark mark. It flashed through her mind that it looked like blood.

Nancy sidled a little closer to Mr Johnsen. 'Who was the original beneficiary?' she asked.

'Her friend, Mabel Rogers,' said Mr Johnsen. 'She'd been the recipient for years and then it was suddenly changed. I checked the papers again just before I came here. I think I'd forgotten because the funny thing was, she never came to the office herself. She always sent a friend, a man called Jim Badgett. I never quite understood why but he only relayed the messages between us so far as I could tell.'

Nancy turned to Guy, who was now standing close by. 'Don't you see?' she said, unable to contain herself. 'It's not who the will was changed *to* that matters. It's who it was changed *from*.'

CHAPTER SEVENTY-TWO

L ouisa looked at the handle and understood. The fur coat. The necklace. The closed window of the train door. It had all happened at Victoria station.

'It was you, wasn't it?' she said. 'You killed your friend.'

Mabel said nothing.

'Did Roland even have anything to do with it at all?'

There was no sound but for the click-click of the windscreen wipers. No sight beyond the pitch black outside the car windows.

Guy and Nancy pushed their way through the guests, one or two of them shouting out after Nancy, bemused at her leaving her own party. They ran from the library and into the Cloisters, the smoke from the stoves still thick and odorous.

'Where is Louisa?' said Nancy. 'Why isn't she here yet?'

'She's with Mabel,' said Guy, his mind a clash of thoughts like a whirligig. 'I see it now: Mabel has come here to frame Roland, not identify him.' He stopped and went still. 'The driver.' The realisation of the danger he had put Louisa in made his heart turn to ice.

'What?' said Nancy. 'Talk sense, for God's sake.'

'The driver,' said Guy, trying not to stammer over his words. 'That is, your regular driver, he was missing his uniform tonight – someone had taken it.'

'You think Mabel has an accomplice? Someone who was here?'

'Of course,' said Guy. 'She didn't do it herself. She had a man with her. Two people, we said, remember?' He ran his hands through his hair and his eyes sprang wide. 'That man, the porter. Jim. How could I have been so stupid?'

'What's going on?' said a man's voice. Nancy jumped. 'I saw you run out. Are you all right?'

'Oh, Roland!' said Nancy as she turned around. 'It wasn't you, it *wasn't* you.' She threw herself into his arms.

'What do you mean?' said Roland, thoroughly at a loss as to what was going on.

Guy hesitated. This man may not have killed Florence Shore but he was not free from suspicion altogether. 'Mabel Rogers is on her way here with Louisa and we have reason to believe she is responsible for the murder of Florence Shore.'

At once, Guy saw the shock register on Roland's face. 'Where are they?' he said.

'Close by, we think,' said Guy, 'they're driving from the station.'

'We need to get a car and find them,' said Roland. 'We need to go *now*.'

CHAPTER SEVENTY-THREE

⁓

The blood rushed in Louisa's ears, momentarily blocking all sound. The black of night outside the car made her feel blind, like a mole. She pushed open the heavy car door and stumbled out, immediately assaulted by the pouring rain, which cleansed her. Though she held the umbrella in her hand, she did not think to open it. A surge of power went through her, as if the fear and the knowledge she now held within her would give her the strength to swim the Channel. She felt unassailable. Then she turned and saw the glint of a knife and knew that she wasn't.

Louisa walked in front of the car, its engine humming, the head-lamps like a lighthouse in the ocean. Everything was happening at the pace of her heartbeat, fast but rhythmic. Mabel and the driver came around from the other side of the car and stood before her, their pale faces like satellite moons to her burning sun, her rage. She thought of Florence Shore, that brave, steady woman who had done so much for so many, met with a violent, undeserved, ignominious ending on a train. Abandoned without dignity some-where between Victoria and Lewes, broken spectacles on the floor, underclothes torn, sentimental jewels ripped from her fingers. Left to be discovered by three slow-moving labourers at Polegate. She had deserved better; anyone deserved better. It enraged Louisa, the anger and the courage engulfing her like flames licking the roof of a tall building.

'It was you,' she said. 'You killed Florence Shore.'

Mabel said nothing, her eyes blacker than the sky above her.

'I suppose he did it for you.' Louisa gestured to the driver, the knife in his hand. He looked old, she thought, too old for this. She noticed a scar on his chin. 'That letter – you knew the batman was shot by his officer, that it wasn't suicide. It wasn't Florence who went to argue with him at the flat. The lady in the fur coat – it was you.' She was almost talking to herself now, daring herself to say it out loud. If you said it, it came true.

In a flash, like lightning in a storm, the driver ran over and grabbed Louisa, holding the knife to her throat.

'Careful, Jim!' cried Mabel, and Louisa heard the fear catching in her voice. 'We don't know who's here.'

The air moved around them; there was a surge from somewhere, Louisa didn't know where. She could no longer tell what was her, what was water, what was another body. Then Mabel shouted and Louisa saw Roland. He came out of the dark, into the headlights, like a dancer stepping on the stage. He ran to Mabel and held her by the shoulders, swung her in front of him and she moved like a rag doll.

'Take me,' he said, looking at Jim. 'If you are looking for vengeance, it's me you want, not Louisa. Let her go.'

Louisa felt the knife, cold, pressed beneath her chin. Jim's grip did not slacken but she felt a faltering, an involuntary movement. The rain sliced almost horizontally on to her, blinding her; she couldn't wipe her eyes and squeezed them shut, hoping to see when she opened them again. The shapes of those around her were blurry but she could hear their voices.

'You know too much,' said Mabel, but she spoke with a tremor.

'Give it up, Mabel,' said Roland. 'The police are coming; you can't run from this.'

There must have been a signal as the arms around her dropped and Louisa found she was shaking on release. She stumbled backwards and was caught by another pair of arms, softer, around her shoulders. There was a murmur in her ear and she knew it was Nancy. They were out of the headlights, cloaked by night and rain. Louisa couldn't take her eyes off the sight before her. Roland had let go of Mabel and his hands were in the air as he walked towards Jim. Mabel looked shrunken, her hat drooping, her fur coat flattened. She looked frightened and very alone.

Roland kept his hands up, his mouth forming a straight line. Jim held the knife before him like Excalibur but his movements were slow, betraying fear and indecisiveness. Whatever he had done, he had not meant it to lead to this point, thought Louisa. As she watched, she felt herself pulled gently further backwards and then another movement in the air beside her. There was the sound of bone on bone, knuckle on jaw. Cracks like ancient branches torn in a storm.

Adjusting to the shapes and the spotlight, Louisa saw it was Guy grappling with Jim – the knife now knocked to the ground. It lay in a puddle by a wheel of the car, useless now. The two men fought, flailing and grunting, their faces soon streaked with mud, then blood. Roland circled them, waiting to step in when the gap was wide enough. Before he could, the fight slowed down, the sound of their short breaths louder than the punches, their legs staggering, their feet slipping.

As the fight lost speed, there was a roar of engines, the clunk of brakes and doors opening. The spotlight on them had enlarged from the added headlights, then several uniformed policemen rushed in and the two men were separated. Guy had his hands on his knees and was gulping air. Roland had receded into the darkness. Louisa saw a policeman's hand pick up the knife from the ground and put it in his pocket.

Louisa and Nancy huddled closer together, their arms wrapped around each other. Nancy's thin dress clung to her but Louisa's coat was heavy on her own shoulders; her hat had long been knocked off. The whole thing had taken only minutes but they were shivering as if they had been standing outside for hours.

Louisa looked for Mabel and saw her step to the side, glancing at Jim, who was now held, arms behind his back, wheezing, his mouth pulled back in pain. Louisa was about to shout out, to stop her, when another man came forwards and stopped her. Detective Inspector Haigh had arrived as the rain eased, the storm over.

'Mabel Rogers, I'm arresting you on suspicion of the murder of Florence Nightingale Shore.'

CHAPTER SEVENTY-FOUR

~~~~~

As the police took off Mabel and Jim, Nancy and Louisa started to run back to the house. Roland was with them, his arm at their backs, worry etched on his face.

'Quick,' said Nancy, 'let's go to the nursery. I'm going to have to change.'

Nobody was in the hall and they were able to run up the stairs without being seen, although they left wet footprints behind them. The fire was still glowing from earlier and Roland stood shivering beside it while Louisa ran to the linen cupboard to grab an armful of warm towels. The nursery was empty, the children having been promised a good eyeful of the party.

They were all still in shock at what had happened and Louisa knew the story wasn't over yet. Roland sat on Nanny's armchair, using a towel to absorb the wet as best he could.

Nancy had left the room briefly and came back in with a dressing gown on. She laughed a little. 'It's a bit like the first time I met you,' she said.

'What do you mean?' said Roland.

'That ball at the Savoy, it had been raining that night too.

Lou-Lou and I thought we looked like drowned rats then! It was nothing compared to this.'

Roland tried to raise a smile but couldn't.

Nancy kneeled before him. 'I'm so sorry but I have to go back downstairs as soon as I can.' Her face was flushed from the warmth after being outside. 'I suppose I shan't see you again, shall I?'

Roland shook his head sadly.

Nancy took his hand and held it gently. 'Perhaps you might write and let me know how you are. I wish you the very best of luck, you know.'

Roland gave her hand a small squeeze and let it go. 'Thank you. Now, get back to your party. Everyone will be wondering where you are.'

Nancy gave a short laugh but her excitement was palpable. As if the party wasn't enough, now there was a tale of great drama in the middle of it. She gave him a last fond look and ran out of the room to change and go back to her friends.

With Nancy gone, the atmosphere changed. Louisa knew that Guy would be occupied with Mabel and Jim. She certainly wasn't going to join the party, nor would the man sitting opposite her, looking worriedly into the fire. It was time to discover the truth. She decided that with everything that had gone on that evening, she may as well be completely direct.

'Who are you? Are you Roland Lucknor or are you Xander Waring?'

'I'm Xander,' he said, and the very act of saying it seemed to change his face, like a chameleon moving from a branch to a leaf, from fear to relief. Louisa waited for him to say more. 'I didn't kill Roland. I mean, I did –' he breathed out, as if he'd held it in for years – 'but not like that. He didn't want to live. If you'd been there, in Ypres, you'd have understood too. He was in constant pain; he woke up screaming every night. He'd been signed off to return to England but he couldn't see the point of living.'

'Did you try to talk him out of it?'

'Of course, every night, we talked all the time. But he became obsessed with it. We knew we couldn't return to our life in Paris before the war; it wouldn't exist any more and France had been ruined for us. But there was nothing in England for Roland. He wasn't like other men; he wasn't strong. The only thing he was afraid of was his father. They hadn't seen each other for years but his father was a missionary in Africa. Roland knew that his father would suffer terribly if his son were to take his own life. The shame and the stigma would never leave him.'

Louisa knew this to be true. Hadn't she learned as much from Bill's death in the summer?

'I argued with him. I told him that his father deserved some suffering – he'd done nothing for his son. They'd barely seen each other for years. Even when Roland's mother died, he didn't see his father. Why shouldn't he understand how unhappy his only son was? Roland wouldn't listen and then he suggested that we swap identities.'

'Why?'

'He knew there would be no one to miss me if I was reported to have died. No one to be shamed by my suicide. I was brought up in an orphanage and there was certainly no one there who still cares for me. I have never known who my parents were. He said it would please him to know that I could enjoy the advantages of being him, the officer status, the possibility of an inheritance when his father eventually died. I told him I cared nothing for all that, I only wanted him to live.' Louisa could see the sadness leaching out of him like moonlight behind clouds. 'When we heard that I was to be sent back to the front line while he was to return to England, that decided it for him.'

'What do you mean?'

'Not only would we be separated but I'd be back in the trenches, in the line of fire. Roland said we were only pre-empting something that would happen anyway. You must believe me when I say I tried to stop this plan but he said either he would kill himself as himself, or we could go through with this plan and he could do it as me. There was nothing I could do to persuade him otherwise. So it came to it – it was the last night before I was to return to the front line and he was to be put on the train to England. We swapped our clothes and identity tags, and Roland shaved off his moustache. I still thought I might be able to talk him out of it but he had his gun and he said goodbye . . .' His eyes were filled with tears now, his voice trembling.

'Go on,' said Louisa gently.

'He said goodbye and he turned the gun on himself but his hands were shaking. He always was a rotten shot; he'd barely managed to shoot even when the Germans were pointing in his direction. He couldn't kill a sodding rat in a trench . . .' The words were thick and fast now, the tears coursing down his cheeks. 'He missed and he started crying, saying he couldn't do anything properly and he . . . he handed me the gun and said I must do it for him. I tried to say no but he was hysterical and he put the gun in my hands, and put the gun in his mouth and I did it. I did it, I killed him, but not . . . I didn't want to, don't you see? Don't you understand? I loved him. He was the only person who had ever, ever cared for me and I loved him.' Roland sank to the floor on his knees, his head in his hands, and Louisa couldn't help herself; she went to him and put her arms around him and held him until his sobs ebbed away.

'I see now,' she said. 'I do see.'

He looked up at her, a man stripped of everything, and begged her forgiveness, as if she was the angel that could absolve him. 'There's nothing to forgive you for, even if it was my place to give it,' said Louisa. She felt as if his own heart ached in her chest. 'But you had better go tonight, and quickly. Guy may come looking for us.'

They walked quietly down the back steps. There were still maids and footmen running back and forth from kitchen to library, with trays of full and empty glasses.

At the back door, Louisa hesitated. 'Wait, before you go, I still have something to ask you.'

'Your uncle.'

Louisa nodded.

'I didn't do anything that you need to be afraid of,' he said.

'You didn't kill him?'

'No.'

Louisa felt light-headed. She had been reprieved. 'What will you do now?'

'I don't think there's anything for me here any more. I'm going to go back to France, or maybe Italy. Try and build a new life. I'd even settle for my old life in Paris, the one I had before the war. I'd like to try and write a novel. I started one before.'

'You should. That sounds like a good idea.'

'There's only one person I'm concerned for and that's Roland's godmother, Violet Temperley,' he said. 'She's in a home and she gets few visitors. I will ensure the bills are always paid but might you go and see her for me?'

'Of course I will. I'm sure Mr Sullivan will, too,' said Louisa,

393

and the fact that she knew she could rely on Guy's kindness of heart felt like a smooth pebble in her hand.

Then Xander Waring went down the stairs and out of all their lives.

CHAPTER SEVENTY-FIVE

In the small hours of that night, when the last of the revellers had been poured into a car and the music had stopped playing, Louisa and Guy were summoned to the drawing room, where they found Nancy with Lord and Lady Redesdale.

Louisa entered the room hesitantly, unsure if she had left the frying pan to leap into the fire. She and Guy had discussed it at length when the police had left. Haigh and Harry had returned to London with Mabel and Jim but before they'd gone, Guy had sat with Haigh while they'd taken Mabel's initial statement down. Afterwards, he had remained at Asthall Manor with Louisa, the two of them reasoning that it wouldn't be right to disappear after they had brought such drama to the house. So they had huddled in Mrs Windsor's sitting room, waiting until it was all over, Guy trying to reassure Louisa that her former employers could only be pleased with her for having saved their daughter from an uncertain fate at the hands of Roland Lucknor.

'I don't think they'll see it that way,' said Louisa, more than once. She had told Guy of Roland's confession and had had to admit that she had deliberately allowed him to leave and evade arrest. 'I know that what he has done is wrong,' she said, 'but I understand his reasons for doing it. Desperation can drive any of us to do things we wouldn't normally believe ourselves capable of.' For which, Guy could only love her more.

Nancy ran over to them as they came into the room. Her hair had come a little loose, her lipstick was long rubbed off and her eyes betrayed two or three glasses of wine drunk. She looked flushed and womanly, though her pleasure at the party having gone well was still delightfully youthful.

'Please, come and sit with us,' said Nancy, gesturing to the sofas where Lord and Lady Redesdale were sitting, the fire burning, the candles low. 'We want to discuss *everything*.'

Louisa could not quite bring herself to sit down in front of them but she did not want to refuse the invitation either, so settled for perching on the arm of the sofa opposite and Guy stood by her. A tray had been brought in with hot cocoa for the women and port for the men, with a plate of savouries.

Lady Redesdale was the first to speak, and Louisa held her breath until she had finished. 'I gather there was quite a to-do at the start of the evening, of which I was unaware,' she said drily.

Louisa wasn't sure what to make of this statement. 'I'm so sorry, my lady—' she began.

'No need to apologise,' Lady Redesdale cut her off. 'The guests were in ignorant bliss, too, and as you brought matters to a successful conclusion, we can only congratulate you both on doing so with such efficacy.'

Louisa was moved. 'Thank you, my lady,' she managed. There was an awkward pause. 'I'd like to explain why I got involved, if I may.'

Lady Redesdale turned her head towards Louisa, her demeanour as cool as a tall glass of iced water.

'I've become very fond of Miss Nancy,' said Louisa, daring herself to look at Lady Redesdale directly. 'Well, of all the children. When I realised that Mr Lucknor posed a danger to the family, I knew I had to do all that I could to get him out of the way.' She saw a thick skin forming on the top of her milky drink. 'I am sorry that it had to be done here, on this night, but there didn't seem to be any other way.'

'Thank you, Louisa,' said Lady Redesdale. 'I can't say that it's all clear to me quite how or why it happened, but I have seen the sincerity of your intentions.'

Louisa wondered if she should find more to say on this but Nancy, sitting on the rug by the fire, broke in impatiently. 'So tell us, Mr Sullivan, why did she do it?' There was no mistaking who she meant or what she was referring to.

Guy was not used to being at the centre of so much attention, but with Louisa at his side he was emboldened to speak. 'It seems that after the war, Mabel overheard Roland Lucknor introduce himself to someone quite by chance. She knew that he wasn't who he said he was, but rather than telling Florence, who was still in France, and turning him over to the police for impersonation and murder, she began blackmailing him with the help of her porter, Jim.'

'That seems an extraordinary thing for someone like that to do. I mean, someone who had worked as a war nurse,' said Lady Redesdale, her silk dress as immaculate at the end of the night as it had been at the beginning. 'They are often marvellous creatures.'

'Absolutely,' said Guy, 'but I gather she felt quite desperate. She said she had returned from many years at war broken by the experience and had nothing at the end of it. No money, no home, only lodgings at a charitable institution in Hammersmith. I have been there and I can tell you that it is not somewhere that you would wish to end your years. She saw the chance for some easy money.'

'But what about Florence?' asked Louisa. 'Wasn't she going to end her years with her?'

'I think that things were not easy between them after the war,' said Guy.

'The war did ghastly things to people,' said Lord Redesdale. 'If you weren't there, you can't imagine what it was like.'

'No,' said Guy, though he felt less ashamed than he did before at this kind of easy reference that former soldiers often made. He knew now that war was not the only way to serve one's country. 'Anyhow, it seems that Florence discovered Mabel and Jim were blackmailing him and demanded that they stop and he be turned over to the police. Mabel refused and the two of them had a terrible row. It was Florence's birthday, she had bought herself a fur coat and Mabel said it enraged her. That she should have nothing and Florence had money to throw around, as she put it. Florence then told Mabel she had cut her out of the will, that she was going to go down to the coast to look for a cottage to buy for her retirement and Mabel was no longer part of that plan.'

'Poor woman,' said Louisa. 'She must have been completely heartbroken.'

'What about the man that was seen jumping down from the train at Lewes?' asked Nancy.

'That was a stroke of luck for Mabel,' said Guy. 'It was a red herring and it sent the police off in completely the wrong direction.'

'Did you ask her if she went to see Roland at his flat? Was she the woman in the fur coat?' Nancy pressed.

'Yes,' said Guy. 'She went to ask him for more money and he said he couldn't. He said he was struggling, that Lord Redesdale had cut him off and he had to pay for the bills at Roland's godmother's nursing home. She said that if he didn't pay up, she would tell the police that he had killed Florence Shore and that she had the letter from Florence that proved he was capable of murder. He knew, of course, that whatever his reasons, he was guilty of shooting the real Roland Lucknor and impersonating him, gaining access to his bank account and flat. That's why he fled.'

Lord Redesdale looked a little shamefaced; his wife was looking at him with her eyebrow raised. 'His business proposition – a golf course – seemed sound,' he shrugged. 'Besides, I understand those soldiers and what they've been through. I wanted to help so long as I knew I could. But after Bill died, I felt guilty that we hadn't lent him the money. When Roland came to France, I asked him for some details, as I'd seen no papers or any sign that the golf course was being built, and he reacted so angrily I knew I was right – it wasn't real. After that, I had to stop giving him anything.'

His wife gave him a look that seemed to indicate they'd be discussing the matter further when they were alone.

Guy carried on. 'When Roland stopped paying out, Mabel was furious with him. Then, when I mentioned Roland, Mabel panicked that I might get to him first and he would tell me about the blackmail. They decided they had to frame him for the murder, to throw us all off their scent. Jim went to see Stuart Hobkirk to try and find out what he knew of the case and what the police were investigating. When we suggested that Mabel come to the party, she saw her chance to identify him as Florence Shore's killer. But before that could happen, Louisa –' here Guy threw her a look of pride – 'realised that Mabel was behind it and then she was cornered.'

'I can't believe what almost happened,' said Nancy.

Louisa drank the last of her now tepid cocoa. 'You and I had better go,' she said to Guy. 'It's very late. My lady, do you think there might still be a driver who could take us to the station? We can wait there until the first train arrives; it won't be all that long now.'

Lady Redesdale stood up and motioned for Louisa to do the same. 'Louisa,' she said, 'you have shown us great loyalty, not to mention determination and courage that I would be proud to see in any of my daughters. Would you do us the honour of staying here and working for us again?'

It was all Louisa could do not to grab Lady Redesdale by the hand. Instead, she restrained herself to little more than a smile. 'My lady,' she said, 'there is nothing I would like more. Thank you.'

'Mr Sullivan,' said Lady Redesdale, 'you are very welcome to stay the night. I'm sure we can have a bed made up somewhere.'

'Thank you, my lady,' said Guy, standing. 'I am very grateful but I have an appointment in London first thing, so I had better return as soon as I can.'

'I'll be coming with you,' said Louisa, 'if I may? I'll be back tomorrow night. There's someone I have to see first.'

CHAPTER SEVENTY-SIX

⟿

At nine o'clock the following morning, Guy was walking up the steps of New Scotland Yard on the Embankment. In all the maelstrom of the night before, as Mabel and Jim were driven away back to London, DI Haigh had asked him to come in. Guy wasn't quite certain whether he would be commended or criticised for the events. Although the evening had ended in two successful arrests, they were not the ones that everybody had been expected to make. What's more, Xander Waring was guilty of murder and he had disappeared. Louisa had had her explanations but Guy was not sure that Haigh would be quite so understanding.

This time, Guy was shown to Haigh's office straight away by a young sergeant on the desk, who had apparently been waiting for his arrival. When Guy came in he saw Haigh sitting behind his desk, and Superintendent Jarvis was with him. They both had stern looks upon their faces and Guy braced himself for the worst. At least he had no job to lose this time.

Haigh asked Guy to sit down, and he perched almost on the edge of the chair.

'Right, Sullivan,' said Haigh, who thankfully had not yet lit his first cigar of the day, though Guy could see one ready and waiting in the ashtray. 'Roland Lucknor, who we now believe to be Alexander Waring, has vanished.'

'Yes, sir,' said Guy.

'He was not, in fact, the man that you had supposed to have been responsible for the death of Florence Nightingale Shore.'

'No, sir.' Was he to be taken point by point through his mistakes? It seemed so.

'Without warrant or official permission, you visited Violet Temperley in her nursing home under police guise and removed a photograph belonging to her. Furthermore, you contacted two further men to verify the identity of those in the photograph, one of whom is extremely close to the heart of the case.'

Guy could only nod. He felt his heart sinking lower with every sentence Haigh spoke.

'Most seriously, you visited Mabel Rogers after the report of her burglary, took away with you a letter that was crucial evidence in the case and did not declare it to your former direct superior – Jarvis, here – as you should have done but came to me.'

'Yes, sir,' said Guy, his voice hardly louder than a whisper.

'Rather than declare your own unofficial interest, you asked your former colleague, Sergeant Conlon, to bear the responsibility of requesting cars and men to a house outside London belonging to one of our esteemed members of the House of Lords.'

Haigh looked up at Jarvis and said, 'Well, my good man. What shall we do with him? As we discussed?'

'Yes, I think so,' said Jarvis.

Haigh folded his arms on the desk and leaned towards Guy. 'Do you acknowledge the very serious errors of policing you have made here?'

'Yes, sir,' said Guy, 'I do.'

'I think, then, that we had better have you under our control. It would be more appropriate, don't you think, that you work *for* us in the future?'

Hope lit inside Guy. 'Oh, yes, sir!'

'Then I invite you to join the Metropolitan Police, Mr Sullivan, as a junior constable. You will start straight away, as you are needed to help prepare the court cases against Mabel Rogers and Jim Badgett.'

Guy stood up. He thought his heart would burst right out of his chest. 'Thank you, sir, I won't let you down.'

Haigh grunted. 'The door's behind you, Sullivan.'

CHAPTER SEVENTY-SEVEN

'**M**a!' called out Louisa. 'Are you there? It's me.'

'I'm in the kitchen,' Winnie called back. 'Is that really you?'

Louisa ran in and found her mother, and they embraced tightly. 'I'm sorry it's been so long.'

'Oh, not to worry, dear,' said Winnie. 'I knew you'd been working.'

Louisa stood back. 'You look well,' she said. 'You're up.'

'Yes, I'm much better.'

Around the room, there were three or four boxes open, and Louisa noticed the books were no longer on the shelf and the framed picture of her parents on their wedding day was not on the mantelpiece.

'Are you leaving?'

'In a few days, yes,' said Winnie. 'I was going to have a note sent to you. It was Jennie who helped me. When she came over to read me your letters and write mine back to you, we used to sit and chat for a bit. I asked her if she might write to my sister, Gertie, in Suffolk.'

'In Hadleigh?' said Louisa.

'Yes, that's it. Gertie's been on her own, as you know, since her husband died ten years ago, and we realised it was silly the two of us living on our own when we could be together, quite happy and share the cost of things. She keeps a few chickens and sells the eggs. I could do a bit of laundry work and mending there if I need to, but we won't need much.'

'Oh, that's a wonderful idea, Ma!' said Louisa.

'It means I have to let the flat go but I don't know that you really wanted it. Do you?' Winnie looked shyly at her daughter. 'I think you're moving up in the world.'

'I don't know about that,' laughed Louisa, 'but I've got work, I'm fine. You don't need to worry about me.'

'You still don't have a husband,' chaffed her mother.

'Give over, Ma,' said Louisa, but the mood was happy. She felt something tickling her leg and looked down to see Socks, licking at her feet. She crouched down to check – yes, those silky ears, that white tail – it was definitely Socks, Stephen's dog. 'What's he doing here?' she said. 'Is Stephen about?'

'No,' said Winnie. 'He came back here a while ago, apologised for everything and said he was going to join the army to straighten himself out.'

'What?' said Louisa. 'That doesn't sound like him.'

'I know,' said Winnie. 'It was the strangest thing. I hadn't seen him for weeks, then he turned up all of a sudden. Gave me a shock because it was at night and I was on my way to bed. He had two black eyes and looked a state. I thought he was going to ask me for steaks.'

'Steaks?'

'To put on his eyes.' Winnie chuckled. 'Anyway, he didn't; instead he started saying sorry for everything he'd done to us and

405

that he'd decided to turn everything around and was going to sign up the very next morning.'

'What?' Louisa wasn't sure if she believed it and she must have given it away on her face because her mother nodded.

'I know, my first thought was that he must owe a lot of money to someone and hiding in the army was the safest place for him. And maybe that is true, but he swore that he'd met a man who had explained to him what could happen if he carried on the way he was going – that he'd end up dead in a ditch before long, but if he went straight, he could save himself.'

'Blimey,' said Louisa, stumped for words. If that was Roland, it was true, he did know what could happen. 'Why the army, though?'

'He said he'd thought about it long and hard, and realised that the army would take him, give him bed and board besides wages, and keep him away from all his old muckers who might try and persuade him otherwise. He fancied travel, he said, and with luck he'd get a posting abroad before long. It was quite something, I don't mind telling you. I saw him smile for the first time.'

Louisa shook her head in disbelief and bent down again to stroke Socks' soft head.

'I don't really know what to do with the dog, though,' said Winnie. 'Fond as I am of him, Gertie doesn't want him there, she says dogs make her sneeze. I was going to try Battersea Dogs Home, but could you take him back to where you work? Haven't they got a nice big garden? They might not even notice him there.'

'No, I can't do that,' said Louisa. 'But I think I do know someone who might look after him.'

CHAPTER SEVENTY-EIGHT

G uy checked his watch. Ten to six. He'd made it home in time for tea, and he knew all the family would be there. Even Walter was back for a few nights, while his wife was visiting her mother in Manchester.

In the front room, the logs in the fire were crackling with the kind of low flames that meant they had been burning for hours. Usually his mother only lit it at midday on Christmas, to really warm the house through. He took in the sight of his brothers and father seated in various chairs, waiting for him, it seemed, and his mother ran over to him.

'Oh, Guy! You've got your old job back!'

'Not quite,' said Guy, though he couldn't keep up the joke, the urge to grin was too great.

'What's the uniform, then?' said Ernest teasingly. 'Got it from the costume shop, did you?'

'Look at the crest on my hat,' said Guy. 'It's not the same as the one before.'

Guy's father walked up to him and peered up at his tall police-man's helmet. 'Blimey, son, Metropolitan Police Force?'

407

'You are looking at a newly appointed junior constable of the London Metropolitan,' said Guy, and the room erupted into cheers. His mother started crying, his brothers were slapping him on the back and at one point his glasses were nearly knocked off, earning another gentle tease, this time from Bertie, but Guy didn't care. He could hear, for the first time in his life, that they were proud of him.

They were interrupted by a knock at the door. 'You'd better answer it, son,' said his father. 'Impress the neighbours, would you?'

Guy grinned and, straightening his hat, went to the front door.

'Goodness,' said Louisa when she saw him. 'I wasn't expecting that!'

Guy laughed, blushing slightly. He felt a bit silly in his hat now and took it off.

'Did you get your job back?' she asked.

'Almost,' he said, unable to keep the smile off his face. 'I'm working for the Met.'

Louisa whistled. 'I say,' she said, 'I shall have to mind my Ps and Qs around you now.'

'Not you,' laughed Guy, relieved that she was in such good humour with him. It had crossed his mind that he had cost her her job with his relentless pursuit of the case, not to mention bringing the police and Mabel Rogers to Asthall Manor. He was about to beg her forgiveness again when he noticed Socks. 'Hello, who's this?' Guy bent down to the black and white dog, wildly wagging its tail and jumping up at his legs. It immediately started trying to lick his face, making him laugh again. 'What a good dog,' he said.

'His name is Socks,' said Louisa, 'and it looks like love at first sight, if you ask me. He's yours, if you can have him.'

Guy straightened up and looked at Louisa. 'Yes,' he said, 'I think it is love at first sight.' She smiled at him. 'But where did he come from?'

'My uncle,' she said. 'He left him with my ma; said he was off to join the army. More likely he's hoping to get posted abroad where no one can find him for money he owes.'

'So Xander . . . ?'

'Seems there was a fight – that explains the blood I saw, and Ma said he turned up with two black eyes. Whatever Xander said, he did only as I asked him and no more,' said Louisa.

This was the cherry on the icing. Whatever Xander Waring had done to Roland Lucknor could be forgiven, even in the eyes of the law, thought Guy, and he hadn't done anything to Stephen Cannon. It was the last arrest that Guy hadn't managed, and it had niggled at him, but no more. Even better, Louisa was completely exonerated.

There was just one more thing. Guy looked at her, standing on the step before him. Her porcelain skin was illuminated by the street lamps and her eyes were nearly black. He saw her shiver slightly from the cold. As he was about to say something, he sensed someone behind him and when he looked, saw his brothers all grinning cheekily, their heads peering around into the hall. Guy gently closed the front door behind him.

'May I come and see you soon, at Asthall Manor?'

'Yes,' said Louisa softly, 'please come. It's not just the family who will be pleased to see you.'

And in the shadows of the doorway, with Socks sitting down and looking up at them, his tail thumping, Guy and Louisa embraced.

CHAPTER SEVENTY-NINE

~~~~~

Some evenings later, when the advent calendars had been put up in the nursery, and all the girls had exclaimed over the darling pictures of robins and holly branches that began to appear behind the cardboard doors, Nancy and Louisa were sitting by the fire on the scratchy rug, Nanny Blor in her armchair, reading and dozing in the warm fug of the little sitting room.

Nancy was writing in a school exercise book that looked as if it had been dug out from the bottom of a cupboard somewhere. She wrote quickly, with words scratched out and replaced frequently, her pen not so much flying as dive-bombing over the page. Very occasionally she would look up, hand poised, ready to resume the writing as soon as the tap was turned on again, then her head would be bent over her lap once more. There was no sound but for the ticking of the carriage clock and the rustle of Nanny's crêpe skirt as she shifted about, moving the cushion behind her back, trying to get a little more comfortable when she closed her eyes.

Louisa couldn't quite concentrate on her own book. She was struggling slightly over a history book on Henry VIII because she had decided that she wanted to educate herself better and Lady Redesdale had given her a list to start with.

'What's that you're writing?' she asked. 'One of Grue's stories?'

Nancy stopped and looked at Louisa, then slightly past her, as if watching something else in the distance. 'No,' she said. 'I've been thinking of writing a novel. A grown-up one.'

'What does that mean?' said Louisa, interested.

'It means, not about imaginary things but real people. About the things that real people do to each other.'

'I look forward to reading it,' said Louisa.

'You shall be one of the first, I promise,' said Nancy. She put her book down and straightened out her legs, pointing her feet to stretch out, like a dog after a long walk. 'It will be my London season next year. Everything is about to change – for me, at any rate.' She laughed.

'I think you are absolutely right,' said Louisa. 'It might even change for me, too, you know.'

Nanny Blor looked up at this, startled. 'Don't say you're planning to go off again.'

Louisa stood up and shook her head. 'Oh no, Nanny, I'm not going anywhere.' She walked across the room and into one of the bedrooms, where the other girls were supposed to be getting ready for bed.

Diana was in her long flannel nightdress with tiny pearl buttons that ran all the way from neck to hem. She was sitting at the dressing table, regarding herself in the looking-glass, with Pamela standing behind her, brushing her hair and counting each stroke. Pamela's own dark curls were tied back and her pyjamas were getting rather short. Louisa thought she might try to let down the hems.

Unity and Decca, in softest cotton jammies, were standing on either side of Debo's cot, teasing her gently with their starfish hands as she gurgled at them. None of them looked up at Louisa as she stood in the doorway, drinking in the pleasure of their presence. She noticed, as if for the first time, the delicate print of flowers on the wallpaper, the three framed illustrations of a hunt on one wall, the spring of the soft carpet beneath her feet. A few toys were strewn about in a way that was untidy but cosy: a yellow doll's dress on the bed, some wooden soldiers knocked over, a drum that had lost its sticks. It didn't matter; she knew where everything went.

'... ninety-nine, a hundred,' said Pamela triumphantly, and suddenly looked up at Louisa as she did so, the hair brush held aloft like a winner's trophy.

Pamela was the oldest child in the nursery now that Nancy was in stockings, planning parties in London and threatening to cut her hair short. Lord Redesdale had roared at the suggestion and Nancy had never looked more thrilled.

It wouldn't be long until Tom would be home for the holidays and the Christmas tree would be standing in the hall, resplendently decorated with lights and homemade baubles that moved in the breeze each time the children ran past. Before midnight mass, all of the family and the servants would gather by the fire to sing carols, to herald in the angels and the new years ahead.

Louisa Cannon didn't know what those years would bring but she knew that, at last, she looked forward to finding out.

15 October 1919
Dunkerque

My dearest one,

I am writing with the joyous news that my war is over. I was given my demobilisation orders this morning. The men we have been nursing here are all now declared either fully rehabilitated or have been found places in homes that will look after them for their remaining years. It is a strange and sad time, somehow, to leave behind this work and the people I have come to admire and respect as my colleagues. After two wars and almost forty years of nursing, I have nothing ahead but a quiet old age.

Yet it is, of course, a happy time, too. You and I will be together in Carnforth Lodge, but not for long. Let us find a cottage by the sea, where we may plant yellow roses around the door and put rocking chairs by the window, so we may look out at the calm and peaceful sea.

We have been given a week or so to pack our things and clear out this field hospital. I will telegram ahead of my arrival to London, probably to Waterloo station.

Wait for me just a little longer. I am coming home to you at last, my darling.

Most tender love,
Flo

28 December 1919

My dearest one,

I'm writing to you now because you are making it impossible for us to talk like the civilised people I know we are. Despite all you have said to me, most cruelly, I feel it only right to let you know of my plans.

I meant it when I told you, if you do not stop the blackmail, I have no choice but to go to the police.

Believe me when I say I do not want to do this. You and I have been friends for so long but you trouble me when your anger rages. Perhaps we were apart too long in the war, and have lost our understanding of each other. It seems you seek only the worst in me and I am finding it hard to remember the best of you, of which I was always so very fond.

I have changed my will, and left the monies I had intended to look after you, should I die before you, to my cousin Stuart instead. As you know, I am an admirer of his work and the money will give him the encouragement he needs to pursue his painting. I cannot, in all conscience, risk you being recognised by my family as someone close to me. You are engaging in an act of duplicity that is nothing less than a twisted perversion of the kindness you and I so long strived to demonstrate in our work. When the new year

414

comes, I will spend a week with Rosa to look for a seaside cottage there, in which I hope to spend my retirement. It has come sooner than expected but I want only for peace and quiet, to tend a garden and listen to the sounds of the waves. Your anger, your ire and jealousy are oppressive burdens I can no longer carry. I would rather be alone than beside you. How sad that is.

Flo

HISTORICAL NOTE

Florence Nightingale Shore was attacked on the Brighton line on Monday 12 January, 1920, and died a few days later in hospital. There was public outrage at her death and money was raised to fund the Florence Nightingale Shore Memorial Hospital (destroyed by bombing in World War Two), of which her long-term friend, Mabel Rogers, became the superintendent. Mabel Rogers was never suspected or charged with the murder of Florence Shore, and all conversations with her outside of the inquests have been completely invented by me.

Interviews with real-life witnesses have been taken from newspaper reports at the time of the inquests. Nobody has ever been found guilty of her murder.

While the Mitford sisters and their parents are, of course, a real family, my scenes with them in this book are all entirely imagined. Other members of their family and their servants also have their roots in reality, but for the purposes of moving the story along, I have had to change some dates (Nancy Mitford turned 18 years old in 1922, not 1921).

First and foremost, this is a novel. It is my hope, however, that in blending fact with fiction, we come closer to understanding the people of the past, as well as remember and commemorate them.

ACKNOWLEDGEMENTS

This book is for Florence Nightingale Shore and all war nurses, then and now, around the world. Florence was, like her godmother and namesake, a woman who worked tirelessly and courageously in extreme conditions during the Boer and Great wars. She refused to take shelter without the men she was looking after and always remained in the hospital with her patients despite the threat of bombing. She deserved a better ending than the one she got and I hope this book does something to earn her the respect and recognition she deserved.

I should like to pay tribute to Rosemary Cook's detailed, factual history of Florence's life and career as a Queen's Nurse, *The Nightingale Shore Murder* (Second edition, Troubadour Publishing 2015), which to no small extent inspired my own fictional account.

The Mitford Murders was raised by a village. Thank you, Ed Wood, for your encouragement and patience from that very first step to the last of the thousand miles. My thanks, too, to Cath Burke, Andy Hine and Kate Hibbert and all the teams of Sphere and Little, Brown that have helped bring this book to life.

For cheering at the corners, there's no better than Hope Dellon of St Martin's Press – thank you.

Thank you to my brilliant agent, Caroline Michel of PFD.

For expert advice and guidance, thank you Nicky Bird and Celestria Hales. Any mistakes that remain are of course my own.

Thank you to John Goodall and Melanie Bryan of *Country Life* magazine, for giving me a peek into Asthall Manor.

Thank you to my family and friends who have always given me life and laughter but especially to: Rory Fellowes, Lyn Fellowes, Cordelia Fellowes, Julian Fellowes, Emma Kitchener-Fellowes, Annette Jacot de Boinod, Celia Walden, Anna Cusden, Emma Wood, Damian Barr and Clare Peake. (Always remembering the ever-glorious Georgina Fellowes.)

And thank you to my family, whom I love more than words. I couldn't have done any of this without you, my darling Simon, Beatrix, Louis and George.

BIBLIOGRAPHY

For my research on the lives of the Mitford family and the murder of Florence Nightingale Shore, I drew inspiration from a number of books, articles and online material. I am indebted to the lively accounts the sisters made of their own lives – whether as autobiography or closely-related novel – as well as the many biographies and collections of their extensive letters. Everything that happens in this novel is completely fictional but interested readers may enjoy discovering snippets of authentic detail within.

For those who'd like to know more, I refer them to: *The Mitford Girls: The Biography of an Extraordinary Family* by Mary S. Lovell; *Nancy Mitford* by Selina Hastings, *Hons and Rebels* by Jessica Mitford, *The Mitfords: Letters Between Six Sisters* edited by Charlotte Mosley and *Decca: The Letters of Jessica Mitford* edited by Peter Y. Sussman.

For novels which seem to draw on Nancy Mitford's earlier years, I heartily recommend *Love in a Cold Climate*, *The Pursuit of Love* and *The Blessing*.

Turn the page to read the first chapter from the second novel in the Mitford Murders series, *Bright Young Dead*, exclusive to Sainsbury's.

CHAPTER ONE

～～～

There comes a moment in every child's life that marks defini-
tively their transition to adulthood. That moment had not yet
come for Pamela Mitford, nearly eighteen years old and peevish on
the steps of a narrow house in Mayfair. Her nursery maid, Louisa
Cannon, had chaperoned Pamela to London for a dinner, where
her older sister, Nancy, hoped to use her as bait: Pamela's coming
out dance was to take place at the family home, Asthall Manor,
the following month, and the men on the guest list were, Nancy
quipped, as few as the dinosaurs in the Natural History Museum
and just as old.

However, Pamela, though fair-haired and with the bluest eyes
of all the six sisters – the only one with a gaze that matched their
father's, in fact – was suffering an attack of nerves on the steps.

'Tell Koko to come and fetch me,' she said, her back to the glossy
black door. 'I don't want you taking me in. It makes me look like
a baby.'

Facing the stubborn back, Louisa rolled her eyes. 'I have to; I
promised Lady Redesdale I would stay. And besides, nobody here
knows I'm your nursery maid. I might be anybody,' she said, not

for the first time. The journey from Asthall Manor to London had felt like a long one, in spite of the familiar train route and a taxi that had appeared at Paddington Station almost the instant they stepped out.

Pamela's shoulders relaxed slightly and Louisa's hopes were raised, but just as she turned around, somebody twitched at the curtains and she quickly spun away again. 'Please,' she said quietly, 'go and fetch Koko.'

Koko was the family name for Nancy, one of a string of nicknames and codes that all the sisters, the brother and their parents switched between when referring to one another. Louisa, in situ now for almost six years, could tick them off like a French vocab test.

She walked to the top and rang the bell, and the door was opened alarmingly quickly by a girl who looked to be almost the mirror of Louisa: of similar height, with the same pale brown hair tied back and a dress that also looked as if it were well made but well worn, most likely a hand-me-down from her mistress, as Louisa's was from Nancy. Her clean face looked tired but the freckles on her small nose livened her, somehow. She noticed Pamela's back and the two maids exchanged a look that acknowledged the boat they were both in.

'Good evening,' said Louisa, 'could you tell me if Miss Nancy Mitford is there, please?'

The girl looked as if she might start laughing. 'I'd better ask who's asking,' she said in an accent that Louisa recognised as coming from south of the river.

'It's her sister, Miss Pamela,' said Louisa. 'Only, she doesn't want to come in with me and I'm not to let her in alone. May I come in and talk to Miss Nancy?'

The maid gave a nod and held the door open. 'Follow me.'

*

Along the hall, the maid pointed to a door then disappeared through another. Louisa thought it was odd she hadn't been shown in formally but when she walked in, she understood why. In a dimly lit sitting-room, two large, shabby armchairs faced a fire that crackled and spat. From each, a long thin arm stretched towards another. The first, a woman's, was clad in a black silk glove to above the elbow; the second was a man's, whose wrist was covered by a stiff white cuff and the sleeve of an evening jacket, his hand naked bar a heavy gold signet ring. The two were playfully entwining their fingers as if in a sort of Punch and Judy Show, the male hand thrusting and parrying, the female lightly poking and withdrawing, allowing itself to be easily caught again.

Louisa had been watching this a beat too long when the head belonging to the gloved hand peered around the side of the chair's wing. The shock prompted by Nancy's bobbed hair had subsided for Louisa some time ago and now she rather admired it. The face was not conventionally pretty but it had its charms, with what moving-picture critics would call 'rosebud lips' painted dark red, a small nose and big round eyes that were half-closed now, focusing on their old nursery maid. Louisa registered a typical mix of fondness and exasperation.

'Beg your pardon, Miss Nancy,' said Louisa. 'I've come to let you know that Miss Pamela is here.'

At this, the man looked out. His face was all angles and planes, with a long nose and hair that had been combed so flat and smooth it looked like a sheet of gold beaten onto the skull. Sebastian Atlas, Louisa knew. He had been down to Asthall Manor with Nancy a few times, in spite of the fact that Lord Redesdale went puce at the sight of him, much to the eldest Mitford girl's delight and Lady Redesdale's displeasure, though hers was indicated at a lower register. If Lord Redesdale hath fire and fury, Lady Redesdale hath ice and ire.

'Well, why doesn't she come in, then?' drawled Sebastian, flicking Nancy's fingers away and sinking back into the chair. His other hand reached out and picked up a tumbler of whisky.

The low lights and the warmth of the room had a soporific effect on Louisa, making her unsteady on her feet. Luncheon felt like too long ago and they'd missed tea. She tried to convey extra urgency in her face but either failed or Nancy was being deliberately obtuse. 'Perhaps you could come downstairs to meet her?' Louisa said.

Nancy gave a dramatic sigh, dropped her head and then stood up. She shook out her dress of crumpled silk, weighted at the hem with hundreds of tiny beads in a black-and-white zig-zag pattern. It was her most, perhaps only, fashionable dress and worn with a frequency that drove Nanny Blor to distraction.

'What on earth is going on?' whispered Nancy once they were out in the hallway. 'I was *alone* with Mr Atlas . . .' The implication was clear. She had not meant to be disturbed.

'I'm sorry Miss Nancy,' said Louisa, quickly deciding not to drop the prefix, though that had been their habit not so long ago. 'But Miss Pamela doesn't want me to come up. She thinks it looks childish to have a nursery maid with her.'

Something of Nancy's old look came back then and she gave Louisa a half-smile. 'What a dunce,' she said. 'Chaperones are almost fashionable again, but she wouldn't know that.'

'Please, won't you come down?'

'I *am* coming. Look, here we are, walking.'

Pamela and Louisa were only staying in London for the one night, with Lord Redesdale's elderly aunt in Knightsbridge, but there had been building tension at home in anticipation for the last month. Lord Redesdale was never less than stoutly against the entire plan. Lady Redesdale was more sympathetic but still felt a show of resistance was necessary in the face of her eldest daughter's determination.

Nancy had proposed to her parents that Pamela come to London for a night, join her for a party or two and make herself known a little, so that they could invite some of the crowd there for the coming out dance.

'Otherwise,' spelled out Nancy, 'you're asking them to come to a stranger's party and they'll think it's because we're desperate. It's not like it used to be. It's 1925, Farve.'

'I don't see what difference the year makes,' her father had replied tersely.

'All the difference. You've got to be in the right crowd. You can't show up for any old thing.' Which wasn't, Nancy told Louisa in confidence, exactly accurate. There was nothing the crowd liked more than turning up for any old thing and every old thing, where free-flowing wine and the promise of hot dance was on offer. They knew that they *were* the crowd, the beating heart of any party and all others were thrown into darkness by their pulsing light. What Nancy really wanted was a chance to open Pamela's eyes a bit – and, Louisa suspected, make sure her younger sister wouldn't squeal alarm when the crowd showed up at Asthall. It may have been Pamela's birthday, but it was clear that Nancy planned to make this her event, one where the friends she had been cultivating for months would finally see her in all her glory – on her own territory, in charge and, yes, at the centre of attention.

The night's function was a dinner at the London house of Lady Curtis, mother of Adrian and Charlotte, with a plan to go on to a dance afterwards. Nancy had met Adrian in the summer at Eights

Week in Oxford, the annual regatta and the only time the female sex were admitted as supper guests within the university's yellow-stone walls. Nancy had taken up the ukelele only a few months before and told Louisa it had worked a spell on the men there as if she were a snake charmer in Marrakesh.

The Curtis house was rather gloomily decorated with dark walls and enormous oil portraits frowning in the narrow stairway. The maid had disappeared and there was no sign of Lady Curtis, but the sound of jazz music from a gramophone player could be heard drifting down the stairs. Louisa had the odd sensation of monkeys taking over the zoo; it made her own presence somehow even more awkward.

'Must you come?' Pamela whispered to Louisa as the three of them climbed the stairs carefully, the eldest sister leading the way. 'I'm with Nancy after all.'

'I promised Lady Redesdale,' reminded Louisa. She felt rather sorry for her charge, who she had heard weeping quietly in the bathroom earlier before finally emerging with a button in her hand that had come off the skirt fastening. Pamela said nothing but passed it to Louisa, who stayed equally silent as she fetched needle and thread and sewed it back on as she stood before her, hiccupping gently.

As the three ascended, the lively chatter of the guests joined the music, talking slightly faster and louder than strictly necessary. Cologne and cigarette smoke drifted down the stairs reminding Louisa to brace herself for what was to come. She had learned from earlier visits of Nancy's friends to Asthall that their passion for change and a world that broke with the past was only about them; servants, apparently, could carry on as before. She would be ignored at best, asked to pick up a dropped glass and clear up the spills at worst. There was nothing so lonely as standing in a crowded room and being seen, if seen at all, as little more than a dustpan and brush. At the same time, there was plenty for her to look at and she couldn't help it, she *was* excited to enter this party. Stepping inside the room felt like disappearing into the Society pages of *The Tatler*, only with colour – it took a moment for Louisa to adjust her eyes to the blur of young men and women standing close together, their features both softened and highlighted by the flickering flames of the fire and Tiffany lampshades dotted around.

Unable to take in the whole picture, Louisa noticed the details: a smear of red lipstick on an empty glass; cigarettes in long holders that threatened to singe the hair of the person standing opposite; headbands with elaborate feathers drooping from them and daring purple socks that revealed themselves when a man crossed his legs. Pamela had been swallowed whole by the crowd, like Jonah into the whale, and Louisa decided the best thing she could do would be to find a chair close to the door so she would know if her charge decided to leave. Not to mention she was wary of being shaken off for the night and spending hours blindly wandering around London searching for the Mitfords. Nancy was certainly capable of executing such a plan even if Pamela wasn't, but Pamela was enthralled by her sister and would do as she was told.

From her vantage point, Louisa had a good view of a huge fireplace, where a man stood, his fingertips resting on the mantelpiece to steady himself. Louisa recognised him as Adrian Curtis, his glass held out for more whisky, blithely ignoring another young man who poured it. She knew him from his photograph in the papers as well as Nancy's description but she was still surprised to hear him; his sonorous voice did not seem to belong to his thin body. His dark wavy hair had not been entirely tamed by the cream he'd applied and his pale blue eyes, though glassy, were paying close attention to Nancy's décolletage as she drew nearer. His bow tie was undone and there seemed to be a wet patch on the front of his shirt from a carelessly handled drink.

'If it isn't the Honorable Miss Mitford,' he said, and Nancy broke out into a wide smile. He tripped as he drew an arm awkwardly around her shoulders, then pulled away again quickly, hand back to the mantelpiece. His eye caught Pamela's and she blushed. 'Who have you brought along, darling?' Adrian asked, looking directly at her. 'She looks like a lamb to the slaughter, the poor dear.' He laughed and drained his glass.

'This is my sister, Pamela,' said Nancy. 'She's still only seventeen, so she really is a lamb. Do be gentle, A.' She gave him a look that Louisa knew to be saying the contrary: don't be gentle at all.

Pamela put her hand out and said in as grown-up a voice as she could manage, 'How do you do, Mr Curtis?', which made him roar with laughter.

'Stuff and nonsense to all that,' he said, flapping her hand away. 'We're the Bright Young Things, don't you know?'

This was accompanied by an ironic raised eyebrow. Louisa knew better: all these people loved it when the newspapers wrote about them.

'Call me Adrian. Now what can we get you to drink?' He turned to tap the retreating man with the whisky bottle on the shoulder but was interrupted by a loud groan from a woman sitting in a chair nearby. She had the same unruly curls as him, hers having been allowed to grow longer and puff out, and though her eyes were brown not blue, she shared something of the man's sulky lips. She was thin, too, but there was a little pocket of soft flesh that sat just below her chin, enough to give her the appearance of someone round. This was something she would resent until she was thirty-five years old, when she would finally realise it was this quirk that kept her looking young.

The woman did not stand but turned to Pamela. 'Please ignore my brother,' she said, 'he's a bore and we are nothing of the sort. That's all nonsense in the papers. I'm Charlotte, by the way.'

'I'm Pamela.' She went silent. Louisa knew this time had been feverishly anticipated – when Pamela had spent a few months in France the year before, her letters home had been mostly about the dresses she would need for her deb season, though that was not until next summer. Otherwise, her whole life had been spent in the nursery, talking to her brothers and sisters, or Nanny and Louisa, and it was obvious she simply could not navigate this unfamiliar territory.

Charlotte pulled herself out of the chair and picked up two drinks from a tray, handing one to Pamela. She wore a silvery grey dress that hung straight and fell just below her knees, with tassels swinging in tiers from collarbone to calves. On her feet were plain buckled shoes of black leather but her legs were covered with silk stockings – yet she didn't look too much older than Pamela. Pamela tugged at her skirt's uncomfortably tight waistband; her cream silk blouse and navy skirt, which she had told Louisa she hoped would speak of simple Parisian chic, in fact had the effect of hospital nurse chic. Louisa immediately felt sorry for the thought. Pamela took the glass from Charlotte and swigged, only to start coughing and spluttering immediately. She wiped her mouth with the back of her hand and it came away covered with the lipstick Nancy had put on her before they'd gone out.

'Oh fiddlesticks!' she exclaimed and Charlotte burst into giggles.

'That's so adorable,' said Charlotte. 'Come here, I've got a hanky, let's clean you up a bit. You must admit, it is quite funny.'

And she laughed again as she wiped Pamela's face. Pamela nodded and then exploded with giggles, too. 'I've been so nervous for weeks and now the worst has happened. It's not so bad really, is it?'

Charlotte shook her head. 'No, it really isn't. Sit down, I'll perch on the arm in a bit. And I'll try and find something easier for you to drink.'

Pamela sat, and Louisa took the opportunity to observe the other members of the party. She could pick out one or two faces of those who had come to Asthall with Nancy. Sebastian, of course. Adrian she knew was considered rather a catch – if he came to Pamela's party, he was the domino that would make all the others say yes. She looked back at Pamela and saw she'd been left alone and was worried until she saw Clara Mayfield, who waved and smiled as she walked towards the fireplace.

Clara, nearly always referred to as 'The American', was closer to Nancy's age but was kind to Pamela. The two of them had spent some time playing with the dogs together at Asthall, chatting easily about their many and varied canine features and how they wished animals could talk, speculating on what they would say. It was Pamela's best sort of conversation and not one she was likely to have tonight. Clara was straightforwardly and enjoyably pretty, with blonde hair tonged into perfect waves, long arched eyebrows and pink, full lips. She always wore pale colours in flimsy, delicate materials, which made her look as if she could be unwound like a reel of chiffon ribbon.

'Hello there,' said Clara, 'I didn't know you'd be here.'

'It was touch and go,' said Pamela, 'Farve wasn't too keen.'

'No, I shouldn't think he was.' She gave a wry smile. 'Can't say I blame him. Bunch of degenerates here.'

Pamela looked around the room. 'They don't look too bad to me.'

'Don't be deceived,' said Clara. 'Here, budge up.'

She sat on the arm and Pamela whispered up to her. 'Charlotte was sitting there, she's just gone to get a glass of water.'

'It's not a dinner party,' said Clara, 'she can change places. Come on, old thing, don't look as if I've sent you to the corner.'

'I keep getting it wrong,' said Pamela.

'No, you don't. You only need to understand that there's nothing to get right. Anything goes except feeling sorry for yourself, so buck up. There's a girl.' She put her hands in her lap and gave Pamela a sideways look, which Pamela returned. At that moment, Charlotte came back with one glass of clear liquid, and another with something green and a thin slice of apple in it.

'Hello, Clara,' said Charlotte, but there wasn't much warmth to it. 'Have you seen Eddie?'

'Yes, he'll be here any minute, I expect.'

'On the phone to that wretched Dolly, is he?'

Clara shrugged in reply. 'What are Adrian and Nancy in such cahoots about?' she said. The two of them were both looking a tad unsteady on their feet, each one barking with laughter before the other had even finished a sentence. Nancy must have sensed the eyes on them because she turned around and waved them over. 'Come over here,' she said, 'we're plotting the most wonderful thing.'

Charlotte walked over straight away, Clara followed and turned back to nudge Pamela along. 'She means you, too.'

'Gather round, chums,' said Adrian. His voice was loud and at this instruction, Sebastian appeared out of nowhere and sidled up close to Nancy, his head in full craning position. Louisa stood to listen. Adrian's voice had lost no volume but started to slow down and slur, like a record played at the wrong speed. 'We're going to do a treasure hunt.'

'What, *now*?' Charlotte's mouth pulled into an even sulkier droop. 'I don't know why you keep going on like those idiots—'

'No, not now,' said Adrian, his lower lip loose as he shook his head, spittle flying. 'These things need planning. At Pamela's dance next month.' He grinned widely and threw his hands up like a circus ringmaster who had just announced that the tigers would be on after the flying acrobats.

Pamela blanched. 'Oh, I don't think that Farve—'

Nancy shushed her. 'Do shut up, Woman. He doesn't need to know. We'll do it at midnight. Then we'll have the run of the house, even the village too if we want.'

'Yes!' said Adrian, 'And Nancy tells me there's even a graveyard just over the garden wall.' He gave a low chuckle and fell slightly backwards before pulling himself upright again.

And so it was that Adrian Curtis, twenty-two years old, planned his own death just three weeks later.

IF YOU LIKED
THE MITFORD MURDERS

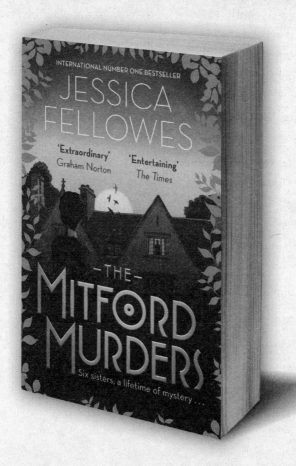

Sign up to our newsletter to be one of the first to hear about the next book in the series, and a chance to win an early signed proof copy.

bit.ly/MitfordMurders

THE MITFORD MURDERS: BOOK 2
BRIGHT YOUNG DEAD

COMING SOON